RACE for REDEMPTION

```
FILE     731*639*1784B      EVENT 98-188 SURV 1003
THREAT   OBS TERM*AP++      PREDICT    LV:075% AV8
SUBJECT  004                MOVEMENT   LV:087%
DRONE    ZEBRA2*SVTM-WP2    TARGET   *2789+VOL=TX
```

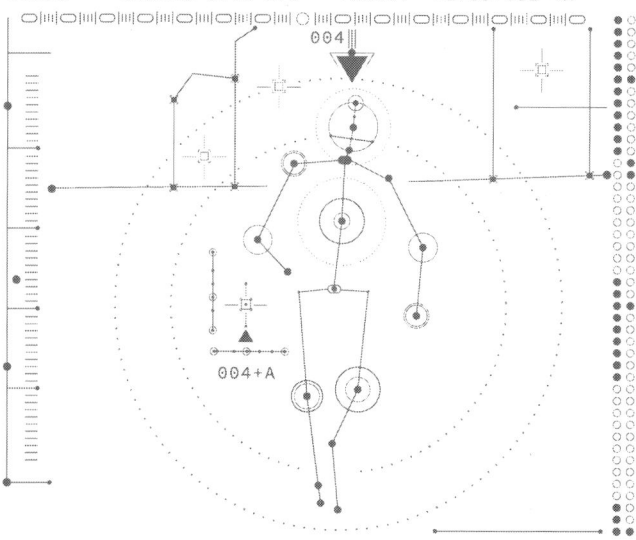

SEQUEL TO
Islands of Deception

CHRIS G THELEN

Will deception run its course?

Race for Redemption

Brookstone Publishing Group
An imprint of Iron Stream Media
100 Missionary Ridge
Birmingham, AL 35242
IronStreamMedia.com

Copyright © 2025 by Chris G. Thelen

No part of this publication may be reproduced, stored in a retrieval system, or transmitted in any form or by any means—electronic, mechanical, photocopying, recording, or otherwise—without the prior written permission of the publisher.

Iron Stream Media serves its authors as they express their views, which may not express the views of the publisher.

This is a work of fiction. Names, characters, and incidents are all products of the author's imagination or are used for fictional purposes. Any mentioned brand names, places, and trademarks remain the property of their respective owners, bear no association with the author or the publisher, and are used for fictional purposes only.

Library of Congress Control Number: 2025930864

Scripture quotations taken from the (NASB®) New American Standard Bible®, Copyright © 1960, 1971, 1977, 1995 by The Lockman Foundation. Used by permission. All rights reserved. lockman.org

Cover design by Brian Preuss

ISBN: 978-1-960814-09-8 (paperback)
ISBN: 978-1-960814-10-4 (ebook)

1 2 3 4 5—29 28 27 26 25

To my amazing daughters, Kristen and Rebecca

MICHIGAN

St. Helena Island
Hog Island
○ St. James
Beaver Island
North Fox Island
○ Charlevoix

Beaver Island
○ Charlevoix
○ Traverse City
Lansing ○
Detroit ○
○ Ann Arbor
Jackson ○

*Pride goes before destruction,
And a haughty spirit before stumbling.*

—Proverbs 16:18

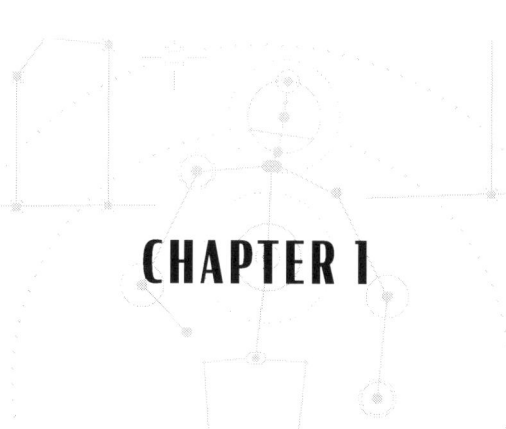

CHAPTER 1

"I'm not a terrorist!" With his eyes locked on his attorney sitting opposite him at the cold metal table, Tom Ferguson experienced a rush of anger.

He turned toward the gray, cinder-block wall in the prison interrogation room and shook his head. "For the last time, I had nothing to do with that drone attack on the *Emerald Isle* ferry boat on Beaver Island last August."

"You've seen the video from the security cameras." The attorney ran a hand through his silver hair and frowned. "It clearly shows you stealing the drone used in the attack from a Caspian distribution warehouse. It's—"

"Someone faked that video with AI."

The chair creaked as the attorney tilted his head, eyebrow raised. He tapped his pen on the legal pad in front of him. "Homeland Security thoroughly analyzed that video. It's real." He leaned in closer. "I don't think you understand the gravity of the charges you—"

"I was never *at* that Caspian warehouse, and never *owned* a cabin on Beaver Island!"

"The feds say you were running a terror cell out of that cabin—that you've owned it for years."

"I've been framed."

"The Charlevoix County records show—"

"It's all fake!" Ferguson clenched his fists, eyes glaring at his attorney, rattling the chains securing his handcuffs to the table.

The attorney shook his head as he pivoted his open laptop toward Ferguson. "The evidence doesn't lie."

"You don't get it," Ferguson said as he glared at the screen on the laptop with the video that showed him loading a large drone into a white cargo van. "All the evidence against me is digital. Whoever created all this fake evidence is still out there."

"Some of your buddies in the crime ring are also facing terrorism charges."

Ferguson shook his head.

"Okay . . ." The attorney closed the laptop screen and crossed his arms over his crisp tan jacket. "I'll play along." He adjusted his wire-rim glasses. "Who would want to frame you?"

"What's the one thing all the evidence has in common?"

The attorney shrugged his shoulders.

"Archipelago."

"The software the State of Michigan uses?"

"And almost half the states in the country."

The attorney's eyes widened. "Do you think someone is tampering with the records on the state's Archipelago system?"

"That has to be it." Ferguson nodded. "All this started last August when someone created a fake hardship release for that prisoner Robert Callahan Junior."

"You mean Cally?"

Ferguson nodded. "That's what his family calls him. Don't you see? Whoever created that fake evidence must've organized his dad's fake funeral that helped him escape from prison."

The attorney slowly shook his head. "You know as well as I do that Marjorie Brogan was head of the state's corrections department. *She* set up the hardship release and fake funeral to capture Cally and get the evidence he had on you and all the other crime ring members."

"Marjorie told me she had nothing to do with it."

"You're all living in a fantasy land." The attorney's eyes narrowed. "You need to face reality. You're going to spend the rest of your life in prison.

CHAPTER 1

That crime ring you were involved with in Detroit was helping fund that terror cell on Beaver Island. Your only hope is a plea bargain in exchange for the names of any others in the terror cell who are still out there."

Ferguson turned his head away and gazed at the window in the door. Sunlight streamed through the opaque glass, which contained a wire mesh. He glanced up at the buzzing fluorescent light overhead and took a deep breath. *No one believes me.*

The attorney sighed. "Your laptop showed you were communicating with a known terror group overseas before the attack. Plans for the attack were found on your computer."

Ferguson leveled his eyes with the attorney's. "It doesn't make any sense. Why would I want to attack a ferry on some remote island in Lake Michigan?"

"You tell me. You were once the warden of the Jackson Correctional Facility, and now look at you."

"I was framed."

"*Cally* was the one framed by you and your crime ring for his friend Chuck's murder. *You* tried to stop Cally from taking the hard drive Chuck gave him to the police. When all the evidence on that hard drive showed up online, it proved *you* and dozens of other state officials and police officers were working for years with the crime ring in Detroit. *Your* laptop showed that the crime ring was funding terrorists. The fact you resisted arrest with a gunfight after the police caught up with you on North Fox Island doesn't help your case."

Ferguson lowered his head as the memory of North Fox Island played in his mind like a movie. Last August had been a disaster. He was so confident that he could capture Cally and Fallon McElliot and stop them from releasing the evidence they had on the crime ring. He could've let them go and fled to Canada or someplace else if he had known the police were coming after him. The whole incident before his capture was still vivid in his mind.

> *He races back to the grass airstrip on North Fox Island, branches slapping against his body and sweat dripping down his face as he grips the automatic rifle. The sick*

feeling in his stomach rises as he sees the plane taxiing and picking up speed down the runway. The automatic gun vibrates in his hands, recoiling as he fires at the plane lifting off, barely clearing the treetops. Dread fills him as he watches the plane disappear from sight, taking away any chance of escaping arrest. They are stuck on the island.

"Tomorrow, they're transferring you from this federal prison in St. Louis back to Michigan. They're locking you up in that new high-security prison on St. Helena Island in the Straits of Mackinac. In a few weeks, you'll face a grand jury in Marquette on domestic terrorism charges. You need to forget this fantasy that you were framed and start working with me on your defense."

Ferguson glared at his attorney. "I don't need you."

"What?"

"You're fired."

"But—"

"If you don't believe I was framed, then I can't have you defending me."

"You need me."

"I'm going to get my freedom one way or another."

The attorney stood, hands on his hips. "What's that supposed to mean?"

"You'll see."

The attorney cocked his head. "Have it your way." He grabbed his laptop, slipped it in its sleeve, and headed for the door. After a couple of knocks, the door opened, and a guard entered the room.

"Are you finished, sir?" the guard asked.

Ferguson glared at the attorney as his heart rate increased by the second.

The attorney turned his back to Ferguson. "We're done here," he said to the guard. Seconds later, the metal door slammed shut behind the attorney with a loud thud that echoed in the room.

CHAPTER 1

* * *

Back in his cell, Ferguson sat on the edge of his bed. He looked at the business card on the small plastic desk next to the bed, picked it up, and read the name: "Nigel Moseley, Attorney." A post office box address in San Francisco was printed at the bottom along with a phone number. He looked at the piece of paper he found in the envelope with the card and read the sentence scrawled across the middle of the page:

Contact me if you're interested in freedom.

What did he have to lose? It seemed no one else was interested in actually defending him.

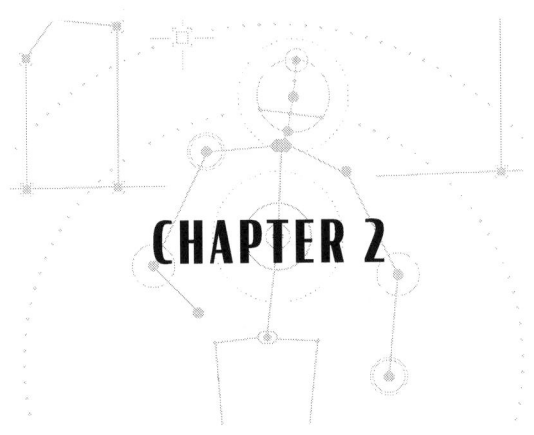

CHAPTER 2

The tip of the cigar glowed in the dimly lit room as Henry Massey pressed the butt between his lips, drew in a deep breath, and exhaled. The overstuffed leather chair softly creaked as he shifted position.

Seated across from him in a matching chair, Daniel Callahan studied the puff of smoke as it curled up and spread along the gold, stamped-tin ceiling.

"Sure you don't want a cigar?" Massey asked. "It's a Davidoff Limited Edition."

"Too expensive for my taste."

"Pocket change." Massey said as he took another draw from the cigar and exhaled. "I pick up as much as I want whenever I'm in Geneva."

Daniel surveyed the large, ornate smoking room in Massey's Colorado mansion. "Quite the room you have here," he said as he noted the dark green walls with rich wood trim and dark walnut cabinets covering the far wall. Behind Massey, through a wall of windows, the lights of Fort Collins were visible below from their vantage point in the foothills of the Rocky Mountains.

"I modeled it after a smoking room I saw in an old estate in England."

CHAPTER 2

Cigar still in one hand, Massey picked up a snifter on the end table next to his chair and took a sip. "The cabinets are an exact replica of the ones in that room, handcrafted in England."

"Beautiful," Daniel said as he looked at the wall of rich walnut cabinets lining one wall. He watched the tip of Massey's cigar glow as he drew in another breath and released a puff of smoke. The rich aroma from the cigar drifted past him. He looked so arrogant and so smug sitting there. Seven months deep undercover for the FBI as Massey's head of security and still no solid evidence to prove he initiated the drone attack on the *Emerald Isle* on Beaver Island. Only his word against Massey's. What other schemes was he cooking up in that twisted mind of his?

Massey took another sip of his drink and set the snifter on the end table next to his chair. "Need a drink, Daniel?"

Daniel picked up his glass from the end table next to his chair. "I'll stick with my Vernor's ginger ale."

"That's what I like about you. You're all business. Just the man I want in charge of my security."

"You said you wanted to show me something."

Massey nodded and set his cigar on an ashtray on the end table next to his chair. The leather chair groaned as he hoisted his overweight frame and walked across the room to the wall of cabinets. He opened a drawer and pulled something out. "My landscaper has been working on remodeling the stone patio and trail behind my mansion," Massey said as he turned to face Daniel. "She found this yesterday near the trail."

Daniel tried to hold back his gasp when he instantly recognized the broken pieces of plastic in Massey's open hand in front of him—pieces of the device he used to communicate with the FBI last November. He should've been more careful disposing of it. His pulse quickened. He steadied his hand as he took a large piece and examined it. "What do you make of it?"

Massey looked at the remaining pieces in his hand, then eyed Daniel. "I'm not sure."

"It looks like a GPS communication device used for remote hiking." Daniel placed the piece back in Massey's hand.

"I'm concerned the FBI is surveilling my estate," Massey said as he plopped himself back in his chair.

Their eyes locked.

"I value loyalty," Massey said.

Daniel leaned closer toward Massey, elbows on his thighs, eyes on Massey with a practiced look of sincerity. "You helped my brother, Cally, escape from prison. You got all the evidence on the hard drive out there to prove Cally didn't murder his friend Chuck. Because of you, the truth came out that the crime ring murdered Chuck. You exposed all the corrupt police officers and state officials working for the crime ring. We shut them down and locked them up. Plus, you framed Ferguson and others for the terror attack on the *Emerald Isle*—the perfect revenge after he framed Cally for Chuck's murder."

"But *you* were a loyal FBI agent," Massey said.

"Until they chose not to help me prove Cally's innocence. They abandoned me when I needed them most. The deal was that if you helped me get that hard drive and prove Cally's innocence, then I would work for you. You're the one who came through for me. That's where my loyalty remains." Daniel watched Massey lean back in his chair, deep in thought. Their eyes locked on each other briefly. Does Massey still believe me?

"I guess it's possible some curious hikers dropped it, and the device was smashed in a rockslide," Massey said as he glanced at the pieces in his hand. "We still need to be careful. Step up the scans on the perimeter of the estate and increase the range of the jamming equipment."

Daniel swallowed, thankful that he'd deflected any attention away from him. "Someone in the mountains could still monitor you with high-power binoculars. Your electronic equipment wouldn't pick up on that."

"Let them." Massey smiled as he clenched the pieces inside a fist. "My most important secrets are buried deep inside my estate out of their sight."

Daniel raised an eyebrow.

"Sometime I'll show you." Massey held his open hand toward Daniel. "Take these pieces and have them analyzed. See if you can find anything on its memory."

"They look pretty weathered," Daniel said as he took the pieces from Massey and studied them. "It's unlikely any of the data survived."

CHAPTER 2

"Check it anyway." Massey leaned back in his chair and picked up his cigar from the ashtray. He took a long, slow draw from it and exhaled, adding to the haze in the room.

"It sure smells good in here."

"I feel like I'm in an English estate." Massey said. His watch dinged. He looked at the screen. "Dinner's ready."

Daniel pocketed the pieces as he left the room and followed Massey down a long hallway. They rounded a corner to a dining room with a crystal chandelier suspended from a high ceiling above the table. Daniel sat down opposite the Masseys' two college-age daughters, Leigha and Carolyn, already seated at the table.

Massey's wife, Helen, smiled at Daniel from the head of the table. "Glad you could join us."

"I'm about done reviewing security for Quick Connect's locations worldwide," Daniel said. He looked at the linen tablecloth, lit taper candles, and crystal vase in the center, overflowing with an exotic arrangement of fresh flowers. "It's good to be back. This beats takeout on the road."

"Roast duck tonight," Helen said as a member of the household staff set a platter in front of her. Two other staff members followed with large trays and set side dishes in the middle of the table.

Daniel sat back. One of the staff members exchanged a lingering gaze with Daniel before he left the room. Could he be an ally?

"You go first," Helen said as she picked up the platter with slices of duck and passed it to Daniel. Their eyes met for a few seconds.

Daniel took the platter and quickly focused on placing a slice of meat on his plate. The routine was foreign to him. The family dug in without saying prayers before the meal. At his parents' house they always prayed before meals. Were they praying for him? None of them knew where he had disappeared to or that he was working undercover. He passed the platter to Henry as he glanced at the expensive place settings. He was accustomed to common dishes, a menagerie of old glassware, accompanied by bent and scuffed stainless steel utensils.

As he exchanged small talk with the Massey family during the meal, thoughts of his younger brother lingered in his mind. How was Cally doing now that he was free from prison? He wanted to be there to help him, to make sure he didn't end up back in prison.

*　*　*

"Daniel and I have a little business to attend to," Henry announced as he slid his chair back after the meal while the staff cleared the table.

Daniel happened to glance up and the staff member who looked at him earlier winked. Could he be FBI? He had no way to know since his last communication with the FBI last November. It was still too risky to try to get a message to them.

Helen stood. "Come on, girls. The Denver Nuggets game is on."

Leigha and Carolyn joined Helen in the adjoining great room.

"Come with me to my office," Henry said.

Daniel followed Massey down another hallway past dozens of photos that showed the story of how they built their company Quick Connect into the largest social media platform in the world.

"You're just a kid there," Daniel said as he stopped and pointed at a photo of Massey in his dorm room at college.

Massey stopped and looked at the picture. "I was such a nerd. No one took me seriously except Helen."

"You met her in college?"

"She was working on her MBA," Massey said as he continued down the hallway. "A mutual friend referred her to me to help her with some statistical modeling. We hit it off right away."

"Is that when you came up with the idea for Quick Connect?"

"It was just a simple program I came up with to make it easy to share what we were working on. Soon our friends were using it, and the rest is history." He stopped to admire a photo showing him and Helen ringing the opening bell for trading on the Nasdaq stock exchange. "Social media wasn't a thing when Helen and I started Quick Connect. Everyone laughed at us." Massey said with a gleam in his eyes. "But the business helped me become a multimillionaire. That's when people finally took us seriously."

"Now your Archipelago software is running twenty states, including Michigan."

CHAPTER 2

"Twenty-two now," Massey said. "We added two more states last month. No one believed us when my venture capital firm Arpa launched our Archipelago software suite to transform government and make it far more efficient. Now we're running almost half the states in the country."

"Do you miss running Arpa since you put Helen in charge of it last fall?"

"I had to separate myself from it now that I'm running for Michigan governor," Massey said as he continued down the hallway. "I need to focus on denying Governor Karen Bauer a second term."

"Why do you want to be governor? You're a billionaire."

Massey stopped at the paneled oak door to his office and turned to look at Daniel. "It's a stepping stone to running for president of the United States." He entered his office.

"I didn't know you had your sights on the presidency," Daniel said. He took a seat in front of Massey's massive oak desk and scanned the empty desktop, which contained only a closed laptop centered on a leather desk pad.

Massey sat behind his desk in a high-back, black leather desk chair trimmed with polished chrome and placed his hands on the desk.

"What did you want to discuss?"

"Helen is well aware of why I formed Arpa as a venture capital firm." He flipped up the laptop screen and rubbed his chin for a moment. "It brought together the richest tech entrepreneurs on the planet as investors. Together, we control most of the world with our digital platforms. Combined, we have more wealth than most countries. I convinced them we could make governments more efficient with my Archipelago software suite."

"What are you getting at?"

Henry lowered his voice. "Only you and I know the real reason I formed Arpa. They have no idea how much power I'll have with all the data I'm collecting from the states running Archipelago. Data is pure gold in the digital world."

"What *exactly* do you plan to do with all that data?"

"You saw how I revised evidence and state and county records in Archipelago to frame Ferguson." Massey grinned. "That was a test.

Imagine what I could do controlling all the data in twenty-two states. Can you imagine what kind of power I'd have if I were president and convinced the federal government to start using Archipelago?"

Daniel suppressed a sigh. He could indeed imagine the power Henry would have. It was the reason he was deep undercover. Daniel leaned forward. "You must have a large server farm to house all that data. Aren't you concerned someone will figure out what you're doing?"

Massey flashed a devious look. "Not as big as you think."

Daniel hesitated on how much to push for details. "Does Helen know you're still collecting data from all the states using Archipelago?"

"It's better if I leave her in the dark. I told the Arpa board last year I was shutting down collecting all the data for our personal use."

"But what if someone finds out?"

Massey draped his arms over the armrests. "You know I have the capability to use force if necessary."

"I think you proved that when you targeted the *Emerald Isle* with your armed drone."

"Everything worked out better than I thought." Massey frowned. "Tomorrow, they're moving Ferguson to St. Helena prison. He'll go before the grand jury a few weeks after that. Everything about the case, all the evidence, will be reviewed again. They'll likely indict him on terrorism charges. Are you sure there's no possibility of them connecting me to the drone attack?"

"The feds have more than enough evidence for the grand jury to indict Ferguson. There wasn't even a hint of your involvement."

"I'm a software coder at heart. I'm always looking for the one line of computer code I might have missed that could create problems."

The room grew quiet for a moment as Massey kept his gaze focused on Daniel.

"Trust me," Daniel said. "We're good."

Henry scrunched his face. "I just think they're moving too fast on this case. I'm sure Governor Bauer had a hand in expediting this so that the trial is over before the gubernatorial primary election in August."

"You were hoping Ferguson's trial would be held a couple of weeks

CHAPTER 2

before the primary election to remind voters to vote for you instead of Governor Bauer?"

"Of course. I am challenging the governor for the party nomination. I want to unseat her."

"No need to worry," Daniel repeated. "The governor's poll numbers have slipped since the terror attack last August. You sure stirred up a lot of fear in the tourist towns."

"Just what I hoped for," Massey said. We still need to consider what might come up in the trial."

"Their case is solid. They have no idea that the video of Ferguson loading the stolen drone into a van is fake. They couldn't even detect you spliced it into the security camera footage."

"My video manipulation software is years ahead of anything out there. Once they stored the evidence in Archipelago, it was easy to modify the video."

"I'm more concerned about Fallon McElliot," Daniel said. "I've known him for a lot of years. He's always been determined to get to the truth."

"Don't worry about him," Massey said with a dismissive wave. "Even if he remembered the details about our meeting in the cabin before the terror attack, no one would believe him."

"They'd think he believed all those phony online conspiracy theories you put on those websites you created."

Massey nodded. "Exactly. Besides, we're keeping tabs on McElliot."

"Are you monitoring his phone?" Daniel asked.

"Not since he took a medical leave from his job with the governor. He's no longer using a phone connected to Archipelago, and I can't track that ancient car of his."

"His Dodge Dart is 1960s vintage," Daniel said. "That thing is all analog. Nothing digital about it. But he must have a cell phone."

"Too risky trying to tap into it. I don't want the FBI to trace anything back to me."

"You think they're tracking McElliot?"

Massey frowned. "Can't be too careful. Besides, I still have Trevor Jackson, Regional Director of Homeland Security, keeping tabs on

McElliot and his friend Alicia Chalmers. We want to be the first to know if McElliot remembers any of the details from the cabin.

"Okay, but I still don't get why Trevor agreed to be a spy for you."

"I promised him a position in my cabinet," Massey leaned back, "when I'm governor."

Daniel ran a hand across his forehead. "Seems risky to me to have him onboard."

Massey shrugged. "He thinks it's just background for my gubernatorial campaign. He isn't aware of anything else. Besides, I'm paying him a nice bonus."

Daniel nodded and stroked his beard. Why did Massey need Trevor? A tech titan running the world's largest social media platform and twenty-two states with Archipelago could digitally track anyone he wanted. Who else was secretly working with him? All the more reason to be careful in trying to reach out to the FBI or Fallon. No doubt Henry was keeping close tabs on him and every piece of communication he used. He looked at Massey. "You're so confident."

"I have to be. You know, Daniel . . ." Henry shifted in his chair. "I'm concerned about Helen."

"Why?"

"With her running Arpa now, I feel out of touch with my board of tech entrepreneurs. I can't afford to have someone suspect what I'm up to."

"I can talk to my buddies at Peninsular who run security for your Arpa board meetings. They can give me a read on the group at next month's board meeting in Geneva."

Henry pointed at Daniel. "I want *you* to go to their board meeting. I'll talk to Helen later tonight about you going with her to make sure Peninsular is still doing a good job handling security for the meeting."

"You want me to keep tabs on Helen?"

"Mainly the Arpa board." Massey stood. "Can you still make next week's campaign planning meeting back in Michigan at my home in Bloomfield Hills?"

"I'll be there." Daniel winked at Massey and stood. "At your official residence."

CHAPTER 2

"Colorado is still fighting me about it. They want my millions in income tax, but Michigan hasn't objected."

"Why hasn't the governor questioned your Michigan residency?"

"Because I've given millions to the party's PAC."

"Are the party officials supporting you?"

"Not publicly. I'm leaving nothing to chance. Next week we'll wrap up plans for my June bus tour of the state. Starting next month we're going to ramp up my campaign with ads. By summer it will be a full court press to the August primary election."

"I'll be there," Daniel said.

"Good." Massey took a step toward the door, then stopped and looked back at Daniel. "You know you can't contact your family while we're in Michigan. It's too risky."

"I'm aware of that."

Massey patted Daniel on the shoulder. "It's good to have you onboard. Let's go watch the Nuggets."

Daniel followed Massey out of his office and down the long hallway, observing the framed photos showing the history of Quick Connect in reverse. Only a couple photos showed Helen and him together. There were so many pictures, and he was always front and center. How many more months could he stand as Massey's right-hand man?

He was deeply embedded in the Massey empire since last summer with nothing to show for it. There had to be some way to get some hard evidence to prove Massey's secret plan. He must be communicating with others, yet the FBI had been monitoring him for years with nothing to show for it. Could he be using a private network to communicate undetected with others involved in his plan? And just where was he hiding his secret computer server farm? It could be anywhere in the world.

"How are our Denver Nuggets doing?" Massey asked as they entered the great room with a massive screen mounted on a wall in front of a semicircle of overstuffed chairs and a couch.

Daniel felt like he was courtside watching the basketball game as he sat in a chair facing the screen. He watched Massey pour himself a drink and sit next to Helen on the couch.

"Help yourself," Massey said as he held his glass up toward Daniel.

"No thanks, "Daniel said.

The golden liquid in Massey's glass—the way Massey held it toward him—a memory flashed in his mind to the moment last August when he, Massey, and Fallon had been in the cabin on Beaver Island just before the drone attack. The same sick feeling in his stomach came back when he recalled the moment Henry released the drone with explosives, programmed to target the *Emerald Isle*. He couldn't forget the bewildered look on Fallon's face as he stood in the driveway while the drone hovered above the cabin, then flew north toward St. James Harbor. That was the last he saw Fallon before he was almost killed stopping the drone from reaching its target.

Daniel looked at Henry sitting next to his wife on the couch, and their daughters sitting in overstuffed chairs flanking it. What would Massey do if he was backed into a corner, if someone tried to stop him? What would he do if he had a fleet of armed drones? They were all smiling, cheering as the Nuggets scored a basket. Suddenly, Helen locked eyes with Daniel as the others stared at the large screen. The corners of her mouth curled up as she raised an eyebrow. He nodded back with a slight smile. Maybe the trip to Geneva would give him an opportunity to see what Helen really knew about Henry's plans.

CHAPTER 3

The jump rope was a blur in front of him as it whooshed through the air. Ignore the pain. Push through. Fallon McElliot continued to rotate his wrists to keep the rope spinning in front of him as it passed under his tennis shoes with increasing frequency. Concentrate.

"Ease up a bit." His physical therapist, Bryce Collins, said.

Bryce's words were lost in the whirring of the rope. Keep the rope spinning. He had to get in shape to return to his job as the governor's state police liaison.

"You can stop now," Bryce said.

Through the blur of the spinning rope in front of him, Fallon's eyes met Bryce's. Nothing was going to stop him from getting to the truth behind the terrorist attack on the *Emerald Isle*. Not even the armed drone that tried to take him out.

Bryce shook his head.

Fallon let the rope drop to the floor. Bent over, hands on his knees, he gasped for air. His legs felt weak.

"I can't believe the progress you've made," Bryce said. "You've come so far since I first saw you in the hospital. That exploding drone sure did a number on your body."

"I don't like sitting around," Fallon said as he wiped the sweat off his forehead, then took a seat by a row of plastic folding chairs lined up along a wall of windows. He scanned the gym full of other patients working with physical therapists trying to restore their mobility.

"I've never seen someone so determined to get better," Bryce said as he sat next to Fallon.

"I've been pushing the governor to let me go back to work."

"You just won't let it go."

"I can't."

Silence lingered for a moment. Only the muffled sounds of conversations, the groans of patients, and the clanking and squeaking of gym equipment filled the air. They observed an older woman gripping a bar to steady herself on the parallel bars.

"That was you a few months ago when I started working with you," Bryce said as he nodded toward the woman.

"I know they're missing something . . ." A tingling feeling across the top of his head interrupted his thoughts. He traced the four-inch scar with his finger through his thick, black hair now streaked with gray.

Bryce opened his mouth as their eyes met.

Fallon turned away to watch a man slowly walking on an inclined treadmill, wobbling with each step as he gripped the handrail. He knew what Bryce was about to say. He had heard it before. *It's the injuries that can't be seen that I still need to overcome.*

"You know, Fallon . . ."

Fallon turned to look at him. "If I could just get my brain in shape like the rest of my body."

"You're lucky you've maintained most of your motor skills and you only have memory issues. A lot of my patients can't do everyday tasks on their own." Bryce smiled. "How does it feel to be driving again?"

"Great being behind the wheel again in my Dart. It's like an old friend."

"Can't believe that old thing is still running." Bryce grinned. "Kind of like you."

Fallon cracked a smile. He leaned back in his chair and rubbed his eyes. "Why can't I remember details of what happened the week of the drone attack?"

CHAPTER 3

Bryce put his hand on Fallon's shoulder. "That's a question for your therapist. I think it's more about the trauma than anything physically wrong with your brain."

Fallon thought of his therapist, Grace Brooks. "Grace told me I have post-traumatic stress disorder."

"Not surprised you have PTSD." His eyes narrowed. "I've watched the online videos that passengers on the *Emerald Isle* recorded of you and Alicia Chalmers in that speedboat, trying to stop the drone from crashing into the ferry. You barely escaped with your life when the drone collided with your speedboat and exploded."

Fallon closed his eyes. *That* memory was still there. He shook his head and looked at Bryce.

"When is your next appointment with Grace?" Bryce asked.

"Next week." He shook his head. "This recovery is taking too long."

"You need to give it time. You can't rush healing."

"I feel like I don't have time."

"You're impossible." Bryce stood up and looked at his watch. "That's enough for today."

Fallon stood. His legs were weak. He steadied himself with his hand on the bar along the window.

"You okay?"

"I'm fine." Fallon straightened his body, gripping the handrail, trying to keep a straight face. "Thanks."

Bryce sighed. "Take care of yourself, Fallon. See you next week."

* * *

In the locker room Fallon changed out of his sweats into his khaki slacks and light-blue oxford shirt. He looked at the empty side holster in his duffle bag, remembering that the state police took his gun and badge away after he was injured. It seemed strange not to have his gun by his side. He slipped on his blue blazer, zipped up his duffle bag, and exited the building.

Outside he smiled when he saw his Dart in the parking lot. Something familiar. It stood tall among the other sleek, newer cars. He set his duffle bag on the hood of the car, unlocked the door with his key, and scanned the parking lot as he opened the door. A dark-blue Dodge Charger caught his attention. The same car that tailed him yesterday.

He tossed his duffle bag on the passenger side of the bench seat and climbed in behind the steering wheel. His leg hurt as he depressed the clutch and started the car. The sound of the engine revving soothed him. He ignored the pain in his leg as he eased off the clutch and backed out of his parking spot. He depressed the clutch again, slipped the column shift into first gear, and drove out of the parking lot. In his rearview mirror, he saw the Charger pull out of its parking spot and follow him.

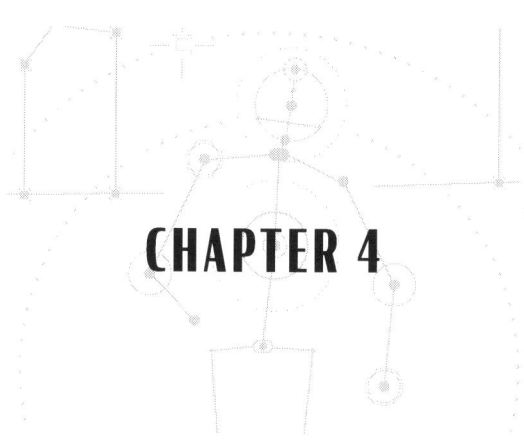

CHAPTER 4

The thumping sound of the helicopter blades above transitioned to a loud whooshing noise as the engine's whir grew louder. Ferguson felt the aircraft lift off and tilt as it moved away from the helipad at Mackinac County Airport. He shifted in his seat, finding it difficult to get comfortable with the seatbelt around his waist and his hands cuffed behind his back. Below, through the rain-streaked window next to him, he could make out a blurry image of the Mackinac Bridge towers.

"I think you'll enjoy the new federal prison on St. Helena Island," the prison guard sitting next to him remarked.

Ferguson shot an annoyed look at the muscular man in a crisply ironed uniform.

"It was made for terrorists like you."

"I'm not a terrorist."

The guard sneered.

Ferguson glanced at the look of disbelief from the two guards seated across from him, then returned to looking out his window.

A minute later, a lighthouse came into view with several outbuildings barely visible on a small clearing at the island's eastern tip. He noted a boat tied to an illuminated dock and several people scurrying in the rain to a vehicle parked nearby.

"Why didn't you bring me here by boat?" Ferguson asked as he glanced at the guards sitting across from him.

"This is a more secure way to transport you," a guard responded.

He looked out the window again as they passed by the lighthouse with an attached, two-story house. A bright light at the top of the tall tower blinked on and off as they passed by. A second later a large prison complex came into view, glowing with bright spotlights, surrounded by a tall, chain-link fence topped with razor wire. In the center stood a large two-story, cinder block building with narrow windows. He recognized that as the cell block for prisoners.

Suddenly, the helicopter banked hard to the right and began its descent. His body tensed as memories of his army years in Afghanistan flooded back, accompanied by the anxious anticipation of being dispatched on another mission. A brightly illuminated helipad came into view, and he took a deep breath. As the helicopter touched down, he felt his body sink into the seat cushion, compressing his cuffed hands against his back. The whir of the rotor faded into a slowing *whup-whup* sound as the engine wound down. The side door opened to reveal the glare of spotlights and the chill of a March evening rain.

The guard seated next to Ferguson unbuckled him while another guard grabbed his arm and pulled him out of the seat. The third guard pushed him from behind toward the open door. Outside, three more guards with rain ponchos stood at attention. One stepped forward.

"Welcome to St. Helena Island Federal Correctional Facility," the guard outside said as he extended his arms to help Ferguson step out of the helicopter. "The Alcatraz of the Great Lakes."

"Keep your head down," one guard inside the helicopter said as he helped Ferguson step down.

"Don't I get a rain poncho?" Ferguson asked.

The guards just laughed.

"He's all yours," the burly guard said as he pushed him toward the three guards standing outside.

The rain soaked his orange jumpsuit as he hunched under the spinning

CHAPTER 4

helicopter blades, chilling him to the bone. Someone grabbed his arm while someone else pushed him from behind.

"Move it!" a guard beside him shouted.

As he walked with the guards, he shook off the rain dripping down from his hair over his eyes and spotted a large, metal entry door in a smaller cinder block building attached to the two-story cell block. "Nice weather," he remarked as he turned his head away from the violent swirl of rain being churned by the spinning blades as the helicopter lifted off.

"The Straits of Mackinac aren't hospitable when it comes to weather," a white-haired guard said. "You're lucky this isn't snow."

A moment later a dry, warm breeze engulfed them as they entered the prison.

Ferguson's soaked sneakers squeaked as they walked across the polished linoleum floor. Someone grabbed his shoulders and pushed him down onto a hard, metal chair. His soaked jumpsuit made it hard to slide into the seat. A guard sat next to him, flipped down the hood of his rain poncho, and revealed his bald head supported by a thick neck.

"Thomas Ferguson, transfer from Missouri for the grand jury investigation," the bald guard said as he gripped his arm.

"We've been expecting this terrorist," a man dressed in a blue shirt with green tie and black slacks said as he appeared with a tablet in his hand. "We should just tie you to a big rock and toss you into Lake Michigan for what you did."

Ferguson noted the warden badge on the left side of his shirt. He frowned at the man. "I'm not a terrorist. I was framed."

"You're a disgrace to our profession," the warden said as he stood in front of Ferguson. "If you think you'll get special treatment because you were once the warden of Jackson Prison . . ." The warden crouched to eye level and locked his gaze on him. "You're wrong."

Ferguson tried not to flinch as he kept silent, eyes focused on the warden. He fought the urge to shiver as his rain-soaked clothes chilled his skin. He clenched his teeth to stop them from chattering.

The warden straightened his body and began tapping on his tablet.

"You're disgusting," the burly guard seated next to him grumbled. "Not only did you try to kill everyone on the *Emerald Isle*, but you killed tourism in Northern Michigan. All our businesses around here have suffered. Everyone is terrified to visit here after that drone attack last August. My mom lost her only source of income from her vacation rental."

"Good thing Alicia Chalmers and Fallon McElliot stopped that drone," another guard chimed in. "They're heroes around here."

Anger surged inside Ferguson. McElliot! That traitor. He knew Fallon was somehow involved in framing him for the terror attack. How could his former partner in the Detroit Police betray him like that. Especially after he saved his life when they were on an army patrol in Afghanistan.

"We'll get you checked into our fine hotel," the warden said as he continued to tap his tablet.

"My dad is a police officer with the Detroit Police," another guard said, glaring at him. "He knew your dad when he was precinct captain, and he said your dad would be ashamed of you and what you've done. You're a disgrace—you and your crooked friends in that crime ring."

"I get to leave here tonight and go home to my family," the burly guard sneered. "I bet your family has abandoned you after this."

Ferguson glared at the guard. Family. He had no family. The crime ring *was* his family before it was broken up with all the arrests last year. None of this would've happened if he had stopped Cally from releasing all that evidence. If only he hadn't threatened Cally's family to force him to hand over the computer hard drive holding all the evidence on the crime ring. Maybe Cally wouldn't have escaped from prison. He'd weighed this a million times in his head.

"Get him out of here," the warden said as he kicked Ferguson in the shin.

A sharp pain rose up his leg as two guards yanked him out of the chair and pushed him forward. They hurried him through a series of corridors to a cell at the end of a long hallway, removed his handcuffs, and shoved him inside. As he tumbled onto the cement floor, the door closed behind him with a loud thud.

"Hey, what about these wet clothes?" Ferguson asked.

The sound of hard-soled shoes clicking on cement faded into silence.

The cold from the floor began to seep into his body. Ferguson pulled himself up, took a deep breath, and sat on a small plastic stool next to a

CHAPTER 4

small plastic desktop attached to the wall. He surveyed the stark, narrow cell with gray cement block walls, a single bunk on one side, and a stainless steel sink and toilet in one corner. He knew the layout well. He had studied the blueprints when he was part of the prison design committee while he was warden of Jackson Prison. This was the thanks he got for lobbying the Federal Bureau of Prisons to build on this site. He had made the case that the federal government already owned the land with a lighthouse and an old Coast Guard rescue station. He never dreamed he would be a prisoner here.

A lot of good it did now, knowing the layout of the prison. There had to be some way out of this place, but how? Not all the members of the crime ring in Detroit had been captured. If he could locate one or two of them, maybe they could intercept him when he was transferred to Marquette for the grand jury. Dream on. Security would be even tighter for the transfer.

He stood and walked to the tiny window in his cell, just large enough for him to put his face near the thick, glass pane. Through the streaks of rain flowing down the narrow window, he could see the Mackinac Bridge now lit up across the Straits of Mackinac against the nighttime sky.

There had to be a way out of this mess. What could Fallon know? Was he faking his memory loss to hide something? He hadn't talked to Fallon since last summer when he sent Fallon to find Cally after escaping prison. Fallon was supposed to find Cally and help locate the hard drive with all that incriminating evidence on the crime ring before the authorities did. Instead, Fallon turned on him. The traitor. If he only knew what Fallon had found on Beaver Island. What was he hiding from everyone? Somehow, Fallon knew the terror attack was about to happen. Did Fallon know enough to prove he wasn't behind the terror attack?

The clunk of his cell door opening startled him. He turned away from the window to see a guard step into his cell.

"Get out of those wet clothes and put these on," the guard said as he tossed a folded orange jumpsuit and underwear along with a pair of dry shoes and socks on his bed. "It's standard issue."

Ferguson picked up the jumpsuit and stared at the guard.

"When you're changed, there's a Nigel Moseley here to see you. Says he's your new attorney." The guard shook his head. "I heard you fired your public defender in Missouri. I'm surprised there's anyone left who wants to represent you."

The guard exited the cell, and the door clunked closed behind him.

Ferguson rubbed his jaw. He was surprised Nigel showed up after his phone call. He unfolded the jumpsuit on his bed and slipped out of his wet clothes. The dry jumpsuit felt good.

A few minutes later, his cell door opened.

"We're here to take you to your new attorney," a different guard said as he stepped into the cell and cuffed his hands.

Another guard joined them. They grabbed his arms, pulled him out of his cell, and closed the door behind them. As they proceeded down a long corridor, Ferguson squinted his eyes against the bright overhead lights and stark, white walls. They wound around a corner and down another long hallway until they reached a series of metal doors with windows. Each door was numbered.

"He's in here," the guard said as he opened a door with the number 3 below the glass.

A man in a crisply tailored suit seated on one side of a small metal table stood as Ferguson entered the room.

"Nigel Moseley," the man said as he sat back down. "Nasty night to visit you. It's pouring out there."

The guard secured Ferguson's cuffs to the metal table. "Tell me about it," he said as he sat across from Moseley.

The door closed behind the guard, and the room became silent. They sat for a moment, looking at each other.

Ferguson eyed the man with suspicion. He looked too put-together, too polished. He eyed his dark, neatly styled hair, clean-shaven face, and round, wire-framed glasses trimmed with gold. The paisley silk tie was over the top, but the look seemed to fit his confident appearance.

Ferguson shifted in his seat. "So Mr. Moseley—"

"Call me Nigel."

"Okay, Nigel. Why *did* you send me that note and your business card?"

"I believe you're innocent—at least regarding the terrorism charges. I know the video is fake."

"What makes you say that?"

CHAPTER 4

"We're going to get you out of here."

Ferguson laughed. "As in free?"

Nigel nodded. His stone-face stare emphasized his seriousness.

"There is no way the feds are going to let me walk. They want me locked away for the rest of my life."

"You didn't do it," Nigel said with a look of indifference as he leaned closer. "When you hear the name Nadia Long, do *exactly* what she tells you."

"What are you talking about?"

"It'll make sense soon enough." Nigel stood.

"Wait! That's it? That's all you have to say?"

Nigel put his hands on the table and leaned closer to Ferguson. "You need to be ready. Make sure you follow Nadia Long's instructions."

"Why should I trust you?"

Nigel's icy blue eyes bore down on him. "We want justice."

"So, you know Fallon McElliot framed me for the terrorist attack?"

"Fallon didn't frame you," Nigel said as he walked to the door.

"Of course he did."

"The video is fake."

"How do you know that?"

Nigel knocked on the door. "Nadia Long. Remember."

"Wait."

A guard opened the door.

"That's it? Aren't you going to discuss my defense?"

Nigel stopped a moment in the open doorway. He grinned, then exited the room.

"Nigel!"

Two guards entered the room and unlocked his cuffs from the table.

One of the guards chuckled. "Some attorney."

"Might as well get used to prison life," the other guard said.

They led him through the doorway. He spotted Nigel at the far end of the hallway.

"Wait! Nigel!"

Nigel kept walking and disappeared around a corner.

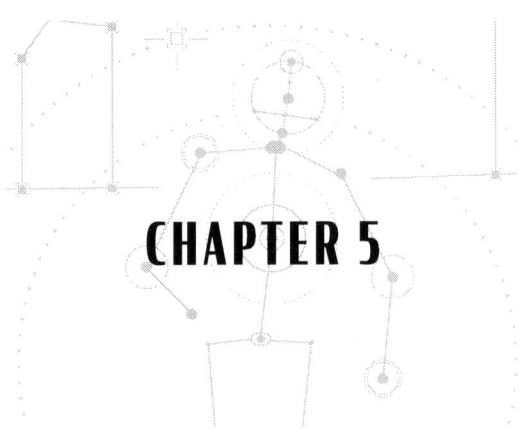

CHAPTER 5

*A*bove, *the drone is closing in on him. The buzzing sound is deafening. He dives into the icy water, feeling the chill of the lake penetrate to his very bones as he swims deeper and deeper. A sudden flash of light, the muffled sound of an explosion, and a strong current of water churn around him; his arms and legs flail. In an instant, intense pain pierces his head, the side of his body, and his legs. The pain surges through him. He tries to move, but then a sudden darkness.* "Fallon!"

His body jerked as he opened his eyes and blinked a few times. He looked at his therapist, Grace Brooks, seated across from him in an overstuffed, tan chair with her legs crossed, notepad on her lap, and pen in hand. Her long, brown hair was pulled back in a neat ponytail. A lone table lamp next to her cast a warm glow on the look of concern on her face. He glanced at the black-and-white Ansel Adams nature scenes displayed on the tan walls and the swinging pendulum on the regulator clock across from him.

"Take a deep breath and try to relax," Grace said. "These are difficult memories."

CHAPTER 5

Eyes closed again, Fallon took a deep breath, then let his stiff body relax as he exhaled. His shoulders lowered as he leaned back on the couch, letting his body sink into the worn cushions. His hands dropped to his side, fingers tracing the soft fabric. He opened his eyes, looked at the gray sky outside the large window to his left, and watched the rain trickling down the glass pane. He focused on the sound of the ticking clock.

"It's pouring out there," Fallon said. "It's been raining all week."

"Tell me what you were just remembering," Grace said.

He continued watching streams of water flow down the window. The memory returned. *He's suddenly immersed in cold lake water*. His hands curled into fists; body tensed as if he was about to be struck.

Fallon turned and looked into Grace's soft, brown eyes. Her calm face eased the tension. He took a deep breath and closed his eyes. "I'm underwater . . . there's an explosion . . . a strong current of water hits me hard . . . then. . ." Tears welled. He blinked to stop them.

The room is silent, except for rain pattering on the window and the clock ticking. "Go on, Fallon."

"Is this really necessary?"

"You went through a very traumatic experience." Grace said, her voice soft. "You survived a terrorist attack."

Trauma. Fallon let the word hang there a moment, suspended in his mind.

"I know this is hard," Grace said.

"Is this really necessary?"

Grace nodded.

Fallon exhaled. "I've watched the video of Alicia and me stopping that drone from hitting the *Emerald Isle* as it left Beaver Island, but I can't seem to piece together how I got there."

Grace flipped back pages in her notebook. "Alicia Chalmers, your friend from Homeland Security?"

"Yes."

"Tell me what *you* remember seeing, not the video."

Fallon closed his eyes and pressed his elbows against his side. He squeezed his hands together on his lap as images resurfaced in his mind. "I'm driving my granddad's Chris-Craft boat, and Alicia is with me.

There's a loud buzzing noise. I see a large drone quickly closing in on us with the name Caspian on the front of it . . ." He rested his right arm on the armrest.

"Do you recall why you had your granddad's boat?"

Why *did* he have his granddad's boat? "No."

"Okay. Go on."

"I push the throttle on the boat wide open," Fallon gripped the end of the armrest with his hand. "The boat's engine is howling, but I can hear people screaming on the *Emerald Isle* . . . I look behind me and Alicia is standing in the back of the boat with an automatic rifle pointed at the sky . . ." He dug his fingers into the foam on the armrest.

The room is quiet, except for the ticking clock. Suddenly a crack of thunder breaks the silence. His hands curl into tight fists. A new image in his mind replaced Alicia.

> *He's wearing fatigues, carrying a rifle, and running into a dark building. More gunfire, more repeated popping. Bullets hit the wall next to him. Another man in fatigues joins him in a dark room. He's holding a rifle. He can barely make out the man's face in the beams of sunlight coming through the holes in the wall. Tom Ferguson? He stares at him as he mouths his name, but he hears a woman's voice.*

"Fallon," Grace said.

He opened his eyes.

"Were you still in the boat?"

"I think . . . I was in Afghanistan."

"Is this the incident with Tom Ferguson when you were in the army?"

Fallon nodded.

Grace gave him an empathetic nod. "You have multiple layers of trauma. That clap of thunder was a trigger. Take a moment to reset."

Fallon took a deep breath, then slowly exhaled.

Grace took a few notes, then shifted in her chair. "Do you recall anything after you blacked out from the drone explosion?"

Fallon looked at the rain outside. "Water was dripping off me as a man

CHAPTER 5

and a woman pulled me onto a boat. The man is wearing a brown sheriff's uniform . . ."

"Keep going."

"Then I was in a helicopter. Alicia is looking down at me. I was in so much pain . . ." Fallon rubbed his forehead and sighed. "These headaches just don't go away."

"What else?"

"That's it. Next thing I remember is waking up in the hospital."

Grace flipped some pages in her notebook. "Last session you mentioned being in a cabin right before the terrorist attack. What do you recall about that?"

"Not much. Just a fuzzy image of a man sitting in a chair across from me in a dimly lit room swirling some whiskey in his glass."

"Who is it?"

Fallon closed his eyes. "I'm not sure."

"Is he telling you something?"

He sat silent for a moment. The memory was so foggy. Did the man tell him drones could deliver something far more damaging than shoes or food? He looked at Grace with a practiced look of empathy. "I'm not sure."

They sat silent, looking at each other.

"I can tell you're frustrated, Fallon. You need to give it time."

"It's been more than seven months," Fallon said as he tapped the top of his head. "And I still can't piece together all the scrambled memories in my head."

"Let's approach it like working on a puzzle. Let's find the corner pieces and try to fill in the border. Grace uncrossed her legs and leaned in toward Fallon, setting her pen down on the notepad on her lap. "Let's try to frame the day you had your brain injury."

Eyes closed. Concentrate. Frame the day. "So many pieces," Fallon said.

"Start with a corner piece, a memory that's clear. How did the day begin?"

"There's this piece where I'm in a plane and someone I know is at the controls."

"Who is it?"

"I'm not sure . . ."

"Was this the day of the terror attack?"

"Maybe?"

"Why were you in the plane?"

"I think we were working a case together, but I'm not sure . . ."

The room was silent as Fallon and Grace looked at each other.

"Let's try another corner piece—the cabin." Grace said. "Try again to recall what the man with the glass told you in the cabin."

A deep breath in, eyes closed. The memory of golden liquid swirling in a glass. "The man across from me is talking about Archipelago."

"A group of islands?"

"No, the software."

"What is he saying about it?"

The conversation is jumbled in his head. "I'm not sure."

"Is anyone else with you?"

Eyes closed. Concentrate. A new memory. "Another man *is* in the room. He's sitting across from me on the couch."

Grace raised an eyebrow. "You've never talked about someone else in the room."

Fallon rubbed his pounding forehead. "We've been over this fuzzy cabin memory for weeks." He stood and stepped over to the window. His mind felt like the gray clouds outside.

"Let's close the memory puzzle box and talk about something else," Grace said.

"No . . ." A stream of water flowed down the glass pane and dropped onto the windowsill. "There is something I need to remember, something that happened in that cabin, something important."

"Okay. Tell me again who is in the room."

Fallon closed his eyes. The outline of the face of the second man on the couch looked familiar. Could it be Daniel, the FBI agent? He looked at Grace. "Just those two men on the couch."

"Any idea who?"

He looked at her and hesitated. "No."

"What else do you recall in the cabin before the drone attack?"

CHAPTER 5

Fallon shook his head and returned to his seat. He bent over and rested his head in the palms of his hands, trying to ease his throbbing forehead.

"You've done great today." Grace set her notepad and pen on a small end table next to her chair. Do you want to finish a few minutes early?"

"There's something else." Fallon looked at Grace. "I think I was in the cabin with them right before the attack on the ferry, but maybe it happened before that. There *is* something about this memory that keeps drawing me back."

They looked at each other for a moment, silent.

She seemed so caring, so concerned, yet at times he was uneasy about her. Was everyone always a suspect?

"You worked law enforcement for years," Grace finally said. "It's possible your detective thinking is like muscle memory, that your brain automatically focuses on the key facts for a case and any potential suspects."

Fallon noted Grace's fidgeting hands in her lap. "I feel like I'm interrogating myself."

"You're a bit obsessed about trying to remember how you knew about the terror attack before it happened."

"That's what made me a great detective."

"Do you remember being a detective?"

Fallon nodded. "I was a detective until the governor made me her state police liaison last year."

"But you don't seem to recall a lot of the details the day of the terror attack."

"Just those pieces I've told you."

Grace grabbed her notepad and flipped some pages. "You talked about being at Cally's parents' house in Detroit in another session." She looked up at Fallon. "Visiting the house might help you remember."

Were he and Daniel at the house? Fallon narrowed his eyes. "I'll give it some thought."

"Or maybe going back to the cabin on Beaver Island would help."

"Ferguson's cabin?"

Grace nodded.

"I haven't been back to Beaver Island since." Fallon's heart rate quickened.

"Give it some thought." Grace glanced at the clock. "Our time is up."

Fallon took a deep breath and got up. He followed Grace as she walked to the exit. He opened the door and looked up and down the hallway.

"Something wrong?" Grace asked.

"I feel like someone is following me."

"It's just anxiety caused by your trauma." She smiled. "Take care, Fallon."

Fallon nodded and stepped into the hallway as Grace closed the door behind him.

Waiting for the elevator, he tried to recall the last time he saw Daniel. Was it a case in Detroit they worked on, or did he really see him at the cabin with Massey?

The elevator doors opened with a ding. A tall man dressed in a trim, dark-blue suit and an open collared shirt stepped out. They exchanged glances as he walked by. He looked familiar. Fallon stepped into the elevator, then put his hand on the door to stop it from closing. He stepped back out and glanced down the hallway.

"Hey, Trevor!" he shouted after the man.

The man stopped and turned. "Fallon? I wasn't sure you recognized me since your..."

Fallon took a few steps down the hallway as the elevator doors closed. "You visited me in the hospital. You're Trevor Jackson, regional director of Homeland Security, Alicia's boss."

Trevor smiled. "You're looking a lot better."

"What are you doing here?"

"Oh...," Trevor nodded toward Grace's office at the end of the hallway. "Same reason as you. You see things you can't forget—horrible things."

"I understand." Fallon raised an eyebrow. "You drove from Detroit to Lansing to see her?"

"She's the best trauma therapist in the state. She understands police work."

Fallon nodded.

CHAPTER 5

Trevor shifted his stance, his eyes darted toward Grace's door, then back at Fallon. "I need to get to my appointment."

Fallon waved at Trevor as he walked down the hall. He pressed the call button for the elevator as he watched Trevor step into Grace's office. Grace smiled, waved, then closed the door. He looked up and down the hallway as the elevator doors opened with a ding. He hesitated, staring at the empty elevator as the doors closed. He stepped toward Grace's office, listening to the muffled voices coming from behind the door, but stopped. Maybe Grace was right. He was just anxious.

Suddenly, a downpour hammered the roof, drowning out the faint voices. Fallon made his way to the stairway next to the elevator. He gripped the handrail as he descended the steps to the ground floor, ignoring the shooting pain in his leg. Why couldn't he remember all the details from the day of the terror attack? Should he go back to Cally's parents' house or return to . . .? He stopped a moment on the bottom step and gripped the handrail.

In the parking garage attached to the office building, he spotted his Dart. He smiled as he unlocked the car door with his key and climbed in. A musty smell greeted him as he closed the door and started the engine. The car rocked as he revved the V8 engine. Music to his ears, so soothing.

His phone dinged. A text from Governor Karen Bauer: "Can you meet me at the Lansing Country Club this afternoon at 2?"

"Sure," Fallon texted back. "What's this about?"

"Just be there."

He responded with a thumbs-up emoji and tossed his phone next to him on the bench seat. As he backed out of his parking spot and drove toward the exit, he glanced at the rearview mirror. A Charger followed him out of the parking garage.

CHAPTER 6

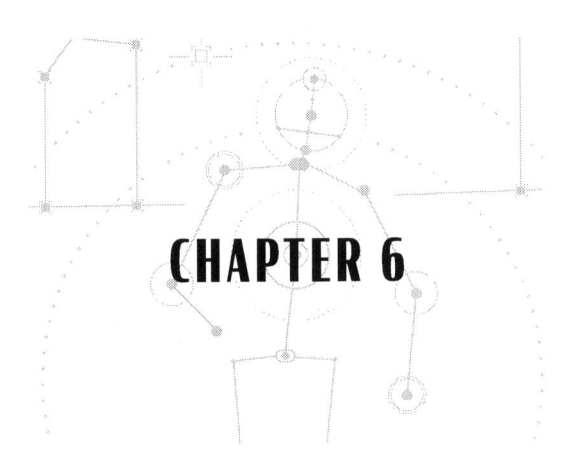

Fallon walked toward the entrance of the stately white building that housed the Lansing Country Club. It seemed familiar. He stopped a moment at the large French doors and looked at his reflection in one of the panes of glass. For a split second, he saw an image of his dad.

"Sorry," a woman said as the door opened and almost hit him.

He waved at her as she passed, then he stepped inside. A member of the governor's security detail met him and escorted him to a room on the far end of the building.

"Thanks for coming, Fallon," Karen said as she greeted him at the door.

Fallon stepped into the large room and looked at the high ceiling with wood beams and a chandelier suspended in the center of the room. He walked to the row of large windows and looked at the golf course outside. "You know my dad liked to come here when he was state attorney general." Fallon turned to look at the governor standing by a long table with a dozen chairs. "My mom told me he had a party in this room for his campaign staff after he lost his primary election for governor to George Romney. She told me his bouts with depression started after that—a couple of years before I was born."

CHAPTER 6

"I didn't know that was the reason."

"That's why I don't like politics."

"Yet here you are—"

"Sorry I'm late," Karen's husband, Jack, said as he entered the room. "The tree-planting ceremony went long."

"What's he doing here?" Fallon asked.

Jack gave Karen a hug, then shook Fallon's hand. "I could ask the same about you."

"I asked him to meet with us before my campaign staff meeting," Karen said as she motioned to her security detail to wait outside. She sat at the table next to Jack and motioned to Fallon. "Have a seat."

"It's never good when you're both talking to me." Fallon sat down at the table opposite them.

"Fallon, I—"

"Karen, before you begin, I have something I need to discuss with you."

Karen raised an eyebrow.

"Ever since I started driving a week ago, a dark-blue Charger has been following me. That's the standard undercover car used by the state police."

"Ever since your head injury, you've been—"

"Admit it. You're having me followed."

Karen folded her arms across her chest.

"Why?"

"No one is following you," Karen said. "You're just paranoid."

"I may have a head injury, but I'm still aware of what's going on around me."

"She's worried about you," Jack chimed in.

"Well, don't be. I can take care of myself."

Karen put her elbows on the table, crossed her arms, and leaned in toward Fallon.

He glared at her. "I know what you're going to say."

Karen's face grew serious. "I wanted to tell you in person."

"Don't say it."

"I can't let you come back to work for me . . . at least not yet."

"How about on a trial basis for just a week?"

"No."

Fallon sighed and leaned back in his chair.

"Chip's handling things for now as the interim state police liaison."

"He's the best analyst I've ever had. We worked together for years until..."

Karen's eyes widened. "He knows you. He's got you covered. This is your time to heal."

"I'm driving now. I've made a lot of progress. I don't doubt Chip's doing a great job, but you need me back there."

Karen and Jack sat staring at Fallon with somber expressions on their faces.

After several seconds, Fallon tapped his finger on the table. "I can handle it."

"We've known each other since grade school," Karen said, her voice laced with concern. "We've always been honest with each other. You may be physically ready, but I'm not sure you're emotionally ready. The state police took your gun and badge away for a reason."

"They had no right doing that."

Karen sighed.

"Look, Fallon," Jack said. "You're a hero for stopping that drone."

"He's more popular than me." Karen's eyes met Fallon's. "Did you see the *Detroit News* poll last week?"

Fallon shook his head. "You know I don't look at the news since the terror attack."

"They put *you* five points ahead of Henry Massey in a hypothetical matchup for governor."

"What she isn't telling you is that Alicia did even better," Jack said. "She polled ten points ahead of Massey. The *News* ran that image of her standing in that Chris-Craft, automatic rifle pointed at the sky, taking out that terrorist drone. She looked pretty tough, like a leader willing to take action."

"Fallon's a hero too," Karen said.

"I just drove the boat."

"Regardless, you're both popular with the public," Jack said.

"The August primary election is still a few months away," Fallon said. "A lot can happen in that time."

CHAPTER 6

Jack pointed his finger at Karen. "You're going to beat Massey."

"That arrogant . . ." Fallon grumbled. "Jack's right. You don't need to worry."

Karen leaned back in her chair and stared at Fallon. "Why won't you let me recognize you and Alicia with a medal for saving all those lives on the *Emerald Isle*?"

"Don't you think it's a little self-serving, especially in an election year?"

"Just because we've been friends since childhood doesn't mean I can't recognize you for being a hero." She shrugged. "Who cares what other people think?"

"You're the one quoting polls."

"That's different," Karen muttered.

"I think Alicia and you should be publicly recognized," Jack said. "You almost lost your life stopping that terrorist drone."

"Technically it *was* a stolen Caspian Corporation drone weaponized by Tom Ferguson's terrorist cell," Karen clarified.

Fallon drummed his fingers on the table. Something about Ferguson being a terrorist didn't set well with him. The pieces didn't seem to fit together to complete the picture. "I'll let you recognize me if you let me go back to work."

"Why are you in such a hurry to come back?" Karen asked.

Fallon locked eyes with his friend.

"You almost died," Karen said, her voice soft.

"Karen—"

"No." Her arms folded in front of her, a look of resolve in her eyes.

"I need to get to the truth about that terror attack."

"You're chasing ghosts, Fallon. The truth is that Tom Ferguson was working for a terror cell on Beaver Island, and he coordinated the entire attack. There's plenty of evidence to support that."

"I have a hunch he didn't do it."

Jack shook his head. "Not another one of your hunches."

"My last hunch was right. I knew that drone was targeting the *Emerald Isle*."

Karen cocked her head and squinted her eyes. "How *did* you know about that terror attack before it happened?"

Fallon shrugged his shoulders. "I'm not sure."

Karen frowned.

They sat a moment in silence, eyes fixed on each other.

"You need to work through the trauma you've been through," Karen said.

"It's been almost eight months. I'm ready *now*."

Karen shook her head.

"You need me for this election," Fallon said. "Henry Massey is going to chew you up and spit you out in the primary election. He'll come at you swinging with his millions of dollars. You know he'll use his Quick Connect for *his* benefit. You *need* me there to help you."

"No I don't."

"Karen, just let me help you. Please."

She shook her head, her lips forming a straight line.

Fallon kept his eyes focused on hers.

"Okay, I'll think about it."

Fallon smiled. "I'll take that."

"There's something else I wanted to talk to you about," Karen said. "They moved Tom Ferguson back to Michigan—to St. Helena Island—until the grand jury meets in Marquette in a few weeks. It's easier to keep the media away on an island."

"Is that the new federal prison?"

"They call it the Alcatraz of the Great Lakes." Karen leaned back in her chair. "When they transfer Ferguson and this whole grand jury investigation starts, it's going to be a media feeding frenzy. You and Alicia are going to be back in the news."

"We can handle it."

"They're going to replay all the events from last August. Are your ready for that?"

"Sure."

Karen frowned. "Whatever you do, don't talk to the media. You need to give yourself space."

"What about Alicia?" Fallon asked. "Are you telling her not to talk to the media?"

Karen smiled. "I hear you're seeing Alicia again."

CHAPTER 6

"I don't remember."

"I think she's good for you. Maybe this time it will stick."

"Maybe that head injury knocked some sense into you," Jack said.

"I doubt it," Karen laughed.

"We're just hanging out together. That's it."

"It seems you've been doing a lot of that lately," Karen said.

"I have a lot of time on my hands right now. I'm visiting her in DC in a few days."

Karen grinned. "Just hanging out together."

"So . . ." Fallon said. "How are your girls doing?"

"I like the way you changed the subject," Jack said.

"Melanie will finish her second year of college at Michigan in a couple months, and Colleen will graduate from high school in May," Karen said. "They have no interest in following in my footsteps."

"Looks like you have no one to carry on your political legacy."

"They've seen too much of the nastiness behind the scenes."

Fallon nodded. "Smart girls."

"But your dad was the Michigan attorney general for a long time," Jack said. "You did carry on his legacy of crime fighting."

Fallon glanced at Karen. "But I didn't have to run for office like my dad."

"It's a pain. At least I'm only running for reelection this time, then I'm term limited."

"How are your boys doing, Fallon?" Jack asked.

"Scott will graduate next year from Wayne State University in criminal justice—"

"Still pursuing the family business of crime fighting," Jack said. "Even after you were seriously injured."

"I think it only encouraged him more," Fallon said. "Trent will finish his first year at the University of Michigan in a few weeks. He's still a social justice major, but he's now looking at law school."

Karen leaned back in her chair. "A lawyer like his grandfather—maybe attorney general someday."

"Maybe he'll follow in my dad's footsteps."

"It seems you're getting along better with your sons now," Karen said. "I know it was difficult after the divorce."

"Since I was injured, they really stepped up to help me with my recovery." Fallon smiled. "So when do I start back to work?"

Karen shook her head. "You just won't let it go."

"I can't."

"We can talk again in a few weeks."

Fallon rubbed his forehead.

Karen's face grew serious. "Just be careful out there."

"Does that mean you'll still have someone follow me?"

"It's for your own good."

"Call off the tail."

Karen stood, tilted her head, and put her hands on her hips. "Okay."

Fallon pushed his chair back and carefully stood, hiding the pain he felt in his leg. "What do you think of me visiting Chip in a week or two for a social visit?"

"You're impossible." Karen sighed. "I'll have Chip arrange security clearance for you to access the Romney Building." She walked over to Fallon and gave him a hug.

As Fallon released Karen, he looked at Jack. "Keep an eye on her."

Jack put his arm around her. "It's a tough job, but I'll manage."

Fallon stepped to the door and looked back at Jack and Karen still standing by the table. "Aren't you leaving?"

"Our campaign staff is meeting here in a few minutes," Karen said.

"I don't think I'll stick around for that." Fallon opened the door and nodded at the security detail standing outside as he headed down the hallway to the exit. In the parking lot, he walked to his Dart and slipped behind the wheel. He depressed the clutch, ignoring the pain in his leg, and tapped the throttle a couple times before turning the key to start the car. The engine groaned as it turned over, then sputtered to life.

A memory surfaced as he listened to the engine. He looked at the empty bench seat next to him. Alicia was sitting with him last summer in this car. He took some deep breaths. They were together, but was it the day of the terrorist attack on the *Emerald Isle*? Were they driving to the cabin on Beaver Island? He tried to piece together the fragments

CHAPTER 6

of memory. His heart beat faster. He closed his eyes as the engine idled, trying to remember.

> *They park the car and slowly advance toward the cabin through a wooded lot . . . sticks breaking beneath their feet, small tree branches brushing by them as they approach a cabin in a clearing. They press against the side of the cabin . . . moving carefully, peering in the windows. It looks like someone is inside the cabin. He tries to identify the person . . .*

A throbbing pain in his head cut off the memory. He rubbed his forehead and checked his rearview mirror. As he pulled out of his parking spot, a Charger began to follow him, then stopped in the middle of the parking lot. He smiled as he drove away without a tail.

CHAPTER 7

Daniel scanned the conference room inside Massey's Bloomfield Hills, Michigan, mansion. The room was empty like most of the rest of the house except for the large oak table where they sat and the half-dozen screens mounted to the wall for video conferencing. This might as well be called his campaign headquarters instead of the home that made him an official Michigan resident so he could run for governor. He studied the faces of young, energetic people on the screens staring back at them. They all seemed so phony, working too hard to look sincere and knowledgeable—too eager to help make Massey the next governor. He leaned back in his leather office chair and looked at Massey orchestrating the meeting, head held high, confident, hands emphasizing his points as he spoke.

"I know Governor Karen Bauer is concerned about her poll numbers. We're in a good position, but we still have a lot of work to do." Massey rolled up his shirt sleeves. I don't like that *Detroit News* poll showing Alicia Chalmers and Fallon McElliot polling ahead of me in a hypothetical race for governor.

"You don't think those two would actually run for governor?" a campaign consultant chimed in.

CHAPTER 7

"I doubt it," Massey said. "What about the media buy during my statewide bus tour?"

"We're placing ads that will hit the markets where you speak each day," a woman replied as she tapped on a tablet in front of her.

"And you're paying list price for ads on my Quick Connect platform?"

"Of course, Henry." The woman chuckled. "We don't want to give any impression of impropriety."

"What about speaking locations?" Massey continued, looking at the tablet in his hand. "Are you getting venues for my speeches in key areas with our targeted voting blocs?"

"We're making great progress, Henry," a woman on another screen said. "We have . . ."

The woman's words began to fade into the background as he watched Massey engage his campaign team. Had he really won his confidence or was he merely playing him—using him? It all seemed too easy, yet hard to win his trust as his global head of security. He glanced at the half-dozen screens displaying campaign aides eager and full of enthusiasm. They're all playing him—only joining him on the ride in hopes of getting a position in the administration if he wins the governorship. What would they think if they knew his more sinister motive for wanting the governorship? Would they still stick with him if they knew he wanted to seize control of all the State of Michigan data as well as the other states running Archipelago?

Daniel took a sip of his coffee and scanned the list of security items he'd identified for the campaign. He glanced at Massey, then back at his tablet. How many others were in on his secret plan? Daniel studied the faces on the screens. How many of them knew the truth about Archipelago?

"You're up, Daniel," Massey said.

Daniel jumped at the sound of his name and quickly glanced at his tablet. "Security details . . ."

He spent the next few minutes reviewing the security plans for each location of the bus tour. He was on autopilot as he outlined the protocols, training for volunteers to spot potential threats, and active AI technology that would be deployed to screen the crowds. "The last thing we want is someone taking a shot at our candidate."

"You really think someone would want to shoot me?" Massey asked, eyebrows raised.

"We can't be too careful," Daniel said.

Massey nodded, deep in thought.

"Any questions?" Daniel asked.

The faces on the screens returned blank stares.

"Good." Massey smiled. "Things are coming together very well. Thank you, everyone. We'll talk again in a week."

The screens went dark as people signed out. Massey pivoted in his seat and looked at Daniel. "I saw you studying each person onscreen."

"I've run background checks on all of them, but I still like to study their mannerisms and facial expressions. I want to know if they're hiding something we don't know."

"Any red flags?"

"Nothing yet."

"I do know they are all ambitious political operatives," Massey said.

"That's what concerns me."

Massey tilted his head and shifted in his seat.

"It seems their loyalty to you is based on how much it benefits them and their careers."

Massey smirked. "Of course. I expect that. It's how the game is played." He narrowed his eyes. "What I really wonder about is whether one of them might be an FBI agent trying to infiltrate my campaign."

Daniel looked at the blank screens, then Massey. "You don't need to worry about that."

Massey nodded and shifted in his seat. "When you go to Geneva with Helen for the Arpa board meeting next month"—he examined the blank screens—"I want you to read the faces of all the tech leaders I have on the board."

"I'm sure Helen's staff is capable of screening them."

"Helen's staff does not attend the Arpa board meetings. Everything discussed at those meetings is strictly confidential. Only Peninsular staff and Arpa's board attends. I want you to go as part of the Peninsular security team. No one will give a second thought to you being there since you used to work for Peninsular."

CHAPTER 7

"You want me to look for signs that someone might turn on you?"

"You have a way of reading people." Massey leaned forward in his chair, face scrunched, eyes focused on Daniel. "You seem to have a sense when someone is lying or covering up something."

"That comes from years of interrogating suspects." Daniel locked eyes with Massey. "If you do it enough, you start to see patterns in people. You learn to read body language." He glanced back at the blank screens. "Things are coming together for your campaign."

"We're going to win, Daniel." Massey stood, rolled down his sleeves, and buttoned them. "Losing is not an option."

"Are you concerned about Fallon remembering what you told him in my cabin on Beaver Island right before the drone attack?"

"Trevor told me Fallon still can't piece together the details of what happened before the attack," Massey said as he threw on his suit jacket. "He just has some vague memories with a few details."

"Does that concern you?"

"Like I told Fallon in the cabin last August before the drone attack, even if he does remember, no one is going to believe him." He straightened his tie.

"The problem is if Fallon does remember every detail, he won't stop until he has hard evidence to support his claim. I saw it in the cases we worked together. He chased down every hunch he had and every suspect until the case was solved."

"I suppose you know Fallon pretty well," Massey said as he slipped his tablet into a slim, leather case.

"What I know is that he helped me solve some of the toughest cases I had at the FBI. He's one of the best detectives I've ever known. I doubt his head injury would cause him to lose that." Daniel noticed the perplexed look on Massey's face. "I know. Maybe I overthink things. I'm always running scenarios to prepare for the worst."

Massey tucked his leather case under his arm. "Fallon is the least of my worries. Last week an attorney named Nigel Moseley visited Ferguson in prison. Apparently he fired his public defender in St. Louis and hired this Moseley guy."

"And how do you know that?"

"The Archipelago software that the State of Michigan Corrections uses has interconnects with federal prisons for prisoner exchanges and visitors. I've been keeping tabs on Ferguson."

"You seem concerned."

"What's more concerning is that we can't find any background on this Moseley character. The phone number Ferguson used to call him ties back to the San Francisco area, but that's all we have."

"Archipelago has nothing on him?"

"California is still using an outdated computer system we can't seem to tap into. Arpa is still in talks with them."

"Do you think someone is on to you?"

"I'm not sure. We're monitoring the situation," Massey said.

Daniel nodded, wondering exactly who was helping Massey gather intelligence on Ferguson.

"Mr. Massey," came a voice from behind them as the door to the conference room opened. "Your jet is ready."

Daniel turned to see a tall, slender woman standing in the doorway, smartly dressed in a navy blue business suit. "Have we met?" he asked her.

"I'm Mr. Massey's new personal assistant."

Daniel glared at Massey.

"Don't worry, she's been thoroughly checked," Massey said as he took a few steps toward the door and smiled at her. "I'll meet you on the jet."

The woman left the room.

The rich aroma of perfume wafted past Daniel as he stood. "You two are traveling alone?"

"Don't worry, there's nothing going on."

"Just the appearance could be bad for you. Does Helen know about her?"

"Of course she does. She's not the jealous type. She trusts me."

Daniel wasn't sure *he* could trust him.

"Well, we're off to California."

"To convince them they need Archipelago?"

"That too, but first, I'm going to watch the last launch to complete my satellite network. I want to be there to congratulate my team. With this launch, my private, global network will be fully operational."

CHAPTER 7

"Congratulations. I remember when you launched your first satellite. Everyone said it couldn't be done."

"My plans are coming together," Massey said with a smug look. "When I win the governorship, I'll have the perfect platform to manage all the State of Michigan's digital assets. As governor, I can convince more and more states to use Archipelago software to manage their operations. Soon I will be able to consolidate all the data from all those states onto one server. They'll be focused on the billions of dollars they are saving, and I'll have control of all their data."

Daniel eyed Massey. "That would have to be a massive server farm to house all that data."

"Not necessarily," Massey said as he headed for the door. "More on that another day."

"I almost forgot," Daniel called after him. "I had those pieces of the satellite communications device analyzed."

Massey stopped at the door and turned to face Daniel. "And?"

"It came back with nothing, but it still concerns me. Do you have architectural plans for your Colorado estate? I want to take a look at potential access points like the climate control system. I want to make sure everything is nailed down tight."

"I assure you, it's sound," Massey said with his hand on the doorknob.

"I still think I should take a look at it just to be sure."

Massey shifted his stance, eyes trained on Daniel.

Daniel let the silence hang for a moment, waiting for an answer.

"Just off the commercial kitchen there's a stairway that will take you to the basement level. On the far end of the basement is a glassed-in service room with all the digital controls for running my estate—that's all I know about that. The blueprint for the house is on a table in that room for the maintenance crew."

"You have a paper copy of the blueprint? I thought you'd only have digital copies."

"I do, but the engineering firm who built the house told us to have a paper copy in the service room for repair people to use in case the computer system was inaccessible."

"*Your* computer system inaccessible?"

"I know. I took that as an insult, but I also believe in expecting the unexpected."

"I'll take a look at the blueprints. Do I have access to that room?"

Silence again as Massey tilted his head slightly.

Daniel maintained his calm stance, but inside, he was tense. Did he push too far?

"I think it's time I give you full access to my estate." Massey nodded. "It'll take a few hours for the system to update the biometric details for your clearance."

Daniel watched Massey leave the room. He looked again at the blank screens. No doubt Massey was monitoring every step he took.

CHAPTER 8

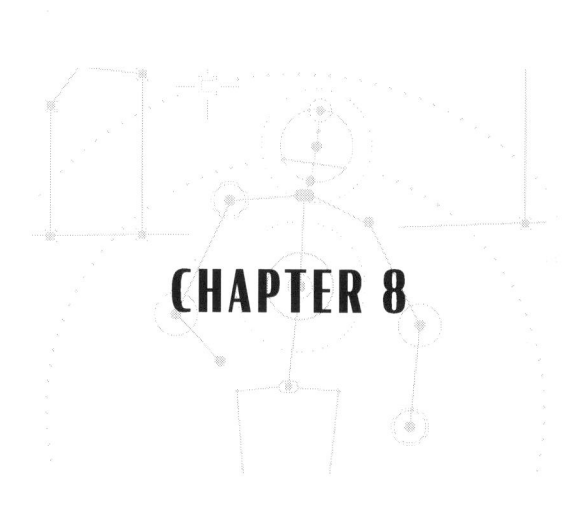

It was nice of you to fly to Washington, DC, to see me," Alicia said as she sat on the couch with Fallon in her condo.

"Are you sure you won't move back to Michigan?" Fallon asked. "I'm sure the governor could—"

"Did you ask the governor to find me a job?" Alicia glared at Fallon.

"Well, I . . ."

"My career with Homeland Security is based here."

"But you're a detective with Homeland Security. You travel all the time. Do you really need an office here?"

Alicia turned away.

"You're scared about us."

Alicia looked at Fallon. "Now's not the right time."

"If not now, when?" He shifted his position and stretched his leg.

"You need to focus on healing."

Fallon leaned back on the couch and noticed a framed picture on a bookshelf of him and Alicia standing on the pier in Charlevoix. "My therapist thinks I should go back to the cabin on Beaver Island." He felt Alicia take his hand and hold it. It felt warm and comforting.

"Are you ready for that?"

"I don't know." He closed his eyes for a moment as his heart rate increased."

"Fallon, talk to me."

"I need to get answers." He looked at Alicia. "What do you remember about the day of the terrorist attack?"

Alicia sighed. "We've been over this a dozen times."

"I want to know what *you* remember."

She looked at her watch. "My mom will be here in thirty minutes."

He kept his eyes focused on her.

"Okay, I'll try."

"I know it's hard for you, too, but I need to try to piece it together. I know there's something important I need to remember."

She nodded.

Fallon listened to her recount the day of the terror attack on the *Emerald Isle*, trying to add her pieces to what he recalled. "How did you end up on North Fox Island?"

"What did I tell you?"

"You told me you were hiding out with Cally and his dad, Robert, at the lighthouse on the south end of Beaver Island." Fallon bit his lip and blinked several times. "Then Ferguson found you, and you escaped to North Fox Island with a boat from the old lifesaving station by the lighthouse."

Alicia smiled. "Yes. Go on."

Fallon closed his eyes. "Ferguson pursued you the next day by plane to North Fox Island with two of his hired guns." He opened his eyes and looked at Alicia. "But you commandeered his plane and flew it out of there with Cally and his dad."

"Good," she said as she let go of his hand and shifted on the couch, so her body faced him.

"Then you made an emergency landing at Welke Airport."

Several moments of silence filled the space between them.

Fallon tapped his chin. "I drove to Welke Airport on Beaver Island, and your plane was there at the end of the runway." He blinked several times. "White smoke was coming out of the front of the plane and firefighters were there."

Alicia smiled. "Go on."

CHAPTER 8

"I drove you, Cally, and his dad to the marina."

"That's right."

He rubbed his forehead and closed his eyes.

"Fallon?"

He looked at Alicia.

"We jumped into my grandad's boat that was docked at the marina." His hands squeezed into fists as pieces of memory flowed in his head.

> *He grips the steering wheel of the boat, and pushes the throttle forward. The engine responds with a throaty roar.*

"Then we . . ." His head dropped. He sighed and looked at the floor.

"Do you want to talk about what happened next?"

He closed his eyes and rubbed his forehead with his fingertips. Fallon opened his eyes and noticed tears forming in her eyes. "I know it's hard for you too."

Alicia's lips pressed tight. Her eyes lowered to look at the couch cushion. "I helped pull you from the water. I thought you were . . ."

Fallon took her hand.

She gently squeezed it. "How *did* you know the drone was going to attack the *Emerald Isle* at that moment?"

"I'm not sure. I think I was in Daniel's cabin before I picked you up at the airport."

"You keep saying Daniel's cabin, but the property records show that Ferguson owned it for years," Alicia said. "Homeland Security thinks Ferguson used it as a base for his terror cell."

"I'm sure it belonged to Daniel."

"Was Daniel at the cabin before you picked me up?"

"In my last therapy session, I recalled sitting in that cabin. I think it was right before I picked you up."

Alicia sat up. "This is new."

"I'm sitting across from someone holding a snifter with whiskey."

"Who was it?"

"I'm not sure, but he was talking about Archipelago."

"The software?"

"Yes, but I just can't remember what he said about it."

"Who was talking to you?"

Fallon paused, focusing on the image in his mind. "I think he kind of looked like Henry Massey, but why would he be on the island? I remember that last year we had several meetings with Massey and the governor's staff about launching his Archipelago software at the State."

"What would Archipelago software have to do with any of this?"

"I don't know. But there's something important about it and that cabin." Fallon rubbed his eyes. "I'm not sure Ferguson is the terrorist."

"They have him on video stealing the drone from one of Caspian's Detroit fulfillment warehouses. There's enough solid evidence to convict him."

"But . . ." The doorbell interrupted Fallon's thought.

Alicia gasped as she looked at the clock. "That must be Mom. She's early. I should've known." She hurried into the kitchen. "Get the door while I finish getting dinner ready."

Fallon opened the door. "Hello, Ms. Chalmers." He noted her bright blue overcoat with a red purse draped over her shoulder and her round glasses with a bright, multicolored frame. "Nice glasses."

"Well, there's our hero," she said as she patted him on the cheek and stepped into the condo. "I've told you to call me Irene, remember?"

Fallon closed the door. "I'm *not* the hero. Alicia is." He reached for her overcoat as she took it off, but she ignored him and tossed it over the back of the couch.

"Your dad would've been proud." Irene smiled as she set her purse on an end table. She looked at Alicia, approaching them and wiping her hands on a towel. "Her father taught her how to shoot. He sure knew how to handle a gun."

"He reminded me every time I picked Alicia up for a date." Fallon laughed as he put his arm around Alicia's waist while they stood in the living room.

"She was still in high school, and you were this college-bound kid," Irene said, smacking his shoulder. "Her father was suspicious of your intentions."

CHAPTER 8

Alicia laughed as she hugged her mom. "He was suspicious of Fallon because your family had that big summer house in Charlevoix."

"Not to mention your dad was the Michigan attorney general," Irene added.

"Have a seat on the couch, Mom. Dinner isn't quite ready," Alicia said as she disappeared into the kitchen.

Irene sat on the couch and patted the cushion next to her. "Sit with me, Fallon."

Fallon sat next to her.

"You made a mistake breaking up with Alicia when you were in college." She poked him in the chest.

"That was a long time ago."

"I heard that, Mom!" Alicia said from the kitchen.

"Well, it's true," Irene said. "It would've saved you from marrying that abusive deputy."

"Don't remind me," Alicia said as a timer beeped.

"You two were perfect for each other. Alicia became a deputy for the Charlevoix County Sheriff, and *you*, Fallon, joined the Detroit Police."

"You need to let it go," Alicia said as she stepped into the living room. "That was more than thirty years ago!"

"Well, at least you two are back together," Irene smiled.

"We're only back together because he's brain damaged." Alicia smirked as she stood in front of them with an oven mitt on one hand.

Fallon watched her move a strand of auburn-colored hair away from her slim face.

"Let's eat," she said as she returned to the kitchen.

Fallon followed Irene into the dining area and pulled out Irene's chair at the small table with place settings for three.

"The table looks great," Irene said as she pushed Fallon's hand off her chair and scooted herself in.

Alicia set a large platter on the table and then sat down across from Fallon.

"Meatloaf, baked potatoes, and green beans," Fallon said as his eyes met Alicia's. "My favorite."

"Pretty boring," Irene remarked, putting her napkin in her lap.

"Boring is okay, Mom," Alicia said as she reached for the platter.

Fallon looked at Alicia. Those eyes, those hazel eyes.

Alicia turned away and handed the platter to her mom. "It is *your* recipe, Mom."

"Well, your dad *was* a fan of it too," Irene said as she took the platter.

* * *

In the kitchen after dinner, Fallon loaded the dishwasher and started it while Alicia stood at the sink rinsing out a pan. He put his arm around her. "Do you think we make a good couple?"

She turned and put her wet hands around him, wiping them on the back of his shirt. "You really are brain damaged."

"Hey!" Fallon said as he pulled away, laughing.

They stood a moment facing each other.

"I should be going," Irene said as she entered the kitchen, holding her coat.

"So soon?" Alicia asked as she stepped away from Fallon.

"I don't want to drive in the dark." Irene gave Fallon a hug. "Remember what I said. Don't let her get away this time."

"Mom!" Alicia said as she hugged her mom.

Irene smiled. "I can see my way out." She slipped on her coat, grabbed her purse, and paused as Fallon and Alicia joined her by the open doorway. "Have a safe trip back to Michigan, Fallon."

"Good to see you, Irene." He clicked the door shut behind her and pulled Alicia close. "I'm really tired. I should get back to my hotel."

"Stay for a few more minutes."

He nodded and joined her on the couch.

"You know Ferguson was transferred to St. Helena Island. They'll move him in a few weeks to Marquette for the grand jury investigation," Alicia said. "It's going to be all over the media again."

"The governor met with me to talk about it."

"Are you ready for that?"

Fallon sighed. "I'm not sure."

"I'm just ready to put this all behind us. The grand jury will indict

CHAPTER 8

Ferguson, he'll be convicted at the trial and that will be the end of it. Case closed."

"This case is *not* closed."

"But what if it *is* really closed and your jumbled mind is playing tricks on you?"

"I just can't get rid of this hunch that there's still a bigger threat out there."

"Fallon—"

"No, Alicia. I know there is. It keeps gnawing at me."

"You need to drop it."

"I can't."

She took his hand.

He looked into her eyes.

"You were always so driven, following your hunches, the littlest details, until you got results," Alicia said. "You used to solve cases that everyone else gave up on."

"If only I could remember all the details from the drone attack." He squeezed her hand. "I know you went through a lot too. You were there with me when the drone exploded."

Tears formed in her eyes. "I was underwater when I heard the muffled explosion. I felt the shock wave. When I surfaced all I saw was floating debris from the boat, but you were nowhere. I kept diving, searching underwater, until I found your body. The sheriff pulled up in a boat just in time to help me. We both pulled you into his boat and I resuscitated you."

"You saved my life," Fallon said as he fought back tears. "I'm not sure who I am anymore—who we are as a couple."

"I'm not sure either," Alicia said as she wiped tears from her eyes.

"You know I like having you around," Fallon smiled. "You calm me."

"Like meatloaf, baked potatoes, and green beans?"

Fallon nodded. "Maybe your mom's right."

"About what?"

"You and me."

Alicia laughed. "My mom couldn't possibly be right."

"Maybe just once?"

"Maybe."

Fallon rubbed his forehead. "I should be going. Can we talk more tomorrow?"

"Headache?"

Fallon nodded.

"You want to have lunch tomorrow—before you fly out?"

He smiled. "I would like that."

* * *

Back in his hotel room, Fallon traced the streams of rainwater tumbling down the pane of glass on his window. He returned to the couch and opened a video of the drone attack on his phone filmed by a passenger on the *Emerald Isle*. That was definitely him at the wheel of the Chris-Craft as it approached the ferry. The view jerked skyward and zoomed in on a large, approaching drone. Suddenly there was a rat-a-tat-tat sound of automatic weapon fire. The view jerked to the floor, showing dozens of screaming people lying on the metal floor of the boat and under benches. Slowly, the camera returned to the railing of the boat, moving back and forth from a view of the drone to the speedboat. Fallon could see himself at the wheel, and Alicia standing in the back of the boat, firing the rifle at the drone. Rat-a-tat-tat. More screams from passengers on the *Emerald Isle*. The camera focused on the smoking drone closing in on the Chris-Craft.

Fallon's teeth clenched and his body tensed as he watched the drone quickly descend from the sky toward his boat. He stopped the video, noting the controlled descent of the drone as if it was pursuing their boat. He started the video again and watched himself motioning to Alicia. She glanced at the drone, dropped the rifle, and dove into the water. The drone continued its steep dive, quickly closing in on their boat.

Fallon's body shook, and the phone almost fell from his hand as he fought the urge to shield his face. He watched himself on the screen dive into the water as the drone impaled their boat. Suddenly everything on the video went blurry as the camera view twirled violently, the audio overwhelmed by the sound of a massive explosion. His body jerked as he recalled the pain that instantly surged through his body as his boat blew up. The phone dropped to the floor as he held his head. So much pain. The screams from the video playing on his phone on the floor echoed in his head. Then silence, piercing silence.

His hands eased down from his head, and he looked at the phone on the floor with an image frozen on the screen with dozens of panicked people lying on the deck of the *Emerald Isle*, faces filled with fear. If he hadn't been there that day—if Alicia had not shot down that drone—all those people might be dead.

He took a deep breath, exhaled, then repeated it. He picked up his phone and looked at the image of panicked people frozen on the screen staring back at him. Ferguson just didn't seem like the type to run a terror cell. Together, they fought terrorists in Afghanistan. Ferguson's involvement with the crime ring was believable, but not terrorism. Yet, if it wasn't Ferguson, then who executed the drone attack and why? No one claimed responsibility and Ferguson denied he had anything to do with it. What if the real terrorist was still out there?

Maybe Grace was right. He should revisit the cabin... he should return to Cally's parents' house in Detroit. It might help him piece together the fragmented memories of being at the house with Daniel the night before the terror attack. He massaged his forehead with his fingertips. Maybe a visit with Chip would help.

CHAPTER 9

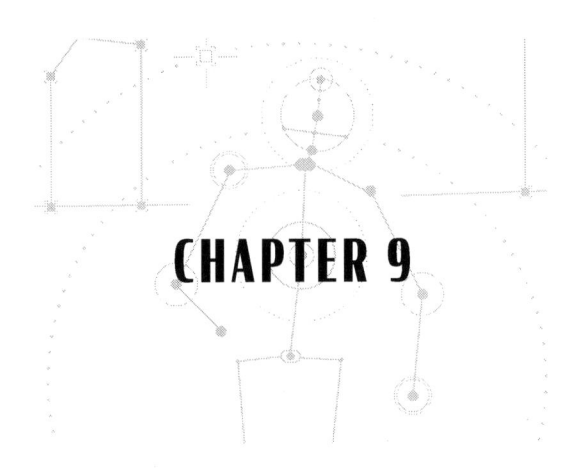

Fallon stood a moment outside the thirteen-story, brick building. He read the name above the main entrance: George W. Romney State Office Building. He glanced at the Capitol Building across the street. Did anyone remember his dad? Politics. It all seemed so meaningless now.

"Mr. McElliot," a guard said as Fallon stepped through the entrance and approached the security screening area. "It's so good to see you. Are you coming back to work?"

Fallon tossed his keys and phone in a small plastic container and walked through the metal detector. It beeped as expected. "I'm visiting Chip."

The security guard nodded as he waved the metal detector wand up and down Fallon. "You're good to go."

As he rode the elevator up, he looked at his distorted reflection in the polished metal walls and listened to the hum of the motor carrying him up. It felt so familiar yet so foreign. He couldn't recall the last time he was here. A ding announced the tenth floor, and the doors opened. There stood Chip in the hallway smiling at him.

"The guards told me you were on your way up," Chip said. "It's been a while."

CHAPTER 9

Fallon looked down the brightly lit hallway with framed pictures of Michigan scenery hanging on beige walls.

"It's good to have you back . . . for a visit."

Fallon anxiously watched people quickly moving up and down the hallway. "Keeping busy?"

"Yeah." Chip patted Fallon on the shoulder. "Come on, let's go to my . . . your office. Sorry."

Fallon nodded and followed Chip down the long hallway. He looked confident. This wasn't the same nerdy kid he knew when he hired him years ago as an analyst.

They stopped at the corner office at the end of the hallway.

"You kept my name on the door." Fallon smiled.

"Of course, we did," Chip said. "After you."

Fallon took a deep breath, then slowly opened the door to reveal a desk, bookshelves, and a small conference table. This *was* his office. He stepped inside and paused by a picture on the wall of his teenage self and his dad standing on the Charlevoix pier. His dad looked out of place in his gray suit surrounded by people in swimsuits and summer clothing. They both looked like rigid toy soldiers standing next to each other. "For some reason my dad had to sign that picture with his title . . . like I didn't know him."

"You remember when that was taken?" Chip asked.

"I think I was sixteen." Fallon walked behind his desk and stood a moment in front of the window behind his chair. He looked at the State Capitol below. "I remember visiting my dad when he was attorney general. Sometimes I would meet him in the Capitol, and we would go out to dinner downtown. Once in a while we would get a couple bags of warm peanuts at the Peanut Shop in downtown Lansing then go to a park and talk."

Fallon shook his head as he sat in his desk chair and scooted it forward. "They still haven't fixed that sticky wheel." He ran his fingers across the aged oak desktop. "Did I ever tell you this was the desk and chair my dad used?"

"Many times." Chip smiled. "I hear you and Alicia are back together."

"Did the governor tell you that?"

Chip shrugged. "Maybe."

"It's nothing serious." Fallon looked at the papers on the desk arranged in neat stacks. "I never kept my desk this neat."

"I'm a bit obsessed about it."

"I always liked that about you. You kept me on track."

They sat a moment in silence as Fallon scanned the room. The pictures on the walls, the small conference table in the corner, and the bookshelves on each side of the door. He looked at Chip. "You don't need me here."

"It's not the same without you. We're a team." Chip sat down in a chair in front of the desk. "When do you think you'll come back?"

Fallon looked at the stacks of papers on his desk and the open laptop with the login window for the Archipelago software system. His pulse quickened. He took a deep breath and exhaled. "I'm . . . waiting for my therapist's okay."

"Any idea when?"

"Not sure. I still have memory issues."

Do you remember the church bombing last summer at Cally's dad's funeral?"

Fallon shook his head. "It wasn't a bombing. They used flash-bangs and a recording of explosions to make it appear to be a bombing. It was all a diversion to help Cally escape."

Chip smiled. "You *do* remember that."

"Not all of it."

Chip leaned forward in his seat with a serious look. "When we first heard your boat was blown up stopping the drone attack on the *Emerald Isle*, we thought we'd lost both you and Alicia. It's *so* good to see you behind that desk again."

Fallon glided his palms along the worn leather on the armrest of the chair. "It does help my memory being here."

"The grand jury investigation with Ferguson starts next week. It's going to bring the whole terror attack, the prison escape, the release of the evidence on the crime ring—it's going to be headline news again."

Fallon closed his eyes for a few seconds, then opened them. "I'm sorry. Tell me again about the evidence on the crime ring."

"Evidence someone put on the internet showed that a bunch of people in the Detroit Police and state government were involved in a crime ring in

CHAPTER 9

Detroit. Marjorie Brogan, head of corrections, was using the prison system to distribute and sell drugs. Tom Ferguson was in on the whole scheme. The feds think the drugs they were selling were funding Ferguson's terror cell on Beaver Island."

"That's not good for the governor's reelection."

"Massey will paint her as corrupt based on the people in her administration involved in the crime ring. I'm sure he's also preparing ads reminding people about the terror attack and her inability to protect the citizens of Michigan." Chip shook his head. "I hate politics."

"Now you're sounding like me." Fallon picked up a plastic container on his desk and examined the splinters of wood and twisted pieces of metal inside. "Did you put this on my desk?"

"You gave that to me last time we had lunch," Chip said.

Fallon rolled the container in his hand and watched the pieces tumble over one another. "These are pieces of my granddad's boat that they pulled out of me." He held the container in front of Chip. "It was so much fun when granddad took me out in his boat, just the two of us. He would push it full throttle and we would fly across the water."

Chip looked at the container. "That drone sure shredded your granddad's boat. I hear the museum on Beaver Island is working on finding a replacement boat."

"The people on the island have been so good to me." Fallon set the container back on the desk. "But you can never replace the boat my granddad sat in."

Someone knocked and the door opened. Fallon was surprised to see the governor.

Karen sat in the chair next to Chip. "How does it feel to be back in your office?"

"Not sure . . ." Fallon said.

"We were just talking about Ferguson going before the grand jury," Chip said.

"I've been pushing the prosecutor to move this case along," she said as she crossed her legs and set her phone in her lap.

"Should be an open-and-shut case," Chip said.

Karen glanced at Chip. "Can you give us a few minutes alone?"

Fallon watched the door click shut behind Chip. He eyed Karen.

She leaned forward in her chair.

"I don't like that look on your face."

"My lieutenant governor is concerned about my poll numbers," Karen said. "He thinks it's hurting his political career."

"Nothing like poll numbers to test someone's loyalty. Is your lieutenant governor having second thoughts about running with you for reelection?"

Karen nodded.

"It's a little late for him to pull out," Fallon said.

"If he pulled out, he'd use some excuse like he didn't want to put his family through another nasty campaign. Besides, people have short memories." She shifted in her seat. "There are days I just get tired of it all." Her face sank.

Fallon studied her face. "No, Karen . . ."

"What?"

"You can't drop out of the campaign. If you do, you'll hand the party's nomination to Massey."

"Who said I'm thinking about dropping out?"

"I know that look."

She sighed. "We've been working so hard at running this state. So many of the numbers are moving in the right direction, but he continues to be ahead of me in the polls."

"*No*, Karen—"

"You have to know when it's time to move on and let someone else take over."

"You can't just hand it over to Massey . . ." A sudden sense of urgency overtook him. "We have to stop him from becoming governor."

They stared at each other for a moment.

Fallon leaned toward her across the desk, face-to-face. "You need to stick with it and run this race."

"People in the party are pressuring me to step down. They don't want a primary fight. They think Massey will give them the momentum they need to win it all in the general election in November."

"There's something about Massey that bothers me."

"Me too."

CHAPTER 9

"You think Massey cares about the party? He's just using them for his own gain."

"But he's ahead of me in the polls. The party just cares about winning."

"Karen, you *cannot* bow out of this race!" Fallon grabbed the plastic container of boat pieces and shook it at her. "If I can overcome this, you can overcome Massey!"

Karen pressed her lips together, staring out the window.

Fallon swiveled his seat to face the window and looked at the Capitol Building below. "You belong there, Karen." He turned and slammed the container onto the desk.

Karen looked at the container, then at Fallon. The room went silent for a moment except for muffled activity in the hallway outside the door and traffic noise on the street below. She sighed. "There *is* another option. You recall the *Detroit News* poll showing Alicia outpolling me."

Fallon's eyes narrowed.

"People are crying for heroes, Fallon." Karen leaned forward in her chair. "Alicia is a hero."

"What are you saying?"

"Do you think she would run with me as lieutenant governor?"

"I doubt it. She hates politics as much as I do."

"The image people have of Alicia standing in your granddad's boat, shooting down that drone with an automatic rifle. Do you know how many million views those videos have on social media? No amount of campaign money can buy that kind of political capital."

"She has no political experience."

Karen chuckled. "She has plenty of *other* experience. Besides, since when is experience required to serve in public office?"

"I don't know—"

"She could be the boost I need to overcome Massey."

Fallon shook his head. "I think she'll turn you down."

"I think she can decide for herself . . . and don't say a word to her."

"So you're going to ask her?"

"I'll think about it . . ." Karen looked around the office, then at Fallon. "How does it feel to be back?"

"Sitting here . . . I'm not sure."

"I don't think you're ready."

"But I feel like I need to get back in the game. There's something I'm missing . . . something we're all missing. I can feel it."

"You need to drop it, Fallon."

"I can't Karen. I'm thinking of going to Cally's parents' house and maybe back to Beaver Island to see if it helps me fill in some of the gaps."

"I don't know, Fallon . . ." Karen's phone dinged. She glanced at it, then Fallon. "I have to get to my next appointment." She walked to the door, then turned to look at him. "Can you stop by my office in about thirty minutes—before you leave?"

"Is there something else you want to tell me?"

She glanced at her watch. "I don't have time right now. Stop by my office."

"Okay."

"Good," she said as she exited the office.

Fallon looked out the window at the Capitol as Chip returned. He swung his chair around as Chip sat in front of the desk. "Chip . . . what do you know about Henry Massey?"

CHAPTER 10

Eight months now deep undercover and what did he have to show for it? How much longer could he continue this deception? Daniel sat in the living room of his apartment inside the lower level of the Massey estate weighing his options. He was now a trusted advisor in Massey's inner circle, or was he merely being played? He now had access to Massey's entire estate, or were there still parts he couldn't get to? Somehow he had to find a way to dig deeper without being detected. Exactly how was Massey communicating with others helping him with his secret plan and just where was he hiding that secret computer server farm where he was collecting all the data from states running Archipelago?

He walked to the wall of windows and stared at Fort Collins below. He could've stopped the planned drone attack on the *Emerald Isle* last August, but it would've blown his cover and years of work. He'd counted on Fallon to stop it, and he did at a great cost. It was his fault Fallon suffered a brain injury and memory loss. He would never be the same. He should've stopped that drone before it ever left the cabin.

Daniel drew in a deep breath and ran his fingers through his hair as he exhaled. If only he had said no when the FBI director personally approached him about infiltrating Massey's empire. What if he had refused to go undercover as Massey's head of security? Would someone else have stepped in instead of him? None of it mattered now. There was no turning back.

He couldn't deny that he was attracted to the sheer thrill of the mission and the adrenaline rush of uncovering the secret plans of a bunch of arrogant tech billionaires who felt they owned the world. He had to admit he was smug about the fact Arpa took the bait he set, hiring the phony global security company Peninsular the FBI created to infiltrate the group. All the years of hard work, and they still were no closer to getting hard evidence that would take down Henry Massey and Arpa. If he didn't stop Massey, he could control every aspect of government in at least half the states in the country—everything from taxes, to permits, to legislation and personnel files housed in Archipelago.

Daniel walked to the kitchen and pulled a Vernor's from the fridge. The can hissed as he cracked it open, went into the living room, and sat on the couch. He took a swallow and stared at the city below through the wall of floor-to-ceiling windows in front of him. It seemed so far-fetched, yet all the pieces were in play for Massey to win the primary in August and the general election in the fall. Once he did that, he could implement his plan. It would be a digital coup of half the state governments in the country and no one would be aware of it—except a handful of people at the FBI.

A server farm to house all the data from twenty-two states and more would be huge and difficult to hide. What did Massey say a while ago? *"My most important secrets are buried deep inside my estate out of their sight."* He now had access to the entire estate, but he had to be careful where he went, knowing his every step was being tracked. A soft knock at his door interrupted his thoughts.

Daniel opened the door. "Helen."

"I need to ask you a question," she said as she pushed past him into the room. She sat on the couch and patted the empty seat next to her.

He joined her on the couch, sitting closer to the armrest than her.

"We leave at eight tomorrow morning for Geneva. Our driver will take us to our jet at the airport. Have you reviewed the security plans?"

"I have. Matias is taking the lead for Peninsular. He was my right-hand man when I organized security for Arpa meetings. He's the best."

CHAPTER 10

"I know he took over for you when you started working for the FBI. They are all highly qualified, but I feel better knowing you're there."

Her focused look on him made him tense. Relax. "There's nothing to be concerned about."

Helen smiled and their eyes locked for a moment. The room was quiet, yet Daniel heard a full conversation in her eyes.

"I just want to make sure we're not missing anything," she said. "Transitions can be an opportune time for someone to cause trouble."

"Are you concerned about anything in particular?"

"No, but you can't be too careful." She blinked a few times. "I don't want to invite trouble."

"I'll look at the security plans again before we leave." Daniel stood and walked to the door. "I still need to finish packing." He opened the door.

She stepped closer to him. "I like your beard."

He brushed his knuckles over his jaw. "I figured it will help conceal my identity during the campaign."

"You didn't do anything wrong. The FBI has nothing to connect you to Cally's escape from prison."

"I think they suspect I might've had something to do with it, but they have no proof."

"And the whole terrorist attack on the ferry—that was all pinned on Tom Ferguson."

Daniel shrugged. "I still need to be careful when I'm in public." The scent of expensive perfume caught his attention.

"You know Henry will be gone a lot this summer during the campaign." Her green eyes focused on him from under her long lashes.

"And I'll be right by his side making sure he's safe."

She took Daniel's hand. "You think there are people who want to take him out?"

Daniel's pulse quickened as her hand squeezed his. "You don't get to his position without making a lot of enemies."

"I suppose," Helen said, moistening her lips with a lingering gaze.

"I'll see you in the morning."

They stood a moment looking at each other before she finally nodded and smiled.

"Are you going to be at the fundraiser tonight?" Helen asked.

"I'm overseeing security."

"We'll see you there," Helen said as she left.

Daniel watched her walk down the hallway for a second before he clicked the door shut and exhaled.

CHAPTER 11

"Thanks for stopping by, Fallon," Karen said as she sat behind her desk in her second-floor office in the Romney Building.

"I always liked the view of the Capitol from your office," Fallon said as he sat in front of her large, oak desk. The look on her face told him he wasn't here for light chit-chat.

"One of the perks of being governor." She took a deep breath and exhaled. Her chair squeaked as she leaned back. "The grand jury investigation for Ferguson starts next week."

"The prosecutor must be convinced she'll get an indictment on terrorism charges."

"The video of Ferguson loading the stolen Caspian drone, the messages between him and an overseas terror cell on his laptop, the explosives they found in his home that match what was in the drone—there's more than enough evidence."

Fallon shook his head. "No terrorist at that level would be so sloppy. Something doesn't feel right."

"I feel like . . ." Karen looked at Fallon as she tapped her fingers on the desk. "I think you've been struggling to recall things that didn't necessarily happen."

"I *have not* lost my detective instincts. I just need to figure out what I'm missing."

"Okay, but have you thought about what happens if the prosecutor puts you on the stand when the case goes to trial?"

"I'll tell him what I remember."

"But there's more to it than that. The defense is going to question you about the video they have of you and Ferguson in his office at Jackson Prison. You agreed to try to find the escaped prisoner Robert Callahan Jr. for Ferguson before the authorities got to him. Do you understand how that made me look—my own state police liaison."

Fallon nodded.

"Do you remember going to see Ferguson before the drone attack?"

"The memory isn't clear."

"You never told me you were doing that. Why?"

"We've been over this before, Karen—"

"Do you see how it looks like you're using your memory loss to hide something—to cover for me?"

Fallon sighed.

"Not only will the defense use your memory loss against you, but they'll try to discredit you based on your friendship with Ferguson."

Fallon shrugged. "I wouldn't call it a friendship."

"You two go way back. You were partners at the Detroit Police Department. You served in the army together in Afghanistan." She leaned forward and rested her elbows on the desk. "Look, I understand why he pressured you to do him a favor by going after Cally—trying to intercept him before the police caught him."

"I remember he was my partner when I was a Detroit police officer, and I remember Afghanistan." Fallon's breathing quickened. A memory interrupted his train of thought. He gripped the armrests.

> *A firefight. Bullets flying, piercing the sandbags in front of him. A vehicle burning.*

He pulled his arms tight against his chest.

"Fallon?"

CHAPTER 11

His body jerked at the sound of his name. It wasn't Ferguson sitting in front of him on the battlefield. "Karen?"

"Are you okay?"

Fallon nodded and tried to slow his breathing.

Karen sighed. "You can't do that on the stand during the trial. It would be a disaster."

Fallon shifted in his seat.

"These episodes of yours concern me, Fallon. You have a lot of layers of trauma to work through, not just from the terror attack, but Afghanistan and your police work."

"I've made a lot of progress. I'm driving again and I don't need help anymore with daily tasks. It's just the gaps in my memory leading up to the terror attack."

Karen bit her lip and sat a moment, deep in thought.

"Karen?"

"Maybe . . ." She leaned back in her chair, folded her arms across her chest, and tapped her chin with her pointer finger. "It might be good for you to go back to Cally's house in Detroit and Beaver Island. If it helps you find the missing pieces of memory, I think you might be able to finally put last summer behind you."

They sat a moment in silence looking at each other.

Fallon nodded. "I appreciate the support."

"We've been friends a long time." Karen smiled as she reached in her desk drawer and pulled something out. "I need to get ready for my next appointment," Karen said as she walked around her desk.

Fallon gave her a hug and felt her slip something in his hand.

"Keep in touch," Karen said pointing to Fallon's hand. "Just give me a call. I don't need you texting or emailing. I get enough of those."

"I will." Fallon looked at the red flip phone in his hand. It was familiar. He exchanged a glance with her. It appeared as if he had done this before.

"Take care," she said.

Fallon slipped the phone in his pocket, exited her office, and headed down the hallway toward the elevator. A woman approached dressed in a trim, black business suit complemented by a string of expensive pearls draped around her neck. He noted the rich leather tablet case in her hand

and the diamond bracelet peering out of her sleeve as she passed him headed toward Karen's office.

"Sophia! Nice to see you." He heard Karen say behind him. "Fallon!" she shouted after him.

He turned to see Karen standing in the doorway of her office with Sophia.

"I'd like you to meet Sophia Doyle, the CEO of Caspian, the world's largest online retailer," Karen said.

Fallon took a few steps back and shook the woman's extended hand. "Nice to meet you."

"This is Fallon McElliot," Karen said.

"What an honor to meet you, Mr. McElliot," Sophia said with an admiring look as she firmly squeezed his hand. "I've heard so much about you and what you and Alicia Chalmers did to stop that terror attack."

The word *Caspian* echoed in his mind. "I've heard about you as well," Fallon responded.

"I want to personally thank you for stopping that Caspian drone from reaching its target," Sophia said. "It could've been much worse."

"I guess so," Fallon said as his body stiffened. He pushed back the memory of the drone closing in on him, the Caspian logo visible on the front.

"I'm eager to have justice served on the perpetrators of the terror attack," Sophia said with a determined look. "Then we can put this whole thing behind us."

"Couldn't agree more," Fallon said.

"Sophia is here to talk about the state's broadband access program," Karen said.

"If you ever need anything, Mr. McElliot, just let me know," Sophia said, her deep-blue eyes projecting sincerity."

"Couldn't I just order anything I need on your Caspian website?"

"I like your sense of humor, Mr. McElliot." Sophia laughed as she followed Karen into her office.

Fallon watched the door close behind them as he stood in the hallway while members of the governor's staff hurriedly passed by him. Something bothered him about Sophia. He sensed she was hiding something. He

CHAPTER 11

pulled out the red flip phone and looked at it. The governor gave him a red flip phone before he went to Beaver Island last summer. She wanted him to go to the island, but he couldn't quite remember why. She was concerned about digital communication and about him using his work phone. He closed his eyes and concentrated. A vague memory surfaced of meeting with Karen here in her office before the drone attack. She was talking about a potential terror plot to attack the *Emerald Isle*.

"Can I help you, Mr. McElliot?" someone asked from behind him.

Startled, Fallon turned to see a young man looking at him. "I'm fine. Thanks."

"I can get you a new phone," the man said, pointing to the red flip phone in Fallon's hand. "I'm surprised you still have that."

"It still works great."

"Suit yourself," the man said as he continued down the hallway.

As Fallon walked to the elevators, he slipped the flip phone in his pocket and pulled out his work phone. He found Cally's contact information and pressed the call button.

CHAPTER 12

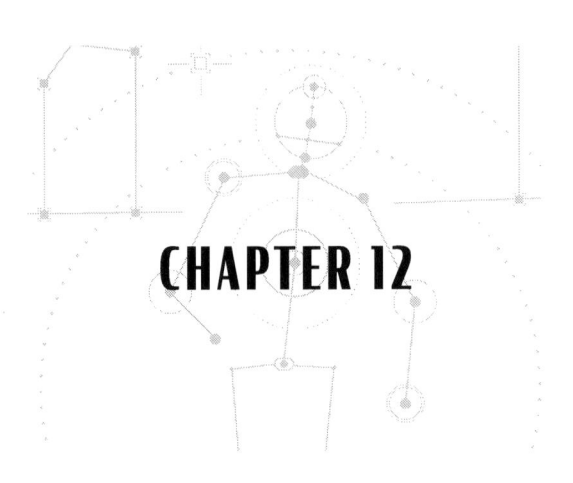

Ferguson sat on the edge of the bed in his prison cell. Could he really believe this Nigel guy could free him? He glanced at the calendar on his wall. April. A month since Nigel's visit and no further word from him. No response to his voice mails. No follow-up on his claim Fallon didn't frame him and that the video of him stealing the drone was fake. And who was this Nadia Long? He'd been waiting for weeks for some word from her to tell him what to do next and nothing. Some attorney he turned out to be.

He was now defenseless facing a grand jury next week. He dreaded the media circus that would follow his every move. There was no way he was going to shake the terrorist label. It had to be Fallon who framed him, but how could he pull off something like that? The question haunted him ever since his arrest last summer on North Fox Island. He'd been over it dozens of times. Somehow, Fallon knew the drone attack was coming and stopped it. It all seemed too convenient that Fallon now had a brain injury and couldn't remember who launched the attack. Fallon was hiding something. He *must* be faking a brain injury to protect someone, but who?

The bed squeaked as Ferguson buried his head in his hands. Hope of beating the terrorism charge was fading fast. There was no way he was

CHAPTER 12

going to avoid forty years in prison just for the terrorism charge. He'd be in his nineties if he served a full sentence. It might as well be a life sentence.

He sat on his bed. He couldn't convince his other attorney that he was innocent. They were simply trying to shorten his sentence with a potential plea deal. So how did Nigel know the video was fake? He seemed so confident. If *only* he was just dealing with the crime ring charges. Some of his friends in the crime ring were already convicted and serving their sentences. They would be out in a few years. Why was he facing terrorism charges and not others? How did Marjorie Brogan, the former head of corrections and mastermind behind the crime ring, avoid the connection to funding terrorism? Everyone had abandoned him—and now Nigel had too. If that idiot Detroit police chief Peters had stopped Cally from getting all that evidence on the crime ring activities, he wouldn't be in this mess. He would—

Thunk!

He jumped at the sound of the door to his cell opening.

"Outside exercise time," a guard said as he stepped through the open door.

He followed the guard through several corridors to an outside exercise area. He walked the narrow strip of sandy soil with scraggly weeds framed by a twelve-foot-high chain-link fence topped with rolls of razor wire. He strolled to the center of the exercise area and assessed the tall fence a few feet on either side of him. It was his idea to narrow the width of the exercise area so a helicopter could not land in it. If *only* he hadn't pointed that out to the prison design committee. He was the only warden to notice it out of the four wardens they tapped to review the plans for the St. Helena Island prison.

Breathing in the cool, damp air, he closed his eyes. A light breeze blew across his face as he imagined a helicopter hovering above him with a winch lowering a rope and harness. He could picture himself being lifted clear of the fence and whisked off the island before the guards started firing at him from the four guard towers at each corner of the prison perimeter. The odds of that happening were zero. They would shoot him and the helicopter out of the sky before they cleared the island.

He opened his eyes. Through the chain-link fence and the clearing in the trees, the horizon was clear enough to make out the Mackinac Bridge in the distance to the east. To his left he could see the lighthouse poking above the trees, its white paint glowing in the early evening light. He took another deep breath and let the cool air refresh him. He looked up at the fence, the sharp tips on the razor wire reflected the low sunlight. It was inevitable he would become a convicted terrorist. He took another deep breath as a guard retrieved him and guided him back inside the prison.

CHAPTER 13

Daniel walked through the large commercial kitchen in the basement level of the Massey mansion. He nodded at a couple of Massey's staff busily at work prepping food.

"Hey, Daniel," one of the staff members said.

"Looks like you're expecting a lot of company tonight," he replied as he stopped to look at the staff member cutting a large pile of vegetables.

"Another fundraiser," the man said. "I'm sure we're going to have a lot more of these events."

"You can plan on it," Daniel said as he continued to the end of the hallway off the kitchen and placed his hand on the biometric scanner next to a door. The system read his palm. Nothing happened. Just a red blinking dot in the upper-right corner. A moment later a green outline of his hand appeared with the word "Access Granted" on the top of the pad.

The lock clicked and Daniel opened the door. Cool air greeted him. He grabbed the cold, metal railing and descended the stairway. His hard-soled shoes clunked on the steps, echoing against the cement walls. At the bottom of the stairwell, overhead lights automatically clicked on. He scanned the room. Large pipes and cables ran everywhere along the ceiling between rows of metal I-beams. On the far end of the large room, he spotted a glassed-in service room. He stepped inside and glanced at the wall of monitors displaying the status of dozens of systems for the estate. He turned to a large stack of blueprints spread out across the entire length of a metal table—just as Massey said.

Bending over the table, Daniel studied the top sheet, smoothing out the curled ends. He scanned the site plan for the Massey estate and noted a dotted line around the edges. He traced it with his finger until he found faint letters reading "Former Military Site."

Military? Massey never mentioned that. He leafed through each subsequent page, working his way down each floor of the estate to the service level where he stood. He traced the infrastructure details with his finger, following electric, gas, broadband, water, and sewer lines until they ran off the page. How did he get all these lines run up here in the foothills? Daniel flipped to the last page, surprised by what he saw. There appeared to be another level below him. No detail, just a large, empty rectangle with the words *Old Military Bunker* in the middle.

Curious, Daniel stepped out of the service room and wound his way along clanking pipes and humming electronics above him searching for an access door to this lower level. Back and forth he moved across the room until he spotted another door near whirring ventilation equipment. He put his hand on the biometric scanner next to the door. A red outline of his hand lit up. "Access Denied" flashed on the screen. *Denied?* He should have full access to the estate by now, or could this be an area off limits to even him?

He looked at the solid metal door with chipped, gray paint and the cement walls. It looked original, like the metal blast doors and walls he had seen in old military nuclear bunkers when he was in the air force. A small, black box mounted on the wall and tucked in a corner caught his attention. He stepped next to it and chuckled. Why would Massey keep a 1960s vintage rotary phone? It looked like the one his parents had when he was a kid. He picked up the receiver, shocked to hear a dial tone. Could this old analog phone still be connected to the copper phone line network, or did Massey tie it into his digital network?

Daniel studied the phone. He remembered seeing a similar phone when he was stationed at an air base years ago and was told it was used

CHAPTER 13

for emergency communications if the digital network had a catastrophic failure. He considered the reasons Massey would keep an old analog phone. Analog, copper lines were not his thing. There was no way this old technology would be useful to a person like Massey. So why would he keep it connected? He slipped the receiver back on the phone.

Staring at the old phone, Daniel wondered if he could contact the FBI without his call being traced. He knew the FBI was tied in with the emergency copper network the military used. Any form of communication, even cell phones, would be monitored by Massey over his digital network. But an analog phone over copper wires—it would not be compatible with digital networks and would be untraceable. Yet it still seemed too risky. He could not afford to blow his cover over a phone call.

Back in the service room, Daniel examined the stack of blueprints on the table. There had to be another page showing the detail for the bunker. He scanned the table and spotted a large drawer under the metal tabletop. Inside, he found a large rolled-up page with the word *bunker* scrawled on it. He unrolled the paper and spread it across the table, surprised to see detailed blueprints for a large room inside the bunker behind the blast door. He scanned the detail on the page and noted a large rectangle in the center with the word *Supercomputer* written inside with the description "(shipping container dimensions)." Of course. That would be why he didn't have access. A supercomputer stashed in an old nuclear bunker would be the perfect place to keep secrets and would be undetectable by even the most advanced surveillance technology.

Tracing a line on the drawing running out of the bunker, Daniel noted it was labeled "Arpanet." He recalled Massey fondly talking about Arpanet with him and Fallon last summer back in his cabin on Beaver Island. It's what his venture capital firm Arpa was named after. Of course, Massey would leave the old Arpanet lines intact. It seemed he had an appreciation for old technology, even if he didn't use it.

Daniel stroked his beard as he studied the drawing. Arpanet once connected research computers back in the 1960s in the days before the internet. He walked back to the old phone on the wall by the blast door and stared at it. He recalled seeing a phone just like it when he did the security sweep for Massey's campaign announcement on the steps of the

Michigan State Capitol last November. The physical plant worker had guided him through the service corridors in the basement of the Capitol as he searched for any signs of bombs prior to Massey's arrival. The worker had pointed out the old wall-mount rotary phone in one of the corridors near the stairway.

"It's an old phone line connecting the state capitols and Washington," the worker told him. "It was top secret, part of Arpanet's emergency preparedness in case of nuclear war." He recalled the worker telling him the phone was once part of a bomb shelter that was removed during the last renovation of the Capitol. The phone was still connected to the old copper network per the instructions of FEMA—emergency communication if solar flares or a solar superstorm disabled digital communications.

He pulled out his phone and swiped through pictures of the Capitol security sweep. He found a picture showing an old rotary phone on a cement wall in the basement of the Michigan Capitol. He enlarged it. The picture was fuzzy, but he could make out a phone number on a label in the middle of the rotary dial.

Walking back to the phone outside the bunker, he contemplated calling the phone in the Capitol to see if it worked. His finger hovered over the rotary dial. Could he trust the phone was not tapped? He took off the old, black plastic cover and studied the guts of the phone. It did not appear to be bugged. He slipped the black cover back on the phone and stood a moment looking at it. *Not now. Be patient.* First, he would have to learn more about Massey's supercomputer. No doubt Massey would want to show it off so he could brag about how he had the most advanced technology on the planet.

CHAPTER 14

Fallon parked the car along the curb in front of Cally's parents' house in Detroit and eyed the worn, two-story house with faded wood siding. He traced the broken cement sidewalk to three leaning, cement steps that rose up to a sagging porch. None of it looked familiar. He barely recalled being here last summer. A neighbor said he talked to him and Daniel in the alley behind the house the night before the drone attack. It seemed they entered the house through the back yard. He closed his eyes and concentrated.

Gun pulled, he followed Daniel. The back of the house was dark. They climbed three steps to a back porch. Daniel fished out a key from under a flowerpot and unlocked the door. The door squeaked as they entered the house. The floorboards creaked as they moved through a laundry room.

He rubbed his forehead. They were after something. Alicia told him he and Daniel came here to get the hard drive that contained the evidence on all the illegal activities of the crime ring. When was the last time he saw Cally? It seemed he was on Beaver Island with him, but where? He looked at the house. The memories were fragmented. Maybe Cally could help him find the missing pieces.

Fallon stepped out of his car and walked to the front steps of the house. The worn door on the screened-in porch squeaked as he opened it. Floorboards on the old porch sagged as he stepped to the front door and knocked.

"Fallon!" An old man with a furrowed face wearing worn jeans and a faded flannel shirt greeted him.

He thought he recognized him. "Have we met before?"

"Robert Callahan Senior," Robert said. "You don't remember?"

Fallon studied the man's facial features, but nothing registered in his mind. He shook his head.

Robert nodded. "I'm Cally's dad. And this is my wife, Liz," Robert said as he pointed to a gray-haired, older woman standing next to him wearing a blue dress with a flower pattern.

"Thank you for all you did for Cally," Liz said as she extended her hand.

Fallon looked into her warm eyes as he shook her hand. "I'm not sure what I did."

"You got the truth out," Liz said. "Cally is free because of you."

Robert waved his hand toward the door. "Come on in, Fallon."

Fallon followed them into the living room and sat on an old wingback chair facing the couch where Robert and Liz sat.

"Cally's upstairs," Liz said. "He'll be down in a minute."

"Can I get you some Cheez Whiz?" Robert asked with a smile.

Fallon looked at him with a blank stare. Why did he ask him that? Was it a joke?

Robert frowned. "I guess you don't remember me liking Cheez Whiz when we were in the cabin."

"Sorry." Fallon leaned back in the chair and sunk into the worn cushion as he looked at a family picture on the mantel—two men and a woman standing with Robert and Liz. Fallon pointed to the picture. "Are those your kids standing with you?"

"Yes," Liz stood, grabbed the family portrait, and handed it to Fallon. "That's Sheila, our oldest. She's a lawyer in Detroit," she said as she pointed to the younger woman in the picture. "She had a trial today, otherwise she would be here too," Liz pointed to the man next to Sheila in the picture. "Then there's Cally. He's living with us right now, and . . ." Liz's face grew somber.

CHAPTER 14

Fallon looked at the other man in the picture. "Is that Daniel?"

Liz smiled. "You remember him?"

Fallon studied his face. "I think we worked some cases together. Is he FBI?"

Robert nodded. "Yes."

"I remember doing stakeouts with him."

Liz frowned as she returned the picture to the mantel. "Do you remember coming here with him?"

Fallon glanced around the living room at the old furniture and the dated wallpaper. "I'm not sure." He eyed the disappointed look on the faces of Liz and Robert.

"Hey, Fallon!" someone said from behind him.

Fallon turned to see a younger man with curly brown hair enter the room. He looked like the man Liz called Cally in the picture. He stood and extended his hand. "You must be Cally."

"Fallon." Cally said as he shook Fallon's hand. "You remember me?"

"Not exactly." Fallon sat down. "Your mom showed me your family picture."

"We were at Daniel's cabin last time we saw each other," Cally said as he sat in the wingback chair next to him. "On Beaver Island."

Fallon studied Cally's face. "You were . . . wait, there were others there?"

"Daniel, my brother," Cally said, pointing to Daniel standing next to him in the picture. "You, me, Alicia, Dad, and Daniel were all there."

"It's hard for me to recall being there," Fallon looked around the room. "Is Daniel here?"

Cally, Robert, and Liz glanced at one another.

Robert sighed and looked at Fallon. "Daniel has been missing since the day of the drone attack. We have no idea where he is."

He looked at their long faces.

"You were the last one with Daniel," Cally said. "Don't you remember anything?"

"The day before the drone attack, we watched you leave on a seaplane with Daniel from the cabin on Lake Geneserath on Beaver Island," Robert added. "You were going to Detroit to get the hard drive with the evidence on the crime ring."

Fallon blinked several times as they looked at him with anticipation. A seaplane. He had walked from the cabin to a seaplane docked on a lake.

> *Daniel sits next to him in the cockpit. He buckles up as the plane's engine sputters and comes to life. He watches blue smoke rise past the windshield as the engine sputters. The smoke slowly dissolves. . . . He had been inside the cabin. There is someone sitting across from him inside the cabin . . . a man holding a whiskey snifter . . .*

"I remember having drinks with someone," Fallon offered.

Cally sighed. "We didn't have drinks."

"Wait." Robert jumped in. "Is that something you remember from the cabin?"

Fallon closed his eyes. "An overweight man was sitting across from me holding a snifter and sipping whiskey. He was wearing a suit jacket."

"That doesn't sound like Daniel," Cally said. "Who was it?"

"I'm not sure," Fallon said, not saying he thought it might be Massey.

They sat a moment in silence.

Cally leaned forward in his chair. "You and Daniel came here the night before the drone attack. Does anything look familiar?"

Fallon looked around the room and spotted the staircase. "Maybe? I remember it was dark inside the house and hard to see."

"You would've gone upstairs to retrieve the hard drive," Cally said as he stood up. "Maybe if we go upstairs it will jog your memory."

"Do you want us to come along?" Robert asked.

Cally looked at Fallon. "I think it's better if I just go with Fallon."

"But—" Robert said.

"Cally's right," Fallon said.

He followed Cally up the long, narrow staircase. Something did feel familiar. He recognized the sound of the creaking boards under his feet. At the top of the stairs, Cally led him to a room at the end of a long hallway. He *had* been here before. He looked at a night-light plugged into

CHAPTER 14

an outlet. It was dark last time he was here. He was following a shadowy figure walking in front of him with a flashlight lighting the way.

The door squeaked as they stepped inside Cally's bedroom. He stood still for a moment taking in the room. A framed picture of two men sitting on the hood of a Shelby Mustang Cobra caught his attention. He picked up the picture. "Who's that with you?"

"That's my friend Chuck. The one who gave me the hard drive packed with evidence that brought down the crime ring."

"Chuck gave you the evidence?"

Cally choked. "The crime ring killed him for that."

"I'm sorry. Alicia told me about that." Fallon set the picture back on the dresser. "The hard drive." He looked at the closet door. "We *were* here to get the hard drive."

"Yes! You and Daniel came back to Detroit to retrieve it."

Something clicked in his brain. He looked at the floor. He *was* standing in this room, in this very spot. It was night.

> *A square of light from the streetlights shining through the window lights up the floor below him.*

He walked to the closet, opened the door, and crouched near the floor, examining the floor molding. "It was in here," Fallon said as he pulled out a loose piece of molding to reveal am empty space in the wall. "The hard drive was hidden in there." Fallon looked up at Cally standing in the closet doorway.

"That's it. That's where I hid the hard drive after Chuck gave it to me, and that's where you and Daniel retrieved it the night before the drone attack."

Still crouched down, Fallon pivoted and looked at the floor toward the back of the closet. Images returned, jerkily spooling like an old movie as they clattered into view in his mind.

> *Shots ring out. A man with a flashlight crouches on the floor of the closet opening a trapdoor in the floor. The man looks at him just before he descends through the square hole in the floor, uncovered by the open*

> *trapdoor. Cool air rises up as he closes the trapdoor and clings to ladder rungs as he descends after the man toward the basement of the house.*

"Daniel and I escaped through that trapdoor in the floor," Fallon said as he pointed to the floor. "It's an old chimney that leads to the basement."

"When we were teenagers, Daniel and I used that trapdoor to sneak out of the house after hours."

Fallon stood and looked at Cally. "Someone was after us. They shot at us."

"After Ferguson was arrested—after all the evidence on the crime ring appeared on the internet—the FBI scoured the house. They pulled slugs out of the walls that matched guns used by police officers connected to the crime ring."

Fallon again crouched down and opened the trapdoor in the floor of the closet. Cool air rushed by his face. The musty smell sparked his memory. He closed the trapdoor, stood, and looked at Cally. "Those dirty cops wanted to kill us. They were trying to stop us from getting the hard drive."

Cally exited the closet and looked at the walls in his room. "I patched the bullet holes and repainted my room."

Fallon stood next to Cally and looked at the freshly painted walls.

"Do you remember going to Coleman Young Airport from here?" Cally asked. "There's video surveillance footage of you and Daniel flying out of there."

Fallon rubbed his forehead as more images appeared in his mind.

> *Police cars chase their plane as they taxi down the runway. His foot holds the plane door open as he raises an automatic rifle and points it at the police cars pursuing them on the airstrip as they lift off. Then a blinding light. A plane bearing down on them for a midair collision. He held his head with both hands.*

"Do you recall flying to Beaver Island after leaving the airport?" Cally pressed.

CHAPTER 14

"I'm getting a blank after that," Fallon said as he took a deep breath and let his hands fall to his side. "It seems the memories that are closest to the time of my head injury are the hardest ones to bring back."

"You met us at Welke Airport on the island—me, my dad, and Alicia. You were driving a Jeep that was registered to Ferguson. You had an automatic rifle that was registered to him." Cally looked intently at Fallon. "How did you know the *Emerald Isle* was going to be attacked by that armed Caspian drone?"

"I don't know." Fallon closed his eyes. The blurry image of the man with the whiskey snifter came to mind. Who was that sitting in the chair across from him? Was it really Massey talking about drones?

"Why wasn't Daniel with you?" Cally persisted.

"I don't know."

"Can you recall anything else?"

"That's all I can remember," Fallon shook his head, then looked at Cally. "When the drone exploded." He lowered his head. "I'm lucky to be alive."

"I'm sorry, Fallon," Cally uttered in a soft voice.

"Something hit my head, hard!" Fallon lightly tapped his head with his finger as he sat on the edge of the bed. "It's like a box of puzzle pieces in here. This is the most I've remembered about that day—about being here in this house—since it happened. It's taken me months to get this far. People just don't get it."

"It's okay, Fallon," Cally said as he sat next to him on the edge of the bed.

Fallon held back tears and stared at the floor. What was happening to him? He felt like he should be strong, but this felt weak.

Cally exhaled, walked to the window, then turned to look at Fallon. "We just want to know what happened to Daniel. We've tried repeatedly to talk to the FBI, but they keep telling us they have no idea. They keep feeding us the line that they are conducting a full-scale investigation. I *know* they're hiding something."

"What would they be hiding?"

"I'm not sure, but I think Daniel was pretty deep into uncovering the crime ring. He had all those videos of Ferguson."

Fallon nodded. "I saw them."

Cally stepped next to Fallon. "Ferguson is your friend."

"*Was* my friend. We go way back. We were partners when I was with the Detroit Police. We were in the army together in Afghanistan after 9/11. Something happened to him. It just wasn't the same the last few years."

"The video showed you meeting Ferguson in his office. You told him you would find me before the police."

"I saw the video. I sounded angry at him when I told him it was the last favor I would do for him. Apparently, all I knew was that you escaped from prison and Ferguson wanted me to find you."

Cally sat next to Fallon on the edge of the bed. "I'm just so frustrated. It's been months with no word from Daniel. I think the crime ring killed Daniel. It's not like him to not contact us."

Fallon put his hand on Cally's shoulder. "I do remember working some cases with Daniel years ago. I liked working with him. I just wish I could remember more."

Tears formed in Cally's eyes. "I feel like I've lost everyone. First Chuck was shot and killed in front of my eyes by the crime ring, and then I lose my brother, Daniel. I'm trying to piece my life back together, and I feel like I don't have anyone to help me."

"What about your dad?"

Cally shrugged. "I don't know. He keeps throwing this Jesus stuff at me. Tells me to have faith, that God wants good things for me, that he's praying for me."

Fallon looked at Cally. "I remember your dad was praying before a meal at the cabin."

Cally's face lit up. "You remember? In the cabin?"

Fallon looked at Cally. "We were all sitting around the table together. It was Alicia, you, your dad, and Daniel."

Cally smiled and nodded.

"Your dad had Cheez Whiz." Fallon smiled. "That's why he asked me if I wanted some . . . then . . ." His smiled sagged as he looked at the worn, wood floor.

"Go on."

CHAPTER 14

Fallon closed his eyes. "That's it." He looked at Cally's disappointed face.

They sat for a moment, only the muffled sounds of traffic outside the window broke the silence.

"You should go back to the cabin on Beaver Island."

Fallon looked at Cally. "Ferguson's cabin?"

Cally shook his head. "I don't get it. Daniel told me he owned it for ten years, but the property records say Tom Ferguson owned it. Why would Daniel tell me that? It's not like him to lie to me."

"I don't know." Fallon walked to the window and looked at the rows of old clapboard houses along the street through the dingy glass. "I haven't been back to Beaver Island since the drone attack."

"Take me with you," Cally said as he stepped next to Fallon.

Fallon looked at the concern on Cally's face. "I need to do this alone."

"I miss Daniel," Cally said as he plopped himself back on the edge of the bed. "He was always here for me."

Fallon sat next to him. "How are you doing?"

"It's hard. I'm learning computers at the community college."

"Don't ask me to help you study for that," Fallon laughed.

"Chuck was so good with computers. I always admired that. I thought I'd give it a try."

"Chuck would be proud of you. Any job prospects?"

Cally looked hesitantly at Fallon. "A recruiter came to the college looking for computer majors to work on the Massey gubernatorial campaign. They specifically wanted ex-cons to demonstrate Massey's plan for rehabilitation. I was on a list of candidates the college gave them."

"That's great."

Cally nodded. "I know you're friends with the governor . . . I hope that doesn't offend you."

"It's a great opportunity." Fallon looked at the picture of Cally and Chuck. "You said the crime ring killed Chuck?"

Silence.

Fallon looked at Cally and noticed the tears streaming down his cheeks and over his quivering lips. "They killed him over that hard drive."

Cally wiped tears from his face with his shirt sleeve. "He was trying to do the right thing. He collected all that evidence on the crime ring to take them all down."

"I heard corrupt police officers shot Chuck at his apartment."

Cally nodded. "They almost got me too. I was barely a step ahead of them. Chuck stayed back to give me a head start. He wanted to make sure I got out with the hard drive and all that evidence."

Fallon put his arm around Cally as he began to sob.

"What if they did the same thing to Daniel?" Cally wiped the tears from his face. "Ferguson told me they were coming after my family."

"Ferguson is locked up along with the people in the crime ring. He can't come after you or your family."

"I'm sure there's still some members of the crime ring out there who escaped arrest." Cally walked to the window and stood in front of it with his back to Fallon.

"If the crime ring wanted to come after you, they would've done something by now," Fallon said.

"That's the way they work," Cally turned to face Fallon. "Let things sit for a while, then go after their enemies when their guard is down."

"The case is closed." Fallon stood. "Once the crime ring people faced charges, they made plea deals to testify against other players. There were more than forty arrested in the Detroit Police and the state government."

"I don't think this is over."

Fallon looked at the closet. He had the same feeling. He glanced at Cally.

Cally raised an eyebrow. "I'm worried."

"It'll be okay," Fallon said as he stood.

They looked at each other for a moment.

Cally pressed his lips together and nodded.

"I should be going," Fallon said.

"Take me to Beaver Island with you. I can help—"

"I have to go alone."

"But—"

"I need to know what I remember not what others do."

Cally took a deep breath and exhaled as he stood. "I get it."

CHAPTER 14

Fallon followed Cally down the stairs, gripping the railing as he tried to ignore the pain in his leg with each step.

"Did it help?" Robert asked as he greeted them at the bottom of the stairs.

"A little," Fallon said as he noticed Robert had a book in his hand.

"Give it time."

"It's a slow process."

"You almost died." Robert smiled. "I know what that feels like."

"Alicia showed me the program from your fake funeral," Fallon said. "Everyone thought you were dead."

"I'm very much alive." Robert held out a book in front of Fallon. "This is for you."

"A Bible?" Fallon asked as he looked at the cover.

"A gift."

Fallon looked at the book, then Robert.

"I highlighted a verse for you," Robert said as he pointed to a bookmark protruding from the pages.

"Thanks," Fallon said as he took the book. "I should be going."

"Be careful," Cally said as Fallon opened the door.

Fallon turned to look at Cally and his parents standing together. "I will."

In his car, Fallon tossed the Bible on the passenger side of the bench seat, slipped the key into the ignition, and started the engine. As he revved the engine, he glanced at the Bible. He opened it to the bookmarked page and read the highlighted verse:

> "'For I know the plans that I have for you,' declares the Lord, 'plans for welfare and not for calamity to give you a future and a hope.'"

He looked at Cally now standing in front of his mom and dad on the front porch. They waved. He waved back and slipped the car into gear. As he drove away, he remembered driving these streets before, but when? A few blocks later he merged onto the freeway. A memory flashed in his mind . . .

He checks the rearview mirror. A police car is following them with its flashers going. He looks at Daniel seated next to him. "See if you can shake them," Daniel says. He presses the accelerator. After a block, he checks the rearview mirror. Now two police cars are chasing them, and they are gaining . . .

Fallon shook his head and eased back on the accelerator. Daniel was with him. He passed a sign for Coleman Young Airport. They had gone to that airport and flew back to Beaver Island. Daniel was flying a seaplane, and they landed on a lake by the cabin. But why did they return to the cabin? What was it that was drawing him back to that cabin?

CHAPTER 15

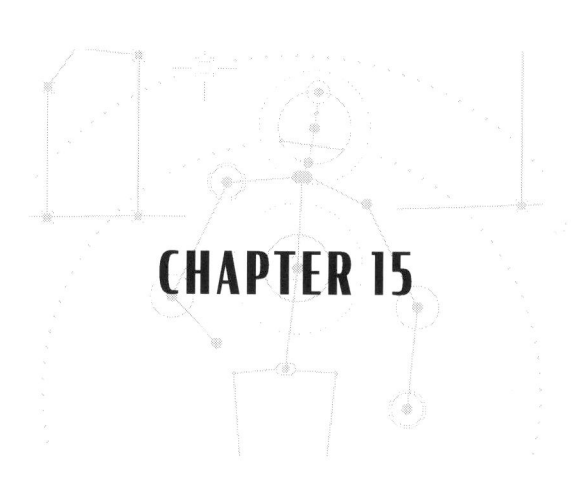

Daniel climbed the stairs to the upper level of the Massey estate and walked toward Helen's office at the opposite end of the hallway that led to Henry's office. As he passed the photos on the walls showing the history of Quick Connect, he stopped at a photo showing Henry and Helen ringing the Nasdaq Stock Market opening bell. This time he noticed Helen did not share the big grins like the other people in the photo.

At the end of the hallway, Daniel tapped on the door and stepped into Helen's office. "You wanted to see me?"

"Come in," Helen said as she spun around in her high-end office chair with deep-blue leather upholstery and gold, metallic trim. "Have a seat on the couch. I need to finish reviewing this food order for Henry's gubernatorial campaign fundraiser here in a few weeks. It's going to be a big event."

"Have you vetted the food delivery company?" Daniel asked as she spun around in her chair and resumed typing on her laptop.

"We've used Food Queen for years. Sophia Doyle owns the company, and she gives us wholesale prices."

"I thought Sophia owned Caspian."

"She bought Food Queen a few years ago to add groceries to her online store. If you need something moved, she's the best in the logistics business."

Daniel sat down on the couch and admired the view of the Rocky Mountains framed by a wall of windows in front of the desk. "Sophia will be at the Arpa board meeting in Geneva this week."

Helen swung her chair around to face Daniel. "Sophia and I go way back. We met in college, and we've been friends ever since. Sophia started Caspian about the same time Henry and I started Quick Connect."

Daniel met her green eyes.

"Is everything buttoned down for Geneva?" she asked.

"I reviewed the latest intel. Peninsular identified some potential threats and addressed them."

"Anything to be concerned about?"

"Nothing out of the ordinary, but they are still on alert for any potential outlier."

Helen nodded, with a protracted stare. "I'm glad you'll be there to personally protect me." A hiss of air released from the office chair as she stood and joined Daniel on the couch.

"Is there something you're concerned about?" Daniel shifted in his seat. "Something we're not aware of?"

"Nothing in particular." Helen delicately placed a hand on his knee. "I've booked a suite at the hotel in Geneva. I'd feel better having you nearby."

Daniel kept his gaze focused on her. What were those green eyes telling him? She might be his ticket to get what he needed, but he would risk losing the trust of Henry. "I have my own room booked."

Helen squeezed Daniel's knee. His heart beat faster. He swallowed hard.

"I think you know what I'm asking," Helen said as she leaned in closer.

Daniel took a deep breath and abruptly stood. "I couldn't do that to Henry."

Helen took hold of Daniel's hand. "You don't think he's been cheating on me?"

"Not that I'm aware of," Daniel said as he tried to keep a straight face.

"Think about it, Daniel," Helen said with a slight smile as she stood.

CHAPTER 15

"Meet me at the front entrance. Our car will be ready in an hour to take us to the airport."

Daniel exhaled, as he watched her leave the room. He turned to look at her open laptop setting on the desk with a messaging app open on the screen. Taking a step toward her desk he noticed a text conversation between Helen and Sophia. He read the last text from Sophia:

Everything is set. Ready to retrieve the package as planned.

Daniel glanced at the open doorway, then back at the laptop screen. He started to read Helen's previous text, but the screen locked out:

Package is ready for pickup. Will wait for . . .

In his apartment in the lower level of the Massey mansion, Daniel pulled his carry-on bag from the closet, thumped it on his bed, and unzipped it. He grabbed some clothes from his dresser near his bed and thrust them into the suitcase. He stopped a moment with a pair of briefs in his hand, balled them up in his fist, then pitched them like a fast ball into his suitcase. He exhaled and put his head in his hands, then sat on the bed next to his suitcase and looked at the walls with generic artwork. Nothing here was his.

Standing up, he kicked the foot of the headboard as he thought about his months undercover since last summer. It seemed the more pieces he uncovered, the further he was from hard evidence to lock up Massey. How did he get himself into this mess? He'd been handpicked from a group of elite air force recruits. The FBI director had flown him to Washington to personally brief him on their secret plans to form the shell security company Peninsular to track the rich and influential.

Maybe the FBI picked him because he was expendable—single with no family of his own. He worked closely with his air force buddies for years to get Peninsular up and running. Their real target all along was Arpa. They were operating on a hunch that all those tech titans were up to no good. Early on he suspected Massey was the ringleader, the one to watch. Now here he was getting deeper and deeper into Massey's empire as head of security and soon his gubernatorial campaign with nothing to show for it. He needed a break.

As he continued packing, he thought about Helen's offer. Could he really leverage it to get to Henry? He added another outfit and checked his bathroom kit. Hidden inside a zippered pocket inside the lid of the suitcase, he carefully pulled out a small family portrait. Mom, Dad, his sister, Sheila, and Cally all posing with him for a family photo. They had no idea it would be the last time they were all together, but he did. He slipped the photo back into the pocket and zipped it shut.

Moving to his desk, he reviewed the security plans for Henry's gubernatorial campaign bus tour one more time. There were so many stops throughout the state, so many vulnerabilities to cover, but everything seemed in order. They had scrutinized every possible security threat they could think of, but there was always that random nutcase out there seeking a moment of fame. He sent a quick email back to the lead on the security detail, "Looks good. Proceed with implementation." The wording was all business. Even though the FBI was likely tracking all their communication, he also knew Massey was as well. He slipped the laptop inside his backpack and changed into his tailored, black suit. Grabbing his suitcase, he headed for the front entrance.

Standing in the stone-walled foyer by the large, castle-like wood front door, Daniel watched Helen approach pulling her wheeled suitcase.

"Ready?" Helen asked as she stepped next to him.

Daniel reached for her suitcase. "Let me get your bag."

She took hold of his hand. "The driver will get it."

They stood a moment looking at each other, her green eyes quickening his heart rate.

"Let's go." She opened the door and walked toward the emerald green Mercedes SUV parked outside with the engine idling.

CHAPTER 16

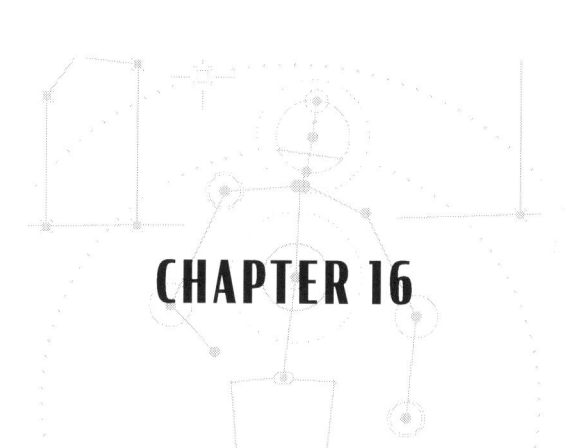

As he drove down Bridge Street in downtown Charlevoix, Fallon looked at the storefronts, the restaurants, and the side streets. The town was fairly quiet with a few people milling about and several cars parked along the dozens of storefronts and restaurants. It looked familiar yet unfamiliar. The memories were there of the summers he spent here as a kid, but why did he come here last summer? Something brought him here. A sign caught his attention. "Blackbird Brewery." He parked his Dart and walked to the entrance.

"Fallon." A familiar man greeted him from behind the bar as he stepped inside.

He studied the man's face for a moment as he sat down at the U-shaped bar in the center of the brewery. They were childhood friends. He was here with him last summer. "Todd Grenshaw?"

"That's me." He looked intently at him. "How are you?"

Fallon shrugged his shoulders. "Pretty good."

"You look pretty good, considering."

"Still have some memory issues." He scanned the large room with its high ceiling, dim lighting, and black bird artwork on the walls. "Is this where your Raven Tavern used to be?"

Todd put his hands on the bar in front of Fallon. "This was the place. You and I had a lot of good times in that old bar. My son Gregg took over a few years ago. He gutted the old bar and reopened it as the Blackbird Brewery."

Fallon looked at the few people seated at booths and tables scattered throughout the brewery. "Was I here with you last summer?"

"Let's go to that booth in the corner and talk," Todd pointed. "I'll have some lunch brought over for us."

"Lunch sounds good, thanks."

Fallon moved to the booth, sat down, and looked around. A couple seated a few booths away. Two men sitting at the bar sipping their beer. He blinked a few times. The brewery was so crowded that night last summer. He watched Todd talk to the bartender. He had seen someone at the bar that night, someone he knew.

"My bartender, Ski, is bringing us a couple drinks," Todd said as he joined Fallon.

"Ski? That's an interesting name," Fallon said.

"It's his nickname. His dad called him Ski-ster when he was a kid, and everyone started calling him Ski."

Fallon looked at Todd sitting across from him. "It's good to see an old friend, a familiar face."

"We go way back, Fallon," Todd said as Ski set two beers on the table in front of them.

"Here's two shorts of the Raven," Ski said as he set the glasses on the table.

"How's Sue doing?" Todd asked Ski.

"She's doing great," Ski replied. "Good to see you, Fallon."

Fallon looked at Ski. "You know me?"

"Doesn't everyone? You and Alicia stopped that terrorist attack. Both of you were here a couple days before the attack."

Fallon frowned at Ski. "We were?"

Ski smiled as he pointed to the bar. "I remember how you kept looking at Alicia at the end of the bar. I saw you film her with your phone."

"I took a video of her?"

CHAPTER 16

"Don't deny it. You two are an item," Ski laughed as he stepped away. "Let me know if you need anything else."

Fallon looked at Todd. "When was I here?"

"Last August, a couple days before the terror attack." Todd turned his head slightly toward the back of the brewery. "We sat in my office in the back. You had a fish sandwich as we talked."

Fallon sighed. "I can remember things that happened years, or even months ago, but not a lot from that week." He took a sip of his beer.

"That was a horrible thing you went through," Todd said.

Fallon watched drops of condensation run down the glass of his beer. He wiped some of it with the tip of his finger. The glass was cold. "I just want to forget everything and move on."

Todd leaned back in his seat, hand still gripping his glass of beer. "Then why did you come back here?"

"It was my therapist's idea. She thought going back to Beaver Island would help me remember details."

"What's the real reason?"

"What do mean?"

"There's something else that brought you here."

Fallon looked around the near-empty brewery, then leaned in across the table and spoke in a hushed tone. "I don't think Ferguson did it."

Todd gave him a curious look. "I'm sure you've seen the video. It's clear he did it."

Fallon leaned back in his seat. "Do you remember what we talked about when I was here last August?"

Todd thought a moment. "You asked about all the old pictures of celebrities The Raven Tavern used to have hanging on the walls. I took you back to my office and showed them to you. I gave you that old, framed photo of you and your dad standing on the Charlevoix pier, the one that used to hang in the old Raven."

"I remember that picture. What else did we talk about?"

"You asked me if I'd seen anything suspicious."

"And?"

"I told you two military-looking people were sitting at the bar a few days ago, and they were packing."

"Open carry?"

Todd nodded. "That's the same thing you asked last summer."

Fallon looked at the bar, then Todd. "You told me you saw a new white cargo van with a rental company sticker on the back at the boat dock. You said it stuck out from the usual trucks you see loaded on the ferry."

"Wait a minute." Todd's eyes opened wide. He pulled out his phone.

"What's wrong?" Fallon watched Todd's finger tap on the screen.

"I don't know why I didn't think of this before."

"What?"

"When the FBI questioned me, I told them about seeing that white van loaded on the ferry a few days before the attack. They said the description fit the same van used by Ferguson to haul the stolen drone to Beaver Island."

"I saw surveillance video from the ferry showing that white van being loaded in Charlevoix and unloaded on the island."

Todd slid his phone on the table to Fallon. "That's the video of Ferguson loading the stolen drone onto a white van at the Caspian warehouse."

"What's your point?"

"I enlarged it." Todd pointed to an area on the screen. "Take a look at the rental company sticker on the back of the van when Ferguson closes the door."

"It says Detroit Rent-all."

"That's not the same sticker I saw on the back of the truck being loaded on the ferry that day."

"Are you sure?"

"Pretty sure."

Fallon looked at the screen showing the fuzzy sticker on the back of the van. He looked at Todd. "We're just going by what you remember."

They looked at each other for moment.

"Who else is with you, Fallon?"

"I came alone."

"Maybe I should go with you."

Fallon slid the phone back to Todd. "I need to do this alone."

Todd put the phone in his shirt pocket. "Last time we talked you went

CHAPTER 16

to the island and . . . well, maybe you should just let this go. I could have it all wrong."

Fallon rubbed his chin. "I have to figure this out on my own. I need to go to that cabin."

"Why don't you stay with me for a few days? I have a guest room. Give yourself some time to collect yourself before you go."

"This can't wait. I'm taking the ferry to Beaver Island this afternoon."

"You're still the same old determined Fallon I've known since we were teenagers." Todd smiled. "Remember when we first met?"

Fallon smiled. "We just graduated from high school. I was in Charlevoix for the summer before I started college. I met you in your dad's old bar, The Raven."

"My girlfriend at the time knew Alicia," Todd said with a distant look on his face. "She set you up with her and we went on a double date."

"We went to that Bryan Adams concert at The Castle." Fallon said with a grin. "I can still hear him playing 'Summer of '69.'"

"The best part is that you and I stayed friends after all these years, even though we eventually broke up with our dates. Well, at least I did." Todd raised an eyebrow. "You and Alicia were on that boat together taking out that drone. Are you seeing her again?"

"I am."

"You two were meant for each other."

"Maybe, but I'm not sure about a lot of things these days."

"For Pete's sake, marry her."

"It's not that simple."

Todd sighed.

"What?"

"I think it's time you retire and get serious about Alicia. Life is too short."

"I can't retire."

"It's time to hand the reigns over to the next generation. My dad held on to The Raven until he died. He never gave me a chance to run things. I was thrown into managing it without him there to help me. I learned from that and handed over the old Raven to my son a few years ago." Todd waved his hand as he looked around the brewery. "And look what he's done to the place. I gave him a chance to put his own stamp on the business."

They exchanged a silent look.

Fallon sighed and rubbed his forehead. "I don't know, Todd."

"What are you waiting for?"

Fallon looked at Todd. "Before I do anything, I have to figure out what happened at that cabin on Beaver Island. I need to find the missing pieces I can't remember."

CHAPTER 17

Daniel stood looking out the tall windows in the large foyer outside the conference room on the seventh floor of the Geneva Grand Hotel. He took in the view of Lake Geneva and the surrounding city below—the towering jet of water in the middle of the lake shooting up almost as high as the hotel; numerous mopeds buzzing along the streets, weaving in and out of traffic dotted with luxury cars; and the Swiss Alps in the distance. So beautiful, so familiar, yet each time he was here there was no time to enjoy it.

He put his hands in his pants pockets and stared at Mont Blanc towering above the peaks of the Alps. The last time he was here he was still working for Peninsular—before he left to be a special agent for the FBI, before he took the undercover assignment. Behind him the rustling of people coming off the elevator caught his attention. He turned to see some familiar faces from Arpa board meetings he managed years ago and took note of the new people mixed in with the group gathering outside the conference room. He studied their interactions with one another, their body language, and their facial expressions, wondering what secrets they might be hiding.

"Hey, Daniel."

Daniel turned to see Matias Phillips, his former coworker at Peninsular, approaching him.

"Great to be working with you again," Matias said as he patted him on the shoulder.

Daniel locked eyes with Matias briefly. It felt good to see a fellow FBI agent after working alone undercover for so many months. He could trust Matias. Together, they built Peninsular into a global security company. There was so much he wanted to discuss with him, but it would be too risky. He would have to speak in code.

"How's it going with Massey?" Matias said.

"He has plenty of security concerns to keep me busy. His Colorado estate is a hub of activity," Daniel added with a wink.

Matias raised an eyebrow. "When are you and Helen heading back?"

"Tomorrow morning on the Masseys' private jet."

"I'm envious." Matias leaned against the wall near Daniel. "What's the range of that jet—do you fly direct to Colorado?"

"One refueling stop in Greenland." Daniel folded his arms over his chest. Was Matias fishing for something—maybe an opportunity for him to provide intelligence to the FBI?

"We're still flying commercial." Matias pulled his phone out of his pocket.

"Are we going to get this meeting started?" a tall man wearing a blue, silky suit said as he approached them, checking his watch. "I have a very tight schedule."

Daniel extended his hand. "Sebastian Tompkin, so good to see you again. Still making those computer chips or have you moved on to potato chips?" He noted how much older Sebastian looked with his graying hair.

"Very funny, Daniel. No, we're now cranking out those AI chips as fast as we can make them," Sebastian said as he firmly shook Daniel's hand. "Are you back working security for Peninsular?"

"No, I'm accompanying Helen Massey on this trip. I'm now managing security for the Masseys."

"I don't understand why you went to work for that devil."

"It's a job." Daniel checked his watch. "Have you seen Helen?"

CHAPTER 17

"There she is now," Matias pointed at Helen confidently walking toward the meeting room door.

"All right, let's get it started," Sebastian said, as he went back to the waiting group of chatting tech billionaires now gathered by the door.

Matias opened the conference room door and checked the security detector arched around the open doorway.

Daniel joined Matias at the entrance and motioned to Helen. "If you could go through first."

"Sorry to keep everyone waiting," Helen said as she handed her phone to Matias, who promptly placed it in a large lockbox by the door.

Matias scanned the access card in Helen's hand and let her walk through the detector in front of the doorway. It promptly buzzed with blinking red warning lights.

"Forgot my Bluetooth device." She took off her necklace and popped out tiny earbuds from her ears. "Earbuds with microphones are not very stylish." She handed the necklace and ear buds to Matias.

"You're looking very sharp, Daniel," Helen said as she walked through the detector again.

"Tailored, black suits—the uniform for Peninsular." Daniel followed Helen through the detector and into the conference room, avoiding Helen's admiring glance. He noted her conservative, navy blue suit with a button-down white blouse. She was all business today.

Standing in the open doorway, Matias waved to the remaining group of people in the foyer outside the conference room. He collected their devices in the lockbox and screened them.

Daniel studied each one as they filed into the room one by one and began to fill the conference table. He made a mental note of a couple of the billionaires who seemed nervous and fidgety. Nicki Navarro, CEO and founder of AirBall Cloud Computing, looked particularly suspicious along with Ted Billings of Level One Investor Software. Then there was Sophia Doyle, CEO of Caspian. He watched her enter the room and take a seat. Below that confident look, he sensed she was hiding something.

When the dozen tech billionaires were all seated around the long mahogany conference table, Matias closed and locked the door. He stood guard by the doorway and nodded to Helen.

RACE FOR REDEMPTION

Daniel stood along the wall opposite Matias and quickly scanned the richly finished, wood wall panels and gold-tile ceiling for anything suspicious. Then he continued to scan the group, noting Navarro fidgeting in her seat as Helen stood at the head of the table and began the meeting with brief introductions for the new people seated at the table. Then she returned to her seat and started with the first page of their thick paper meeting packet in front of each seat.

Daniel listened to the conversations as they worked through the packet page by page. The talk was textbook and boring, full of tech terms pertaining to the rollout of Archipelago in the twenty-two states. Five more states were now considering proposals made by Arpa to implement the software. At this rate, most of the states in the union would be consolidated under Archipelago. He studied Nicki Navarro's facial expressions, as she expressed interest in the proposals, mentioning she had cloud storage in four of the states. Perhaps that was why she was fidgeting, waiting to argue her reasons why she should get the cloud storage business. As the meeting dragged on, he also felt restless.

"You'll see on page forty-two in your packet—"

"Do we really have to keep using paper?" Sophia remarked with a disgusted look on her face.

"Yes," Helen replied. "It's more secure than digital documents."

"But one of us could walk out with the packet," Sophia said, waving the packet in the air.

"We account for every packet and shred them after the meeting," Matias cut in.

"I have a question about the investment listed on this page," Sebastian asked as he thumped his finger on his open packet. "Why are we investing so much in mini storage units in twenty-two states?"

"I know it seems odd," Helen explained. "But we were spending a lot of money to rent storage facilities for computer components to support Archipelago software rollouts in these states. It made more sense to build our own storage facilities. Then we realized how profitable mini storage is, so we decided to expand our investment."

Daniel caught Helen and Sophia exchange a glance. Sophia smiled. *What was that about?*

CHAPTER 17

"I'm going to be blunt with you, Helen," Nicki responded with a firm voice, her face scrunched up in frustration. "From now on you need to vet these investments with us. I'm still angry with Henry for even thinking about misusing all the data Archipelago is storing."

"His run for governor better have nothing to do with him resurrecting that idiotic idea," another investor chimed in. "We made it clear he needed to drop it and erase any evidence of it from the Arpa servers. We need to stick to our initial reason for forming Arpa—to make governments run more efficiently with Archipelago software and build goodwill with the state and federal governments."

"We're making good money on Archipelago," Sebastian remarked. "We don't need to get mixed up in Henry's idiotic plan."

"I assure you Henry has abandoned that plan and erased any reference to it," Helen said. "Besides, he's focused on his run for governor."

"Well, good luck with that." Ted chuckled. "I tried running for the US Senate two years ago and I was hammered in the election for being rich and out of touch. Politics is a lot different than running a business."

"Henry is convinced he can win and model a more effective way to run government," Helen insisted.

"How do we know for sure that Henry erased all the communication we had about his plan to misuse all that government data for our advantage?" Sebastian pressed.

"Trust me," Helen said in a firm tone. "I've reviewed the data myself and it's been erased."

"I trust you, Helen," Sophia remarked.

"Thank you," Helen said, smiling at Sophia.

Daniel looked at the exchange. It appeared staged.

"Where exactly is Arpa's data stored?" Nicki piped up.

"Each state has its own server farm with contracted backups at other cloud computing companies," Helen explained.

"But Henry told us last year that Arpa also had a backup of all the state data as an additional backup service for the states," Nicki said with a skeptical look on her face. "What happened to that?"

"We dropped that plan when more states came onboard," Helen

quickly responded. "It would've required an enormous server farm to keep up with that amount of data."

Nicki's eyes narrowed as she silently stared at Helen.

"Now, if there are no more questions . . ." Helen scanned the room. "I'll continue with the agenda."

The room was silent.

As the meeting continued, Daniel eyed Helen as she lightly tapped a pen on the table and glanced at Sophia. They exchanged a smile.

* * *

Daniel stood with Matias at the exit door as Arpa board members filed out of the room after the meeting. Matias collected meeting packets to shred while Daniel returned cell phones and other devices to the attendees as they left.

Sophia stopped at the exit door as Daniel handed her phone to her. She stood a minute, facing him with a confident stance. "I didn't expect to see you here today. I thought you left Peninsular."

"The Masseys wanted me to review Peninsular's security," Daniel responded with a businesslike tone.

"I don't know why anyone would want to work for Henry Massey," Sophia said. "You deserve better, Daniel."

"It pays well."

"I'm sure it does." Sophia looked at her phone, then Daniel. "Be careful."

"What makes you say that?"

"Just be careful," she said as she exited the room.

"What was that about?" Matias asked.

"She's always been jealous of our success," Helen said as she stepped next to them.

Daniel handed Helen her phone, necklace, and earbuds. "I'll help Matias shred the documents, then we'll pack this up if you want to get going."

"I just need a minute," Helen said, as she went to the wall of floor-to-ceiling windows facing Lake Geneva and stood looking at the view. She

CHAPTER 17

removed the diamond-studded hair comb from the back of her head. Her long, blonde hair fell to her shoulders along the side of her face.

"Do you want us to leave you alone for a few minutes?" Matias offered.

"No," Helen said as she turned and pushed the long strands of hair over her ears. "But I would like Daniel to join me for dinner."

Matias raised an eyebrow at Daniel. "I'll go get the cart for all this equipment."

"Let me help," Daniel said.

Matias put up his hand. "I got it."

They looked at each other for a second. Matias tilted his head toward Helen then left the room.

The conference room door clicked shut. Daniel turned toward Helen.

"What do you say?" Helen walked to him and took his hand. "Just you and me at my favorite restaurant. I can change into something more comfortable."

They stood a moment, eyes locked on each other, as Helen took his other hand. His heart rate increased. Those emerald-green eyes. Her hands felt warm in his. Hadn't he compromised his morals enough letting the drone attack proceed last summer? He couldn't do this, not to Henry, not for his own sense of right. Something told him it was wrong.

"I can't." He took a deep breath and pulled his hands free from her. "I need to help Matias pack up, then I'll get room service back at my hotel room."

The corner of Helen's lips curled up slightly. "You're a good man."

Daniel pressed his lips together and nodded slightly as they looked at each other a few more seconds.

"I'll see you in the lobby tomorrow morning at seven," Helen said as she opened the conference room door and looked back at Daniel. "There will be a car waiting to take us to the airport to catch our jet back to Colorado."

"See you in the morning." Daniel watched the door slowly close behind her and click shut. He kicked the leg of the conference room table and pressed his hands against his head. Did he just miss an opportunity to get the evidence he needed? What did she know that she wasn't telling him?

CHAPTER 18

"You sure you're okay?" Alicia asked over the phone.

Fallon held the phone close to his ear as he looked at the calm water of Lake Michigan through the window next to his seat inside the *Emerald Isle* ferry. "I'm fine."

"You don't sound sure."

"I'll be okay." He looked at a freighter in the distance. "Thanks for letting me use your house on the island."

"Do you remember how to get there?"

"I have the address and my phone to get me there if I don't."

"I still don't like the idea of you going alone."

"I need to do this."

The phone went silent for a moment.

"You still there, Alicia?"

"Yeah. Call me when you're settled in."

"I will . . ."

He hesitated. Should he tell her how much he cared for her, or that other word he just couldn't seem to get out? He ended the call with a simple goodbye. With a sigh, he leaned back in his seat and closed his eyes. Muscles tensed as he listened to the sound of the boat engines and

CHAPTER 18

the vibration of the metal floor. Fragmented thoughts came to mind as the boat's engines slowed. He glanced out the window and spotted Beaver Island coming into view. An uneasy feeling rose up inside of him.

He exited the cabin and stood a moment looking at the stairway to the upper deck. Taking a deep, shaky breath, he ascended the metal stairs. He paused a moment at the top, then walked to the bow and eyed the small town of St. James along the shore in the distance. The clear, blue sky and the calm water looked peaceful, but his body tensed as a green buoy came into view, bobbing in the boat's wake. He pressed his lips together as he noted black marks and dents on the buoy. He tightly gripped the railing on the boat. This was the spot where the drone bore down on them and exploded.

The memory slowly came into view.

> *His hand clamps tightly to the steering wheel of his granddad's Chris-Craft. He presses the throttle all the way forward as the silhouette of the ferry comes into full view. His hair blows in the wind, water spraying off the bow, as he spots the green buoy coming into view. He turns to see Alicia standing in the boat with him, pointing an automatic rifle skyward. The rat-a-tat-tat of repeated gunfire echoes across the water and off the side of the ferry, blending with a loud buzzing noise from the drone and people screaming. He looks up. The large drone is closing in on them.*

Fallon shook his head and released his grip on the metal railing. The boat slowed as they approached the dock and the town of St. James. He walked toward the back of the boat, stopping abruptly near the stern to look at the orange life ring hanging on the railing. The video of him and Alicia stopping the drone was filmed from this spot. He grabbed the railing, noting the fresh paint.

"That sure was a smooth crossing," came a voice from behind him.

Startled, Fallon turned to see a man joining him at the railing.

"First time on the island?" the man asked.

"No." Fallon turned his attention back toward shore as the boat neared the large dock and loading area.

"Wait a minute," the man said. "You're Fallon McElliot! The one who stopped that drone with Alicia Chalmers."

Fallon smiled politely at the man. He just wanted him to leave him alone.

The man held up his phone. "Can I take my picture with you?"

"No," Fallon curtly replied.

"Oh," the man said with an embarrassed look as he hurried to the stairwell.

Fallon walked to the stern of the boat as it pivoted and backed into the dock. He watched as the boat was tied up and the large ramp lowered on the rear of the boat. Cars, trucks, and cargo were unloaded. He took a deep breath, exited the boat, and walked to the parking area where cars were unloaded from the ferry. He smiled when he spotted his Dart being driven off the ferry.

He stood a moment by his car and looked at the people milling about the dock area. Alicia had been on the island with him last August. She was here investigating a potential terror plot against the *Emerald Isle*. Was he here to pursue Cally for Ferguson or was he also checking out the potential terror plot for Karen? He rubbed his forehead and climbed into his car.

As he drove to Alicia's house a few blocks from the ferry dock he recognized some of the sights. He parked his car on the gravel driveway in front of the small house with two dormers and faded green siding. Opening his car door, he stood a moment gazing at the white posts with flaking paint propping up a sagging roof on a small cement porch. Tall trees shaded the house and lot. They had been here . . . together.

Inside the house, he set his suitcase in the bedroom and walked into the kitchen. The old oak floorboards creaked beneath his feet. A memory emerged when he saw the small metal table with a white top.

> *He sits across from her at the table, comparing notes.*
> *He shows her the address that Chip gave him for the*
> *cabin on the island owned by Daniel. The suspected*

CHAPTER 18

terror cell has to be at the cabin. He follows her out the door to drive to the cabin.

He pulled out a chair and sat down. Elbows on the table, he propped his head in his hand. Moving his other hand beneath his hair, he winced as he touched the scar on top of his head, trying not to think about the plate under his scalp. He started counting the months as he traced the scar from the front of his head to the back, one, two, three . . . how many months since the terror attack? So much time had passed, and the events of that day were still unclear. He pulled out his phone and called Chip.

"Are you on the island?" Chip asked.

"Just arrived about a half-hour ago."

"Something wrong?"

"No, but my friend Todd at the brewery in Charlevoix claims the van he saw loaded on the ferry a few days before the drone attack is not the same van in the video with Ferguson at the Caspian warehouse."

"What makes him say that?"

"The one he saw had a different rental company sticker on the back."

"Give me a second. I can call up that video."

Fallon could hear Chip typing.

"Here it is. I'm fast-forwarding through it to a rear view of the van coming off the ferry on Beaver Island. It's the same make, model, and color as the van at the Caspian warehouse, but there is not a clear view of the back of the van."

"Any way to check the VIN numbers?"

"No, they never found the rental van."

"Is it possible someone faked the video of Ferguson loading that drone?"

"That video was scoured. With a terrorism case like this, the prosecutor has taken every precaution to make sure all the evidence is authentic. There's no doubt that Ferguson planned and executed the attack."

"But it's possible someone could've faked the video and overlooked a small detail like a rental sticker."

"Perhaps, but not in this case."

"I don't know Chip . . ."

"You just won't let it go—"

"I can't. I need to figure out what I'm missing."

"It's good to hear you talking like the detective I knew before. Call me if you need anything, Fallon. I'm here for you."

"Thanks, Chip. I know I can always count on you."

Fallon ended the call and looked at his phone. He called up the video of Ferguson loading the drone at the Caspian warehouse and studied the rental sticker on the back of the van. Why would someone go to so much trouble to frame Ferguson? He set his phone on the table and stared at the empty seat across from him. They had gone to the cabin from here. Alicia thought the cabin was the location of the terror cell, but for some reason he didn't think that was right. He needed to visit the cabin this afternoon.

CHAPTER 19

Pieces of memory flooded his mind as Fallon pulled into the driveway of the Lake Geneserath cabin on the south end of Beaver Island. He climbed out of his car and looked at the faded, yellow tape that circled the cabin with dim letters spelling "CRIME SCENE DO NOT PASS." He stood a moment surveying the woods across the road, then the driveway and the cabin. He had stood on this driveway, on this very spot last August right before the drone attack.

> *Gravel crunches as he watches two men leave the cabin and walk down the driveway. One man turns to tell him he wants to give him a fighting chance. They continue to the end of the driveway, then cross the road toward the woods. A loud buzzing noise catches his attention. He stands on the end of the driveway and looks up at a large drone hovering over the cabin, then shouts to the men. One stops, looks at him, then winks.*

He thought a moment of the man who winked at him when he was here last summer. He looked like the man in the family picture Liz Callahan showed him. Was Daniel with him in the cabin? A sheriff's car pulled into the driveway and parked next to his Dart.

"Good afternoon, Mr. McElliot," a man dressed in a brown uniform said as he climbed out of his car and approached Fallon. "I'm the deputy sheriff. It's great to see you again."

"Have we met before?"

"Not exactly. I was handling crowd control at the marina when they took you from the sheriff's boat to the medevac the day of the drone attack. You look like you're recovering well."

"I'm getting there." Fallon turned and scanned the cabin with its rustic log siding. "So this is the cabin."

"The feds officially seized the property last fall. It's been locked up pending the trial."

"Thanks for getting me permission to go inside."

"No problem. Anything you remember will only help the prosecutor's case."

"Is everything the same as it was the day of the drone attack?"

"It's been locked up and under 24-hour video surveillance since the day of the attack," the deputy said as he ducked under the yellow tape draped across the porch and walked to the front entrance.

Fallon stepped next to the deputy as he unlocked a padlock, then the door. They stepped into the kitchen area. The room smelled musty.

"Shouldn't we have gloves on?" Fallon asked as he stood in the kitchen.

"It's been thoroughly dusted for fingerprints," the deputy explained. "Just don't move anything. We want to leave it as we found it."

Fallon stood in the kitchen and observed chewed pieces of paper plates and napkins with mouse droppings scattered all over the table. Silverware and glasses were set for five people. A layer of dust covered everything. He looked at the table, then at the deputy. "What did the fingerprints say—who was here?"

"They collected prints for Robert Callahan Sr., Jr., Alicia, Daniel, and you."

"That's what I was told. Any DNA samples?"

"Same story."

"No one else was here?"

CHAPTER 19

"Except . . ."

Fallon raised his eyebrows.

"They collected prints and DNA off two snifters, one on the table by the couch, the other on a table by the chair opposite the couch. One snifter had your fingerprints on it, but they could not identify who the other prints belong to."

"No match in the databases?"

"None."

Fallon looked at the living room. If it was Massey, they should've been able to identify his prints. Better not tip off the deputy about Massey. "Would it be okay if you leave me alone in here?"

"Sure," the deputy said as he headed for the door.

Fallon watched the door close behind him, then turned to look at the table again. They were all here last summer. Fallon pointed to each chair around the table where Robert, Cally, Daniel, and Alicia sat last summer. He looked at the worn tabletop and empty chairs around the table. Robert prayed before the meal—he prayed for wisdom and safety and something about knowing God's peace. Fallon looked at the chair where he sat that day, then looked at the chair opposite it on the other side of the table. Daniel was sitting across from him. Daniel was here with them. Fallon looked at the back door. Did he go somewhere with Daniel?

Through the living room windows next to the back door, Fallon could see Lake Geneserath and a dock protruding out from the shore. The memory became clearer as he walked to the windows and looked at the calm water.

> *The dock creaks as he walks to the seaplane. The back door on the plane screeches as he opens it, climbs inside, and sits in the front seat next to Daniel. Through the windshield, he sees a puff of blue smoke rise up from the front of the plane as the engine sputters. He looks out the side window and watches the plane's float skim the water as they sail down the glassy water of Lake Geneserath. A wave of nausea comes over him as the plane lifts off from the lake. He looks out his side*

window again at the streams of water shedding off the floats, then he looks down at the disappearing cabin below. A beautiful orange hue lights up the sky in the west as they fly south over Lake Michigan toward the mainland and Detroit.

He watched the deputy climb the steps to the back porch and unlock the back door. Fallon opened the door and joined the deputy. Planks moaned beneath his feet as the door clicked shut behind him. The damp smell of cedar trees filled the air.

"What do you recall about the boat dock?" the deputy asked.

He looked at the dock. "A seaplane was tied up there."

"The FBI obtained transponder data from the morning of the drone attack," the deputy said. "They verified a seaplane took off from this lake."

"And where did it go?"

"We have no idea. The transponder was turned off once they were airborne. But we do know that another pilot saw the plane leaving Beaver Island, and she said it looked like it was headed toward Chicago. She recalled the tail number."

Fallon looked at the deputy. "Were they able to trace the number?"

"It didn't show up in any databases of registered planes."

"I'm not surprised." Fallon turned to go back inside. He tensed as he gripped the doorknob.

"Are you okay?" the deputy asked as he stepped next to Fallon.

"I think so." The cold metal felt familiar in his hand. He opened the door and stepped into the living room. "Which whiskey snifter had the unknown prints and DNA?" Fallon asked as he noticed the empty glass on a small table next to the couch as well as one on an end table next to a chair.

"The one by the couch."

Fallon walked toward the couch.

"You were here, but we're not exactly sure when," the deputy added. "Alicia, Cally, and Robert all say you were with them, here with Daniel, but they all separately insist that no one had any whiskey to drink while all of you were here together."

CHAPTER 19

Fallon stood next to the couch. He remembered sharing a drink of whiskey with someone, but if it wasn't them, was it really Massey? It had to be. Why did his name keep popping up in his mind?

"Do you recall having a drink with someone here?" the deputy asked.

"I do, but it's not too clear." Fallon paused as he thought about the memory Grace resurrected in therapy. "I'm sitting in this cabin holding a snifter filled with whiskey and someone is with me."

"Who?"

Fallon focused on the fuzzy image of someone sitting across from him. A lone floor lamp illuminated his face. He has a snifter in his hand with an amber liquid. He looks familiar. Suddenly anger began to surge in Fallon's body.

"Can you tell me who it is?" the deputy pressed.

The fuzzy image in his mind had to be Massey, even though it did not make sense. Why would he be here? "I'm not sure," Fallon said.

Massey must have had something to do with the drone attack on the ferry. If he could remember exactly what Massey told him that day, it would give him a lead, something to go on. A bigger, clearer picture was beginning to take shape.

"Can you give me another minute alone?" Fallon asked.

The deputy nodded and exited the cabin.

Fallon sat in the chair facing the couch, trying to bring the fuzzy memory into focus. He studied the empty snifters now covered with dust.

> *He sits in the chair, eyes locked on Massey seated across from him. So smug and arrogant, telling him something about his Archipelago software. They talk about Arpa and running state government more efficiently. Something about taking control of the government. If that was true, how could he possibly prove it? For now, he had to keep this to himself. He would have to figure out if the memory was real.*

"Thank you," Fallon said to the deputy as he exited the cabin.

"I hope it helped," the deputy said as he locked the door, then secured the padlock.

Fallon nodded.

As he drove back toward town, he could feel fatigue overtaking him. He convinced himself to take the remainder of the day to rest, have a good dinner, and get a good night's sleep. Tomorrow he would return to Charlevoix on the ferry.

As Fallon drove through town, something caught his eye. He pulled into the parking lot of the municipal marina, parked his car, and looked at an empty slip near the parking lot. His granddad's boat had been docked there last August. He and Alicia used that boat to pursue the *Emerald Isle* and stop the drone. But how had he known the drone attack was about to happen? He looked at the empty dock. More pieces of memory began to connect in his head as he looked at the calm water in St. James Harbor. Massey had talked about drones delivering something far more damaging than shoes or food.

He opened his car door and stepped out. Muscles tensed as he took a few steps toward the dock. A cabin cruiser moved slowly across the glassy water as it approached the marina. In the distance, on the far shore of the bay, he could see a lighthouse. He walked up to the dock where the Chris-Craft was docked last summer. He recalled the drone closing in on them. The pounding in his head was too much. It was hard to think, to process so many thoughts. Above, he noted the darkening sky as evening set in. He needed rest. He took a deep breath and returned to his car. Tomorrow he would revisit the empty dock before he left the island.

CHAPTER 20

The anticipation was eating him up inside. Ferguson sat on the small stool by the tiny desk in his cell tracing the mortar lines of the gray cinder block wall in front of him. The walls seemed to be closing in on him. He felt short of breath. There was nothing to stop this. Soon he would be whisked away to the grand jury. He clenched his hands into fists. Somehow he would get even with Fallon . . . or whoever set him up. Was Nigel right? If so, then who framed him? He jumped at the thud of his cell door opening. Three guards stepped into his cell.

"I can't believe the grand jury isn't having him appear by video conference," the lead guard said as he helped Ferguson put on his coat.

"At least we're getting rid of him," the second guard said as he cuffed Ferguson's hands behind his back.

The third guard grabbed Ferguson's arm and guided him to the door. "They want him there in person for all the business it will bring to the Marquette area. I heard all the hotels in the area are filled."

"We just need to get him on that helicopter," the lead guard said as he shoved Ferguson through the cell door. "The FBI can deal with all the security headaches and the media storm."

The other guard grabbed Ferguson's arm and steered him out of his cell. The door slammed shut behind them, sending the sound of metal on metal echoing down the hallway. This was it. He was on his way to be indicted and eventually a convicted terrorist.

"Don't worry, it's almost May. Most of the snow has melted in Marquette by now," the lead guard laughed as he guided Ferguson down the long hallway.

"What about my dress shirt and pants for the grand jury appearance?" Ferguson asked.

The lead guard pushed him along. "Your attorney is supposed to have them for you when he meets you in Marquette."

"But I haven't heard from him since he visited me."

"Not my problem," the guard on his right said.

They continued down a maze of hallways until they stepped outside to the helipad. Ferguson squinted at the early evening sun low in the sky. He scanned the tall chain-link fencing topped with rolls of razor wire. A *whup, whup, whup* sound caught his attention. He turned to his left and spotted a black helicopter approaching with bright gold letters *FBI* on the side. The guards circled around him as the helicopter touched down. The hum of the engine slowed as the blades continued to spin. The side door opened. A man and woman climbed out and walked toward them. He noted the gold embroidered *FBI* letters on the front of their dark-blue jackets.

Ferguson watched the tall, fit woman approach. She pushed her long brown hair back from her face as she stopped in front of them. The man following behind her was slightly shorter with a muscular build that shaped his jacket. He brushed his long bangs of black hair away from his face as he stood next to the woman.

"We're taking Thomas Ferguson to Mackinac County Airport to catch a plane to Marquette," the woman said as she handed the lead guard a piece of paper. "He's scheduled to appear before the grand jury in a couple days."

"Paper!" the guard smirked. "You feds need to get with the times and get onboard with Archipelago software."

The word *Archipelago* caught Ferguson's attention. He wouldn't trust it. When he was warden at Jackson prison he saw too many glitches in

CHAPTER 20

the system. Somehow it generated an approved hardship release for Cally when the director of corrections never saw it. That's what started this whole mess. The feds claimed the head of state corrections arranged the fake funeral for Cally's dad that helped him escape. He didn't believe it for a minute. Who would go to so much trouble to help Cally escape? If only he had someone to help him escape.

The guard looked at the tablet in his hand, then the sheet of paper. "It all looks in order."

"We'll take him from here," the woman said.

Ferguson eyed her menacing look.

The lead guard stood in front of her. "Not so fast. I need to see your ID."

"You have your paperwork," she snapped, eyes locked on the guard.

Ferguson looked at her staring down the lead guard. If the guard knew what was best for him, he wouldn't mess with her.

"I'm required to see your ID," the guard insisted. "Both of you."

Ferguson rolled his eyes. The guard was such a stickler for protocol. *Let's get on with the transfer.*

"Okay," the woman said as she pulled out her ID.

The man with her sighed and handed his ID to the lead guard.

"Nadia Long?" the guard said as he glanced at the ID, then her.

A shock wave surged through Ferguson's body at the sound of the name. Nigel told him when he heard that name to do exactly what she told him. His heart beat faster as his breathing rapidly increased. He carefully scanned the area. The helicopter was still sitting on the helipad, blades spinning, ready for takeoff. He exchanged a glance with Nadia. She raised an eyebrow.

The guard looked at the two IDs, then ran them through a scanner attached to his tablet. "I can't let you take him," the guard said as his tablet buzzed.

"What are you talking about?" the man with Nadia grumbled.

"A secret code is generated each day by the Archipelago software for prisoner moves," the guard explained. "It's tied to the IDs of the people doing the transfer. Your IDs have yesterday's code. I can't let you take him."

The man and woman looked at each other, then the guard.

"We're FBI. We have orders to take him," Nadia protested. "It's *your* job to match our IDs with *your* stupid code. This is on you. We're taking the prisoner! We have a schedule to keep."

Ferguson tensed. Suddenly he felt Nadia grab his arm. She turned away from the guard and began to pull him toward the waiting helicopter. He felt someone grab his other arm and turned to see the lead guard pull him back toward the building. Nadia resisted the move. This couldn't possibly end well.

"Let him go!" Nadia firmly snapped at the guard.

"No!"

The two guards joined him. One tried to pull Nadia's hand off Ferguson's arm.

Nadia pushed the guard away.

Ferguson looked at Nadia then at the guard as he felt them both tugging at him; both determined to get their way.

"Take him back to his cell," the lead guard barked at the other two guards. He gave Nadia an icy stare. "We'll hold him until we clear this up. This prisoner is too important. I'm not letting him go until we have the correct authorization. Not on my watch!"

Ferguson felt Nadia tighten her grip until one guard pulled her hand off his arm. The other guard quickly pushed him back toward the entrance to the prison. He looked at Nadia's hardened look of determination. His money was on her to win this duel.

The guards began to forcibly move Ferguson toward the door leading back into the prison.

"Hold it right there!" Nadia shouted.

Ferguson looked back, startled to see that Nadia and the man now had guns pulled and pointed at them. A shootout? This was not a good position to be in.

"We're doing this our way now," Nadia insisted. "Let him go and raise your arms."

The guards released their hold on Ferguson's arms as they raised their hands.

"Walk this way slowly, Ferguson," Nadia instructed.

CHAPTER 20

He turned and slowly walked to Nadia and the man. The man grabbed his arm and started to lead him toward the helicopter.

"You're not FBI!" Ferguson heard the lead guard shout. He turned around and saw all three guards now had guns pulled and pointed at them. He looked back at Nadia. Panic surged through his body. He was caught in the middle.

"Drop your guns!" Nadia shouted.

"Stand your ground!" the lead guard shouted. "Ferguson's not escaping on my watch."

"I advise you to look at the helicopter door before you do anything rash," Nadia said.

Ferguson caught a glimpse of a man standing in the open doorway of the helicopter with an automatic rifle pointed toward the guards.

"It's not worth it!" one guard said as he tossed his gun to the pavement and raised his hands.

The other guard tossed his gun to the pavement and raised his hands. "I have a family."

Ferguson looked at the two guards, faces filled with fear, hands raised in the air. He looked at Nadia.

"Let him go!" the lead guard said, gun still pointed at Nadia.

"They're right," Nadia said. "It's not worth it. Think of your family."

"I don't have a family!" the lead guard snapped back.

"What about your mom?" Nadia smiled. "She lives alone. She needs you."

The guard visibly choked. "How did you—"

"Just drop the gun."

They stared at each other for a moment, guns drawn. Ferguson could see the gun visibly shaking in the lead guard's hand. He glanced at the gun in Nadia's hand, steady and firm.

The lead guard sighed and tossed his gun onto the pavement.

"Lay on the ground—all of you!" Nadia barked at the guards, then made a swift glance at Ferguson. "Get in the helicopter. Hurry!"

Ferguson hesitated as he watched the guards lie on the pavement. He had no idea who these people were other than Nigel's mention of Nadia Long. He glanced at the helicopter, then back at the prison building.

"Move it!" the woman shouted at Ferguson as she turned and ran toward the helicopter with the man. "Get in the chopper, now!"

He turned and started to run, but suddenly felt someone tackle him. As he fell to the pavement, he saw the lead guard lying next to him, his gun drawn. Suddenly automatic rifle fire erupted. The lead guard screamed and grabbed his leg.

"Run, Ferguson!" Nadia shouted as she jumped into the helicopter.

Ferguson sprinted for the helicopter and dove in through the open door as it lifted off the ground. He hit the metal floor of the helicopter with a thud and instantly felt someone cut off his handcuffs. Through the open door he caught a glimpse of the helipad quickly disappearing from view. He could barely hear the loud, echoing sound of an alarm as flashing red lights lit up the helipad.

"Sit down and buckle up," Nadia said as she grabbed an automatic rifle attached to the side of the helicopter and braced herself against the open door. "This is going to be a rough ride."

Ferguson strapped himself into a seat as the helicopter abruptly tilted. His body pushed against the seat belt as the force of the turn pushed him toward the fuselage. He rubbed his wrists as he looked out the window at waves crashing on the shore of St. Helena Island. In the distance he could see the lighthouse on the eastern tip of the island, its white tower touched with hints of orange from the setting sun. The light at the top was now blinking. As they leveled out over Lake Michigan, shots rang out from the prison. Bullets began to pierce the fuselage. He watched the woman brace herself, point the rifle rearward, and return fire. The shooting intensified.

As the firefight continued, memories of Afghanistan flooded his mind. Sitting across from his army buddies inside the helicopter, dressed in desert fatigues as they clutched their rifles. Nervous glances at one another as they hunted terrorists hiding out in the desert terrain below. Sudden gunfire sent them all scrambling for positions to return fire. He gripped the edge of his seat. Now he was the terrorist.

He glanced at Nadia and the man, rifles pointed out the side doors, returning fire. This couldn't end well. Nigel told him to follow their lead. What other option did he have?

CHAPTER 20

More bullets pierced the fuselage. More return fire, then the shooting stopped.

"We're out of range," Nadia shouted above the roar of the helicopter as she set the rifle on the seat next to her and closed the side door. She waved at Ferguson. "I'm Nadia Long."

"I heard," Ferguson shouted back. "Are you with the crime ring?"

"No," Nadia chuckled as she sat next to him and buckled herself in. "Your crime ring friends had nothing to do with this."

"You know my friends?"

"We know a lot about you. Probably more than you know about yourself."

"You knew the lead guard's mom lived alone," Ferguson said.

"We do our homework."

"Who *are* you, and where are we going?"

"Patience," Nadia replied.

They sat in silence for a few minutes. Ferguson looked at the man sitting across from them. "I didn't catch your name."

"That's not important," the man said with a stern face.

Suddenly a buzzing alarm rang out from the cockpit. Ferguson instantly recognized the warning sound from his army days. "Engine trouble," he shouted as he looked back at Nadia.

Nadia swore as the helicopter shuddered and began to wobble. "How bad is it?"

"Buckle up!" the pilot replied. "Oil pressure is dropping fast. We're about to lose our engine."

Ferguson glanced out his window at the large waves below on Lake Michigan. He'd done this before, only with waves of desert sand below.

> *The helicopter engine sputters as they begin to lose altitude. "We're going down!" He grips the handrail next to the open doorway of the army helicopter and looks at Fallon next to him firing at something below. Fallon turns to look at him. There is fear in his eyes. He gripped the edge of his seat. The sights. The sounds. The*

smell of burning oil. The familiar sick feeling in his gut that they were about to crash.

"Is there someplace to put us down?" Nadia shouted.

"No!" the pilot responded. "Wait, I see something ahead. I think I can get us there."

A few seconds later, Ferguson spotted treetops out his window. An island.

CHAPTER 21

Still shaking, Ferguson looked at the helicopter wedged into the sand in a clearing surrounded by woods. "I can't believe you made a controlled landing with no engine."

"Thank the marines for training me for emergency landings," the pilot said as he flipped open a panel on the side of the helicopter and looked at the engine.

"I was army," Ferguson said.

The pilot looked at him. "Afghanistan?"

Ferguson nodded as he pointed to the engine. "How bad is it?"

"We're stuck here," the pilot said.

Ferguson scanned the large open area surrounded by a dense stand of trees, scraggly brush, and large rocks protruding from the ground. "And where exactly are we?"

"South end of Hog Island, not far from Beaver Island," the pilot said.

Ferguson saw Nadia and the man step out of the wooded area and approach him. "Now what?"

"First, we have to get you out of that bright-orange jumpsuit," the man said as he climbed into the helicopter and reemerged. He tossed some clothes to Ferguson. "Here, change into these."

"Do you have a name?" Ferguson asked as he caught the clothes and looked at the man.

"Lance." The man said as he started walking toward an opening in the woods. "I'll scout the island and see what our options are."

Ferguson took off his jumpsuit and slipped on the jeans. Perfect fit. "How'd you know my size?"

"It's part of your prison record," Nadia said.

Who are these people and how did they access his record? "Well, we're off to a great start," Ferguson scoffed as he put on the shirt. "I went from prisoner on one island to stranded on another."

"I think you're cursed," Nadia said in an annoyed tone as she sat on a large rock nearby.

He looked at Nadia, then the navy-blue helicopter with bright FBI letters painted on the side. How did they pull off something as bold as pretending to be the FBI picking him up? "Who are you working for?"

"Let's just say an interested party who wants revenge."

Not the answer he expected. Ferguson frowned as he leaned against the helicopter's fuselage. "On who?"

"Henry Massey."

"What does he have to do with anything?"

"He's the one who set you up as the terrorist with the fake video of you stealing the Caspian drone, messages from terrorists overseas on your laptop, and the explosives in your home that matched the drone targeting the *Emerald Isle*."

The pilot emerged from the helicopter. "Here's some bottled water." He tossed a bottle to Nadia and Ferguson, then disappeared inside the chopper.

Nadia caught the bottle and took a drink. "Massey also changed the county records to show you owned the cabin on Beaver Island, which prosecutors labeled as the location of your terror cell. You fell right into their trap." She rubbed her leg.

"What's up with your leg?"

"Just a bruise."

"I'm still knotted up from that landing," he said as he rubbed his neck. "Why would Massey go to so much trouble to frame me?"

CHAPTER 21

"To get revenge on you and the crime ring for going after Cally's family."

"Why would that matter to him?" Ferguson asked, stretching his arms. His joints cracked, releasing the tension.

"Does the name Daniel Callahan mean anything to you?"

"He's Cally's brother. Cally was in Jackson Prison when I was warden there."

"Daniel is the one who staged his dad's funeral to help Cally escape from prison."

"I doubt Daniel could do something like that alone."

"Daniel worked with Massey. They're the ones who put all that evidence on the crime ring on the internet so his brother, Cally, could go free. They shut down your whole crime ring."

"Then who was behind the drone strike?"

"Massey."

"Why would he do that?"

"It's part of a much bigger plan of his."

"What plan?"

"We'll tell you soon enough," Nadia said as she looked up at the sky, then started walking to the helicopter. "It'll be dark soon. We need to figure out how to get off this island before the feds catch up to us."

"Wait!" Ferguson followed behind her. "Can you at least tell me why you helped me escape? What do you need me for?"

Nadia turned to look at Ferguson. "When you get the whole story, you'll be just as motivated as we are to get revenge on Massey. I'll tell you this much right now. You have nothing to lose going with us. You were going to spend the rest of your life in prison just on the terrorism charges."

"What if I don't want to help you?"

"Then we leave you here and you go back to prison for the rest of your life."

Ferguson looked at the desolate surroundings. "And if I help you, what's in it for me?"

"Freedom."

"How?"

"It's a big world. When you have a lot of money backing you, there are a lot of options."

"Who's backing you?"

"Someone with more money than you can imagine."

"I can imagine quite a bit."

"Then think about where in the world you would like to live after we pull this off."

"Hey!"

Ferguson turned to see Lance running toward them.

"I think I found a way out of here," Lance said as he stopped next to them. "There's a boat beached on the shore with the keys in it. I think whoever brought it here might be camping on the island."

Nadia's eyes widened as she quickly scanned the clearing. "We need to move fast. Those campers may have seen us land here. I'll grab our backpacks." She quickly ran to the helicopter and climbed inside.

Ferguson looked up at the darkening sky. "Where are we going?"

"Beaver Island," Nadia said as she jumped out of the helicopter holding a couple backpacks. "Come on! Let's move."

Ferguson followed Nadia, Lance, and the pilot to a boat beached on the western shore of the island. He felt the cold Lake Michigan water soak his shoes and the lower portion of his jeans as he helped push the boat from the beach. He jumped into the boat and sat in a seat near the stern. He glanced to the west and saw the sun nearing the horizon, casting an orange glow over the water. The boat's engine started, and he turned to see Nadia at the wheel. As the boat powered up and started skimming across the smooth water, he spotted Beaver Island directly ahead. The last time he was there, he was in handcuffs after the police apprehended him on North Fox Island.

Nadia eased the boat into a dock at the municipal marina on Beaver Island and tied it up. It was almost dark as they climbed out of the boat. Ferguson pulled his hood over his head as they walked to the shore.

"Now what?" Lance asked.

"There's a hotel across the street," Nadia said as she pointed to a sign with *Harborview Inn* on it. "We'll stay there tonight. In the morning we'll be on a jet out of here."

CHAPTER 21

Ferguson nervously eyed his surroundings as he started to follow her, skeptical of her plan. But Nigel had told him to do what Nadia said. As he glanced around one more time, he spotted a familiar car in the marina parking lot. A green Dart. Could it be? He stopped a moment and saw someone get out of the car. Could it really be Fallon? If it was, how did he get here so quickly? He quickly turned his head away.

"Come on," Nadia motioned. "Step it up."

Ferguson followed Nadia and Lance across the street toward the hotel. He recalled Fallon telling him the location of Alicia's place on the island. It was only a few blocks from the marina and the hotel. Could he be staying there? He would keep this to himself for the moment. This could be his last chance to confirm what Fallon knew about the drone attack—to see if Nadia was telling the truth.

CHAPTER 22

A buzzing sound pulled him out of deep sleep. Fallon sat up in bed and blinked a few times, remembering he was in Alicia's cabin on Beaver Island. He looked at the nightstand next to the bed and saw his phone screen glowing in the darkness with Karen's name and picture.

"Hello?"

"Where are you, Fallon?"

"Karen?"

"Are you on Beaver Island?"

"What's wrong. You sound panicked."

"Where are you?"

He put the phone on speaker and dropped it on the bed as he rubbed his eyes. "Alicia's house on the island . . . What time is it?"

"Two a.m.—You need to come back to Lansing as soon as possible."

"What . . . why?"

"Ferguson's escaped."

Was he dreaming? He stared at the phone.

"Fallon? Are you there?"

"What did you say?"

"Ferguson has escaped."

CHAPTER 22

"How? He's in that maximum security prison on St. Helena Island."

"Was . . . they think someone hijacked the helicopter they were using to transport him to Mackinac City to catch a plane to Marquette for the grand jury."

"How did he pull that off?"

"I don't have a lot of details . . . Fallon, you need to come back as soon as possible."

Fallon swung his legs around off the side of the bed and touched the cold floor with his bare feet as he rubbed his forehead.

"Fallon?"

"I'm here . . . I'm still waking up."

"You need to listen to me, Fallon. It's a short flight from St. Helena Island to Beaver Island."

"What are you saying?"

"Someone with enough guts to hijack an FBI helicopter to help Ferguson escape might be crazy enough to come after you for revenge."

Fallon stood and ran his fingers through his hair. "Who?"

"Did you forget they think the crime ring was funding terrorists? Ferguson's laptop had messages from a terror group overseas."

"My memory isn't what it used to be . . . remember?"

"Fallon—"

"How would they know I'm here?"

"I don't know, Fallon; I just have a bad feeling about this. Please catch the first flight back in the morning. I'll have the state police pick you up at the airport."

"You know I hate flying . . . besides, I'm booked on the morning ferry."

"You need to leave the island as soon as possible. Catch the first plane out of there in the morning."

"I can't leave my Dart—"

"Listen, Fallon—"

"Don't worry, Karen. I'll be back with my car in Charlevoix by noon tomorrow."

Fallon ended the call and put the phone back on the nightstand next to the bed. He was wide awake now. He walked to the back porch and stood a moment leaning against a post looking up at the stars glowing brightly against the night sky. He took a moment to breathe in the rich, moist aroma of cedar trees and the sound of a chorus of crickets. Suddenly someone grabbed him from behind and tackled him to the floor of the porch. He twisted his body back and forth, thrashing his arms and legs, resisting the attempts of the person on his back to pin him down. He turned his head, trying to see who it was, but he was greeted with a smack across his cheek that jerked his head against the floorboards. As a sharp pain radiated through his head, he stopped thrashing for a second. Suddenly his arms were pulled behind his back. A plastic band looped around his wrists. The band tightened with a zipping noise. Still lying on his stomach, hands secured behind his back, a foot pressed against his side.

"Get up," a man's voice grumped as he pushed him on his side with his foot.

Fallon looked up into the darkness at the silhouette of the man standing over him. Who was he and what did he plan to do to him?

"Stand up," the man said as he grabbed his arm and tugged at him.

He managed to get up on his knees, catching his breath for a moment. The man tugged at him again and he stood up. Feeling lightheaded, Fallon wobbled a bit.

"Get inside," the man said as he shoved him through the open back door then guided him through the dark hallway and into the kitchen. A lone nightlight in an outlet by the sink cast a dim light in the room. Fallon's breathing quickened as he tried to get a look at the man's face.

"Sit down," the man said as shoved him onto a chair by the kitchen table.

Suddenly the light over the table came on. He gasped when he saw Ferguson's face. He felt his pulse quicken as he watched Ferguson sit in the chair across the table from him.

"Well, this is like the old days when we would interrogate suspects at the Detroit police precinct." Ferguson folded his hands in front of him on the table. "Do you know what it's like to be cuffed to a table like a criminal and grilled by FBI agents?"

"How did you find me?" Fallon asked.

Ferguson twisted his lips and tapped his chest with his pointer finger. "How did *you* find *me*?"

CHAPTER 22

"I wasn't looking for you," Fallon said, noticing Ferguson's gloved hands. No fingerprints. His body tensed. What did he plan to do with him?

Ferguson shook his head. "So, it's just a coincidence I spotted you at the marina."

"It's no coincidence you're here. What do you want?"

Ferguson stood, pulled out a handgun, and pointed it at Fallon. "I ought to shoot you right now and leave your body to rot in the woods on this island."

Fallon could feel his body stiffen as he stared down the barrel of the gun. Muscles tightened as he drew his shoulders in toward his neck, pulling his zip-tied hands tight against his back. He tried to push back the memory but felt powerless under its force.

> *Gravel crunches under his boots as he cautiously enters a bombed-out building in Afghanistan, rifle pointed in front of him. Someone suddenly appears from the shadowy darkness with a rifle, his face barely visible. He stares down the barrel of the gun pointed at him. They are frozen in time for a moment, eyes locked on each other, guns pointed at each other. For a split second he sees a person, another human being. Gunfire erupts. His body instantly coils up, waiting for the bullets to pierce him, but they never arrive. The strange man falls to the floor. He stares at the body sprawled on the ground—the enemy—then he turns in the direction of the gunfire and sees Ferguson standing there wearing fatigues, gun pointed in the direction of the man that was just shot.*

"Fallon!" someone shouted.

Shaking his head, Fallon blinked several times and looked up at Ferguson staring at him with a serious look on his face, gun still pointed at him.

"What's wrong with you?" Ferguson asked.

"Flashback from Afghanistan."

Ferguson nodded and sat back down in the chair across from Fallon.

Still clutching the gun, he lowered it into his lap and stared at the floor for a moment. "I saved your life that day in Afghanistan." He looked at Fallon.

"You never let me forget it."

"The terrorist in that bombed-out building could've shot you. You both choked. That split second almost cost you your life."

"Every time you needed something from me, you reminded me how you saved my life that day. I told you last summer going after that escaped prisoner Cally would be my last favor for you, that we would be even after that."

"I thought your memory was shot."

"Mostly from the week of the drone attack. I saw the videos of you and me in your office in Jackson Prison talking about going after Cally. I know I agreed to try to find Cally for you."

"You were supposed to find Cally for me before anyone else." Ferguson stood up. "I needed to get him back before . . ." He turned away from Fallon and sighed.

"You wanted me to help you stop Cally from giving the police all the evidence he had on your crime ring activities," Fallon said. "You were using me."

Ferguson whipped his head around. "You betrayed me! I wouldn't be in this mess if you had kept your word."

"You have only yourself to blame."

"Some friend you are." Ferguson leaned forward, put his face in front of Fallon and pointed at him. "I saved your life in Afghanistan and that's the thanks I get?"

Fallon could feel each word move across his face with Ferguson's breath. "Enough about your heroics in Afghanistan!"

"Shut up!" Ferguson plopped himself in the chair across from Fallon. He held up his gun in front of him and stared at it. "I thought you might betray me." He glared at Fallon. "How *did* you know we were coming after you at the cabin last summer?"

"I don't know what you're talking about."

"Stop hiding behind your brain injury."

"I wish I could remember all the details."

CHAPTER 22

"You and Alicia stole my plane. You left me and my buddies stranded on North Fox Island for the police to capture."

"I was never on North Fox."

"You liar." Ferguson's lips pressed tightly together. "*You* framed me as a terrorist."

"What are you talking about?"

"I don't know how you did it, but somehow you got a lot of fake evidence to frame me for the drone attack on the *Emerald Isle*."

"That's ridiculous." Fallon shook his head, searching for any fragment of memory that pointed to him framing Ferguson. Could it be true? "Why are you wasting your time with me? Shouldn't you be on the run? Every cop in the country will be looking for you by daybreak."

"Unfinished business." Ferguson leaned forward. "You came after me on North Fox Island. You hunted me down like some animal. Who was with you? You don't know how to fly. Someone helped you steal my plane so you could escape and leave me stranded on North Fox for the police to capture."

Fallon stared blankly at Ferguson. He had no memory of being on North Fox Island. He tried to recall if he had pursued Ferguson to North Fox, but there wasn't even a fragment of memory to draw from. "What makes you think I chased you to North Fox Island?"

"We found your duffel bag at the abandoned log house on North Fox. We knew you were there because I tracked you."

"A tracking device?" Fallon frowned. He recalled having a ready bag he always kept in his car—a duffel bag packed with essentials for emergency travel. Alicia had told him about Ferguson pursuing her, Cally, and Robert to North Fox Island, and how they took his duffel bag with them.

"After we met in my office in Jackson Prison, while you were interrogating Cally's prison friend Louis, I put a tracking device in the ready bag I knew you always kept in your car."

Fallon frowned. Alicia had mentioned flying a plane from North Fox to meet him at the airport on Beaver Island. A faint memory popped in his mind.

> *He pulls the Jeep over to the side of the road next to an airstrip by an airport. Through the side window, he can see Alicia, Cally, and Robert standing next to a plane with smoke coming out of the front of it.*

"Don't give me that blank look," Ferguson grumbled. "I *know* you found Cally on Beaver Island. Who flew the plane for you from North Fox?"

Memories circled in Fallon's head from the day of the terror attack. His head began to pound. A fuzzy image came to mind.

> *Seated in the passenger seat of a seaplane, he looks over at Daniel at the controls. He looks out the side window as they approach an airport. Was it in Detroit? "You know I suffered a traumatic brain injury—"*

"Enough about your brain injury!" Ferguson pounded the table with his fist. I think you *do* remember details from that day and that you're bluffing. *You* framed me, Fallon. *You're* the one who told the Feds I was behind the drone attack."

Fallon closed his eyes, concentrating on what Ferguson was telling him. His mind was blank. "I never told the Feds anything like that. You framed yourself. I saw the evidence—the video of you stealing the drone."

Ferguson leaned forward again, spittle flying. "That was a fake! I *never* stole a drone! I admit I was in the crime ring, but I was never involved in any terrorist plot."

"I'm not the one who framed you."

"Then why didn't you contact me when you found Cally?" Ferguson pressed as he stared down at Fallon.

Fallon closed his eyes, pulling at the pieces he could remember. Alicia told him they were together when they found Cally at the cabin on Beaver Island.

"Who was with you when you found Cally?"

Fallon tried to ignore the throbbing pain in his head. He recalled that Alicia was in the cabin with him. Daniel, Cally, and Robert were there seated around the table. "Alicia was there. We tracked Cally to the cabin."

CHAPTER 22

"How did you know he was there?"

"I'm not sure." Fallon paused as another memory surfaced.

> *Chip is talking to him on the phone giving him information on a parcel from the online property records from Charlevoix County.*

"Someone gave me the address to Daniel Callahan's cabin."

Ferguson shifted in his seat. "Wait a minute, are you saying Cally's brother, Daniel Callahan, owned that cabin? The Feds had property records from Charlevoix County that showed *I* owned that cabin for ten years. I kept telling them I never owned it. This is the first time someone told me otherwise."

"On one of the stakeouts we did together, Daniel told me he owned a cabin on Beaver Island."

Ferguson leaned in toward Fallon. "What else do you know that can prove I'm not a terrorist?"

"I'm not sure," Fallon said as he took a deep breath.

"If Daniel owned that cabin," Ferguson narrowed his eyes, "who changed the property records?"

"Archipelago," Fallon said as the fuzzy image from the cabin started to clear. He could now clearly see the man seated across from him taking a sip from the whiskey snifter. "The guy who created the Archipelago software."

"What are you talking about?"

"Henry Massey. I remember him reviewing the software at the governor's cabinet meeting when the state started using Archipelago."

"That's ridiculous. You really are brain damaged."

"I'm telling you—"

"Enough."

Fallon looked at Ferguson sitting in the chair across from him. He'd been here before, someone sitting across from him. Was it Daniel with a gun in his lap? Was it Alicia? Who exactly was sitting across from him in the cabin on the day of the drone attack? "Henry Massey," Fallon whispered.

"What are you mumbling about?"

Suddenly a clear thought entered Fallon's mind. A piece of jumbled memory stood out. A clear image of who was sitting across from him in the cabin. "Henry Massey is the one who launched the attack on the *Emerald Isle*."

Ferguson shook his head and stared at Fallon. "That's ridiculous. Why would a billionaire want to attack a ferry boat in a remote part of Michigan?"

Fallon shrugged his shoulders. "You tell me."

CHAPTER 23

The clouds drifted effortlessly outside the window of Daniel's seat on the Masseys' personal jet as they flew over the Atlantic on their return trip to Colorado. His mind wandered back to a family camping trip on Beaver Island when they were kids—*sitting with Cally and his sister, Sheila, around a campfire laughing as the embers drift skyward into the night sky.*

"You look tense," Helen said as she raised her glass. "Have some wine and relax."

Daniel looked at Helen seated across from him in the plush, black leather seat with her legs crossed. "No thanks." He picked up the mug from his cup holder. "I'll stick to coffee."

Helen took a sip of wine and set the glass in a cup holder next to her seat. She folded her hands in her lap as she eased back.

They sat a moment looking at each other.

"I'll be blunt with you, Daniel. I respect you turning down my proposals. You're a man of integrity."

"I just couldn't do that to Henry."

She raised the corners of her mouth as she nodded back at him. The soft hum of the jet engines filled the cabin as they sat silent for a moment.

"There's something you should know about Henry." Helen looked out the window for a moment, then back at Daniel. "When I met him in college twenty years ago, he was a rumpled geek going nowhere. He excelled at coding computer software, but that was about it. I'm the one who helped him turn his little program he created into Quick Connect and the billion-dollar company it is today."

"That's not the story I heard from Henry."

"All this success has gone to his head. He's gotten a little arrogant and forgotten how it all began and what I did for him."

"But you're still part of the day-to-day operations, and you're chairing Arpa now."

"Actually I'm doing less and less with Quick Connect, *and* he sent you to this Arpa meeting to check up on me."

"He wanted me to monitor the board members."

"You don't need to defend Henry."

He could hear the frustration in her voice. Where was this going? It was hard to read her intense look. Was it anger or something else?

She shifted in her seat. "Didn't you fly jets in the air force?"

"That was a while ago."

"But you still fly. Last year you flew Henry off of Beaver Island."

"Yes, I—."

"It had to be hard for you to let that drone leave the cabin, knowing it was targeting the *Emerald Isle*."

"So, you knew about his plan?"

"After the fact. When I saw that a stolen Caspian drone was used in the attack, I became suspicious. I knew Arpa was providing drones for the delivery test project in Detroit. I confronted him and he told me all about it. He admitted he used it to set up Ferguson as a terrorist—revenge for him coming after your family."

"I asked Henry as a favor to pull down all those fake racist posts Ferguson created on Quick Connect in my dad's name to come after our family—to try to force Cally to hand over the evidence he had on the crime ring that would put them all in prison. He offered me something better: a way to help Cally escape from prison and get revenge on Ferguson. If he pulled it off, I agreed to leave the FBI and work for him."

CHAPTER 23

"And here you are heading up our global security."

"It was part of the deal."

"You and Henry had justice served on the crime ring. You sent all those corrupt people to prison where they belong. And you cleared your brother of the murder conviction. I admire what you did."

"You would do the same."

"I suppose I would," Helen said with a distant, thoughtful look on her face.

"We're making our approach to Greenland to refuel," came the pilot's voice over the speaker in the ceiling. "Fasten your seat belts."

* * *

On the ground, a customs agent boarded the plane and stood in the aisle of the jet by Daniel and Helen's seats.

Daniel handed the customs agent his passport.

"We're just refueling," Helen said to the agent.

"I'm aware of that," the agent responded. "We're checking landings as a precaution. The US has raised the terrorism risk level."

Daniel locked eyes with the agent who winked at him. He watched him slip a piece of paper in his passport and hand it back to him. Daniel quickly slipped his passport back in his shirt pocket as the agent checked Helen's passport.

"Have a good flight," the agent said as he left the plane.

Daniel watched the captain close the door and walk back to them.

"Buckle up," he said. "We should be back in Fort Collins in about seven hours."

Daniel buckled his seat belt and looked at Helen. She smiled back at him as the jet engines accelerated and the jet began to taxi to the runway.

* * *

After they reached cruising altitude, Daniel unbuckled his seat belt. "I have to use the toilet," he announced to Helen as he climbed out of his seat.

"Too much coffee," Helen said as she looked at her phone.

Daniel laughed and headed to the back of the plane. He closed the door behind him and pulled the piece of paper out of his passport. One side had a handwritten message:

Customs agent in CO is us. Give update on back.

Flipping the piece of paper over, Daniel quickly jotted down a short note:

Supercomputer in old military bunker at CO estate is key.

He exhaled deeply as he carefully slipped the small piece of paper back into his passport, hoping it would not fall out, hoping the customs agent in Colorado was an FBI agent. He relieved himself, flushed the toilet, and returned to his seat. Helen's probing eyes met his as he sat down. Did she suspect something?

"Do you miss your family?"

"Sometimes," Daniel said. "Most days I don't miss the drama."

"But you miss your brother, Cally."

"I do."

"You abandoned your FBI career to save him and correct the injustice done to him."

"My little brother needed me."

Helen sat silent for a moment. Then she looked at Daniel. "When Quick Connect took off, we became billionaires. It changed our relationship with family and friends. Many of them distanced themselves from us for some reason."

"Do you have siblings?"

"I have a sister." Helen turned her gaze to the window. "We used to be close, but we don't talk anymore."

"What about Henry?"

"He has a brother," she said as she looked at Daniel.

"He never told me that."

"His brother was an early investor in Quick Connect. About a year before we took the company public, they had a falling out. His brother wanted to keep the company private, but I wanted to take it public so

CHAPTER 23

we could scale up the business to take advantage of the growth of social media. I convinced Henry to take it public, and he bought out his brother for a few million."

"Is he still in touch with him?"

"No, they're estranged. Henry blamed me for that." Her face softened, eyes empathetic. "I think that's why Henry wanted to help you free your brother. He admired your sacrificial love for Cally. He secretly envied your relationship. In some ways I think he looks at you as the brother he lost."

Daniel nodded. He couldn't help feeling some attachment to Henry. He looked at Helen. Did he have feelings for her as well—for both of them? "I guess he's kind of like a brother to me as well."

Helen smiled, then her face fell.

"You miss your sister, don't you?"

He watched her take a deep breath, slightly nodding in agreement. "That's okay. Sophia is like a sister to me."

"Sounds like Sophia is a good friend."

"She is," Helen said as she straightened up in her seat, pulled out her laptop, and flipped open the screen. "I do have some business I need to attend to."

Daniel watched her start typing on her keyboard. She paused, gave him a smile, then went back to typing.

CHAPTER 24

"I've heard enough." Ferguson stood. "I'm wasting my time here. You've got nothing to help me prove I'm not a terrorist."

"You're going back to prison," Fallon said.

Ferguson stood next to Fallon and stared down at him. "Some friend you turned out to be."

Suddenly he felt a quick kick to his shin. He pushed Fallon out of the chair and watched him fall to the floor, the chair tumbling on top of him. He watched Fallon squirm on the floor, with his hands still zip-tied behind his back, as the chair rolled from him onto the floor. Ferguson bent down on his knees and pulled another zip tie out of his pocket.

"I hope I never see you again, Fallon," he said as he wrapped the tie around his legs and pulled it tight with a zipping noise.

"Don't worry, I won't visit you in prison."

Ferguson grabbed a dish towel and gagged Fallon's mouth. "I don't have to listen to you anymore." He stood and looked around the room. "Now, where is your phone?"

He could hear Fallon mumbling under the gag as he went into the bedroom and spotted a phone and car keys on the nightstand.

"I'm taking these with me," Ferguson smiled as he walked past Fallon,

CHAPTER 24

waving the phone. "There's no way Siri is going to call 911 for you." A second later he was out the door, walking the few blocks on dark, deserted streets back to the hotel.

* * *

"Where have you been?" Nadia asked as Ferguson stepped back into the hotel room.

"I needed some fresh air." Ferguson closed the door behind him.

Nadia threw her hands up in the air. "What were you thinking?"

"We're on a remote island—"

"Your face is all over the media right now."

"It's dark out. No one saw me."

"What's going on?" Lance asked as he entered the room rubbing his eyes.

"This idiot decided to go for walk in the middle of the night." Nadia shook her head. "I should just turn you in right now and forget this whole thing." She glared at him. "Do you realize you're now on the FBI's Most Wanted list?"

"I just needed a minute to clear my head."

Nadia pointed her finger at him. "Don't take any more chances like that!"

* * *

Ferguson looked through a slit in the window blind in their hotel room. He squinted as the sun rose above the horizon, casting an orange-and-yellow glow on the water in the bay. Straight ahead he could see the *Emerald Isle* docked with forklifts loading cargo onto the boat. A county sheriff's car passed by. Ferguson turned to look at Nadia, Lance, and the pilot in the living room area of the motel suite. "When are we leaving?"

"Soon," Nadia said.

"Not soon enough," Lance said as he peered through a slit in the window blind while holding his coffee cup. "It was pretty risky spending the night in town."

"Even more risky to go for a walk." Nadia scowled at Ferguson as she poured a cup of coffee. "Our ride will be here soon. He's meeting us in the marina parking lot across the street."

"I hope he's here soon," Lance remarked.

"Any minute," Nadia said as she handed Ferguson a cup of coffee.

"I need this," Ferguson said as he took a sip.

"And keep that gun I gave you hidden," Nadia added.

"Tucked in my belt under my jacket."

"That's a show of trust," Nadia said as she locked eyes on him. "Don't give us a reason to send you back to the Feds."

Ferguson nodded.

"It's been good working with you again," the pilot said as he threw his backpack over his shoulder and headed for the door. "Until next time."

Ferguson watched the door close behind the pilot. "Where's he going?"

"He never tells me, but he always shows up when I call him, with the equipment we need." Nadia glanced at her phone. "The jet just arrived and is waiting for us at Beaver Island Airport."

"Jet?" Ferguson asked.

Nadia smiled. "We like to travel in style."

Where are we going?"

"One step at a time."

"A red SUV just pulled into the marina parking lot across the street," Lance said.

Nadia stood next to Lance and looked through the slit in the blinds. "That's him. Let's go." She paused and handed Ferguson a hat with "Beaver Island" stitched on the front. "Put this on."

Ferguson pulled the hat close to his eyes and lowered his chin.

They exited the room and walked down the sidewalk toward the waiting SUV across the street.

CHAPTER 25

Fallon opened his eyes and looked up at the kitchen cabinets. He took a deep breath through the damp towel gagging his mouth and noticed the dim light in the window over the sink. How long had he been sleeping? His side hurt from lying on it, or was it from all his effort trying to get to the drawer with the knives? Glancing at the clock on the wall, he could only speculate that Ferguson had left the island by now, but there might still be a chance to catch him.

He rolled onto his back and rocked back and forth until he managed to get himself sitting, then he tried several times to get on his knees, but he fell over on his side. This was his chance to get Ferguson. With a deep breath, he rolled onto his back again and rocked until he was sitting up. Carefully wrenching his body, he finally managed to get onto his knees and stand up.

His leg throbbed with pain as he hopped to a drawer and turned so his hands, secured behind his back, could open the drawer. He could feel spoons, forks, and butter knives. Sliding his hands to the side of the drawer, he felt the handle of a steak knife. With his fingers, he carefully maneuvered it and began sawing at the zip tie, the flat metal of the back of the knife sliding over his wrists. His arms ached, his side hurt, as he pressed the sharp edge against the plastic tie. Suddenly the zip tie snapped from his wrists.

The knife dropped to the floor as he let his arms drop to his side. He rubbed his wrists, then picked up the knife and cut the zip ties around his ankles. Then he wrestled the towel off his mouth and threw it on the floor. He grabbed a screwdriver from another drawer in the kitchen and ran out the door. There's more than one way to start that Dart. He quickly popped the hood and hot-wired the car. The engine roared to life. He closed the hood and climbed behind the wheel. He would check the marina first to see if he could catch Ferguson and his accomplices leaving by boat at first light.

A few blocks later Fallon pulled into the marina parking lot where he had seen the empty slip the previous night. About one hundred yards away he could see the *Emerald Isle* docked and forklifts moving back and forth loading cargo into the boat. He sat in his car surveying the spot where his granddad's Chris-Craft had been docked last summer. He glanced at a red SUV as it parked next to him, then returned his focus to the empty slip looking for any sign of Ferguson.

As he scanned the boats in the marina, a door slamming broke his concentration. He looked at the SUV backing out of the parking spot next to him and exchanged a glance with a man in the back seat. They locked eyes for a second. His heart beat faster when he suddenly realized it looked like Ferguson.

Fallon slipped his car into gear and followed the SUV down King's Highway. The vehicle picked up speed as he pursued it. If it was Ferguson, he needed to call someone, but then he remembered Ferguson took his phone. He pulled his car into the left lane and tried to pass, but the SUV accelerated. An oncoming car forced him to retreat to the right lane behind the SUV as they passed Welke Airport.

They were trying to flee from him. He glanced at the speedometer now marking seventy miles per hour and climbing. It must be Ferguson. Suddenly he remembered the red flip phone Karen gave him. He pulled it out of his pants pocket just as the SUV made a sharp turn onto Sloptown Road. The phone flew out of his hand onto the passenger side of the bench seat as he grabbed the steering column shift lever and downshifted for the

CHAPTER 25

turn. The car fishtailed onto the gravel road. A dust cloud quickly rose up in front of him and obscured the SUV from view.

He let up a bit on the accelerator, straining his eyes as he tried to spot the SUV in the thick, brown dust cloud. Suddenly red brake lights materialized in the swirling dust. A fork in the road. The SUV swerved left as he went right. He hit the brakes. The Dart abruptly stopped, locked wheels growling as they dug into the gravel. The SUV disappeared down the other road, quickly masked by a rising dust cloud. He jammed the car into Reverse, backed up to the intersection, then hit the accelerator. The rear tires spun as they dug into the gravel, thrusting the car forward down the other road. He continued his pursuit, frantically searching in the thick dust that encircled his car for any sign of the SUV. Whether it was Ferguson or not, someone didn't want him to catch up with them.

He turned on the wipers to clear the windshield of accumulating dust. With his left hand clamped to the steering wheel, he grabbed the phone sliding around on the seat next to him with his free hand. He tried to punch the small redial button on the flip phone, but his thumb was too big. Fallon tossed the phone back on the seat. Looking back at the road ahead, he suddenly saw brake lights appear through the dust. He hit the brakes, feeling pain radiating up his leg as he stiffened his legs against the brake pedal and clutch. The back end of the car fishtailed as loose gravel pinged against the underside of the car. He cranked the wheel trying to correct the skid, but the car was sliding out of control. Suddenly his body was thrust against the driver's side as the car began to flip. He caught a quick glimpse of a deep ditch out his side window. He closed his eyes as he felt himself tumbling inside the car like the splinters of wood and twisted pieces of metal from his granddad's boat inside the plastic container on Chip's desk.

CHAPTER 26

Ferguson looked out the back window of the SUV as the dust cleared. A few yards back he spotted the Dart. He watched Nadia open the passenger side door and jump out with her gun drawn. She stood a moment next to the SUV. He jumped out and stared at Fallon's car resting upside down in a deep ditch, steam rising from the front and a tree branch jammed into the rear window. The front wheels slowly spun to a stop as dust settled on the floor pan of the car. He pulled Fallon's phone and keys out of his pants pocket and tossed them into the woods.

Lance opened his window holding his phone. "The jet's waiting. They want to know where we are."

"Tell them we're almost there," Nadia said as she climbed back into the SUV.

Pulling the door shut, Ferguson felt himself pressed into the back seat as they accelerated down the road. A few minutes later, Ferguson saw a sign for the Beaver Island Airport. Through the chain-link fence, he spotted a private jet parked near the small terminal building.

"That's our ticket out of here," Nadia said.

"Not soon enough," Ferguson said as he gripped the armrest between him and Nadia.

CHAPTER 26

Doors flew open as the SUV stopped near the terminal building. Ferguson noticed the waiting area inside the building was empty as he pulled the brim of his hat close to his eyes and lowered his head. As he followed Nadia and Lance through a small gate in the tall chain-link fence that surrounded the airport, he could hear the whine of the idling jet engines. He followed Nadia and Lance through the open door to the interior of the aircraft.

"Welcome aboard," the pilot said as he quickly closed the door behind them.

Ferguson looked down the aisle at the two rows of four single leather seats on each side of the jet facing each other.

"Have a seat," Nadia said as she sat down and pointed to the seat facing hers.

He parked himself in the seat and buckled his seat belt. "Nice ride."

Nadia smiled. "I told you we had money behind us."

"Exactly *who is* behind you?"

"Hopefully you'll get to meet her soon."

The jet engines revved, and the aircraft began to move. Soon they were airborne. Ferguson looked out his window at Beaver Island disappearing below. "Where are we going?"

"Settle in, it'll be a few hours." Nadia said as she tapped on her phone.

Ferguson looked out his window at the waves on Lake Michigan until all he saw was clouds.

* * *

The drone of the jet engines slowed as the plane turned off the runway. Ferguson watched through his window as they passed a sign that read "Welcome to Boulder, Colorado." He pressed his face closer to the window. Ahead he saw a wide door sliding open as they approached a large hangar. A bright, blue oval painted on the building above the door made him gasp—the Caspian logo. Eyes widened; he turned to look at Nadia.

"Surprised?"

Ferguson nodded. Were they going to get him back for the weaponized Caspian delivery drone he never stole?

"Just relax," Nadia smiled. "We're going to lay low for a while until things cool down."

He looked out his window as the jet pulled into the hangar. Were they going to dispose of him in the mountains? Relax was the last thing he wanted to do.

"Where are you taking me?" Ferguson asked, noticing a black SUV parked nearby.

Nadia glanced out her window. "Just a little road trip. Follow Lance."

Ferguson watched Lance walk by them and open the door as the jet engines wound down. He pressed his arms against his side and felt the gun in the side holster under his jacket. Why would they give him a gun? He followed Lance as he exited the jet with Nadia directly behind him. Maybe a life sentence would've been better.

"After you," Nadia said as she opened the back door of the SUV parked inside the hangar.

He climbed in and sat on the back seat as she closed the door.

"You need to trust us," Lance said as he sat next to him and closed the door.

"I don't think I have much of a choice."

The engine started and Ferguson caught Nadia's deep blue eyes in the rearview mirror. He took a deep breath as a garage door in the back of the building opened. A moment later they were driving down a state highway toward the mountains.

Ferguson tried to get his bearings as he looked at the scraggly brush along the roadside. Soon they turned off the highway onto a two-lane road, then a gravel road that led to a long, paved driveway. A few minutes later they arrived at a large log cabin nestled in a remote part of the foothills of the Rocky Mountains. He climbed out of the SUV and followed Nadia toward a large front porch. Noticing he was winded, he stopped to catch his breath.

"The air is thinner up here," Nadia said as she climbed a dozen wooden steps and stood on the front porch. From the bottom of the steps, he watched her place her hand on a small touchpad next to the entry door. A light blinked green, and the lock clicked. She opened the large wooden door and entered the cabin.

CHAPTER 26

Taking a few deep breaths, Ferguson followed Nadia inside.

"Have a seat," she said, pointing to a couch by a massive stone fireplace.

He sat on the rustic couch with a log frame and sank into the worn, corduroy cushion. The fireplace next to the couch drew his attention as his eyes traced its rugged stone chimney to the peak of a vaulted ceiling with log rafters. "Quite the place you have here."

"It's not mine," Nadia said as she stepped next to a bar along one wall and poured two drinks. "Need a drink, Lance?"

Lance walked by her and into the kitchen next to the great room. "I'm fine," he said as he opened the refrigerator door. "Looks like we're well-stocked to stay here for a while."

Nadia sat on the couch next to Ferguson and handed him a drink.

He took the glass from her and stared at the liquid as he held it in his hand.

"Don't worry, it's just scotch and water, nothing else." Nadia took another sip.

Ferguson took a sip and closed his eyes as he enjoyed the smoothness of the drink. How long had it been since he had a good, stiff drink of scotch, or anything like it? Too long.

"I'm sure glad to be here after that chaotic trip," Nadia said as she propped her feet on a footstool in front of the couch. "I can't believe they got the wrong code for our IDs at the prison. I was assured we would have the right code."

Ferguson raised his glass to his mouth, then lowered it and looked at Nadia. "When I was warden of Jackson Prison, the employee suite of the Archipelago software generated a random code an hour before a prison transfer only to the people handling the move. I didn't even know the code. How did you get access?"

Nadia smiled, raised the glass to her lips, and took a sip.

"Why did you bring me here?"

Nadia set her glass on the end table next to the couch.

They watched Lance sit in a large leather chair facing the couch.

"You ask too many questions," Lance said as he folded his hands on his lap.

"What's your game?" Ferguson said as he eyed Lance, then looked at Nadia.

"You'll find out soon enough," Nadia said. "For now, you might as well relax. We're going to be here for a while."

He nodded, taking deep breaths to compensate for the thin air. He looked at the glass in his hand and noticed the Caspian logo etched in the side. "How did you know I like scotch?"

Nadia smiled. "We know a lot about you."

CHAPTER 27

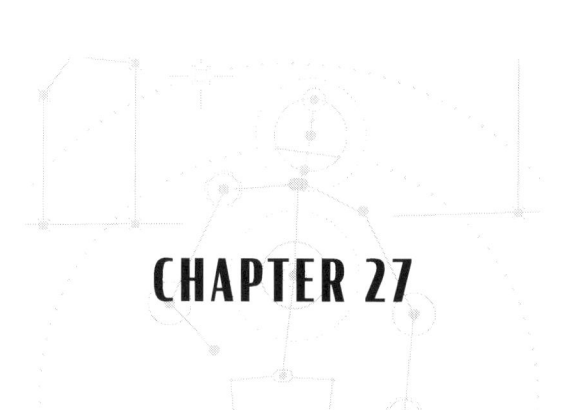

"Henry is meeting us at the airport," Helen said as she ended her call and looked at Daniel. "He wants to review the campaign bus tour with you."

"We're about six weeks away from the start of his bus tour," Daniel said as the plane descended onto the runway, wheels thumping the tarmac. Through his window he could see they were approaching a familiar, gray metal hangar. The jet taxied through the open hangar door and parked next to another private jet parked inside. The captain opened the door after the jet stopped and a customs agent entered.

"Passports please," the agent said as he stood in front of Daniel, blocking Helen's view.

Daniel handed the agent his passport. The agent immediately took the piece of paper Daniel had placed in his passport, slipped it in his pocket, and returned the passport to him with a wink. He then turned and reviewed Helen's passport.

"You're good to go," the agent said.

Daniel spotted Henry walking toward them as he followed Helen out of the jet. They stopped as Henry approached, arms extended.

"Helen!" Henry said as he greeted her with a tight embrace. "I missed you, my love."

She looked at Daniel over Henry's shoulder. "Hello, Henry," she said as they released.

"How did the Arpa meeting go?" Henry asked, still holding Helen's hand.

"The usual complaints," Helen said.

"You reassured them?"

"Of course."

"She handled the meeting well," Daniel added.

Henry let go of Helen's hand. "Sophia cause any trouble?" He looked at Daniel.

Daniel looked at Helen.

"Nothing out of the ordinary," Helen replied.

"Good," Henry said.

They stood a moment looking at each other.

"Daniel and I will be here an hour or so reviewing campaign details," Henry said as he turned to walk away.

"I'll see you back at the estate." Helen waved as she walked toward a waiting emerald-green Mercedes.

Daniel followed Henry to a stairway in the hangar that led to an upstairs conference room.

"Anyone else coming?" Daniel asked as he looked at the empty conference table.

"Just us," Henry said, pointing to a small table near the door with a few sandwiches and side dishes. "Help yourself."

Daniel scanned the small conference room with windows overlooking the airport.

"Something wrong?"

"Just habit." He reached for a sandwich and a small container of coleslaw and sat at the table.

Henry joined him with a sandwich and a bag of potato chips. As they ate, they made small talk about the flight, the Arpa meeting, and the accommodations in Geneva.

CHAPTER 27

"The Geneva Grand Hotel always treats us well," Henry smiled, wiping his mouth with his napkin.

"They should for what you pay."

Henry pushed his plate away from him, leaned back in his chair, and brushed crumbs from his silk suit pants. The room was quiet except for the buzzing of a small plane taxiing outside. Daniel watched the small Cessna move toward the runway as he poured coffee into two cups from the carafe on the table. "How are the campaign plans looking?" He slid a cup to Henry.

"Great," Henry said as he took a sip of coffee. "I need to level with you before we get started." He set his cup on the table and eyed Daniel sitting across from him. "Loyalty is something I hold in high regard."

Daniel tried to relax and manage his facial features. "As do I."

"Are you familiar with the story of Joseph and Potiphar in the Old Testament?"

He nodded, trying not to roll his eyes. Was he trying to teach him Bible stories like his mom did when he was a kid? Had Henry gotten religion while they were away? "I'm familiar with it."

"Potiphar trusted Joseph with everything in his household." Henry paused, leaning in toward Daniel with a scrutinizing look. "Even his wife."

Daniel caught a gasp rising up his windpipe, but stopped the rush of air before it reached his mouth. He lowered his eyebrows, eyes firmly focused on Massey. "You and Helen were testing me."

Massey grinned. "You're quick."

"Helen purposely tried to seduce me." Daniel tilted his head. "You were testing my loyalty."

"And you passed with flying colors."

They continued to look at each other in silence for a moment.

"And what if I had given in?"

Massey glanced up at the ceiling, opened his mouth, then looked at Daniel. "Like Joseph, you rejected my wife's advances. He maintained his character, his loyalty to Potiphar, just like you."

"But Potiphar's wife falsely accused Joseph of trying to solicit her, and Potiphar threw Joseph in prison." Daniel said. He wouldn't put it past Massey to do something like that to him if he double-crossed him—if he knew the truth. After all, he framed Ferguson for the drone attack and now he was in prison.

Massey chuckled. "Helen wouldn't do that to you." He tapped the table with his hand and pointed at him. "I value your advice, your loyalty, Daniel."

He looked at Massey, smiled and nodded. Who exactly was he loyal to, the FBI or Massey? He felt like he was serving two masters.

"Maybe someday I can put you in charge of my kingdom like Pharaoh did with Joseph."

"I'll stick to security, thank you."

"Don't shortchange yourself. You—" Henry's phone rang, and he answered it.

As Massey talked, Daniel watched the color drain from his face as he suddenly looked concerned.

Massey ended the call and blankly looked at Daniel. "Ferguson escaped from prison."

"How?"

"Apparently someone hijacked the FBI helicopter they were using to transport him."

"Should we be concerned?"

Massey flashed a nervous smile, trying to regain his composure. "I don't think we have anything to worry about."

CHAPTER 28

The hum of the jet engines filled the cabin of the small Homeland Security jet bound for Charlevoix, Michigan. Alicia reclined her seat a notch as she gazed at Trevor, seated directly across from her focused on the clouds outside his window. Sunlight peered through the oval windows on the fuselage, casting beams of light across his face, tan blazer, and white shirt. She watched him tapping his finger on the small tray table extended over his lap, his other hand holding a paper cup filled with coffee.

"You really think the terror cell was behind Ferguson's escape?" Alicia asked.

"The bigger question is why Ferguson is such a valuable asset to the terror cell," Trevor said as he turned away from the window. He picked up his paper cup and slurped his coffee.

"Because he almost pulled off a successful drone attack on an unlikely target." The memory flashed forward. Alicia refocused on the blanket of clouds below them, but she couldn't shake the recurring image.

> *She tightly grips Fallon's limp body, treading water, trying to keep them above the surface of cold Lake Michigan water. Debris from the explosion scatters*

everywhere on the surface of the water. The smell of oil and gasoline burns her nose. A large piece of wood floats by with metal letters attached spelling Chris-Craft. She looks at his bloody face. She blinked several times, pushing the memory back.

"Don't worry, Fallon will be okay," Trevor said. "I talked to the doctor."

She nodded and looked at Trevor leaned forward in his seat, coffee cup in his hand.

"Alicia... What you went through last August was very traumatic. You should get help processing it."

She shook her head. "There isn't time."

"You need to make time."

"The threats don't stop coming. It seems there are more and more leads to investigate."

"You don't have to do this." He set his coffee cup in the cup holder next to his seat and folded the tray table down. "We got this. The FBI has set up an operations center in Charlevoix. The state police, Homeland Security, and sheriff are all working on finding Ferguson. We have more than enough people looking for him."

"I need to be there."

Trevor nodded. "Look, I'll work with the FBI's operations center. When we get to Charlevoix I want you to catch the next plane to Beaver Island."

"But—"

"Go. Be with Fallon."

Alicia leaned back in her seat and exhaled.

***

On the ground Alicia parted ways with Trevor and caught the next flight on Island Airways to Beaver Island. Seated in the small plane, she watched the island come into view as the plane approached Welke Airport. Was she ready for this? She gripped the armrest as the propellers on the plane buzzed outside her window. Ahead she could see the landing strip. She tried to block the memory...

CHAPTER 28

Hands clamp to the yoke of the plane as the engine sputters and they lose altitude. "Cessna five, five, seven. Emergency landing at Welke." She glances at Cally seated next to her, then ahead. A wide, two-lane road is just ahead. She tilts the plane to line up with the road as they buzz a Jeep driving on the road. The engine quits. Just the sound of the wind passing by the wings. The smell of burnt oil fills the cockpit.

A thud shook her body. She looked out the window as the plane slowed on the runway and taxied to a small terminal building with "Welke Airport" on a sign on the side.

As she climbed out of the plane and collected her suitcase, she spotted Sheriff Conlan Cooper walking toward her.

"Welcome back to Beaver Island," the sheriff said as he gave her a hug. "First time back since—"

"Yes," Alicia said as she drew in a deep breath. "Where's Fallon?"

"He's still at the health center. He's refusing to go to the hospital in Charlevoix."

"Is it bad?"

"It doesn't appear to be, but it really shook him up, particularly with his previous injuries. They wanted to send him to Charlevoix to have him checked out as a precaution."

"He shouldn't have come here." She followed the sheriff to his car and climbed in the passenger seat. "I thought you'd be in Charlevoix at the FBI operations center."

"There's more than enough horsepower there. They're keeping me updated on the search."

"What's the latest?"

"Enbridge pipeline company has cameras on St. Helena Island by the lighthouse to track ships on the Mackinac Straits, checking to make sure they aren't dragging their anchors. They caught the hijacked FBI chopper on camera last night heading west before it disappeared from sight."

"Did they confirm it was hit?"

"They did pick up a trail of white smoke coming out of the helicopter just before it was out of camera range."

"Any idea where it was headed?"

"Hard to say."

"It could've gone down in Lake Michigan."

"Coast Guard is looking for a debris field."

"So they didn't get far?"

"Let's hope."

Alicia took a deep breath as they pulled into the parking lot of the clinic. She followed the sheriff inside where he led her to a room where Fallon was lying on a hospital bed.

"I'll be in the waiting area," the sheriff said as he closed the door behind him.

Sitting next to the bed, Alicia looked at Fallon lying there, eyes closed. She looked at a large bruise on his cheek, small cuts on his face, and the tightly wrapped arm next to his side outside the sheet. In a flash she was back to last August . . .

> *The sheriff next to her, both strain to pull Fallon's limp body out of the water and into the boat. His body hits the floor of the boat with a thud. The vibration from the boat engine starts while she frantically does mouth-to-mouth.*

"Alicia?"

She jumped at the sound of her name and looked into Fallon's eyes.

"Where am I?"

"The health center on Beaver Island."

"Where's Ferguson?"

"They haven't found him yet."

"I saw him."

Alicia tilted her head and touched his shoulder. "What?"

"He attacked me at your house on the island. I was standing on the back porch of your house talking to the governor on the phone. After I ended the call he tackled me."

"It's likely his chopper went down in Lake Michigan."

CHAPTER 28

Fallon shook his head and winced. "He attacked me—tied me up." He started to sit up. "We need to get him."

Alicia gently pushed him back onto the bed. She opened her mouth as she looked at the distressed look on his face. "What happened?"

"After he tackled me, he dragged me into the kitchen, tied me up with zip ties, and sat me on a chair. He thinks I framed him—"

"You must have hit your head—"

"No." He tried to lift his arm but dropped it back on the bed, closing his eyes tightly.

"The sheriff told me you went off the road and flipped your car. What happened?"

Fallon opened his eyes and looked at her. "I managed to cut myself loose after he left the house. I drove to town, and I saw Ferguson in a red SUV. I chased him but I lost control of my car." Fallon rubbed his head with his other hand.

"Did you hit your head again?"

"Maybe." Fallon rested his hand on his chest and looked at Alicia. "I'm not imagining it."

Alicia sighed and placed her hand on his. She looked into his eyes. "Your memory hasn't been right since last summer. You're chasing ghosts, Fallon."

They sat a moment, looking at each other. Alicia could feel tears welling up. She blinked them away, tamping down her emotions.

"You have to believe me."

His pleading eyes. Was there a tinge of truth in what seemed impossible? "He tied you up in my house."

Fallon nodded.

The doctor came into the room and introduced herself.

"Alicia Chalmers, Fallon's friend," she said as she shook the doctor's hand.

"I know who you are," the doctor smiled. "I saw the video—"

"How is he?"

"He hit his head pretty hard when his car flipped. Given his previous injuries, I'm having him airlifted to Charlevoix to have him checked out."

Fallon tried to sit up. "No, doc." He scrunched his face and lay back down.

"We can't take any chances," the doctor said.

Two nurses came into the room and unlocked the wheels on the bed.

"Stop them, Alicia," Fallon said as they started to wheel him out of the room.

"They need to check you out." Alicia stood.

"Do you want to ride with him?" the doctor asked as she stopped in the doorway.

"That's okay. He's in good hands." She stepped out of the room and watched the bed roll down the hallway with the doctor.

"Alicia!" Fallon's voice echoed against the walls.

"Everything will be okay, Fallon!"

"You're not going with them?" the sheriff asked as he stepped next to her.

Alicia shook her head. "Can you take me to the spot where his car ran off the road?"

"Sure."

They exited the hospital and stood a moment outside the doors watching the ambulance drive away.

The sheriff patted Alicia on the shoulder, his eyebrow lowered, the corner of his mouth raised. "It'll be okay."

Alicia looked at him. "That's what you told me when I divorced your son."

"Hmph . . . that was a while ago." The sheriff stuck his thumbs in his belt near his radio and gun holster.

"You've always stuck by me."

"I never stopped being your father-in-law, especially after your father died."

Alicia smiled. "Let's go."

She followed him to his patrol car, and they drove to the site where Fallon's car left the road.

"Someone called it in a couple hours ago," the sheriff said as he climbed out of the car. "Paramedics pulled him out, and I had the car towed to the station."

CHAPTER 28

Alicia stood in front of the patrol car and looked down the tree-lined road, then at the deep cuts in the gravel that ended in the ditch. "Looks like he fishtailed into the ditch. He must have been going pretty fast."

"Fallon told me at the health center that he was chasing someone."

"Who?" She bit her lip as she stared at the ruts in the road and torn up dirt and weeds in the ditch.

"He wasn't sure . . ."

She turned to look at the sheriff. "Frankly, I think he's chasing ghosts. I'm not sure if he knows what's real anymore."

The sheriff bent down and ran his hand along the rut in the gravel road. "Something caused him to go off the road."

Alicia looked down the road. "What's that up there?"

The sheriff followed her as she walked a few yards and stopped at a pair of deep ruts.

"Looks like someone left here in a hurry."

The sheriff bent down, looked at the ruts, then down the road. He stood and looked at Alicia. "Maybe this was the ghost he was chasing."

She looked back at the spot where Fallon's car left the road. "Or not." She glanced at the sheriff. "Can you take me to my house?"

They climbed back into the car and headed back to town.

Alicia watched the scenery pass by her window. Every time she saw the sheriff the memories were there—the history with the sheriff's son. It was old history. She felt the awkward silence as they sat quietly in the car.

"I'm still sorry about what happened between you and my son," the sheriff said. "You know, the divorce and all."

"Forget it." She caught herself almost calling him "Dad." "That was a long time ago."

"Hardest thing I ever had to do was fire my own son from being a deputy under me," he said. "He never forgave me. I just couldn't have his uncontrolled temper on the force. It was too dangerous."

"I'm so grateful you confronted me about it and believed me when I told you he was abusing me."

"I suspected as much. He was always such a hothead. The drinking didn't help."

"Where is he now?"

He kept his eyes focused on the road ahead, not saying anything.

"Did you ever see him again?"

He cleared his throat. "I haven't seen or heard from him since he left Charlevoix a few days after I fired him. It's been more than twenty years now."

Alicia sighed. More memories to push down—the beatings, abuse, and hateful words. She looked at the sheriff focused on the road. "Thank you."

"I lost a son, but I gained a daughter," he said as he glanced at her. "Thanks for keeping in touch."

"I owe you."

"You owe me nothing," he said. "Sometimes doing the right thing is hard, but it's always the right thing to do."

She nodded as they pulled into the driveway of her house.

"You okay?"

"Yeah, I'm fine," she replied as she opened the door.

"Do you have a ride?"

"I left my truck at the repair shop in town last time I was here. I can pick it up if I need it. It's just a short walk."

"Let me know if you need anything."

"I will."

She watched him back out of the driveway and drive off. Stepping up to the porch, she opened the front door and went inside. Walking into the kitchen, she froze. A tipped-over chair, an open drawer, a knife on the floor next to a wadded-up dish towel, and there, lying next to the knife, pieces of curled zip ties.

CHAPTER 29

"I think you should be worried," Daniel said. "Whoever had enough guts to hijack that FBI helicopter and free Ferguson probably has the guts to come after you for revenge."

"There's nothing pointing to me framing Ferguson." Massey took a deep breath and looked at his phone. "Besides, it appears the chopper was shot down by the prison guards and it crashed into Lake Michigan. This could be the end of it all."

Daniel eyed Massey. "How do you know that?"

"I have sources." He smiled and sat upright as he grabbed his laptop and opened it. "Regardless, we need to make sure everything is buttoned down for my bus tour." He glanced at the screen. "We'll start at Huntington Place in downtown Detroit in June," Massey said as they continued their discussion about the upcoming bus tour in the upstairs conference room inside Massey's private hangar.

"Huntington Place?" Daniel questioned. "Isn't that too much flash?"

"It's all about image. We're taking on a sitting governor. They need to know we're serious about this campaign."

"Are you using Peninsular for security?"

"They would not be good for our image. They're tied to covert security and high-powered people."

"Like you?"

"Yes, like me." Massey smiled. "We're using the same security company the mayor uses. I want you to oversee security for the event."

Daniel glanced at his tablet. "That looks like your biggest event. It's all small towns after that, winding your way through the state to the Upper Peninsula, then back down to Grand Rapids."

"We want to win the heartland of Michigan," Massey added.

"I'm no political consultant, but the population centers are where the votes are at."

"That's why no one wants to campaign in the small, rural areas. It's very expensive per vote to campaign that way. We've run the scenarios. I know I can get enough support from the more rural areas of the state to tip the primary election in my favor."

"And money's not an issue for you."

"Exactly."

"But the governor still has a lock on the party faithful, and she's favored in the urban areas."

"I've stirred up enough doubt in the current governor to erode her support. The latest polls show it."

"What if you lose the party primary election in August, then what?"

"I won't lose."

"But—"

"I'm used to people telling me what I can't do and then proving them wrong. I'm gaining more and more support from younger voters. They would rather vote for an entrepreneur like me who helped build the digital tools they use every day—someone who understands them. They don't want an entrenched party favorite like the governor."

"I have to admit, that's appealing to me."

"Exactly," Massey said as he stood and walked to the door. "Well, I must be going now."

"One more thing," Daniel said as he stood. "When I was checking the service area in the lower level of your estate, I came across another room I did not have access to."

CHAPTER 29

"That's my supercomputer room," Massey said with a proud look. He sat back down. "That's my pride and joy."

"Is it secure?"

"It's more than secure. You saw on the plans that my estate was built on an old military base used during the Cold War. The supercomputer is in an old bunker designed to withstand a nuclear blast."

"I think I should inspect that room."

Massey grinned. "I want you to see it for yourself. I'll give you access to it. Check it out. I think you'll be impressed. That supercomputer is the culmination of my life's work. It uses technology that is light years ahead of anything out there. For years I've been privately funding a research lab experimenting with advanced computer chips, memory, and data compression technology. I now have the ability to store data from several server farms in a computer the size of a shipping container. No one on the planet has the capability to do that, and they won't for years—if ever."

"Does anyone else know about this?" Daniel asked, trying to tolerate the glowing pride on Massey's face.

"Just you, me, and the research lab," Massey said, still grinning.

"Where is this research lab? Can we trust them to keep it a secret?"

"We have a signed confidentiality agreement. If they break that agreement there will be consequences."

"Like what?"

Massey examined his watch. "I really need to be going." He walked to the door and opened it. "Be sure to check out that supercomputer—I know you'll be impressed."

"Where to now?"

Massey stopped in the doorway. "Off to New York to prep for the release of Quick Connect's first quarter financials. It's another record year of revenue." Massey paused in thought.

"Was there something else?" Daniel asked.

"I think it's time I give you some stock options in Quick Connect. You should have a sizable bonus for all your hard work in shoring up the security of my global enterprises."

"I don't need any stock options."

"This is something I want to do for you," Massey insisted. "I'll talk to my financial people when I'm in New York," he added as the door closed behind him.

Daniel exited the conference room and stood on the stairway as Massey boarded his jet parked inside the hangar. He was getting drawn deeper and deeper into Massey's lair. His campaign was about to move into full speed ahead. Time was running out. The supercomputer had to be the key. If he could figure out a way to tap into it, he would likely find all the evidence he needed to convict Massey. Yet any attempt to hack it would be discovered and traced by Massey.

The door to Massey's jet closed. He's going to get away with it. Who was he kidding thinking he could stop him? The slip of paper to the customs agent would tip off the FBI about the supercomputer, but what would they do about it? They would never get approval for a search warrant based on his little piece of paper. If only there was some way to get word to Fallon or the governor. Any form of digital communication would be discovered by Massey's advanced artificial intelligence. At what point should he risk blowing his cover?

Daniel watched the ground crew connect the aircraft tug to the front of Massey's jet then back it out of the hangar. He could feel his chances of stopping Massey slip away as the tug released the jet and it began to taxi toward the runway. As the jet passed a parking lot near the hangar, a blue post office box caught his attention. There might still be one way to communicate without the risk of being detected. Old school.

CHAPTER 30

Ferguson shifted in the mission oak chair next to the stone fireplace as he watched the glowing cinders in the fire. Across from him on the couch sat Lance tapping his fingers on his phone. For all he knew he was on Quick Connect monitoring his friends' social lives. He looked at the clock on the wall. Nadia had left some time ago and still hadn't returned. It was just the two of them in the cabin. *I could take him, overpower him.* But were there others outside?

Suddenly the front door opened. Nadia appeared, accompanied by a woman casually dressed in expensive jeans and a trim blouse wearing a confident look that instantly seized control of the room. Ferguson felt himself automatically sit upright at attention as if a five-star general had just entered the room. He watched the woman sit in a large, overstuffed chair by the fireplace and drape her arms over the armrests like a queen on her throne.

Nadia seated herself next to Lance on the couch facing Ferguson.

"I could use a drink, Lance," the woman snapped.

Ferguson watched him instantly pocket his phone and scurry from the room to the kitchen.

The woman smiled, crossed her legs, and leaned back. She looked so relaxed. Should he be concerned? Their eyes locked on each other. She remained silent. He knew this tactic. She was more than likely using the silence to make him squirm. It was the same tactic he used when interrogating suspects when he was a police officer. He remained silent as the minutes passed, keeping his eyes focused on her with an expressionless face.

Lance reappeared with her drink. "Here's your anarchist martini."

"Do a perimeter check around the cabin," the woman snapped as she looked at Lance.

"But we just—"

"Do it now." She stared at Ferguson. "There's a national manhunt right now for our guest. We can't be too careful."

Lance nodded and went outside.

The woman took a sip of her drink. "I must say, Lance is an excellent bartender."

Ferguson studied the woman's face. "You look familiar."

Her frown gave way to a smile. "I think you know who I am."

Suddenly, it came to him. "You're Sophia Doyle, the CEO of Caspian, the world's largest online retailer. You went to a lot of trouble bringing me here."

"And I saved you a lot of trouble. You were facing forty years just for the terrorism charge on top of the hefty list of other charges related to your crime ring activity."

"I'm not a terrorist."

Sophia shrugged. "You might've been able to plea a deal on the crime ring charges down to twenty years, but they don't negotiate with terrorists." Sophia shifted in her chair, took another sip of her martini, then leaned forward and smiled. "How did it feel to be cornered on North Fox Island by the police and hunted like an animal?"

"How do you know so much about me?"

"You were all over the news. The story was a global sensation. The media couldn't get enough of it. Social media is still on fire about it. I'm surprised you weren't approached about a book deal."

"I was."

Sophia smirked. "Of course."

CHAPTER 30

"I turned it down."

"How noble of you." She swirled the skewer with an olive on it in her drink.

"And your company was accused of lax security in letting that drone get stolen from your company warehouse in Detroit right before your pilot program to test drone deliveries. That was all over the news too."

"You're catching on," Sophia said. "You and I both know that you did not steal that drone, and that the video of you loading it into a van is fake."

Ferguson raised an eyebrow. "So you also know someone used my identity for the rental van used to steal the drone."

Sophia smirked. "And I know who did it. *He* gave my company a bad name."

"Who?"

"Henry Massey."

"The tech billionaire?"

She pointed the skewer at him. "That's the guy."

Ferguson watched her put the skewer in her mouth, clamp the olive between her teeth, and pull out the skewer. She chewed the olive while appearing to be deep in thought.

He swallowed hard. "That doesn't make sense. Why would someone with a social media empire like Quick Connect that's worth billions mess around with a terrorist attack?"

"He's a very ambitious man. I think you understand how ambition can cause you to do certain things."

"I think he does," Nadia chimed in. "Your crime ring had a lot of influence and money before it was taken down."

Ferguson nodded. He understood all too well as he looked at Sophia. He was getting an angry vibe off her. Maybe she shared his interest in revenge.

"You must have heard about Arpa," Sophia said.

"Arpa created the Archipelago software used to run state governments. When I was warden at Jackson Prison, the prison system used it as part of the State of Michigan's computer operating system."

"Arpa is Massey's thing. He was the force behind the creation of Archipelago. At first it was his desire to make government more efficient that drove him, but then he saw something else," Sophia said, appearing as if she wanted to say something more.

A few moments of silence passed.

Nadia raised an eyebrow, seeming to relish the suspense created by Sophia's silence.

"What else?" Ferguson prodded.

"He saw it as a way to commandeer all the data state governments hold on people and businesses."

Ferguson laughed. "That's ridiculous. It sounds like some sort of conspiracy theory on the internet."

"Exactly. It sounds so absurd; who would believe it? Who do you think created all those conspiracy websites with theories about tech people secretly controlling government?"

"Massey created those sites?"

"It's a diversion, a distraction to hide the truth."

"Why would someone publicize their secret plan?"

"As ridiculous as someone faking a video of you stealing a drone. Or documents showing you rented a van that you never did. Or faking property records that show you owned a cabin on Beaver Island for ten years when you had never been to the island. Or fake messages on your laptop from terrorists overseas?"

"Don't forget the fake hardship release form that helped Cally escape from prison," Nadia smirked.

"What do you want with me?"

"You're the one person I know who wants revenge as much as I do. You've proven you're willing to break the law to get what you want. Massey's little stunt almost locked you up in prison on terrorism charges for the rest of your life, and it hurt my business. Our stock is in the tank since the terrorist attack with one of our drones. I'm sure you saw the picture of the drone wreckage that divers pulled from Lake Michigan after the attack. One of the pieces had our logo on it. It was all over the media. That put our drone delivery program on indefinite hold. Now we're facing government scrutiny. I'll probably have to testify before Congress—*again*."

Ferguson frowned, his body tensed. "You want me to take out Massey?"

"I wish," Nadia scoffed.

CHAPTER 30

Sophia laughed. "That would be too easy. I want him to suffer."

She wanted blood. He imagined the horrible things she would do to Massey for crossing her. What would she do if *he* crossed her? "What do you have in mind?"

"In our business, data is gold," she said as she leaned back in her chair and took another sip of her drink. "Without the user data on our platforms, there's no money to be made. Massey is planning to make his own personal copy of all the state data they're collecting from the twenty-two states currently using Archipelago."

"To what end?"

"Imagine what you could do if you had access to everything the state government controlled."

Ferguson nodded. "Like change property records."

"Or arrest warrants and evidence," Nadia added.

"What do you have in mind?" Ferguson leaned forward, elbows on his thighs.

"I want *you* to steal his copy of the Archipelago data."

"Look, I want revenge as much as you, but I'm not a computer guy. I'm sure Massey has all kinds of firewalls protecting his data." Ferguson leaned back in his chair. "I don't know any hackers with that kind of expertise. The crime ring had just a tech nerd running its computer network."

Nadia propped her feet on the coffee table in front of the couch and chuckled. "And he's the one who stole all that incriminating evidence on the crime ring from your network and gave it to Cally, which found its way to the internet and led to your arrests."

"Don't remind me."

Sophia leaned forward; her sinister smile made Ferguson uneasy.

"Everyone thinks that to steal data you have to hack the system. No one considers that data has to be physically stored, that it needs physical infrastructure to survive."

Ferguson let the thought sink in. "You'd have to steal an entire server farm to physically grab all the data Massey has stored on Archipelago. Even I know that. But even *if* you did steal it, he would have it backed up at another location."

"True, but Massey has a supercomputer hidden away that keeps his most secret stuff stored in a compact space. That is *his* baby, *his* pride and joy."

"And what's on this secret computer?"

"Arpa is just a shell company acting like a venture capital firm. In reality, it is the vehicle that has given Massey the ability to seize all the data from state governments."

Ferguson let that thought stew for a moment. Everything state government needed to operate was now inside the Archipelago operating system. The amount of information Massey could harvest seemed infinite.

"Years ago, Henry Massey floated the idea that Arpa could act as a force to make governments more efficient. At the time we were all angry about constantly being hauled into Congress to testify before committees and subcommittees. When Massey showed us a sample of his Archipelago software, we all thought it would be a way to win the approval of state and federal governments by showing the good we could do for them. All the tech billionaires were sold on the idea and became investors in Arpa to launch the software."

Sophia stood and walked to the large windows facing the Rocky Mountain peaks. "Then Massey saw something else. He presented to us the idea of how we could use all that data to our advantage." She turned around, one hand on her hip, the other holding her drink. "We could tap into the tax records of our competitors, show permits as approved that were denied, tap into all kinds of information on residents, or monitor lawmaker communication for incriminating evidence that we could use for our advantage. It seemed the possibilities were endless."

"You could even clean up my driving record," Nadia chuckled.

"That might be more challenging," Sophia laughed and returned to her seat. "Everyone who is part of Arpa told him we didn't want any part in it. We made him agree to drop the plan and delete any mention of it in the Arpa computer servers. He kept reassuring us he had dropped it and erased everything, but then he told us he was considering a run for governor of Michigan."

"Why would he want to be governor if he already has all the state data at his disposal?"

"That is another ambition of his," Sophia explained. "He wants to use

CHAPTER 30

the governorship as a platform to make a run for president of the United States."

"You make it sound like he has all that data on a laptop he carries with him."

"Not exactly. Massey is into advanced computing. He's developed a way to compress petabytes of data into compact memory chips. His supercomputer is the size of a shipping container and can fit in an enclosed semi-trailer. That gives him a copy of all that data in a portable container he can move anywhere."

Nadia demonstrated a crane dropping a load with her hand. "Just plop it on a semi-trailer or ship and he could take it anywhere in the world without a trace."

"What's the point of that?" Ferguson asked.

Sophia leaned forward in her chair and gave Ferguson a serious look. "I'm not sure what he plans to do with it, but if for some reason the server farms hosting all that state data were destroyed, he would have the only copy."

"Are you saying Massey would destroy all those server farms to put himself in that position?"

"I think it's his backup plan, a fail-safe if he gets caught. He could use that threat to gain immunity from prosecution."

Ferguson shifted in his chair. "How could he possibly take out all those server farms in twenty-two states—not to mention all their backup server farms?"

"You saw the damage one rogue drone did last August," Sophia said as she leaned back in her chair and took a sip of her martini. "Imagine what an army of drones could do."

"You think he has a fleet of those drones?"

"Arpa is also an investor in the company that made the delivery drones Caspian was using for our pilot delivery program in Detroit."

"But your whole drone delivery program was shut down after that," Ferguson said.

"And because of that, they had nearly a thousand drones stockpiled that Henry Massey purchased from them at a heavily discounted price."

"Where is he keeping all those drones?"

Sophia sighed. "We're not exactly sure."

"His estate is big enough to hide all those drones," Nadia suggested.

Sophia shook her head. "There's no evidence of that in the satellite images we've reviewed."

"But he still needs a network to download all that data to his supercomputer," Ferguson said, deep in thought trying to figure out why she needed him and not some high-powered techie. "Can't the states trace where the data is going?"

"Recently he completed his private satellite network—the last piece of his plan to consolidate all that data."

"All compressed into something the size of a shipping container, not a server farm." Ferguson tried to picture a computer of that magnitude fitting into something that small. "How do you know all of this?"

Sophia smiled. "I have my ways."

"And you want *me* to stop this lunatic?"

"By stealing his supercomputer—the key to his whole plan."

"And just where *is* this supercomputer?"

"It's in an underground bunker beneath Massey's estate in Colorado." Sophia glanced at her watch. "I must be going."

"Just when do you plan to steal this supercomputer?"

"Not just yet. For now we need you to lay low for a while until things cool down."

"They're not going to give up looking for me."

"No, but as time goes on, they're going to think you fled the country and they'll scale back the search in the US." Sophia set her drink on the coffee table in front of the couch and stood.

"Why would Massey link your company to a terror attack with one of your drones?" Ferguson asked. "Why would he double-cross you like that if you're part of Arpa?"

"Because I was very vocal about my opposition to his plan to use the state government data for ulterior motives. He thinks I'm the reason everyone else on Arpa voted him down."

"What's in it for you?" Ferguson remarked.

"The same thing you want—revenge. I'm ambitious, but I'm rational. I don't let power go to my head. It's important to listen to other people. He

CHAPTER 30

totally rejected me. The man belittled me in front of all my tech billionaire peers for aggressively disagreeing with him. He doesn't like people who question him."

Nadia pointed her finger at Ferguson. "You can't let a guy like Massey get away with that."

"Exactly," Sophia added.

Ferguson could see the anger on her face. She seemed as if she definitely wanted blood. "What's in it for me?"

"You steal that supercomputer, and you're a free man."

"Hardly. I might be cleared on terrorism charges, but there's still that long list of other charges—stuff I actually did."

Sophia smiled. "I have connections all over the world. There are a half-dozen places I can relocate you where you *will* be a free man."

"Maybe the Caribbean?"

"I prefer Paris," Nadia chimed in.

"Think bigger." Sophia smiled. "How about the Mediterranean? Maybe you can manage one of my islands."

"Why go to all the trouble to bring me here, to help me escape? Why not just have Nadia or Lance steal the computer?"

Nadia's face lit up.

"If anything goes wrong, we won't have any connection to you or the heist of Massey's supercomputer. And you are motivated to get revenge on him. Plus, if you do get caught, you're no worse off than you were before. You were going to spend the rest of your life in prison anyways. It doesn't matter how long your prison sentence is, you only have one life to live."

"But what about the evidence from my escape?" Ferguson asked.

"None of it will tie back to us." Sophia headed toward the door. "I must be going."

"Wait! What am I supposed to do?"

"Relax. You're going to be here for a while," Nadia said.

"How long?"

"Until the time is right."

"How will I know that?"

"Someone will show up to brief you on the operation when it's time,"

Sophia said as she opened the door. "Come on, Nadia. We need to get to the airport."

"But—"

"Make yourself at home," Nadia said as she closed the door behind them.

CHAPTER 31

The sheriff bent down and examined the pieces of cut zip ties on the kitchen floor in Alicia's house. He picked up the knife and stood. "I don't think they were having a steak dinner," he said as he examined the knife in his gloved hand. "There's plastic bits on the blade."

Alicia looked at the table and the turned-over chair. "Fallon said that Ferguson was here, that he tied him up." She looked at the sheriff.

"It doesn't make any sense that Ferguson would waste his time coming here." The sheriff scanned the room. "If he really wanted revenge, he would've—"

"But he didn't."

The sheriff nodded.

"Fallon said he was on the back porch when he was tackled."

They walked down the hallway to the back porch, stopping when they both saw the door wide open. Carefully, they stepped out onto the porch.

"No sign of a struggle," Alicia said as she surveyed the porch and back yard.

The sheriff leaned against a post. "They think the hijacked FBI helicopter went down in Lake Michigan. If that's the case, I doubt anyone survived that. But is there any chance someone from his terror cell is on the island?"

Alicia sighed. "This is between you and me," she said, her voice low. "Homeland Security thinks Ferguson's terror cell may have been behind his escape. My regional director is at the FBI Operations Center in Charlevoix."

Looking around the yard, the sheriff nodded. "So, it's possible someone from the terror cell came after Fallon, but why?"

"Revenge."

The sheriff looked at her. "They would've killed him if that's all they were after. If it's true what Fallon said—that they tied him up and sat him in the kitchen—I think they were trying to get some information from him."

"I don't know." Alicia put her hands on her hips as she stood on the porch looking at the trees lining the yard. She turned to look at the sheriff. "If Fallon was chasing someone with his car, where were they headed?"

The sheriff rubbed his chin. "The Beaver Island Airport isn't far from where Fallon's car went off the road."

"It wouldn't hurt to check departing flights at the airport."

* * *

At the airport, they leafed through the log of arriving and departing flights.

"Nothing of note," the sheriff said. "looks like the usual flights in and out."

Alicia noticed an open door in the back of the waiting area inside the small terminal building. She walked toward the door and noticed a man standing inside a janitor closet with a broom.

"Excuse me," she said as she approached the man. "Did you see any unusual planes leave here this morning?"

The man turned and looked at Alicia. "Who wants to know?"

"I'm Alicia Chalmers, Homeland Security," she said as she showed him her badge.

"Hey, you're that lady who took out that drone last summer."

CHAPTER 31

Alicia nodded, trying to hold back her annoyed look. "Did you see anything out of the ordinary?"

"Are you guys looking for that guy who escaped from prison yesterday?"

"Yes," the sheriff said. "We're checking outbound flights and other routine stuff."

"Well," the man said as he shifted his position while still holding his push broom. "There was this private jet that flew in this morning. Those jets make quite the noise."

"Did you see who got onboard?"

"A couple men and a woman. They weren't on the ground long. Looked like the jet came in to pick them up. I'm guessing it was corporate types vacationing here."

The sheriff thanked the man, and they walked back to the patrol car.

"Are jets that common here?" Alicia asked as she stood with the passenger side door open.

The sheriff opened his door. "Occasionally we get private jets landing here."

"Any way to find out who it belonged to?"

"Pilots are required to communicate landings and takeoffs. I can talk to the airport manager. If they didn't, it can only mean one thing—"

"That they didn't want anyone to know they were here," Alicia said as she climbed into the car.

The sheriff sat behind the wheel and closed his door. He started the car as his phone rang.

Alicia noted his surprised look as he talked. "Who was that?" she asked as he ended the call.

"They found the helicopter." The sheriff looked at her and pressed his lips together.

"Did they find a debris field in Lake Michigan?"

"No, they found it ditched on Hog Island. Some campers on the island went back to their boat in the morning and it was gone. They followed some tracks from the beach and found the FBI helicopter."

Alicia took a deep breath. "Maybe Fallon was right."

"We need to figure out who was on that jet and where they went."

CHAPTER 32

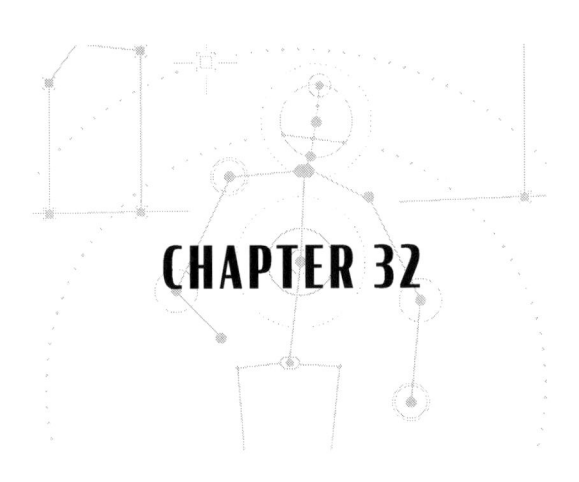

Everything is so green," Fallon said as he looked out the window by his seat on the State of Michigan jet. "I didn't have a good view from my window during those ten days in the hospital."

"Spring is finally here," Alicia said from the seat across from him. "It's almost May."

"There's the Capitol," he said as he looked at the white dome glowing in the morning light. "It will be good to be back home." Fallon turned to face Alicia, glaring at him. "I know that look."

"This accident you had on Beaver Island has set back your recovery. Even though the doctor said you didn't hit your head when you flipped your car, it still shook you up. He still wants you to take it easy for a few more weeks."

Fallon looked at his hand and arm still wrapped with an elastic bandage. "I still have one good arm."

"Even though it's a greenstick fracture, you still have to be careful that it doesn't break."

"You don't think I'll be careful?"

"I'm going to check on you every day, and if you're not taking it easy, I'm going to have my mom fly out and stay with you until you're better."

CHAPTER 32

"Not Irene."

"She'll make you take it easy until you're healed. She won't—"

Just then, Alicia's phone rang, and she answered the call.

He watched her face droop as she nodded.

"Okay, thanks." She ended the call and stared at Fallon, her mouth slightly open.

"Who was that?"

"My analyst at Homeland Security in DC. They've been trying to find out who flew that jet into the Beaver Island Airport." She paused as she set the phone on a small shelf by her seat. "They can't find anything. It's like it never happened. No pilot would fly a jet without communicating the landing and takeoff. They could get in a lot of trouble with the FAA. It's against regulations."

"Unless you were doing something illegal like helping a fugitive escape."

Alicia took a deep breath. "Are you sure it was Ferguson you saw at my house on the island?"

"Positive. I chased them in a red SUV until I skidded off the road."

Alicia shook her head.

Fallon groaned. "You don't believe me?"

She dipped her head and rubbed her forehead. "It's just that—"

"You're not sure if I'm mentally all here, if I can sort out if my memories are real or imagined." He clenched his jaw as his heart rate increased. "I *know* what I saw. Besides, you found pieces of zip ties on your kitchen floor. Didn't you?"

"Yes. I believe you, but I can't find any other evidence to back up what you saw," Alicia said, her voice soft. "We couldn't even find the red SUV on the island that matched your description."

He frowned. "What about the plate number?"

"It doesn't exist."

"Someone's messing with the records. Ferguson told me he was framed, that the video was fake."

"The FBI has some of the best tech people in the business. I had them take another look at the video and they confirmed the video is real."

Fallon looked out his window as they flew past the State Capitol

Building and turned toward the airport. Beneath his feet the floor vibrated as a humming noise signaled the lowering of the landing gear. "You know I had a dream while I was in the hospital in Charlevoix." He turned to Alicia. "I dreamed I was running toward the Capitol with a computer bag. I had this sick feeling that if I didn't get there in time, something horrible was going to happen and that the governor was in danger."

Alicia's eyes widened.

"I believe I had something important in that bag I needed to get to the governor."

"And what was in the bag?"

"I'm not sure." Fallon glanced out the window. No one believed him. His mind drifted to last August when he was in the cabin on Beaver Island with Daniel and Massey. What exactly did that arrogant billionaire tell him? He closed his eyes.

"Fallon, what else can you recall?"

He opened his eyes and looked at Alicia. "Massey wants to take control of Michigan and all the other states running Archipelago. He wants to hold them hostage with his Archipelago software." More pieces of memory fell into place. "That's what he told me in the cabin last summer. It's what I've been trying to remember all these months."

"You *were* in the cabin before you met me at Welke Airport, before we stopped the drone attack," Alicia said.

"Massey was at the cabin when Daniel and I returned from Detroit."

"That can't be right."

The jet engines grew louder. Fallon looked out his window as the jet touched down.

Alicia's phone rang. "Oh, hi, Governor . . . Yes, we just touched down . . . okay, great." She ended the call and looked at Fallon. "The governor is meeting us at the State of Michigan hangar."

"I hope she can give me a ride to my place," Fallon said, as a wave of sadness washed over him.. "I don't have a car anymore."

"Is your Dart totaled?"

"That's what the body shop on the island told me. I've had that car since I was in high school—through my whole career. It's been through a lot with me."

CHAPTER 32

"So have you and I."

Fallon took in her warm eyes and affectionate gaze. She had been there for him so many times. He turned his head back to the window and ran his hand over his mouth as the jet taxied. "I never told you this." He took a deep breath and exhaled, turning to face Alicia. "My dad gave me that car my senior year in high school, a year after my granddad died. That Dart was my granddad's car. I feel like I'm losing everything."

Alicia smiled. "I'm still here."

He smiled back at her as the taxiing jet came to a stop. The engines wound down as the captain opened the door.

"Thanks," Fallon said as he unbuckled his seat belt and followed her out of the jet.

"Nice of you to meet us here," Fallon called to Karen as she walked from the State of Michigan hangar with her security detail following a few steps behind her.

Karen frowned as she looked at Fallon's bandaged arm. "I'm glad you weren't hurt worse."

"Me too," Alicia added.

"Any word on Ferguson?" Fallon asked.

"Every lead has dried up." Karen sighed. "It's been a couple of weeks, and it seems he's disappeared into thin air." She turned to Alicia. "No leads on that jet that was at the airport on Beaver Island?"

"There's no record of a jet being in the area that day. Only the janitor at the terminal saw it. We interviewed people around the airport, and some say they heard a jet but didn't see anything."

Karen nodded. "I'm headed to Charlevoix for a press conference with the FBI. They think he may have left the country. Every exit point in this country is being scoured for a lead."

"What about the two people posing as FBI agents?"

"There's no record of them anywhere," Karen said. "It's like they don't exist." She narrowed her eyes and looked at Fallon. "But you saw Ferguson at Alicia's house on the island."

Fallon nodded.

"I saw the pieces of zip ties he used to tie up Fallon," Alicia said.

They stood a moment looking at one another.

"Well, I need to get going," Karen said. "My driver can take you where you need to go." She gave Alicia a hug, then Fallon. "Take care of yourself, Fallon, or else—"

"Or else I told him I would have my mom stay with him," Alicia said.

Karen smiled. "That should motivate you, Fallon," she said as she walked toward the jet.

Fallon watched her board the plane, then he glanced at Alicia. "You headed back to DC?"

"There's nothing more for me to follow up on here. Trevor is handling the potential terrorist threat with the FBI. My flight leaves in an hour. Are you headed back to your condo?"

"Yeah, but I'll ride with you to the terminal."

Inside the terminal, he embraced Alicia outside the security checkpoint. He held her close for a minute, feeling the warmth of her embrace.

"You'll have to stay at your condo and rest now that you don't have a car," Alicia said as she released Fallon.

"I guess I'm stuck there."

Alicia lightly tapped him on the chest. "You take care of yourself," she said. "Get better."

Her hazel eyes captivated him. He didn't want her to leave. "I will," he said, his voice low.

He watched Alicia check in with security and disappear down a corridor to her gate. He stood a moment staring at the people coming and going, then turned to head for the escalator and the ground floor. His leg hurt as he walked; so did his bandaged arm. He stopped a moment at a window and watched the Jetway pull away from Alicia's plane. It pained him to see her go. What was he waiting for? He sighed and continued toward the exit.

As he rode the escalator down to the ground floor he noticed a rental car counter. He pulled out his phone and called Chip. This conversation he had to do in person.

CHAPTER 33

Daniel followed Massey through the empty commercial kitchen in the basement level of the Massey mansion. They passed by large pots and pans suspended from a rack mounted to the ceiling and long stainless steel tables that reflected the bright overhead lights.

"You could feed an army with this kitchen," Daniel said.

"I often do," Massey said, his attention focused on a door at the end of the hall. "I can't wait to show you my baby." He placed his hand on a biometric scanner next to the door. A moment later a green outline of his hand appeared with the words "Access Granted" on the top of the pad. The lock clicked open.

A rush of cool air greeted them as they descended a stairway. At the bottom, Daniel stepped onto the polished cement floor behind Massey. Overhead lights automatically clicked on. They passed large pipes and cables running along the ceiling between rows of steel I-beams. In the far corner of the room they stopped at a solid metal door with chipped, gray paint.

"This is the original door from the old military base that leads to the old bunker," Massey said as he tapped on the door. "You have to love the patina on this old door from the Cold War era."

"What's with the old rotary phone?" Daniel asked as he pointed to the black box on the wall.

"It just seemed right to keep the old phone that once connected to Arpanet."

"Is it still connected?"

"I severed all connections with the government when I built my estate. It's now connected to my digital network."

Daniel nodded, glad he didn't make a call with it.

Massey placed his hand on the biometric scanner next to the door. A large clunk echoed in the room as the door popped open. He pulled it open, and Daniel followed him down another set of stairs to a loading dock area.

"This was the place where they loaded missiles and other equipment," Massey said as he stopped a moment by several truck bays with heavy overhead doors sealing them off from the outside. "Hard to believe this was once the site of a military base with missiles."

"That must be the bunker," Daniel said, pointing to a large blast door on the other end of the loading dock. He followed Massey to the door and watched him open a control panel. The door of the panel blocked his view of Massey's hand. He could hear buttons clicking.

"There's no biometric scanner?"

Massey smiled as he pressed a few more buttons. "The blast door locks are all mechanical so they would still be operational in the event of a nuclear attack. I kept that in place so no one could unlock the doors digitally."

"To protect you against someone hacking into the bunker?"

"Exactly. If anyone wanted to hack into this computer, they would have to be physically on-site to open this door."

"But couldn't they hack into your private satellite network?"

"Only I have access to it. The software running it is unique to my network and the encryption is so advanced that anyone breaking into it would be immediately lost in a wilderness of unfamiliar programming."

"You really are a computer coding genius."

Massey closed the control box door and strained to open the heavy blast door. "Inside here is my pride and joy."

CHAPTER 33

"What if someone managed to get through this door?" Daniel asked as he helped open the door.

"You ask a lot of questions."

"I want to make sure everything is secure, especially your supercomputer."

"I have an alarm system inside the bunker," Massey said as he stepped inside. "It uses facial recognition. We're both cleared to enter. Anyone else would trip the alarm and lock down the supercomputer."

Daniel followed him inside. Motion sensors turned the lights on, revealing a sterile room with white-paneled walls. On the far wall he spotted a gray metal desk with a keyboard and two large screens with a large office chair pushed against the desk. In the center of the room sat a shipping-container-sized computer with sleek, deep-blue metal panels and large cables running to it from the ceiling.

"This is it," Massey announced with a big grin on his face. "The only one of its kind in the world. I've spent years putting this together, and here it is." He patted the metal side panel. "Advanced chips and processors along with my exclusive data compression software. This baby is light years ahead of any computing technology on the planet."

"It's a beauty."

"Think about it, Daniel—the data from twenty-two states all compressed into this box."

"That's an amazing accomplishment."

They stood a moment looking at the supercomputer.

"You know, Henry . . . When I look at this supercomputer, I wonder why you bothered with something as small and risky as sending an armed drone after the *Emerald Isle*."

Massey pressed his lips together and stared off into the distance. "My granddad had a ferry service to Beaver Island from Harbor Springs in the 1920s. The government shut it down and sold off the boat."

"Why?"

"That's a story for another time," Massey said. "My mom and grandmother fought to get the boat back—it was their livelihood. They depended on that boat, on tourists, to put food on the table. I wanted the people in the area to feel the pain my family felt."

"But that was more than one hundred years ago."

Massey took a step closer to Daniel. He could feel the anger radiating from him.

"Before my mom died"—Massey swallowed hard—"Quick Connect was starting to take off. Helen and I were getting rich. A few days before she died she made me promise I would use my wealth to somehow get back at the people who stole their livelihood when she was a kid."

"It's personal," Daniel said, seeing the anger in his eyes.

"When you came to me about helping you free Cally, I saw my opportunity. I didn't have to think about my target. I knew I could create all kinds of chaos with just one drone." Massey smiled. "I'm finally going to make the governments bow to me. When we start my bus tour in a few weeks, it will be a new day for Michigan, a new day for this country, and a new day for me."

Daniel watched Massey run his hand over the supercomputer, gently caressing it with admiring eyes. He had to stop this guy. He was out of options . . . except . . . the paper letter he sent to Fallon in a regular old, stamped envelope through the postal service.

CHAPTER 34

From the tenth floor of the Romney Office Building, Chip looked down at the State Capitol visible across the street from the window behind Fallon's desk. The dome rose above the trees surrounding the building, glowing in the afternoon sunlight. He swiveled his chair around and glanced at the framed picture on the desk of Fallon and Alicia sitting together with big smiles on the Charlevoix pier. Would Fallon ever return to this chair?

He began to go through a stack of fan mail addressed to Fallon. Even after all these months, the letters still arrived filled with appreciation for stopping the drone attack. Fallon told him to toss them, but he couldn't bring himself to do it. After opening a dozen letters, an envelope with a Fort Collins, Colorado, postmark caught his attention. Most had a postmark from Great Lakes states. The address was handwritten: "Mr. Fallon McElliot, Romney Building, Lansing, Michigan." He opened it and pulled out a handwritten note. No letterhead, just a note on a torn page of lined paper, in fairly legible handwriting.

> *Dear Mr. McElliot: I want to thank you for your heroic efforts in saving all those lives on the Emerald Isle. I admire your bravery*

and hope that you continue to heal from your injuries. I would love to meet you in person . . .

It read like so many other letters Fallon had received since the attack last August, except the sentence at the end where he said he wanted to meet Fallon on a specific date in the service tunnel below the Capitol at 7:20 a.m. It was oddly specific. Could it be a hoax or possibly a threat? His heart beat faster when he noted Daniel Callahan's signature at the bottom. Then he read the postscript at the bottom of the page with an obscure fact about a case he, Fallon, and Daniel worked on a few years ago. Only he, Fallon, and the person writing the letter would know that fact.

Setting the letter on the desk, Chip read it again. Could it really be Daniel after he had gone missing since the drone attack last August? Apparently Daniel wanted to confirm it was really him and he wanted to meet Fallon. Could it be true that he would meet them in person after being missing all this time, and why now? Then a thought occurred to Chip. He quickly pulled up the Massey campaign website and reviewed the schedule of locations for his bus tour. Massey would be at the Capitol on the date mentioned in the letter.

His phone rang as he quickly pocketed the note. He saw "Romney Lobby Security" on the screen.

"Fallon McElliot is here to see you," a security person said.

"Send him up."

Chip ended the call, pulled out the letter, and read it again. He swiveled his chair toward the window and looked at the Capitol. What could it mean that Daniel wanted to meet Fallon? Was he somehow tied to the Massey campaign? A few minutes later Fallon entered and sat in front of the desk.

"Did you break your arm?" Chip asked.

"Fortunately it's only a greenstick fracture."

"I heard what happened. You're lucky you weren't hurt worse."

Fallon looked at his arm. "Just a little accident."

"Little? You totaled your Dart."

"That's the worst part . . ." Fallon rubbed his forehead.

"I think I know why you're here," Chip said. "And I'm not sure I want to hear what you have to say."

CHAPTER 34

Fallon rested his wrapped arm in his lap. "I've had a lot of time to think lately."

Chip could see on his face what he was about to tell him. "No, Fallon—"

"It's time, Chip . . . I just can't—"

"I don't want to hear it." Chip leaned across the desk and locked his eyes on Fallon. "You can't retire."

"I have to face the reality that I'm never going to get back to my old self."

They sat silent for a moment, looking at each other.

"It's time, Chip."

"No, Fallon. At least not for now." He waved the letter at Fallon. "We have one more case to work on yet."

"Do you have a lead on Ferguson?"

"No, I'm sorry we don't."

"What about Massey? Did you follow up on what he told me in the cabin?"

"Sorry. There's nothing to prove Massey initiated the drone attack last August."

"So what do you have . . . what's that piece of paper you're holding?"

"This is a different lead for us to follow."

CHAPTER 35

Thirteen credible threats from the intel they collected online before the campaign rally. Daniel's senses were on high alert as he stood in the shadows of the elevated stage at Huntington Place and scanned the massive crowd. People packed in tightly, shoulder to shoulder among waves of "Massey for Governor" banners. As he surveyed the bleacher seating and the growing crowd pressing around the stage, he could not get rid of the gnawing feeling inside that they were missing something.

"Legend One ten minutes out," a voice said over his earpiece.

"Check," Daniel replied with a businesslike tone that masked his disdain for Massey's self-important Legend code name.

"Team in place, coming to you," another voice said over his earpiece.

"Copy."

Daniel moved to the locked access door in the corridor adjacent to the stage. "Positions," he said over the microphone on his earpiece. Other security team members moved into position around the elevated platform. "Ready to receive," he directed.

The door clicked open, and Massey emerged with his team of a half-dozen campaign staff dressed in casual business attire flanked by his security detail. Daniel watched Massey sprint up the steps to the elevated

CHAPTER 35

platform with a big grin on his face as the crowd erupted in thunderous applause, chanting "Massey, Massey, Massey." Another scan of the crowd. He noted his security detail doing the same. Good. He watched Massey standing by the podium waving at the massive crowd, gorging himself on all the attention. The catchy hip-hop song playing in the background ignited the crowd.

"Hello, Detroit!" Massey exclaimed as he stood in front of the podium with his arms open wide. "It's great to see so many of you here as we launch a new era for Michigan."

He had never seen a crowd so excited, so on fire, jumping up and down, screaming and waving their hands. "Are the facial scans picking up anything?" Daniel asked over his earpiece.

"Negative," came the reply.

"Ready to respond onstage," Daniel instructed. He knew the elevated noise was the perfect opportunity for someone to take a shot at Massey.

"Keep scanning for potential threats," Daniel urged as he watched the frenzied crowd.

"Negative so far," a voice responded over his earpiece. "AI is reviewing facial recognition against any potential online threats."

"Turn up the house lights and keep scanning," Daniel added. "Let me know if you get any matches."

"Check," came a voice over his earpiece.

"You *should* be excited!" Massey shouted. "It's a new day for Michigan!"

The crowd went wild again but began to quiet as Massey started to speak. Daniel had heard the speech so many times before. A bright vision for the future, blah, blah, blah. So much puffery. The minutes dragged on as Daniel continued to study the crowd.

"Hey Daniel, AI identified a positive off to your left," a voice said over his earpiece.

He slowly turned to his left.

"Female. Blue denim jacket. Dark-rimmed glasses."

"In my sights," Daniel said as he inched closer to the person. "Background?"

"Anti-capitalism group. Some strong online posts calling Massey all kinds of names."

Now positioned a few feet from each other, he made eye contact with the suspect. The person looked nervous as Daniel steadily closed in on her. She began to move her hand toward her open jacket.

Daniel's arm tensed as he moved his hand closer to the gun under his jacket, assessing if he could take her down without his gun if she pulled out a weapon. He noticed people in the crowd around the woman looking at him as he moved toward her.

The woman swung her head in Daniel's direction as she reached for something under her jacket.

He grabbed her arm before she could wield a rolled-up banner, restraining her as he grabbed the banner with his other hand.

She swore and shouted, "Capitalist!"

"Should we remove her?" someone asked over his earpiece.

Daniel noted people around her taking in the unfolding scene, phones in hand. "No," he replied as he took the rolled-up banner away and moved away from the woman. "We don't want a scene that will make the news. That's what she wants us to do." He released his grip and noted the disappointed look on her face.

Daniel returned to the side of the platform. "I'm guessing it's a protest sign," he said as he handed the sign to a campaign aide.

"How did the screeners miss that at the gate?" the aide asked as he disappeared through a side door with the banner. A second later Daniel heard the aide say over his earpiece. "The banner starts out 'MASSEY,' but then it's filled with some choice words. Apparently, security at the door never unrolled the whole sign."

Daniel looked at Massey droning on, arms waving, voicing words with a practiced tone. He could almost see Massey's ego growing before his eyes in front of the adoring crowd.

Suddenly three loud *crack* sounds echoed in the auditorium. Screams filled the arena as chaos erupted. Instinctively, Daniel bolted toward the platform. He climbed over panicked people as they dove to the floor while he watched Massey's body tumble backward. The security detail behind Massey was already on him, grabbing him as two more popping noises echoed throughout the massive arena.

"Get him out of here!" Daniel shouted, but the team had already

CHAPTER 35

whisked him off the stage. He followed them through the exit doors. The screams and shouting in the arena were now muffled by the doors locking behind them. "To the safe room!"

Daniel stayed close to the security detail as they quickly moved through the brightly lit corridor behind the auditorium. He glanced back and saw two or three people running after them, media credentials flapping against their chests as they pursued the detail. "Stop them!" Daniel pointed to a member of the security detail running with him as they continued down the long corridor. His heart was racing as he watched the rest of the security detail practically carry Massey along. Red spots of blood began to appear on the floor.

"Was he hit?" a police officer shouted as they approached the safe room.

"Get the paramedics in here!" Daniel motioned to the officer. "Get an ambulance."

"I've been shot," Massey groaned as they pushed him into the safe room.

Daniel quickly closed and locked the heavy metal door behind him. He noted blood dripping from Massey's head as they laid him on the couch. "How bad is it?"

"He has a bulletproof vest on," one of his security detail people said.

"I listened to your advice, Daniel," Massey said as he sat up and smiled. He removed his jacket and pointed to three bullet holes in his shirt near his heart.

Daniel scowled at him. "I'm glad you listened to me, or this campaign would be over right now."

"It's only beginning," he smirked as a security agent handed him a wet washcloth to wipe the gash on the side of his head.

"How did you cut your head?" Daniel asked as he crouched next to the couch.

"In all the chaos onstage, I think I hit my head on the corner of the podium." Massey dabbed the washcloth on his wound. He winced as he pressed the cloth against his head. "Whoa, bit of a headache."

Daniel looked at the security detail crowded around Massey. "Nice work. You responded exactly as we trained."

"The police chief wants an update on Massey's condition," a security detail member said, tapping his earpiece.

"Tell him he's okay," Daniel said as he motioned to the security team in the room. "Why don't you go help with crowd control? I'll stay with Massey."

Daniel watched the room empty out as he sat next to Massey on the couch.

"Great way to kick off the bus tour," Massey said as he examined the holes in his shirt.

Daniel noted Massey's suit jacket on the floor had no bullet holes, then he examined three holes in his shirt near his heart. "Someone had good aim." He scrutinized the size of the holes. Something didn't seem right. He thought back to the second he heard the familiar sound of a sniper rifle. He was right next to the stage, and he never heard the subsequent hissing sound of bullets piercing the air.

"What's wrong, Daniel?" Massey asked with a puzzled look.

"Your jacket has no bullet holes and the holes in your shirt look more like they were done with a handgun at close range, not a sniper rifle."

"What makes you say that?"

"I've seen enough victims in my career to know the difference." Daniel firmly tapped his finger on one of the holes in Massey's shirt. "No one was at close range to do that. The gunfire I heard was more like a sniper rifle."

"What are you saying?"

Daniel studied Massey's face as he thumped his chest with his hand. "You're not even flinching. If you were hit, you would definitely feel a bruise on your chest from the force of the bullet, even though the vest stopped it."

"What are you implying?"

"You . . ." Daniel could see he was hiding something. "You faked a shooting. Just like you helped me fake the bombing at the church to help my brother, Cally, escape from prison."

Massey laughed. "You're good."

"If the media gets wind of this, you're done."

"But they won't. The police will find sniper rifle bullets in the vest."

"You had someone shoot at your vest?"

CHAPTER 35

"Exactly. Only I forgot about the shirt, so they had to use a handgun on it."

"But the police will notice the difference and they'll see your suit jacket has no bullet holes."

"They won't care about my shirt, just the bullets in the vest. My security detail will dispose of my suit jacket and say it was lost in all the commotion."

Daniel couldn't argue with that logic. The police would focus on the slugs in the vest and try to find the rifle it came from.

"Don't worry. The sniper rifle was scrapped. They'll never find it."

"And they'll never find the phantom sniper."

"Exactly."

"So now you start your bus tour looking like some heroic tough guy who just survived an assassination attempt."

"Everything is going as planned. We'll monopolize the media for days. Social media is going to be on fire about this. We'll have a press conference in a few hours. I'll explain how we took precautions with me wearing a bulletproof vest, knowing there are people out there who hate us. Then I'll tell them we're going to press on despite those who are trying to stop us and our campaign to shape a new future for Michigan."

Daniel deeply exhaled. The next stop would be the State Capitol. If Fallon received his letter, he would be waiting for him in the service corridor underneath the Capitol. Together they might be able to devise a plan to stop this guy.

"I'm sorry I scared you like that, Daniel," Massey said as he patted him on the shoulder. "It had to be a surprise to make it look real. At least you were able to test your response to an attempt on my life."

Too disgusted to say anything else, Daniel politely nodded, trying to hide his distaste for this man who lacked any scruples.

"I'm sure security will be even tighter at our next stop on the tour," Massey said with a smug tone.

"You can count on that," Daniel added. "The State Capitol is going to be on lockdown after this."

CHAPTER 36

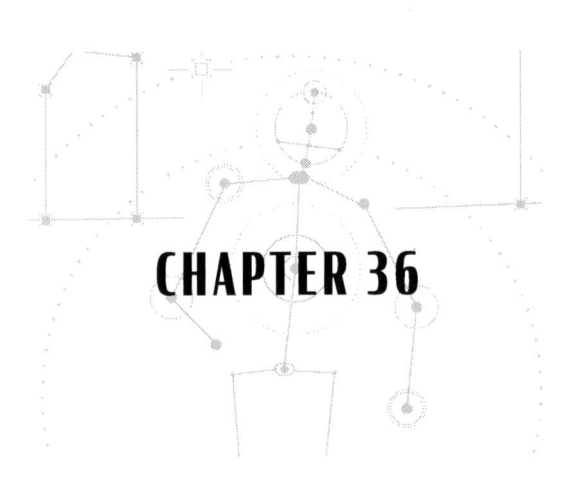

Sitting at a large table in a conference room in the cabin, Ferguson glanced at the rustic wood walls and framed scenic wilderness pictures. He turned his attention to Lance standing in front of a large screen mounted on the wall, then Nigel sitting across from him in a leather desk chair.

"It's about time I learn what this is all about," Ferguson said. "I've been cooped up here for weeks."

"Things have cooled down since your escape," Nigel said. "It's time to act."

"Are Sophia and Nadia joining us?" he asked.

Nigel returned a composed look. "No. We're handling this from here." He pointed at Lance. "Let's get on with the briefing."

Lance grabbed a tablet off the table and clicked to the first slide. An image appeared showing an aerial view of a sprawling estate nestled in the foothills of the Colorado Rockies. "The Massey estate sits on the site of a former military base." He pointed to a section on the far end of the home. "Our surveillance shows that Massey's supercomputer is in a former bunker located here, next to the loading dock."

"How long have you been running surveillance?" Ferguson asked.

CHAPTER 36

"Lance has been making food deliveries to the Massey estate for Food Queen for the last few months," Nigel replied.

"I have a good idea on the layout of the loading dock and the former military site," Lance added.

Ferguson surveyed the aerial image of the massive mansion, surrounded by beautifully landscaped grounds. "That had to cost a fortune."

"Pocket change for him," Nigel remarked.

"Why build there?" Ferguson asked. "It looks remote."

"He made himself out to be an environmental hero by personally paying to clean up a site that no one wanted to touch," Nigel explained. "When some claimed he was taking shortcuts, he built his home there to prove that the site was clean. That silenced his critics."

"This site was part of his plan when he formed Arpa," Lance continued. "The original idea was to build his computer server farm there, but as technology advanced, he opted to build his own supercomputer and place it in the nuclear bunker on the site so he could start consolidating all the data from state governments running Arpa's Archipelago software."

"He's making his own personal copy of all the data from twenty-two states . . ." Ferguson said. "All that data would be a gold mine."

Nigel leaned back and put his hands behind his head. "Imagine having the power to manipulate data in almost half the states in the nation."

"Is that the real reason you're interested in this supercomputer?" Ferguson continued as he studied Nigel, trying to read their motive.

Nigel leaned forward and put his hands on the table. "We also think all his communication about his plans are housed on that supercomputer. We think it has all the evidence we need to send Massey to prison for the rest of his life."

Ferguson folded his hands across his chest. "If you know all of this, why don't you just go to the FBI and work with them?"

Nigel chuckled. "Let's just say that we can do things faster and more efficiently than the FBI—things the FBI isn't allowed to do. We also need to do a little house cleaning on that computer to make sure nothing points to us."

"So, what do you want me to do?"

"All you have to do is load it inside a semi-trailer and drive off," Lance said in a calm voice.

"You make it sound so easy." Ferguson eyed Nigel. "I still think it would be easier to hack into that computer and steal all the data."

"We have no way to access his supercomputer," Nigel explained. "Massey's been using his own private satellite network to download all the data from the states running Archipelago to his supercomputer. He now houses a master copy of all that data. Any changes he makes will be replicated to the other state servers."

"But he still has to be linked to state computers to get daily updates from the data they collect..." Ferguson thought a moment, trying to think of some alternative. "Can't you just hack that connection and divert his downloads?"

"It was hard for Sophia to admit that Massey could out-program her. He anticipated every move the best hackers in the world would make to try to break in," Nigel said with a long face. "His firewalls are like nothing I've ever seen. Plus he's using some software code our programmers have never seen."

"So physically stealing his computer is the best option," Lance added, sitting down at the large conference table across from Ferguson. "It's so outrageous that I don't think he anticipates anyone doing it."

"We'll never be able to break into that bunker. It must have massive, reinforced concrete construction," Ferguson surmised.

"There's an access door on the loading dock where the Massey estate receives deliveries." Lance touched his tablet to advance to the next slide. He pointed to a large steel door in the image on the screen. "At some point he took delivery of that supercomputer and installed it. We just need to reverse the process."

"I don't see how you expect me to steal his supercomputer."

Nigel pointed at the large screen at the front of the room. "Go to the next slide, Lance."

An image appeared on the screen of a semi equipped with a trailer bearing a Food Queen logo. "Often the weakest link in a company's security is the lowest-level supplier."

"Like the SolarWinds hack a few years ago," Lance remarked. "Russia

CHAPTER 36

used a software update in a program from a low-level supplier to gain access to government and corporate networks."

"Exactly," Nigel agreed. "Only we're doing a physical hack of Massey's computer."

Ferguson looked at the screen and shook his head. "You want *me* to just drive up and load his supercomputer. That's ridiculous."

"Exactly," Nigel grinned. "Right now, Massey is preoccupied with his bus tour campaign. Someone tried to shoot him in Detroit."

"What?" Ferguson gasped.

"It's all over the news," Nigel said in an annoyed tone. "He's acting like some hero because he's carrying on his campaign. I wouldn't be surprised if he staged the assassination attempt."

"You really think he'd do that?"

"He fooled you when he faked the church bombing to help Cally escape," Nigel said.

"Good point."

"All his security is focused on his bus tour," Lance pointed out. "Their defenses are down at his estate. Massey wouldn't dream of someone stealing his prized possession in broad daylight."

"It's one thing to drive a truck up to the loading dock, but how do we get in?"

"The final sale of the former military base was contingent on the Defense Department approving the final plan for reusing the site, which included detailed construction blueprints," Nigel explained as Lance clicked to the next slide showing the blast door and loading dock. "We were able to obtain those plans through the EPA with a FOIA request under the context of an environmental group reviewing compliance with the environmental plan."

"I'm guessing it's a group you formed."

"Of course. Sophia is all for saving the environment and making sure crooks like Massey don't pollute."

"What's interesting," Lance explained, pointing to the image on the screen, "is that the blast door locks are all mechanical so they would still be operational in the event of a nuclear attack. Massey kept that in place so no one could unlock the door digitally."

"Someone has to physically be on-site to unlock the door," Nigel said. "It can't be done remotely."

Ferguson studied the image of the blast door. "And you know how to open it?"

Lance advanced to the next slide showing the control box next to the blast door. "We found the instructions for opening it in the Department of Defense reuse plans for the site."

"But won't alarms trip if I open the doors?"

"It's mechanical and not tied to his digital security system."

"But that supercomputer has to weigh a ton," Ferguson objected. "How am I supposed to move it?"

"There's a forklift on the loading dock you can use," Nigel said. "We'll review everything with you on how to disconnect the supercomputer and load it."

"I can't believe I can just walk into the bunker and load the supercomputer," Ferguson said with a sarcastic tone. "There must be security inside that bunker."

"True. Massey does have advanced sensing equipment inside the bunker for twenty-four-hour security," Nigel said. "If facial recognition doesn't match those approved to enter, the sensors will trigger an alert."

"So how do I get around that?"

The room was silent for a moment as Lance and Nigel looked at each other. "Tell him, Lance," Nigel said.

"We have an operative inside the Massey estate who will disable anything that might alert them to you stealing the supercomputer," Lance explained.

"What about the advanced sensing equipment inside the bunker?" Ferguson asked.

"Those will be shut down as well."

Ferguson looked at Lance, then Nigel. "How will I know this operative will have disabled everything?"

"They will meet you on the loading dock and make sure you get a clean getaway with the supercomputer," Lance said. "Keep in mind that the security cameras showing the outside loading dock area will still be

CHAPTER 36

recording the semi backing into the dock to unload the food delivery and its departure. It will appear to be a routine shipment."

Ferguson couldn't avoid the uneasy feeling he had about the whole thing. "This all sounds way too risky."

"If you're having second thoughts," Nigel smiled. "I can take you to the authorities and they'll be happy to send you back to prison."

"Some choice," Ferguson sighed. "What happens after it's loaded?"

"You drive the supercomputer to a rail terminal, and it gets loaded onto a train," Nigel answered. "Then it travels by rail into the Moffat Tunnel under the Rocky Mountains. Once it's in the tunnel, the train engine will mysteriously break down halfway through and the container will be invisible to satellite tracking and hidden from aerial surveillance. That will give my technicians time to access the supercomputer and wipe any information about us from it. Then the FBI will get a tip on the whereabouts of the supercomputer. They'll be able to confiscate it when it comes out of the tunnel."

"Remember, all you need to do is get that truck to the train," Lance added.

"Once you do that," Nigel said. "I'll pick you up and take you to the airport. We'll then ship you to Sophia's Mediterranean island with her private jet. By the next day you'll be a free man basking in a tropical climate."

Ferguson nodded. What did he have to lose? A risky theft of a supercomputer and a chance at freedom were far more appealing than life in prison.

CHAPTER 37

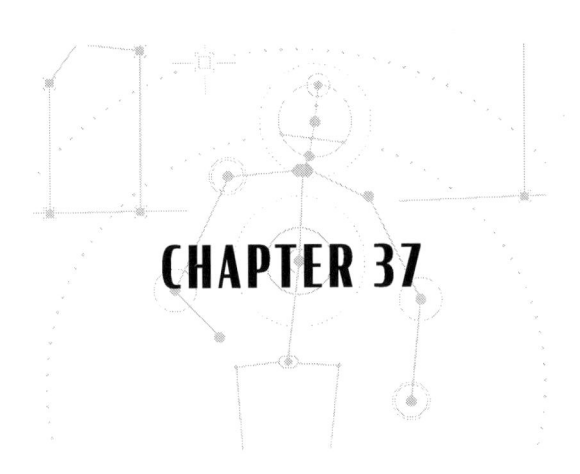

Daniel stood on the glass floor in the rotunda of the Michigan State Capitol, looking up at the stars painted on the ceiling of the dome. The sound of hard-soled shoes clicked on the glass floor and echoed underneath the dome. He turned to see four members of the Massey campaign security detail approaching him.

"Upper floors are secure," a member of the detail said as they joined him in the rotunda. "Capitol is on full lockdown. No one is coming or going."

"Let's do a final sweep..." Daniel paused as he spotted a Capitol police officer dressed in a neatly pressed, blue uniform walking toward him at a brisk pace.

"This is highly unorthodox," the officer said. "We don't need your security team rechecking the building after we've completed our sweep."

"No offense," Daniel replied. "But—"

"Look," the officer said. "We've been on lockdown and heightened security since someone took shots at your boy Massey. We advised his campaign manager to cancel this event."

"We're sticking to the schedule."

CHAPTER 37

"He's not helping us," the officer grunted. "His careless attitude makes all our jobs harder."

Daniel kept a stern face but totally agreed with him. If only he knew Massey faked the shooting in Detroit. "Regardless, it's what we have to work with so let's get through this without an incident."

"Do what you need to do," the officer said with a huff as he turned and walked away. "I'll be glad when this is over."

"Each one of you take a wing and check the offices on this floor," Daniel said to his security detail standing near him. "They should all be vacant. Look for anything suspicious. I'll check the service tunnels. Once it's secure, we can bring Massey in through the Heritage Hall and escort him to the outside balcony facing Michigan Avenue."

The security team split up, each member walking down a wing of the Capitol to the first office. Daniel quickly made his way to the floor below and the access door to the service tunnels. Would someone be there waiting for him? He opened a metal hatch in the floor leading to the basement service tunnels. The hatch clicked shut behind him as he descended the metal stairs into the dark basement area. A lone light illuminated the steps. Cool, moist air greeted him. He flipped a light switch at the bottom of the stairs. A row of lights mounted to metal conduit attached to the low ceiling clicked on, lighting the old, brick walls and worn, cement floor.

Slowly, he moved along the tunnel beneath the Capitol. Large steam pipes mounted to the walls hissed and clanked alongside the sound of water moving through adjacent smaller pipes. He turned a corner, expecting someone to be there, but the tunnel was empty. Had they received his letter? He glanced at his watch: 7:23 a.m. There wasn't much time to make contact. Carefully he advanced down the tunnel as he scanned the corridor ahead. Suddenly a shadowy figure emerged, then another, stepping into the dim light from a single overhead bulb. He clutched his gun under his jacket. "Who's there?"

"It's Chip . . . and Fallon."

Daniel stopped and watched Chip's face light up, followed by Fallon. He stood a moment staring at them, his mouth half open. "You two are a sight for sore eyes."

Fallon took a step closer to Daniel. Their eyes met.

"Is that you, Daniel?" Fallon asked as he studied his face.

"Yeah."

"You've never had a beard."

They stood a moment looking at each other as the sound of clanking and hissing pipes filled the silence.

"Fallon . . . I'm sorry I had to leave you like that on Beaver Island." Daniel watched Fallon's face tighten, his lips pressed together.

"At the cabin . . ." Fallon said. "With Massey."

Daniel nodded.

"What are you doing here?"

Daniel glanced up and down the tunnel. "Does anyone else know you're here?"

"No one," Chip said. "It's just me and Fallon."

"Where have you been?" Fallon asked with a somber look.

"I've been deep undercover in Massey's operations acting as his head of global security." Daniel glanced at Fallon's bandaged arm.

Fallon frowned. "You left me . . . at the cabin."

"Look, I'm sorry—"

"You left me alone . . . to stop that drone."

"I know . . ." Daniel looked at his watch. "Look, I don't have much time to explain—"

"All clear," a radio clipped to Daniel's belt blared.

"Still checking the tunnels," Daniel said as he put the radio to his mouth. "Meet you in the rotunda in ten minutes."

"You were with Massey at the cabin," Fallon said.

"We can talk about this later," Daniel said as he glanced at his watch.

"I need to know—"

"Please . . . Not now, Fallon."

"But—"

"Look . . . I'll get to the point. I think I can get proof that Henry Massey was behind the *Emerald Isle* drone attack."

"That doesn't make sense," Chip said as he looked at Fallon.

"It *was* Massey," Fallon said, his eyes lighting up.

"But there's more, a lot more." Daniel glanced up and down the tunnel again and lowered his voice. "Massey wants to seize control of all the State

CHAPTER 37

of Michigan's data, as well as all the other states running the Archipelago software. Last August he used a Caspian drone sourced from Arpa to test his ability to use force, if needed, to stop anyone from getting in his way."

"But the video shows Ferguson stealing the drone," Chip said.

"He framed Ferguson with a fake video."

"I knew he didn't do it," Fallon said.

"But that video has been thoroughly screened and verified as authentic," Chip said.

"Trust me, it's fake." Daniel checked his watch. "I need to get back to Massey. Walk with me to the stairs."

"How can you prove it?" Chip asked.

They walked together through the service tunnel as Daniel continued. "Massey has a supercomputer at his Colorado estate where he is making a master copy of all the data from the states running Archipelago."

"He must have a massive server farm there," Chip said.

"Actually it's a supercomputer about the size of a shipping container. He told me it uses some sort of advanced computer chip with data compression technology."

"I know the military was doing research into it," Chip said. "The goal was to compress several server farms of data in something the size of a shipping container."

"So it would be transportable?" Daniel asked as he approached a corner to an adjacent service tunnel.

"I hadn't thought of that," Chip said. "But yes."

Fallon shook his head. "I'm glad you two understand all of this."

Daniel stopped abruptly just before rounding the corner. He put his finger to his lips, then stood silent.

"I think I heard someone," Daniel whispered.

A clanking noise echoed down the adjoining tunnel and faded.

"Steam pipes," Chip sighed.

Daniel rounded the corner and walked toward the exit. "Massey could move that supercomputer, along with all the evidence of his plan, if he suspected we were on to him. We wouldn't be able to trace the movement of the data if he physically moved it."

"He could also hold hostage the data from twenty-two states," Chip said.

Daniel glanced over his shoulder and saw Chip right behind him. A few steps back he saw Fallon limping toward them. He looked at his watch, then at the exit stairs just ahead. "That's all I have right now."

"What should we do?"

"I tipped off the FBI about his supercomputer, but it's too risky to try to follow up with them." Daniel started up the stairs and reached for the latch to open the metal access door in the ceiling. Someone grabbed his arm. He turned to see Chip directly behind him.

"Wait!" Chip said as he let go of Daniel's arm. "Specialized chips like that would have to be custom manufactured. You can't just buy them off the shelf."

"Where would he get those chips?" Daniel asked.

"I was talking to a buddy of mine a few weeks ago. He works for an overseas supplier that has been shipping components to a lab in China that he thinks is building a supercomputer with highly advanced computer chips. It appears some tech entrepreneur in the US is funding the lab."

"Who else has access to those computer chips?"

"No one. They're custom and cost prohibitive to use commercially."

"Unless you're a billionaire," Daniel said. "If that supercomputer was built in China with Chinese sourced components and shipped here, he's in violation of the US ban on importing Chinese technology."

"Massey doesn't have a good reputation in the international tech community," Chip said. "There are people I know who may already have evidence to prove he took delivery of that supercomputer. I think they would be happy to help me. If I can get a shipping manifest, bill of sale, or some other type of record showing he took possession of those chips."

"The FBI can get a search warrant for his estate, bust him on that, and confiscate his computer to gain access to all the other incriminating evidence," Daniel patted Chip on the shoulder. "I miss working with you two. Do you think you can get some form of evidence that he took possession of Chinese technology?"

"If anyone can, Chip can," Fallon said.

Daniel looked at Fallon and noted his tired appearance. "Just like

CHAPTER 37

those cases we worked on, Fallon. Chip always came through with the evidence."

Fallon smiled. "Just like the good old days. We were a great team."

"What should I do if I get the evidence we need?"

Daniel wrote a number on a piece of paper and gave it to him. "Fax it to this number using old analog copper lines that connect the states and the Feds for emergency communication. Don't try to contact me. I'm sure Massey is monitoring all communications over Archipelago with his AI bots. He would be able to track my voice."

"Where am I supposed to find a fax machine and an old copper line?"

"The Capitol should still be connected to old copper lines for emergency communications with Washington," Daniel explained. "There's still an old rotary phone down here." He pointed to the phone mounted on a nearby wall.

"I think the governor's ceremonial office may have a fax machine connected to that emergency communication network." Chip looked at the piece of paper with the phone number. "How can I be sure the FBI is on the other end of the line?"

"Fax the word *Copper* to them first," Daniel explained. "If you get the response 'Fred B Innis,' you'll know they received your fax, and you can send them whatever you get."

"Fred B Innis—FBI. Clever." Chip nodded.

"Somehow you need to document that Chinese technology went to the Massey estate. We need probable cause that they are at that address to get the search warrant."

"Do you think Massey would be so sloppy as to leave a trail documenting importing Chinese technology?" Fallon asked.

"He's arrogant enough to wave a middle finger at the federal government's Chinese technology ban to get what he wants."

"Good point."

Daniel's radio blared. "We're waiting for you in the rotunda."

"On my way," Daniel responded into the radio. "Don't tell anyone about meeting me, not even the governor. We can't risk blowing my cover."

"Not even the governor?"

"No," Daniel insisted. He pulled his buzzing phone from his blazer pocket and saw Massey's name on the screen. "I need to go. Make sure no one sees you exiting the service tunnel in the Capitol."

"We used the governor's secret underground tunnel from the Romney Building," Chip smiled. "But you didn't hear me say that."

Daniel paused with his hand on the access hatch and looked at Fallon standing next to Chip. "I hope we get more time to talk soon."

"Me too," Fallon said.

"Good luck," Daniel said as he exited the service tunnel.

CHAPTER 38

Daniel followed Massey into a conference room in the Heritage Center attached to the Capitol. He nodded to the security detail, and they took their positions outside the door.

"Don't let anyone in," he said as he closed the door and took a seat across from Massey at a long oak table with a dozen chairs. He looked at the framed, scenic pictures of Michigan landscapes on the walls, then at Massey busily tapping on his tablet.

"There's a large crowd gathered on the Capitol lawn to hear my speech," Massey said as he set his tablet on the table and looked at Daniel.

"Aren't you worried about Ferguson being on the loose?"

Massey smirked.

"But it's been weeks," Daniel said. "No one has a clue where he's hiding."

"Ferguson is a small-time player."

"Someone had some horsepower to pose as FBI agents. Doesn't that concern you?"

Massey picked up his tablet and waved it at Daniel. "I know more about the search for Ferguson than anyone. My advanced AI gives me a daily update and immediately alerts me if anything new comes up. Remember,

I'm tapped into the Michigan servers. Plus, Trevor is also keeping me updated from the field."

"Exactly how did Ferguson escape?"

"They think it was an inside job."

"Why would two FBI agents suddenly turn and help him escape?"

Massey smiled at Daniel. "It happens."

"I suppose it does." Daniel tilted his head. "You're not worried he'll come after you for framing him?"

"He'll never find out. I'm too smart for them."

Daniel pointed to the video conference equipment on the other end of the room. "What about your Archipelago software? Isn't it recording our conversation right now?"

"I record *all* conversations from the states using Archipelago's video conference module, whether they're active or not. My AI bots constantly search for and store any potentially incriminating recordings in case I need them later for leverage. I already have thousands of files on elected officials and government workers from the states using Archipelago that I can use when needed. Besides, I deactivated it when I arrived here."

"You've covered all your bases."

"You're always weighing different scenarios. I like that about you, Daniel. You're thorough."

"I guess I can't turn it off."

Massey waved his pointer finger at him. "I recall the first time I met you—the first time Peninsular managed security for an Arpa meeting."

"That was a big job." Daniel leaned back in his chair with his arms folded across his chest. How nervous he had been when he took on his first deep undercover job posing as the founder of Peninsular. Massey took the bait, hook, line, and sinker.

"From the moment we first met, I knew there was something different about you." Massey paused, his deep-blue eyes locked on him.

They sat silent for a moment.

Daniel could feel his body tense up. Where was he going with that statement? What would he do if he suspected he was undercover?

"I knew I could trust you," Massey said.

"I take my work seriously," Daniel said, feeling his body relax.

CHAPTER 38

"What did you think of my supercomputer?"

"Impressive." He eyed Massey. "I still can't grasp how you could squeeze an entire server farm into such a compact package."

Massey flashed a look of satisfaction. "Very specialized technology."

"Something you built?"

"Sort of. A lot of people don't know that the Chinese have some of the most advanced computer chips on the planet. All they needed was a little funding to take them to the next level."

"Funding?"

"I signed an agreement with one of the best labs in China a few years ago and boy did they deliver."

"You know there's a ban on using Chinese technology in this country. There are national security concerns."

"Of course I do." Massey frowned. "If the Feds are stupid enough to block access to some of the most advanced computing power available, that's their problem.

"If the Feds find out—"

"The Feds have no idea that I have Chinese technology at my estate, nor do they know I have a supercomputer with capabilities that far exceed what they could ever imagine. The federal government is such a barrier to innovation."

"I can't argue with that."

The door to the conference room opened a crack. "Five minutes, Mr. Massey," a security detail member said as he opened the door.

"Time to move," Daniel said.

They followed the security detail up the connecting stairs to the Capitol entrance. Daniel opened the tall, ornate wood door. They proceeded down the long hallway and across the checkerboard-patterned marble floor, passing beneath the high-arched ceiling with Victorian-era painted trim and old, gas chandeliers. As they walked across the glass floor of the rotunda, Massey stopped a second to glance up at the stars high above, painted on the top of the interior of the dome.

"Beautiful. In January, this place will be ours," Massey said.

They took the elevators up to the next floor, entered a large office area, then went outside to the east-facing balcony of the Capitol. As

Massey took to the podium, Daniel couldn't believe the number of people gathered around the Capitol lawn. He stood in awe as the crowd roared at Massey's appearance, chanting "Massey, Massey, Massey." Suddenly, he felt a sense of urgency. Massey might just win it all. He had to stop him before the primary election in August.

"This is a new day for Michigan!" Massey shouted.

The crowd roared again.

From Daniel's vantage point in the shadows of the limestone pillars, behind the podium on the balcony, he estimated several thousand people chanting Massey's name. The bus tour was just getting started, and he could already feel the momentum building.

CHAPTER 39

Chip quickened his pace down the hallway toward the governor's second-floor office. Something was so urgent she needed to see him immediately. He noted the governor's staff gathered by the windows facing the Capitol with tense looks on their faces, no doubt amazed and concerned about the massive crowd assembled to hear the governor's opponent speak.

He stood a second in front of the governor's door, took a deep breath, and knocked.

"Come in," the governor responded in a curt voice.

He entered and closed the door behind him. The governor was standing in front of the window facing the Capitol watching the growing group of Massey supporters.

The governor abruptly turned. "Can you believe that crowd?"

"For all we know he paid all those people one hundred dollars each to attend," Chip offered as he took a few steps toward her.

"Wouldn't surprise me." She sighed. "Thanks for coming so quickly."

"What's so urgent?"

The governor stood for a moment next to her desk, head down, deep in thought.

Chip stood awkwardly near the door.

She lifted her head. "You've been filling in for Fallon as acting liaison to the state police for nine months now," Karen said. "You've earned my trust."

"Governor . . ." Chip didn't like where he thought the conversation was going. "Fallon will be back."

Karen shook her head and took a couple steps toward Chip. "We need to be realistic. He's never going to be the same."

"But governor . . ." Chip inhaled deeply. He knew it too. Fallon was not the same person he knew before his injuries. He wasn't ready to accept that Fallon was considering retirement.

"I want you to formally assume Fallon's position. We'll publicly keep you as acting liaison out of respect for Fallon, but formally you would have a cabinet-level position. That also means I can share with you a level of confidential information I could not before."

"You're giving me clearance for what you're about to tell me."

"Yes, but not here." Karen opened the door and stepped into the hallway. "Follow me."

"Governor?" Chip called out as he closed the door behind him and kept pace with her brisk stride. Curious staffers watched them hurry as they moved through the reception area to the elevators.

"Will you be back, Governor?" the receptionist shouted after them.

"Yes," the governor replied as an elevator dinged on its arrival and the doors opened.

They stepped inside and the doors closed. She slipped a key into a slot below the floor buttons on the control panel. The elevator jerked as it moved upward. Chip watched the display counting off the floor numbers. They stood silent for a moment with only the hum of the elevator. When the doors opened, Chip was surprised to see they were on the roof level of the building. They stepped outside the elevator and a warm, June breeze ruffled his hair.

"Why are we here?" Chip asked as Karen fought to keep her own hair in place.

"I need to tell you something confidential," Karen said. "And I'm concerned about my office being bugged."

CHAPTER 39

"Who would bug your office?"

"That's secondary right now," Karen continued.

Another muffled roar of the crowd rose up from the Capitol lawn. They stepped to the edge of the roof and looked at the crowd thirteen stories below.

"There must be five thousand people there," Chip said, observing the mass of people pressed against the north, south, and east side of the Capitol. "Traffic is still jammed on Michigan and Capitol Avenues." He turned to the governor. "Couldn't you stop him from speaking at the Capitol?"

"It's a public building. Preventing him from speaking there would only make me look bad." The governor turned her attention back to the Capitol.

A figure walked to a podium on the east-facing balcony.

"That must be Massey," Chip remarked.

Karen swore.

The crowd roared, chanting Massey's name as he waved.

"This is a new day for Michigan!" Massey's amplified voice rose up from massive speakers on the Capitol lawn, echoing off nearby buildings.

The crowd roared again.

Chip noted Karen's disgusted face as they stepped away from the edge of the roof. He had never seen her with such a grave look. "What did you want to tell me that you couldn't say in your office?"

Karen looked intently at Chip.

Suddenly Massey's raised voice echoed across the roof as he shouted, *"This current administration is as corrupt as they come. They have failed on the most basic elements of government—to protect the health, safety, and welfare of the citizens of this state. It's up to you to fix it. A vote for me is a vote for honesty and integrity. I will defend this state against the tyranny of terrorists!"*

Karen sighed and rolled her eyes. "Such arrogance. The people down there have no idea what I'm dealing with or what Massey is really about." Her face tightened as she looked at Chip. "The FBI came to me last summer and told me they were investigating Massey. They were concerned about his Archipelago software, especially if he won the Michigan governorship."

Not what he expected to hear. Daniel told him and Fallon not to tell anyone they met with him, not even the governor. "What made them think that?"

"You've heard of Arpa."

"The venture capital firm behind the Archipelago software."

"Because Arpa is funded by the world's leading tech billionaires, the FBI became suspicious about the real intent of the group."

"Sounds anticompetitive to me."

"It was more than that. They were concerned about so much money and power in the digital world sitting around one table." The governor pushed her hair away from her face. "They had some agents infiltrate the group and verified their concerns."

"What exactly are they concerned about?"

She rubbed her neck, then straightened her stance. "That Massey might misuse the data he's collecting with Archipelago software. He could have inside knowledge of all kinds of records, and he could manipulate them for his gain. Because of the efficiency it's shown in so many other states, the Feds have started using it on a trial basis in a couple of agencies. Imagine the power Massey would have if he was able to manipulate and use state and federal data at will."

Chip glanced toward the Capitol as Massey's voice echoed between the tall buildings in downtown Lansing.

"When a Massey administration takes over this state next year, Michigan will be a star set apart from the US," Massey said. *"We will be our own independent star, shining brighter than any other state in the union."*

Excited screams from the crowd below followed Massey's words.

Chip turned to the governor. "What does the FBI want you to do about it?"

Karen put her hands on her hips. "Win this election at all costs. They're willing to help me do it."

Chip raised an eyebrow. "What does that mean?"

"They told me"—she paused and took a deep breath—"they have an operative inside the Massey campaign. If they find any dirt on him, they'll feed it to me immediately."

"But that's—"

CHAPTER 39

"Extreme times call for extreme measures," Karen cut in as she turned toward the Capitol and frowned as Massey's voice continued to reverberate among the tall buildings.

"Michigan will be a light for the world, a state set high on a hilltop for all to see and admire," Massey shouted, his voice echoing around Karen and Chip. *"I will lead you out of this wilderness of government ineptitude to the land of prosperity!"*

"Did I just hear that correctly?" Chip said with a tone of disbelief. "Is he misquoting the Bible?"

"Worse," the governor quipped. "He thinks he's a god."

"Have they found any dirt?" Chip asked.

"They haven't sent me anything yet."

"I'm sure he's monitoring every form of communication running through Archipelago and his estate."

"Can't be too careful," Karen said.

Massey's voice continued to drone on around them. *"As you have heard, there are some who want to try to stop this campaign of mine to transform Michigan, even resorting to violence."*

"If only they'd been successful," Karen mumbled.

"Governor!"

"Sorry." She threw up her hands. "That just slipped out. It would've made things a lot easier for me."

Chip watched the governor begin to pace. "Do you by any chance have access to an analog phone using old copper lines?"

Karen stared at Chip and tapped her chin with her finger. "There's an old phone in the governor's ceremonial office in the Capitol. It's part of the Cold War era emergency communications network between state capitols and Washington, DC. The Feds wanted it left intact in case the national digital networks ever failed."

"Join me as we dethrone this current administration and move forward to victory this fall!" Massey's voice echoed between the buildings as the crowd roared.

"Is there a fax machine there too?"

"In the storage closet. Why?"

"I need to fill *you* in on some confidential things," Chip said.

CHAPTER 40

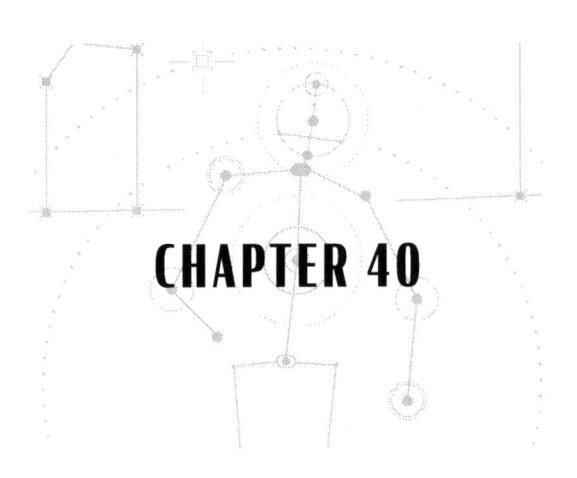

"What kind of car are we looking for?" Fallon asked as he scanned the parking lot of the Meijer store in East Lansing.

"A blue Ford Escape," Chip said as his head darted back and forth.

Fallon looked at Chip tapping his fingers on the steering wheel. "Relax."

"How can I?" He looked at Fallon. "I don't know how you and Daniel managed to do it."

"What?"

"Police work . . . all those stakeouts, undercover work . . . I'd rather hide behind my laptop at a desk."

"And you were darn good at it," Fallon said as he looked at his watch. "What time are you meeting the courier?"

"She was supposed to be here five minutes ago."

"And she has all the documents confirming Massey's purchase of Chinese technology?"

"I hope so . . ." Chip sighed. "It took me more than a week to network through my supplier contacts, but I finally hit pay dirt a few days ago. If

CHAPTER 40

she comes through, we'll have hard evidence that Massey violated the ban on purchasing and using Chinese technology."

"This is like the old days," Fallon smiled. "When we only had paper documents."

"I didn't want to risk sending anything digitally," Chip said, taking a deep breath.

"Smart move."

Chip looked at Fallon. "Did Massey really tell you he launched the drone attack on the *Emerald Isle*?"

"I'm pretty sure." He rubbed his head. "I can't prove it."

"If we can get that search warrant and get into his supercomputer, we might get all the evidence we need to prove it."

"It would be nice to confirm if my memories are correct." Fallon looked at Chip. "It was nice of you to include me on this—to loop me in on the meeting with Daniel too."

"You know I have a lot of respect for you, Fallon. You were my mentor when I started as an analyst with the state police. You've been good to me."

"You didn't need me. You proved yourself." Fallon took a deep breath and looked at Chip. "You've got this."

Chip looked at him with concern.

"When I totaled my car on Beaver Island a few weeks ago . . . well, it made me realize I just can't do police work anymore."

"Fallon—"

"No . . ." He put his head in his hand for a moment, then looked at Chip. "I know you don't want to hear it, but it's okay. It's time."

"But—"

"You've earned it, Chip. You've proven over the last few months that you can do the job."

"I still don't know, Fallon . . ."

"I have a good friend in Charlevoix who seemed to know when it was time to hand over the reins to the next generation."

"Who's that?"

"Todd . . . he handed over his old Raven tavern to his son who turned it into the Blackbird Brewery."

"I've heard of that place."

"I'll have to take you there sometime for a beer." Fallon pushed back the tears. "It's been great working with you."

"We're not done yet," Chip said as he pointed to a blue Escape parking in front of them.

Fallon opened his door and followed Chip as he approached the vehicle. The driver's side window opened and a woman wearing sunglasses turned to look at them.

"Hey, Chip," she said.

"Hi, Victoria," Chip responded.

Fallon noticed he was blushing.

"Who's your friend?" Victoria asked.

"Fallon McElliot."

"No kidding . . . the guy who stopped that drone attack last summer."

"That's me. Nice to meet you."

"Did you get the documents?" Chip asked, stepping next to the door.

Victoria handed over a large manila envelope. "It's all there. A shipping manifest, purchase orders, and a bill of sale showing Massey bought a supercomputer with specially manufactured Chinese computer chips. We were also able to get some documents showing the money trail to fund the lab in China."

Fallon looked at the envelope, then Victoria. "He had it built in China?"

"That's right," Victoria said.

"Sounds like all we need," Fallon said.

"The frosting on the cake," Victoria said as she tapped the envelope. "Henry Massey signed the delivery receipt himself."

"Of course he did," Chip said. "I owe you, Victoria."

She smiled. "I'll remember that."

They watched her window go up and the car back away.

"You never told me about Victoria," Fallon said.

"It never came up."

"You were blushing."

"Come on . . . let's get this envelope to the governor."

CHAPTER 41

Chip followed Karen up the stairway in the Capitol. He looked back at Fallon gripping the railing with one hand, following behind him with his other hand pressed against his thigh. Late afternoon sun cast long rectangles of light on the stairs. Their footsteps echoed in the now-quiet Capitol.

"We can take the elevator, Fallon," he said.

"I'm okay," Fallon said.

Clutching the large manila envelope, Chip continued to the fourth-floor hearing rooms behind the governor with Fallon a few paces behind them. At the top of the stairs, they followed the governor into a conference room and then a closet.

"Where are you going?" Chip asked as he watched her slide a panel open on the back wall.

"It's time you learned about her secret meeting room," Fallon smiled as he stood in the closet doorway.

"Stick with me," Karen said as she moved through the small opening.

Chip followed Karen into the closet, then through a small door on the back wall. His eyes opened wide when he saw a narrow, curved hallway with a winding stairway lit by a single bulb. "Where are we going?"

The governor stopped a few steps up the stairway and looked at him. "To the top of the dome."

"Are you coming, Fallon?" Chip asked as he started up the stairs, then stopped and looked at Fallon rubbing his leg.

"I think I'll wait here . . . in case anyone comes."

Chip looked down at Fallon.

"It's okay," Fallon smiled.

"Fallon—"

"Go."

Clutching the envelope, Chip squeezed the metal railing and continued to follow the governor up the narrow stairway nestled between the inner and outer wall of the Capitol dome.

"This leads to a secret area at the top of the dome," the governor said as she continued up the stairway.

At the top of the stairs, Chip stepped into a small circular room with a shiny, gold railing separating them from an opening at the top of the dome. "I didn't know this was here," Chip said as he looked up at the stars, just an arms-length away, painted on the top of the Capitol dome. He carefully peered over the railing at the glass floor in the rotunda, six stories below where they stood. "Who else knows about this?"

"Only Fallon and a handful of others. This top part of the dome used to be open to the public until it was closed off in the 1950s for safety reasons. Most people have forgotten about it," Karen said as she looked at the Capitol grounds below through the small windows that circled the room. "Up here, I know no one is listening. What did you want to show me?"

Chip opened the envelope and handed a small cassette tape recorder to the governor. "First, I wanted to show you this."

The governor looked at the recorder in her hand. "I haven't seen one of these in years."

"I slipped this into the conference room in Heritage Hall before Massey arrived, hoping I'd catch something incriminating on tape."

"Why didn't you tell me about this before?"

"I didn't want to get your hopes up. I grabbed the recorder after the Massey rally cleared out this morning." Chip pushed the play button. "It's cued to an interesting part."

CHAPTER 41

"I signed an agreement with one of the best labs in China a few years ago and boy did they deliver."

"You know there's a ban on using Chinese technology in this country. There are national security concerns."

"Of course, I do. If the Feds are stupid enough to block access to some of the most advanced computing power available, that's their problem.

"If the Feds find out—"

"The Feds have no idea that I have Chinese technology at my estate, nor do they know I have a supercomputer with capabilities that far exceed what they could ever imagine. The federal government is such a barrier to innovation."

Chip hit the stop button on the recorder. "He confessed."

Karen smiled. "Massey has no idea you recorded it because it's not digital."

"Exactly."

"But is it enough evidence? Massey only admits to violating the ban. We don't have anything that proves he took delivery of the Chinese technology."

"I also received these documents by courier this afternoon," Chip said as he pulled out a dozen pieces of paper from a folder. "A contact of mine drove them here from Detroit. I didn't want to risk digital communication."

"What am I looking at?" the governor asked as she handed the tape recorder back to Chip and examined the papers.

"A shipping manifest, purchase orders, and a bill of sale showing Massey bought a supercomputer with specially manufactured Chinese computer chips. Plus a portion of the money trail showing he funded a lab in China."

"But none of this connects the Chinese technology to the address of his Colorado estate. The FBI would need that for the search warrant."

Chip pointed to the last couple pages in the stack of paper. "These show the supercomputer was shipped from the lab in China to his Colorado estate. Check out who signed the shipping receipt for the supercomputer at his estate."

"Henry Massey himself," Karen said with a grin.

"I'm sure he wanted to be there in person to see it."

"Do I want to know how you obtained these documents?"

"I know a few people in the tech business who have operations in China and are well connected. As I suspected, they already had a lot of these documents and were waiting for the right opportunity—"

"Don't tell me any more about who you talked to." The governor held up her hand. "Why would Massey be so sloppy? This seems too easy."

"My source tells me the contractor who assembled the supercomputer managed Massey's research lab in China. The company wanted documentation to show the Chinese government that Massey is an ally and willing to invest in China to give them the upper hand in technology. That's how Massey was able to continue to operate his Quick Connect platform in China when other social media companies were forced to pull out. I'm guessing it's a lucrative arrangement for both."

"Why did he go to China to build his supercomputer? Why not someone in the US?"

"I'm sure it was the best way for him to keep it secret. He partnered with a Chinese tech company to help manage the research lab. I'm digging into it, but I suspect Massey has a stake in that company."

"This all sounds suspicious. Why would they readily give up Massey like this?"

"My source tells me the company is tired of Massey's arrogance and his rude treatment. They liked his money, but they're fed up with him bossing them around. Now that they have the supercomputer technology, they don't have to put up with him anymore. I get the impression they want to see him taken down as much as we do."

Karen stared at the documents. "Once we fax these to the FBI, they should be able to get a search warrant for Massey's estate."

"Even if the supercomputer has no evidence of his real intentions with Archipelago, what we have here is enough to start an investigation into his company and Arpa. I'm sure there's a lot of dirt hidden inside his empire."

"If they can find the money trail linking him to the Chinese company

CHAPTER 41

that built the supercomputer, and any other money ties to the Chinese government, that alone is enough to take him out," Karen smiled.

Chip looked at the documents, then Karen. "Let's get these to the FBI."

"Not yet," Karen said as she looked at her watch. "I don't want to stir any suspicion. I have a bill-signing in an hour in the ceremonial room. The old fax machine tied to copper lines is in a closet in that room. We can send it after the ceremony."

* * *

Chip stood with Fallon in the governor's ceremonial office in the Capitol as Governor Bauer posed with a group of people in front of an ornate wood desk with intricate carvings of robins, pine trees, and trout. He looked at the excited faces of the half-dozen men and women standing with her as she held the signed legislative bill. Others in the room took pictures with their phones as they stood wearing smiles. A moment later a Capitol police officer escorted the large group out of the room. He closed the door behind them, then looked at the governor.

"If you could wait outside for a minute," the governor said to the officer.

He nodded and stepped outside.

"If you have a minute, Governor, we can test the emergency communication system," Chip said as he opened the closet door.

"When was the last time you sent a fax?" Fallon asked as he looked at the governor.

"I don't remember . . ." she said. "I kind of miss that era before emails."

"Here we go." Chip slipped a single piece of paper with the word *Copper* into the fax machine and keyed in the phone number Daniel gave him.

"What's that?" the governor asked.

"A test page," Chip said as he observed the paper being pulled into the fax machine. He watched a light scan the page as it was pulled into the front of the machine and ejected out the back side.

"Now what?" Fallon asked.

"We wait for a reply."

Chip tensed. What if no reply came? How else would they be able to contact the FBI and who could they trust to tell them what they found? They certainly couldn't trust any digital network.

The fax machine remained silent as the ticking sound of the old regulator clock on the wall filled the room. Chip took a deep breath and exhaled as he looked at the nervous glance from the governor.

"Fax machines are slow," Fallon said. "Remember?"

Chip shook his head. "No."

Karen smiled.

Suddenly the fax machine beeped. The thermal printer started to buzz, and a paper emerged from the lower portion of the machine. When it finished printing, Chip tore off the page, looked at the name printed there—Fred B Innis—and grinned.

"That confirms it was received," Chip said as he excitedly waved the page.

The governor nodded, pointing to the folder in Chip's hand. "Let's try several pages for another test," she said with a wink.

He bit his lip and stepped to the fax machine again. He opened the folder and looked at the documents. He glanced back at the governor and Fallon.

She nodded.

The buzzing of the fax machine filled the room. Chip stood in front of the fax machine, with Fallon and the governor on either side of him, as he watched each page scan through the fax machine. He stared at the pages piling up in an uneven stack, feeling the heaviness of each sheet. He imagined the FBI agents on the other end viewing each page with growing excitement.

When the fax machine finished sending the documents, Chip returned the pages to the folder in his hand. They all stood a moment, waiting for what seemed like hours for another confirmation. Suddenly the fax machine beeped and started to buzz as another sheet emerged.

Chip chuckled as he held up the page with a large smiley face scrawled on it. "Another confirmation," he said as he slipped the page into the folder. "I'll hold on to these."

CHAPTER 41

"Good," the governor said as she looked at Fallon. "It was nice to have you here with us tonight."

"There's something I need to tell you, Karen," Fallon said.

Chip looked at Fallon, resisting the urge to stop him.

"Let's talk later." Karen put her hand on Fallon's shoulder. "It's been a long day. I need to get some rest."

CHAPTER 42

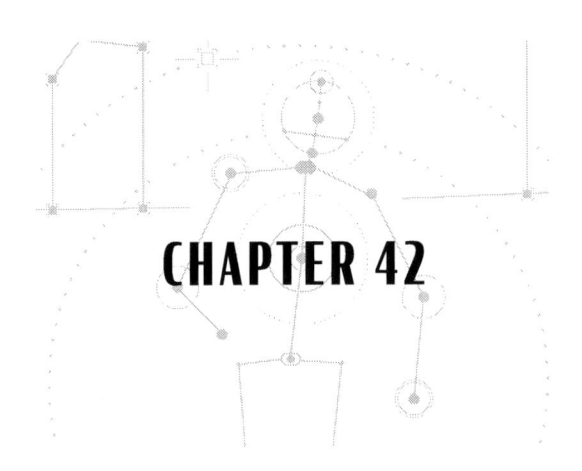

Daniel looked up at the clear, blue sky, feeling the warmth of the early evening sun. He pressed through the packed crowd as Massey bellowed on with his canned speech, standing on a platform on the green space in Clinch Park in Traverse City. The same speech, over and over. By now he could almost recite it word for word. He looked at the surroundings. It was such a picturesque setting except that the giant campaign banner behind the platform blocked the view of the West Arm of Grand Traverse Bay. As Daniel made his way around the side of the platform, a man bumped into him.

"Sorry," the man said as he slipped a piece of paper into his hand.

Their eyes met for a second.

"No problem," Daniel replied, glancing at the note.

The man disappeared almost as quickly as he had appeared.

Daniel stepped behind the large banner, opened the folded piece of paper and read the note:

Bug spray, $8, tomorrow only.

Daniel chuckled as he translated the code in his head: "Raid at 0800 tomorrow." Chip must have found the necessary evidence to convince a

CHAPTER 42

judge to grant a search warrant of Massey's estate. His body relaxed as he took a deep breath and exhaled. Tomorrow he would be free of this undercover nightmare.

Loud applause erupted as Massey finished his speech and descended the stairs. Daniel watched him take a few minutes to shake hands with his admirers before he joined Daniel behind the platform.

"Another rally done." Massey grinned. "This bus tour has been great—such large crowds turning out." He pointed to the paper in Daniel's hand. "What's that?"

"Oh, I just found this on the ground here."

"Is it a death threat?"

"Only if you're a bug," Daniel handed him the paper.

"Bug spray, eight dollars, tomorrow only. Someone must have a really big pest problem," Massey chuckled.

Daniel pocketed the note as he laughed along.

"Ride with me to the airport, Daniel. I want you with me at my estate in Colorado."

"The plan was to have me go on to the next campaign stop with the advance team to prepare security," Daniel said, surprised by the sudden change in plans.

"I want you at the fundraiser tomorrow night at my home. A lot of big-name political donors will be there. They smell victory and want to buy some influence with me."

"Why do you need me in Colorado?"

Massey put his hand on Daniel's shoulder. "You're my most trusted advisor. I want you to study the faces of the people there and tip me off if someone looks suspicious. I want to know if they're there to spy on me or betray me."

"What makes you think I'm such a good judge of people?"

"You were always good at the meetings you handled for me when you were with Peninsular. I'm also sure you were very good at it when you interrogated suspects for the FBI."

"I don't know . . ."

"Remember when we toured our campaign headquarters in Detroit, and you spotted that campaign worker you thought looked nervous?"

"Oh, that."

"She turned out to be someone who tried to infiltrate our campaign. After we monitored her, we discovered she was sending information to the governor's campaign." Massey squeezed Daniel's shoulder. "You're the only one who suspected her just by looking at her."

Daniel nodded, laughing inside. Massey had no idea the woman was an FBI plant for him to point out to prove his skill.

"Grab your bag, Daniel. We have a plane to catch."

Daniel grabbed his duffel bag from the campaign car parked behind the stage. He passed workers tearing down the platform and banners as he joined Massey inside his GMC SUV.

"Where's your Mercedes?" Daniel asked as he sat next to Henry in the back seat and buckled his seat belt.

"It would be bad optics, and this is a Michigan-made vehicle," Massey pulled out his phone. "Excuse me, I need to return some calls."

As the driver pulled away from Clinch Park, Daniel sat in silence watching the traffic and buildings pass by. He tried to contain his excitement that he would be there tomorrow when the FBI showed up to serve the search warrant.

Once they boarded Massey's private jet and were airborne, Massey set his phone down on the shelf next to his seat and looked at Daniel sitting across from him.

"What's on your mind?"

"I appreciate you giving Cally a job at your campaign headquarters."

Massey sat back with a smile. "It was the least I could do. Besides, I've been able to promote how we're helping ex-cons get back into the work world. Plus, the state pays a portion of his salary."

Daniel looked out the window at the landscape below, disgusted by Massey's self-serving attitude.

"What else is on your mind, Daniel?"

"I've been wondering. What happens to me after you win the governorship?"

"I like your confidence."

"You *are* ten points ahead in the polls."

CHAPTER 42

"True." Massey folded his arms across his puffed-up chest. "When I win the primary, I'll have to select a lieutenant governor."

Daniel raised an eyebrow. "I would not make a good running mate. Besides, I've disappeared under suspicious circumstances. Most people don't know where I've been since last August."

"The public doesn't care. We'll just tell them you've been managing global security for me. I also think your military and FBI record would make you a great candidate."

"I'm not so sure I would stand up to media scrutiny."

"You forget that I own one of the biggest media platforms in the world."

"What happens if your plot is uncovered?"

Massey frowned; arms still folded across his chest. "You recall what I told Fallon back on Beaver Island before the drone attack on the *Emerald Isle*?"

"Basically, that you can use force if necessary."

"You know the alleged terrorist drone attack on the *Emerald Isle* was a test of my capabilities to launch a strike."

"Alleged? It actually happened."

"Everyone *thinks* the *Emerald Isle* was the target, but actually Fallon was the intended target all along."

"You planned to kill Fallon?"

"He was becoming a nuisance. I told him about my whole plan at the cabin on Beaver Island last August, knowing he would try to stop the drone from hitting the *Emerald Isle*."

Daniel stared at Massey in disbelief.

"I planted a homing device in the boat Fallon used." Massey spread his hands wide. "In business, you kill off your competition by outsmarting, buying, or burying them. Sometimes you have to eliminate your enemies to stop them."

"You mean kill them."

"You fought in war. I'm sure you had to kill to defend your country."

Daniel fought to keep his anger in check. He nodded as if to agree.

"You were defending a set of ideals. It's no different than what I will do if necessary."

Daniel glanced out the window at the clouds below, trying to calm his rage.

"You're a man of high moral character, Daniel," Massey said. "Yet last year when it came to saving your family, you did what was necessary to stop the crime ring from finishing them off. You were willing to compromise your morals."

"I did what I had to do," Daniel reluctantly agreed.

"I was testing you back at the cabin last August," Massey said, his eyes locked on Daniel. "When I said the drone was targeting the *Emerald Isle*, I was testing your loyalty to me and my plans. You did nothing to stop that drone and at that moment I knew you could be one of my most trusted advisors."

Daniel cleared his throat. "I knew at the time it was a test of whether I could leave my old life behind and join you. You proved to me that you could help me get the truth out about Cally being framed by the crime ring."

"I'd say we've become good friends, Daniel. Better yet, you're like a brother to me. From the moment I first met you in Geneva at your first meeting running security for Arpa, I knew you were the right man for the job. After all, Peninsular only hires the highest caliber, ex-military personnel."

Daniel grinned to hide his annoyance. He recalled the moment it all began when his air force commander called him into his office for a special assignment. *"You are one of the select few who have been chosen for the Peninsular assignment,"* his commander had told him. He felt privileged at the time, but now he was weary from the grueling months of pretending to be someone he was not.

"Now, if you'll excuse me," Massey said as he picked up his cell phone. "I have a long list of calls to return. I want to make sure everything is set for tomorrow's fundraiser. There will be a lot of people to feed so I want to make sure everything is in order."

Daniel turned his attention to his window and watched the colorful grid of passing farm fields far below them. After tomorrow morning he wouldn't have to put up with this arrogant man any longer. He just had to endure one more night at the Massey estate in Colorado.

CHAPTER 43

Ferguson sat on the edge of the bed and stared at the fake Food Queen ID in his hand. The moment of truth. After weeks of laying low, it was time to carry out Sophia's outrageous plan. It was all on him. Could he trust Nigel that everything would go as planned? He stared at his picture on the ID. What if someone recognized him? This felt so different than any army mission he had been on. *His* freedom was at stake. If anything went wrong, he would be locked up the rest of his life. No, he would not let that happen.

His hand shook as he grabbed the paper on his bed showing the layout of the Food Queen warehouse and reviewed the plan, tracing each step with his finger:

1. Use the ID to access the main entrance of the Food Queen warehouse.
2. Go to the main office and grab computer tablet 47 off the wall mount.
3. Make sure the delivery instructions for the Massey estate are on the tablet, including the number of the semi-truck you will use.
4. Pick up the truck keys from the fleet management desk.

5. Drive the truck to the Massey estate and unload all the food.
6. Once Massey's staff leaves with the food delivery, wait for Sophia's accomplice in the Massey estate to arrive on the loading dock to deactivate the bunker security system.
7. Follow the instructions to load the supercomputer into the semi-trailer.

Every step was detailed . . . but no plan survives once the shooting starts. He heard it often in the army.

He took a deep breath as he flipped over the Food Queen warehouse diagram and studied the photos of the supercomputer access doors and the forklift he would use to load the computer inside the truck trailer. The process for disconnecting the supercomputer from its power source and network cables looked complicated. He took a deep breath.

"Daily data updates finish an hour before your arrival," Nigel had assured him. "The computer runs a self-diagnosis to ensure it can operate independently before it automatically disconnects from the satellite network."

The last thing he wanted to do was short out something by yanking a plug too quickly. If he ruined the computer, the whole point of the mission would be lost.

Setting the papers on the bed, he lay on his back and stared at the yellowed, popcorn ceiling. Nigel could've at least put him up for the night in a nice hotel. Sophia certainly could afford it. When he questioned Nigel about his accommodations, he insisted that fewer questions are asked at a cheap motel. It seemed they had thought of everything.

As he lay on his bed, he thought about the moment he decided to help the crime ring when he was a Detroit Police officer. At the time it seemed like a simple way to get a little more money to make ends meet. He was never paid enough as a police officer for what he had to put up with on the street. All he had to do was turn his back on some minor crimes and receive some money. How had things gotten so out of hand that he ended up on North Fox Island wanting to kill Fallon? Prison seemed a remote possibility at that time.

He and Fallon used to be good friends, but his involvement with the

CHAPTER 43

crime ring ruined that. If only he had said no to the crime ring and joined the state police with Fallon. If only he had left temptation behind. If only he had just been content with his middle-class lifestyle, with having meatloaf, mashed potatoes, and green beans. If only . . .

He laughed at the way he was interrogating himself like a suspect. A memory emerged from deep inside his brain:

> *His mom looks down at him with a stern face, pointing her finger at him, rattling off some Bible verse . . . "Be content in all circumstances." He turns his head away and tunes her out. What does she know? He is a junior in high school, and he can think for himself. He doesn't need her lecturing him about poor choices and consequences. What does she know about playing on the edge of right and wrong? He is old enough to make his own decisions. He looks up at her angry face as she mouths words at him that he doesn't hear. Resentment is all he feels toward her.*

He took a deep breath and recalled how he resented Fallon preaching at him about right and wrong. Everyone seemed to know better than he did.

Ferguson sat up on the edge of the bed and shook his head. In a huff, he went to the mini fridge, grabbed a beer, and took a big swallow. At least Nigel had bought him a couple cans of quality craft beer. He chuckled at how Nigel had sternly warned him not to get drunk. "Yes, Mom," he'd responded with a condescending tone.

Propping himself against the headboard of the bed, he settled himself on the lumpy mattress, grabbed the television remote, and turned on CNN.

"*It's astounding what is going on in the Michigan governor's primary race,*" the newscaster remarked while a clip of Massey standing at a podium played in one corner of the screen.

Ferguson almost spilled his beer as he heard the crack of gunfire and watched Massey fall to the floor of the stage. He'd been isolated all this time and had not seen the video clip.

"After surviving an assassination attempt a few days ago," the newscaster continued, "Henry Massey has fearlessly continued his campaign to deny the current governor, Karen Bauer, a second term."

Ferguson felt disappointment at hearing Massey survived the assassination.

"Governor Bauer is facing some serious headwinds since the attempted terrorist attack last August on a ferry in Lake Michigan," a political analyst added.

Ferguson about choked on his beer when he saw a picture of himself on the screen.

"Then the alleged mastermind behind the terror attack, Thomas Ferguson, escaped from a federal prison in Northern Michigan just before he was to appear before a grand jury," the analyst continued. "That reflected poorly on Governor Bauer."

Swearing at the screen, Ferguson felt even more motivated to steal Massey's supercomputer and send that jerk to prison for framing him.

"But, Bob, that was a federal prison," the newscaster said.

"It still is a negative for the governor because it happened in her state. She's now trailing Massey in the latest polls by almost ten points, and we are only a few weeks away from voting day in the primary election in early August."

He took another swallow of beer and cursed the picture of Massey on the screen, determined to make him pay for what he did to him.

CHAPTER 44

The tense look on the governor's face was the first thing Chip noticed when he entered her office. He closed the door and approached her desk.

"Thanks for coming over," she calmly said as she slid a piece of fax paper to the front of her desk. "I wanted to talk with you about prison reform legislation. The Colorado prison system has one of the lowest recidivism rates in the country."

Chip looked at the paper, then her solemn face. He eased himself into a chair in front of the governor's desk, picked up the paper on the governor's desk, and read the sentence printed there:

> Executing 0800 tomorrow. Accompaniment
> welcomed. Boulder Airport tonight.

He looked at her then the paper. The FBI must have gotten the search warrant, and they would be executing it tomorrow morning at 0800 hours. He smiled when he read "Accompaniment welcomed."

He peered over the edge of the paper in front of him. "What are you thinking?"

"I want you to go to Colorado and interview their director of corrections—talk to the people who manage their release programs. Get some ideas on how we might reform our system." She cleared her throat as she looked at the paper in Chip's hand, then him.

"I can do that," he said.

The governor folded her hands with her elbows resting on the armrests. "The director of Colorado corrections will pick you up this evening at the Northern Colorado Regional Airport. My jet will be ready to take you in about an hour."

"Okay," Chip slid the paper back across the desk to the governor. "You're not joining me?"

"I wish I could be there, but my schedule doesn't permit it." She leaned forward, adding emphasis with her solemn face. "Please keep this between us, I don't want the Massey campaign to get wind of this."

"Understood," Chip replied with a somber tone. "I'll give you a call tomorrow to give you an update." As they stood together, the expression on the governor's face concerned him. "You okay, Governor?"

"I'll just be glad when this campaign is over."

"Me too," Chip agreed. "Do you want Fallon to come with me?"

They stood a moment in silence.

"Better do this one on your own," the governor said.

He nodded and exited the room.

* * *

An hour later, Chip arrived with a small carry-on bag at the State of Michigan hangar where a small jet was parked, door open and staircase extended.

"Just you today?" the pilot asked as he greeted Chip.

"Just me," he responded as he boarded the jet and sat in a seat in the middle of the aircraft.

The jet taxied, and they were airborne a few minutes later.

The hum of the jet engines filled the cabin as Chip gazed out his window watching the clouds pass by below. His thoughts drifted to Fallon. He always expected Fallon to recover from his injuries and return to work with him. They had been an unbeatable team. He looked at the empty seat

CHAPTER 44

facing him and felt tears welling up inside of him. So many memories. He looked back at the clouds, trying not to think about it, trying to focus on tomorrow. Then he smiled. Once the FBI executed the search warrant, they could finally rid the campaign of Massey. He relished the thought of seeing Massey's face when the FBI showed up at his front door.

* * *

On the ground in Colorado the jet pulled up to a federal hangar and parked just outside. The pilot opened the door and extended the steps. As Chip exited the aircraft he spotted a silver-haired man in a gray suit standing about one hundred yards away.

"You must be Mitch Egan?" The man extended his hand as Chip approached.

"Call me Chip," he said as he shook his hand.

"I'm Evan Bryce, FBI. Glad you're here."

"Thanks for inviting me."

"That was some nice detective work getting those shipping manifests and other documents. I don't know how you did it."

"I've worked in tech for a long time. I have a lot of connections all over the world."

"We may need your expertise to access Massey's supercomputer once we're inside his estate. We've been trying to hack his systems for years. He has the most complex code our tech experts have ever seen. We need someone who thinks out of the box."

Chip nodded. "You have the search warrant?"

"Yes. I'll give you a ride to the hotel where I have you booked for the night. Remember, no contact with anyone until after we execute the search warrant."

"Understood."

"Follow me," Evan said as he climbed in the driver's side of a black SUV.

Chip sat in the passenger side and buckled up, feeling like he had been thrust into the deep end of the pool. He folded his hands together in his lap to stop them from shaking.

"Governor Bauer said she filled you in on everything?" Evan said as he drove to the hotel.

"She told me you've been running this undercover operation for some time."

"It's taken years to get us to this point."

"What tipped you off on Massey's plans?"

"Someone in the Arpa group came to us early last year about Massey talking about using the Archipelago software to seize state government data that he could leverage for nefarious purposes."

"The governor told me you infiltrated Arpa with undercover agents like Daniel Callahan."

Evan flashed a surprised look. "You know about Daniel?"

"Daniel met me in the basement of the State Capitol in Lansing right before Massey's speech. He gave me your fax information."

"I had a hunch that might've been Daniel," Evan chuckled. "Daniel and I have known each other for some time now. Was the Chinese technology thing your idea?"

"If you're into tech like me, you know a lot about who has the latest technology in development. Even the most secret development projects need suppliers and equipment. People talk and word gets out."

"But then you were able to get those documents proving Massey was using Chinese computer chips—that was some pretty good detective work. And that recording was a bonus. That really helped convince the judge to grant the warrant."

"I learned from the best how to capitalize on a hunch."

Evan smiled. "Fallon McElliot. When he and Daniel paired up on a case, they were unstoppable. The Feds and the State always had a hard time working together, but those two could do the impossible." Evan's tone lowered into concern. "How *is* Fallon doing?"

Chip sat silent for a moment watching the passing landscape through his side window.

Evan glanced at him with concern.

"I don't think he'll return to work . . ." Chip glanced at Evan. "Any leads on Ferguson?"

CHAPTER 44

Evan sighed. "Nothing. After weeks of searching, all leads have come up with dead ends. It's like he's vanished into thin air."

"I heard Homeland Security has a theory that a remnant of his terrorist cell freed him."

"Trevor Jackson, the regional director, is chasing that lead, but I haven't heard anything else." Evan glanced at Chip. "He's not sharing much with us."

"Too bad we don't all work together like Daniel and Fallon did," Chip said as he took a deep breath.

"It would save us a lot of resources and grief," Evan said as they exited the freeway.

They stopped in front of the entrance to a small, two-story chain hotel. "The reservation is in your name. I'll pick you up at 0600 hours. Be ready," Evan said as he handed Chip a large, folded document. "Study this tonight. It's a diagram of the Massey estate."

Chip took the document.

"Get some sleep. Tomorrow's a big day."

"You're not staying here?" Chip asked as he grabbed his carry-on suitcase from the back seat.

"I'm going home," Evan said. "I work out of the Denver office."

Chip stood alone at the hotel entrance with his suitcase and watched the SUV disappear into the dark streets. Tomorrow would be a new day.

CHAPTER 45

Chip wrung his hands as he watched the black SUV pull up to the front entrance of his hotel. He climbed into the passenger side, closed the door, and greeted Evan seated behind the steering wheel. He looked so calm as he took a sip of coffee from his travel mug and returned it to the cup holder.

"There's a coffee there for you," Evan said as they pulled away from the hotel.

"Breakfast didn't sound good," Chip said as he picked up the cup and took a sip of the coffee.

"Relax, Chip."

"You've probably conducted hundreds of these raids."

"A few in my day."

He wrapped his other hand around the paper cup and let the warmth of the hot coffee sink into his hands. "I've never been on a raid."

"This isn't a raid. We're only serving a search warrant."

"What if they resist?"

"They won't."

"But what if they do?"

"Don't worry, we have a dozen agents descending on Massey's estate."

CHAPTER 45

"Do the other agents know Daniel is undercover?"

"No. I don't want to blow his cover unless we have to."

Chip eased back in his seat and tried to focus on the snow-capped Rocky Mountains in the distance as they wound their way up the foothills before pulling into a scenic overlook where four unmarked black SUVs were parked. Evan pulled up next to one of the SUVs, checked his watch, then waved at the driver. The driver waved back and pulled out of the parking lot. The other vehicles followed behind in a single file with Evan bringing up the rear.

"How far to the estate?"

Evan slipped on his dark, aviator sunglasses. "Just a few minutes away."

Chip took a deep breath, then several more.

"The air is thinner up here," Evan smiled.

"What if he moved his supercomputer. That's the key to this whole thing. If we don't get that, we'll blow years of your undercover work."

"We'll still have evidence he violated the ban on purchasing Chinese technology. Thanks to you."

"Somehow that doesn't seem enough. We need that supercomputer to prove his full plan."

"It *will* be there," Evan said as the line of cars stopped in front of a thick, steel security gate framed by a stone arch marking the entrance to the Massey estate. He leaned his head out his open window. "Looks like they're having a little argument with the security guard."

Chip took a sip of his coffee and tried to steady the cup in his shaking hand as the minutes passed.

"The guard is telling us we can't enter," Evan's radio blared.

"Tell him we'll arrest him if he doesn't let us through," Evan snapped back as he removed his sunglasses and tossed them on the dash.

A moment later the brake lights went off on the SUV in front of them and they followed the caravan up a long drive. They parked in a line in the circle driveway in front of the main entrance by a massive fountain. Chip climbed out with Evan and spotted Massey standing in the open doorway with a surprised look.

"I wish Fallon could see this," Chip said.

"Me too," Evan said.

Chip trailed two agents and Evan as they walked toward Massey.

"What is this about?" Massey balked, silk pajama pants protruding from his silk bathrobe.

"We have a search warrant for your estate," an FBI agent announced as he held a piece of paper in his extended hand. "Please move aside."

Massey stood firm in the doorway as he read the paper. "This is absurd! I'm calling my attorney. Don't take another step."

"Please stand aside, sir," the agent demanded as he pressed forward.

"Who else is here with you?" Evan asked as the other agents assembled in the foyer.

"My wife, Helen, is upstairs in her office." Massey pointed to Daniel walking toward them. "And my head of security, Daniel Callahan."

"Make sure Mrs. Massey stays in her office," Evan said to an agent, pointing to the stairway. "Anyone else in the house?"

Massey shook his head. "My kids are at college. The only other people here are my staff in the kitchen in the basement preparing for my fundraiser tonight."

Chip stepped next to Evan and tried not to make eye contact when he saw Daniel approaching them.

"What's going on here?" Daniel asked as he stepped next to Massey.

"I'm talking to my attorney now," Massey said with his phone to his ear, waving the search warrant in his other hand. "FBI served me a search warrant."

"For what?" Daniel asked as he took the search warrant from Massey. He glanced up from the paper at Chip and Evan. "Chinese technology?"

"That's what it says," Evan said. "You're in possession of Chinese technology in violation of the federal ban."

Chip watched Daniel review the warrant and hand it back to Evan. "It all looks legit."

Evan and Daniel exchanged a protracted stare.

"We're moving forward," Evan said. "Lead on, Chip."

Chip pulled out the diagram of the estate from his pocket. He glanced at the large, richly appointed living room to his right and the wide, curved stairway going to the upstairs. "Follow me. The supercomputer is this

CHAPTER 45

way," he said as he walked toward a narrow stairway to his left, descending to the lower level.

"Let's split up," Evan shouted, directing the large group of agents now standing in the wood-paneled foyer. "You cover this floor and the upstairs; we're headed to the basement."

Massey stepped in front of Evan, cell phone in his hand. "My attorney says the basement is off-limits. Your search warrant only covers my home. The basement is separate and part of my business."

Daniel stepped next to Massey, handing the warrant back to Evan. "You heard him. It's off-limits."

Evan calmly pointed to a section on the warrant in his hand. "If you read the language on the search warrant, it says 'the Massey estate' with a legal description of the entire property."

"My estate is my home!" Massey persisted as he grabbed Evan's arm. "You have no right to be here."

Evan forcibly removed Massey's hand from his arm and locked eyes with him. "Out of my way or I'll have you arrested for assaulting an agent."

Massey's face contorted in anger. "You wouldn't dare."

"Try me," Evan said as he pocketed the warrant and pulled out handcuffs.

Daniel stepped in front of Evan with his back to Massey. "Better do as he says."

Standing behind Evan, Chip caught Daniel glance at him and wink. It was a joy to see the panicked look on Massey's face. He had something to hide. He knew he was in trouble.

Massey tried to push Daniel away. "You go in that basement and every one of you will face criminal trespass charges."

Daniel stopped him from grabbing Evan.

"I'll see you in court." Evan pushed Massey aside.

"This way," Chip said, as he stepped forward with the diagram in his hand. Another agent joined them as they descended a stairway to the basement, shoes clanking on the metal stairs.

"Here." Chip motioned as he walked through the expansive commercial kitchen filled with surprised cooks prepping food. He stopped a moment, looked at the diagram, and spotted a heavy metal door in the far corner of the kitchen. "There's the door to the basement."

They walked to the door and Evan jiggled the door handle. "Locked."

"Biometric access," Chip said as he looked at the screen next to the door.

"Get Massey!" Evan told the agent accompanying them.

Chip looked at the diagram of the estate in his hand, then Evan. "The computer is below this level."

Evan took a deep breath. "I still get nervous when we get to this point."

Two agents returned with Massey, Daniel following close behind him. Hands on his hips, Evan glared at Daniel. "Unlock this door."

"Don't do it," Massey protested.

Daniel walked to the door and placed his hand on the screen next to the door. "They have a warrant."

The door latch clicked, and an agent opened the door.

Massey glared at Daniel. "Why did you—"

"In my experience, it's better to cooperate," Daniel replied.

"Keep Massey here," Evan said to an agent behind him, then turned to Daniel. "You're coming with us."

Chip's eyes met Daniel's for a second, then he turned and followed Evan and Daniel down the stairs into the basement, past pipes and I-beams to another door. Daniel placed his hand on another scanner. The door unlocked and they proceeded to the loading dock area. He stood a moment scanning the three empty truck bays. The large overhead doors in each bay were open, letting a breeze blow in. On the far end of the loading area, a heavy-duty forklift caught his attention. Then he noticed a massive blast door on the far wall.

"The supercomputer is this way," Chip said as he looked at the diagram, then walked to the blast door. "Looks like an analog locking mechanism that's separate from the security system."

"Open it," Evan said to Daniel.

"I can't," Daniel said.

"Get Massey down here to open this door," Evan said to the agent standing next to him.

CHAPTER 45

A moment later, two FBI agents brought Massey into the loading dock area next to the blast door.

"How does this open?" Evan snapped.

Massey shrugged his shoulders.

Evan grabbed Daniel and looked him square in the eye. "Open it!"

"I don't know how," Daniel replied.

"I know," an agent said as he stepped next to Evan. "I helped decommission this site when I was with the army."

They watched the agent manipulate switches and levers until the door opened with a loud, metallic thud.

Chip followed Evan as he walked into the room. Motion sensors turned the lights on, revealing a sterile room with white-paneled walls. He noted a gray metal desk against the far wall with a keyboard and two large screens sitting on top of it. A large office chair with a tall backrest was pushed against the desk, blocking part of the screens.

"What the . . ." Evan paused as he stared at the empty room.

"It's supposed to be here," Chip said, feeling his stomach tighten. He looked at the diagram in his hand. "The supercomputer is supposed to be here."

Suddenly a loud buzzing noise filled the room with flashing, bright strobe lights flashing in all directions.

Evan looked at an agent stepping into the room. "Get Massey in here and tell him to shut down this alarm system."

Chip squinted against the bright strobe lights as he walked to the middle of the room. He bent down and examined the dark lines on the floor that formed a large rectangle about the size of a shipping container. He traced the train tracks that ran from the spot to the open blast door. The tracks had fresh scrape marks that indicated something heavy recently rolled on them. Then he looked up and noticed large cords dangling from the ceiling.

"The power cord is still warm," Chip shouted as he held the largest cable and waved the end at Evan. "The supercomputer was moved not too long ago."

An agent entered the room with Massey.

Evan looked at him. "Shut that alarm off!"

Massey winced and put his hand on a biometric scanner. The room immediately went quiet, and the strobe lights stopped flashing.

Evan glared at Massey. "How did you know we were coming?"

"I didn't," Massey replied with a panicked look on his face, his eyes frantically darting around the room.

"Don't give me that!" Evan grabbed Massey by the shoulders and shook him. "Where is it?"

"I don't know!" Massey replied with a monotone voice, face frozen in shock as he continued to survey the room.

CHAPTER 46

Daniel stepped into the empty supercomputer room and looked at the cords dangling from the ceiling. He felt a pit in his stomach as he scanned the empty room. All this time undercover and nothing to show for it. Massey must have known about the search warrant. Someone warned him. He looked at Evan.

Evan winked at him before he shoved him against the wall. Their eyes locked for a moment. "Who tipped you off?"

"Evan!" Another agent shouted as he pulled Evan back from Daniel. "Calm down."

"You have no grounds to be here," Massey said, "Your whole warrant is based on Chinese technology being here, and as you can see, there is nothing here."

Evan stepped in front of Massey. Their eyes met. "We have evidence your supercomputer was delivered here. We're going to tear apart your entire estate until we find it—or you can tell us right now where it is."

"I don't know!" Massey said, as he leaned in toward Evan with wide eyes.

Daniel studied Massey's response. He looked genuinely surprised . . . or was it all an act? In all his time undercover, he had never seen him look so panicked. His usual swagger and self-confidence were gone. But how could someone steal his supercomputer right from under their noses without them knowing it?

Evan looked at two agents standing by the doorway and pointed to Daniel and Massey. "Lock them up in the SUV!"

"My lawyers will see to it you never work for the FBI again!" Massey shouted back as an agent escorted him out of the room.

Another agent guided Daniel through the open blast door.

"Wait!" Evan shouted. "Hold Callahan here for a minute."

Daniel saw Massey look back at him as the agent guided him up the stairs and through a door at the top of the stairs.

"You honestly don't know where the supercomputer is?" Evan whispered.

"I was just as surprised as you."

"Security cameras," Evan said. "Show me what you have recorded from the loading dock this morning."

"Follow me," Daniel said as he guided Evan, Chip, and another agent down a hallway from the loading dock. At the end of the hallway, they entered a room with a dozen large screens showing images of the entire estate.

Daniel sat down and tapped some keys on a computer keyboard. "The software automatically monitors the estate and sends an alert if anything out of the ordinary is identified. I received no alerts this morning."

He called up video footage from outside the loading dock earlier in the morning. He played it in fast-forward until a semi came into view backing a trailer into the loading dock area.

"This is routine," Daniel said as they watched the video. "The surveillance software knows what a scheduled delivery is."

"Wait. Back up." Evan pointed. "What does that say on the side of the truck?"

"Food Queen," Daniel said as he rewound the video of the truck backing into the loading dock and played it again. "Early this morning, the kitchen took delivery of a load of food for Massey's gubernatorial fundraiser tonight."

"A semi load of food?" Evan tapped his chin. "That's not believable."

CHAPTER 46

"Believe it," Daniel said as he stopped the video showing the truck leaving. "A few hundred people will be here tonight."

"Based on the imprint on the floor in the bunker . . ." Chip stepped closer to the screen. "That supercomputer would fit inside a semi-trailer."

Daniel looked at the frozen image of the departing semi on the screen. He noticed the tires on the trailer had a slight bulge at the bottom. "That trailer looks like it's loaded with something very heavy even though it just unloaded a truckload of food."

Chip squinted as he studied the image on the screen. "I have a hunch that supercomputer left here in that trailer."

Daniel pointed at the screen. "You can see a plate number on the trailer."

"That's as good of a lead as any." Evan tapped on his phone and put it to his ear. "Scour the state for a Food Queen semi-truck with license plate BYE-MSY."

"Is there a security camera showing the front of the truck?" Chip asked.

Daniel typed on the keyboard to a view showing the approach road to the loading dock. He rewound the video to earlier in the day until it showed the front view of the semi backing into the loading dock area.

"Wait!" Chip said as he put his fingertips on the screen and zoomed in. "Take a look at the driver."

Daniel gasped. "Is that who I think it is?"

"That's impossible," Chip said.

"Is that Ferguson?" Daniel heard Evan remark from behind him.

Chip held up his cell phone with an image of Ferguson to the enlarged image of the driver on the screen. "That's him."

"Looks like we have a hot lead on that terrorist Thomas Ferguson," Evan said into his phone. "He may be driving a Food Queen truck with plate number BYE-MSY on the trailer. He's likely armed and dangerous, apprehend with caution!"

"When was that video taken?" Chip asked.

Daniel looked at the time marker on the lower right of the screen. "Almost two hours ago."

"Wait a minute," Chip said as he zoomed out on the image with his fingers on the touch screen. "It looks like someone is waiting for him on the loading dock. Can you enhance the image?"

Daniel tapped on the keyboard. "It's too grainy to tell, plus they're standing in a shaded part of the dock."

Chip rubbed his chin. "That person may have helped Ferguson access and load the supercomputer. Do you have video from inside the loading dock?"

Daniel typed on the keyboard. "Oh, great," Daniel said as he stopped the video at the same time the truck backed into the loading dock. "Nothing but static."

"Looks like someone disabled the cameras."

Daniel switched to the view of the truck cab. "How did Ferguson get way out here?" He turned to look at Evan.

"I'm putting you in the SUV with Massey," Evan said. "We need answers."

"Do you know any more about who helped Ferguson escape?" Daniel asked as Evan cuffed his hands behind his back.

"No," Evan said. "We did locate the names of the two agents and the pilot who commandeered the helicopter in our employee database. They were assigned to transport Ferguson. We're still not sure who they are. There's no further record of them—no home address, no passports, no work history—nothing."

Daniel chuckled.

"What?" Evan asked.

"Massey, or anyone with knowledge of Archipelago's computer code, can change at will any document stored in its software," Daniel said. "Did you consider the records on those FBI agents were fabricated?"

Evan frowned. "We don't use his Archipelago software."

"Massey told me last year he sold an HR module to the Feds to manage personnel files," Daniel said. "It was on a trial basis so the Office of Management and Budget could evaluate whether they wanted to start using Archipelago."

CHAPTER 47

Ferguson tensed as he slowed the semi-truck and stopped at the entrance to the rail yard. He checked the mirrors on the truck. No one had followed him. It just all seemed too easy disconnecting the supercomputer in the computer room, rolling it on tracks that led to the loading dock, using the forklift to load the supercomputer inside the Food Queen semi-trailer, and driving off the Massey estate seemingly undetected. He still wondered about that DEFCON 2 flashing on the screen inside the computer room, but Sophia's inside person who met him on the loading dock told him not to worry about it.

Air brakes whooshed, bringing the truck and trailer to a jerky halt, lurching Ferguson's body forward in his seat as he slipped the transmission into Park. He leaned back in his seat, exhaling to relieve some of the tension he felt. As he put the driver's side window down, he grabbed the access card from the packet Nigel gave him and slipped the card into the reader. He nervously scanned the rail yard, studying the dozen or so Food Queen trucks moving trailers into position for loading onto flatbed railcars lined up on a rail spur. He expected federal agents to suddenly appear, guns drawn, screaming at him to turn off the truck's engine and put his hands in the air.

His hand shook as he pulled the card out of the reader and waited for the gate to open. He noted cameras mounted on a pole a few feet ahead pointed at the front of the truck—likely scanning him, the license plate, and whatever intel they could glean. Seconds seemed like hours as he slipped the card back into the packet. The idling diesel engine and the whirring motor closing his window were the only sounds in the cab as he waited for the gate to open. He tilted his head left and right to relieve the tightness in his neck.

Suddenly something beeped, drawing Ferguson's attention to the opening gate in front of him. He exhaled with relief as he slipped the transmission into Drive and maneuvered the semi-truck to the designated bay next to the railcars. As he backed the trailer into position, he continued to keep an eye on his surroundings. Were federal agents waiting for him to exit the truck before they made their move? The truck's air brakes screeched as he stopped. He shut off the engine and spotted a man in the driver's side mirror approaching from the back of the trailer. He opened his door and watched a tall man wearing a leather jacket, low-brimmed hat, and sunglasses step next to the cab.

"Sophia wanted me to congratulate you on a job well done," the man said.

Ferguson climbed down from the cab and stood in front of the man. "Who are you?"

The man removed his sunglasses.

"Nigel," Ferguson said, muscles relaxing. "Everything worked just as you planned."

Nigel put his hands on his hips. "You doubted me?"

"I couldn't have done it without Sophia's inside person who met me at the Massey estate on the loading dock and disabled all the security systems in the bunker," Ferguson said as he glanced at a crane arm swinging into position over the trailer. Several rail yard workers approached the truck.

They stepped away and watched the workers disconnect the trailer and prepare it to be moved to the railcar.

"Who met me at the loading dock?" Ferguson asked.

Nigel grinned. "I can't tell you."

They watched the crane load the Food Queen trailer onto a railcar.

CHAPTER 47

"What now?" Ferguson asked.

Nigel smiled. "There's a jet waiting for you at the airport."

"How do I know you won't turn me in now?"

"Sophia keeps her promises. Just be glad you're on her good side."

A loud *thud* of metal hitting metal echoed in the rail yard. Ferguson turned to see the semi-trailer now sitting on the railcar.

Nigel started walking toward a nearby parking lot. "Time to go."

Ferguson hesitated for a second, then followed Nigel to a rusty old pickup. He settled into the worn vinyl passenger seat, closed the door, and rested his arm on the open window. They exited the rail yard and drove to the nearest state highway.

Nigel's eyes were fixed on the road ahead. Only road noise and the hum of the engine broke the silence. Ferguson looked back through the rear window at the snow-capped Rocky Mountains in the distance. "Under different circumstances, it would be nice to spend a few weeks here hiking and camping."

"You'll have to settle for a Mediterranean island instead," Nigel said.

"Are you joining me?"

Nigel glanced at Ferguson. "No, but save a room in that beachside house for me in case I need it in the future."

"Beachside sounds really nice."

"I've been there. It's real nice."

"Where exactly is this island?"

"Not my place to tell you."

Ferguson smiled, looked at the road ahead, and watched the pavement passing in front of them. "Thanks for everything, Nigel."

Nigel remained focused on the road.

He closed his eyes and soaked in the wind blowing across his face from the open windows. It smelled so fresh. Suddenly he felt alive; his worries seemed to disappear. Could he accept there were no longer bars separating him from living free? Now what would he do with his life? He opened his eyes, looked at the passing scenery, then back at the Rocky Mountains. This would likely be his last time in the United States.

He glanced at Nigel, hands firmly planted on top of the steering wheel. "What's next for you?"

"I'm not sure until the next job comes."

Ferguson nodded and turned his attention to the passing scenery until they pulled up to a waiting jet at the airport. He climbed out and watched Nigel walk around the front of the truck. They stood a moment facing each other, then shook hands.

"Have a nice flight," Nigel said.

"I will," Ferguson replied. "Is Sophia coming with me?"

"She's on the jet."

Ferguson waved at Nigel, then boarded the jet. He smiled when he saw Sophia sitting in a leather seat in the middle of the aircraft.

"Welcome aboard," Sophia said, pointing to the seat opposite her.

"It's good to be here," Ferguson said as he settled into the soft, leather seat.

The door closed and the jet began to taxi.

Out his window, Ferguson spotted Nigel standing by the truck, arms folded in front of him.

"You'll want to see this," Sophia said as she handed him her cell phone.

Ferguson looked at an aerial shot of a CNN broadcast showing a swarm of FBI agents and vehicles at the Massey estate. A crawler on the bottom of the screen read "Henry Massey arrested this morning in FBI raid."

"What would they arrest him for?"

"I'm guessing they were after his supercomputer." Sophia smiled. "We got it just in time."

"How did you know?"

"That's not important."

Ferguson smirked as he handed the phone back to Sophia. "I wish I could've seen Massey's face when he saw his prized supercomputer missing."

"Me too," Sophia said. "Nice work. Buckle up."

Ferguson secured the seat belt around his waist as the jet stopped at the end of the runway. The engines accelerated. A moment later he felt himself being pushed in the seat back as the jet sped down the runway. Out his window he saw the truck, Nigel, and the airport grow smaller and smaller. Nothing like escaping prison in style.

They sat in silence until the jet leveled out.

CHAPTER 47

"This is cause for celebration," Sophia said as she popped the cork off a bottle of champagne. She filled two glass flutes and handed one to Ferguson. "To Henry Massey. Oh, how the mighty have fallen!"

Ferguson took the glass. "You looked pleased."

Sophia raised her glass toward Ferguson and smiled. "Someone will have to be king in his place, or should I say queen."

Ferguson tapped her glass and took a sip.

Sophia had a smug look on her face as she took a sip. "You're going to like island life."

"I don't have much choice," Ferguson said. Sophia looked at him for a moment. It made him uneasy. "Why are you looking at me like that."

"I was just thinking that you did such a good job getting that supercomputer, I might have use for you in the future," Sophia said.

"If you mean another heist like the one I just did, no thanks."

"I'm guessing you're going to get bored after a few months of being stuck on my Mediterranean island."

"I doubt it."

"You know I can always turn you in to the authorities."

"So I'm working for you now?"

"Something like that."

Ferguson took another sip from his glass. He didn't like the sound of that, but it was better than life in prison.

CHAPTER 48

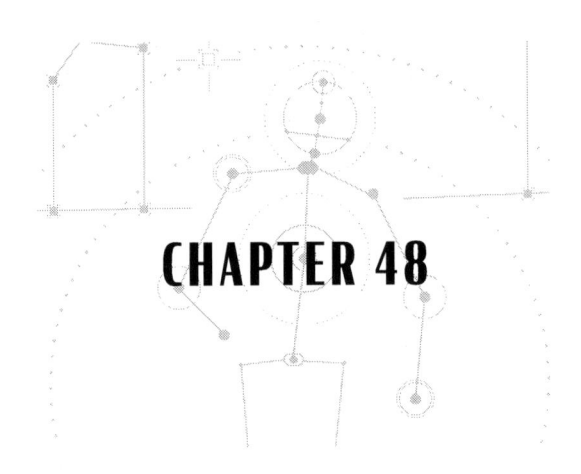

The door slammed shut behind Daniel as he repositioned himself in the back seat of the SUV, hands cuffed behind his back. Massey glanced at him, then returned his gaze to the side window.

"They're not getting away with this," Massey said.

There he sat on the edge of the seat, hands cuffed behind his back, and he was still as confident as ever.

"My attorneys will see to that." He turned to look at Daniel, lips pressed tightly together, a determined look in his eyes.

Daniel caught his gaze. "I warned you about using Chinese technology. You told me the Feds didn't have a clue."

"How *did* the Feds know about my supercomputer?" Massey's face scrunched into a scowl. "It's too much of a coincidence that I gave you access to the supercomputer room and now it's missing."

"What are you saying?" Daniel fired back.

"You were once an FBI agent . . . And now the FBI is here with a search warrant claiming I have Chinese technology."

"I thought I was like a brother to you." He forced tears to well up. "And now you doubt my loyalty?"

Massey turned away.

CHAPTER 48

Taking a slow, deep breath, Daniel looked out his window. He watched agents going in and out of the main entrance of the mansion.

"You *have* proven your loyalty," Massey said.

Daniel turned and looked at him.

"You didn't try to stop the drone attack last August . . ." The frown on Massey's face softened. "You've enhanced the security of my global enterprises and made it harder for the Feds to penetrate my operations." He shifted in his seat. "And you didn't give in to my wife's advances." He sighed. "I just can't figure out how the FBI found out about my supercomputer."

"Who *would* tip off the FBI? Who would want revenge?"

Massey laughed. "It's a long list. You don't get to my position without making a boatload of enemies. Just the fact I'm rich makes me a target for all kinds of people."

"But who would want to do this to you?"

Massey nodded in deep thought. "The people at the Chinese lab I funded always seemed annoyed with me, like they were just tolerating working with me on my supercomputer."

"Do you think they tipped off the FBI?"

"It's possible." Massey's head dipped downward. "Once they shipped my supercomputer, they would've had the blueprints to build their own and no reason to keep working with me."

They sat in silence for another moment.

"You're the richest man in the world," Daniel said. "Why did you need this supercomputer and your whole scheme to seize state government data for your own use?"

Massey's head tilted toward the ceiling, face somber.

"Why are you so determined to get revenge on the government?"

Slowly Massey's head turned toward Daniel. The expression on his face looked distant, deep in thought. His mouth opened, but he didn't speak.

"What is it, Henry?"

"The government killed my grandfather."

Not the answer he was expecting.

"Remember when I told Fallon at the cabin last summer about how my grandfather provided grain for his grandfather's distillery?"

271

"I remember that."

"During Prohibition, the Feds put my grandfather in prison for supplying grain to Fallon's grandfather's distillery on Beaver Island, and for transporting liquor for him." He looked intently at Daniel. "He died in prison a few years after his conviction. Fallon's grandfather was also imprisoned, but he had political connections and was pardoned after Prohibition ended. It wasn't right. Ever since I heard about it when I was a kid, I've wanted to make it right."

"That's a long time to hold a grudge."

"When Congress kept hauling me in to their committees to grill me about Quick Connect and invasion of privacy, when they kept harassing me in front of the media, my mom reminded me of what the government did to my grandfather during Prohibition."

Daniel looked at the far-off look Massey had as he gazed out the window. He had never seen him so emotional.

"Don't you see?" Massey turned to look at Daniel. "You know that there never seems to be justice. I owed it to my grandfather and my mom. I realized I had the means to finally get back at the government and free us once and for all from their tyranny." His face suddenly grew stern. "I realized that if all of us tech leaders joined forces, nothing could stop us. With our digital resources, we could control everything from government operations, currency, and even the military. Unlike some members of Arpa, I haven't lost my resolve to pursue my plan."

"Why did you need the supercomputer? You already control almost half the states in the country with Archipelago software and your server farms across the country."

Massey smiled. "With my own personal copy of all that data at my estate, I could use it however I saw fit to advance my cause, correct injustices, or blackmail anyone who came after me with incriminating information. Plus, its compact size made it easy to transport with an enclosed semi-trailer to wherever I wanted to and still continually update it via my private satellite network."

Daniel's stomach tightened. "Or was it part of a deal with the Chinese government? You get a supercomputer, and they get all the data from

CHAPTER 48

twenty-two states running Archipelago—and maybe the Feds in the future?"

"Now you're questioning my loyalty to my country. Do you really think I would give China all that data?"

"Where *is* your supercomputer?"

"I wish I knew," Massey said with a panicked look. "Whoever took it has all the data from twenty-two states."

Daniel eyed Massey. Was he telling the truth? "Why didn't the security system alert us to someone stealing it? How could they steal it in broad daylight without anyone knowing it?"

"You're head of my security," Massey fired back. "You tell me."

"This is why you should've let me review the bunker security earlier."

"That's the least of my worries . . ." Massey's words trailed off as his head drooped toward the floor.

"I don't like that look."

Massey raised his long face and looked at him.

"Tell me," Daniel pleaded.

"There's one more piece of security for my supercomputer. A fail-safe to give me leverage in case things didn't go as planned and someone tried to seize it."

The sinister smile Massey flashed at Daniel made him uneasy. "What would that be?"

"The minute that supercomputer was unplugged and moved, it triggered a countdown."

"For what?"

Massey looked at his watch. "If I don't enter a passcode in less than two hours, fleets of armed drones I staged across the country will destroy all the server farms in the twenty-two states hosting Archipelago as well as their contracted backup server farms. All their data will be lost and that supercomputer, wherever it is, will have the only copy."

"A military-like strike on their data centers? From where?"

Massey just smiled. It was the same content smile he flashed last summer when he launched the drone strike on the *Emerald Isle*. That was a demonstration of what he was capable of doing to accomplish his goals. There was no doubt in Daniel's mind that he was telling the truth.

273

"And where do you have to be to enter this passcode?"

"There's a desk on the far end of the bunker with a keyboard and two screens. I enter the passcode there and it will send out a command via my satellite network to stop the countdown. If the FBI gives me immunity from prosecution, I'll give them the passcode."

Suddenly the back door opened, and Evan appeared. He grabbed Daniel's arm and pulled him out. "We're going to interrogate you two separately. I need some answers."

"You may want to talk to me first," Massey offered.

Evan looked at Daniel, then Massey. "I'll get to you in a minute." Then he slammed the door shut, leaving Massey inside the SUV.

CHAPTER 49

"I'm telling you Massey is about to initiate a drone strike on all the data centers running Archipelago." Daniel rubbed his wrists as he sat down next to Chip inside the FBI's command center van.

"What makes you so sure he's not bluffing?" Evan said as he took a seat next to Daniel in front of a wall of computer monitors and communications equipment.

"Because he was behind the drone attack on the *Emerald Isle*."

Evan raised an eyebrow. "Homeland Security told us it was a terror attack."

"I was there when he launched it from the cabin on Beaver Island."

"Why am I just hearing this now?"

"Because it was too risky communicating with the FBI since I went undercover." Daniel leaned in toward Evan. "He has a fleet of drones ready to attack. It's his last line of defense. He'll call off the attack if you give him immunity."

"I'm not giving him immunity. What if he's bluffing?"

"He's not. Massey just told me the minute the supercomputer was disconnected it triggered a countdown to the drone attack on all the state government server farms in the twenty-two states using Archipelago. He's the only one who knows the passcode."

"I'm not buying it. There's no way he could hit all the server farms running Archipelago at the same time," Evan said. "There must be hundreds of sites."

"It's possible . . ." Chip opened his laptop, placed it on the metal desk in front of him, and typed on the keyboard. "Arpa purchased several thousand delivery drones over the last year, and they were shipped to all the states running Archipelago."

"How do you know that?" Daniel asked.

"It's in their latest SEC filing online."

"And you just . . . never mind."

"It was a large enough expense that they reported it."

"Exactly where were they shipped?" Evan asked.

"It appears they were shipped to the same states running Archipelago."

"Is there a shipping address?"

"No, but I have a clue on where they might be staged," Chip pointed to the laptop.

Daniel looked at the map of Michigan on his screen with more than a dozen red dots all over the state. "What are those?"

"Those are mini storage facilities across the state that Arpa invested in."

"Also reported in the SEC filing."

Chip nodded.

"That's a strange thing for them to invest in," Evan said. "They usually do tech investments."

Daniel examined the locations of the red dots. "Can you tell me what's near all those red dots?"

"I'm not positive, but they appear to be located near State of Michigan server farms," Chip said as he zoomed in.

"How many total locations?"

"I count at least a dozen across the state, including the Upper Peninsula." Chip looked at Daniel. "I have a hunch Massey may be housing armed drones in those mini storage facilities."

"What about the other states using Archipelago?"

CHAPTER 49

"It also appears . . ." Chip said as he typed on his laptop, then stopped and pointed at the screen showing red dots scattered across a map of the United States, "Arpa has mini storage facilities in all the states running Archipelago."

Daniel looked at his watch. "There's no way we could stop all those drones in the time we have left."

"It would take days and dozens of agents to confirm those drones are actually in all those mini storage facilities across the country," Evan said. "Even if they did, I'm not sure we would be able to disable them."

The back door to the van opened. An FBI agent stuck his head inside. We've located dozens of Food Queen trucks all over the state, but none that matches the license plate on the trailer at the loading dock."

"They must have changed the plate." Evan ran his fingers through his hair and sighed.

"Do you want us to put a call out to stop all those trucks and start searching?" the agent asked.

"No. Have the agents follow them to see where they go." Evan looked at Daniel as the agent left the van. "We're out of options."

"There must be some way Massey is communicating with those drones," Daniel said. "Some central way he issued the command."

"He said it was triggered when the supercomputer was unplugged," Chip said. "There was a desk on the far wall of the bunker with a keyboard and screens."

"Let's go back to the supercomputer room," Daniel said as he held his hands behind his back. "Cuff me in case Massey sees me coming out of the van."

Evan cuffed Daniel and held his arm as they hurriedly exited the van with Chip. Once they were out of sight of the SUV holding Massey, Evan uncuffed Daniel and they sprinted down a driveway to the loading dock area and the bunker. Chip stopped by the open blast door, hunched over and breathing heavy.

Daniel stopped, wiped the sweat off his brow, and put his hand on Chip's shoulder. "You okay?"

"I'm not used to this thin air," Chip said.

"What are we looking for?" Daniel asked as he stepped inside the empty bunker room and looked at the rectangular mark on the floor where the supercomputer once sat. He glanced at the shiny, white walls and the dangling cables.

"There." Chip hurried to a desk on the far wall, sat in the desk chair, and pointed to one of the screens. "DEFCON 2"?

"It looks like Massey is using the readiness levels the military used during the Cold War to ramp up to all-out nuclear war," Evan said. "DEFCON 1 means war is imminent—basically prepare to send nuclear missiles in response to an attack."

"We're now a little over one hour from DEFCON 1 and an imminent launch of the drones," Daniel said as he watched a countdown clock displayed next to the DEFCON 2 flashing on the screen. "If Massey destroys state server farms, what will happen to all their data?"

"They usually run backups every night at off-site cloud computing facilities," Chip said.

"Where are the backups housed?" Evan asked.

"I know Michigan does a backup with an out-of-state cloud service company in case of a catastrophic event," Chip said as he typed on his laptop.

"So the supercomputer won't have the only copy," Daniel said.

"I'm not sure," Chip pointed to the laptop screen. "It looks like Arpa also has a mini storage facility near the cloud server company Michigan uses in Chicago. I'm guessing it's the same in the other states."

Daniel sighed. "It looks like Massey has really thought this through."

Evan stood with his hands on his hips and nodded at the screen blinking DEFCON 2. "Somehow those mini storage units are communicating with this computer in front of us tracking the countdown."

"His satellite network," Daniel blurted out. "His personal satellite network just became fully operational a few weeks ago."

"If we can find the satellite dish on his estate, we can take that out," Chip said.

"Even if we shut down the satellite dish on his estate, couldn't the drones still operate independently?" Daniel asked. "They could still execute their attack when the clock runs out without further commands from here."

CHAPTER 49

"You're right."

"And without the satellite dish the drones would not get the signal to shut down the attack and return to DEFCON 5 if Massey gives us the passcode." Evan looked at the screen, then at Daniel and Chip. "The only way to stop them is to get the code out of Massey."

Daniel stood up. "I'll go see if I can talk some sense into him."

"No, you stay here," Evan said as he looked at his phone. "I'm putting in an immunity request for Massey, so I'll at least have the form ready if we need it."

Daniel grabbed Evan's phone. "You can't give him immunity. We've come too far to get to this point."

"At least we haven't blown your cover yet," Evan grabbed his phone from Daniel. "Immunity may be our only option."

Daniel watched Evan leave the room. He pounded the wall with his fist. After all these months he wasn't about to let Massey off the hook with immunity. He took a deep breath and looked at Chip. "Can we verify that those mini storage sites actually have drones?"

Chip looked at his laptop and enlarged the area around a red dot near Lansing. "There's a site not far from the governor's mansion." He turned to look at Daniel. "Alicia and Fallon are at the governor's mansion right now waiting for updates. They could confirm they're there without causing a stir."

Daniel nodded. "There's no time to get a search warrant, and I don't necessarily want to get the state police involved just yet . . . give them a call."

CHAPTER 50

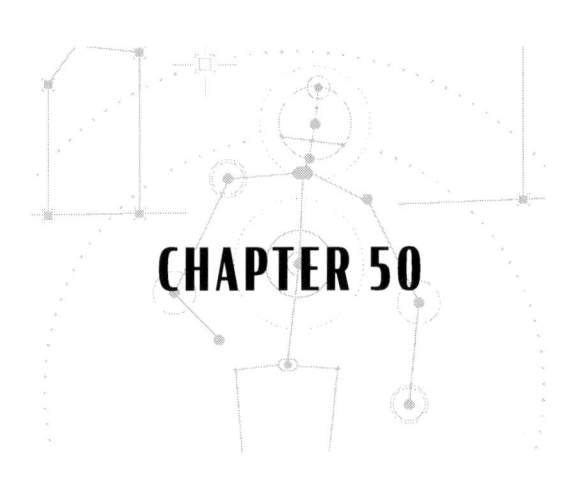

"Thanks for the aspirin," Fallon said as he sat in the dining room of the governor's residence with Alicia and Karen seated across from him. He popped two tablets in his mouth and rubbed his arm.

"Is it healing?" Karen asked.

"It's still a bit sore since they took off the wrap, but my arm is feeling better."

"Any word on what the FBI found at the Massey estate?" Alicia asked.

"Nothing yet." She set her phone on the table.

"How *did* the FBI get the tip about Massey's Chinese-built supercomputer?" Alicia asked as she picked up her coffee cup.

"Daniel gave Chip the tip about the supercomputer," Fallon said.

"Chip was able to get proof Massey took delivery of the computer at his estate," the governor added. "That was enough proof to get a search warrant."

"Chip always comes through." Fallon glanced at the governor.

She smiled and took a bite of her bagel.

"You okay, Fallon?" Alicia asked.

"I think I'm just hungry," he said as he picked up a piece of toast from his plate and took a bite.

CHAPTER 50

"Any word on Ferguson?" Alicia asked. "It's been weeks since his escape."

The governor sighed. "Nothing."

"I don't get how such a high-profile prisoner could just vanish," Alicia said.

The governor shook her head. "I don't either." Her phone on the table buzzed. She picked it up. "Excuse me."

As they watched her leave the room, Alicia turned to Fallon. "You sure you're okay, Fallon?"

"Honestly, I don't know what that means anymore. I keep thinking I'll be who I was before my head injury, before we left the dock to stop that drone, but I don't think I know who that person is anymore."

She reached her hand across the table. "You're still the Fallon I've known for so long."

He put his hand on hers and met her hazel eyes. "I don't think that's true."

"You need to give it time."

"I have, but what if this is it? I'm beginning to think my new reality is scattered thoughts and difficulty concentrating. I can't go back to my old job."

"Of course you can. Karen will work with you."

"The governor needs someone that's all there—someone sharp."

"Fallon—"

"No, Alicia. It's just a hard reality I need to face."

She sat silent with a penetrating look focused on him. It still felt uncomfortable to be vulnerable, but he knew he could trust her.

"When I went to Cally's house, his dad, Robert, told me that sometimes God humbles us to help us see things about ourselves."

She snickered. "Doesn't surprise me he's throwing religious stuff at you."

He swallowed hard. He was getting choked up. He pulled his hand off the table, rubbed his eyes, then looked at her. "I almost died. If you hadn't pulled me out of the water . . ."

Alicia nodded, tears in her eyes.

"I've been a detective all my life. It's all I know." He paused. The words weren't there to describe his feelings.

"This isn't the end," she said as she reached across the table and took hold of his hands. "Look at it as a new beginning."

He sighed. "I'm so disoriented, I'm not sure if can look at it that way right now."

"That was Chip," Karen said as she entered the room. She paused and looked at Fallon and Alicia. "I'm sorry; am I interrupting?"

Alicia leaned back and wiped her eyes. "It's okay."

Fallon bit his lip, welcoming the interruption.

"Unfortunately, they didn't find the supercomputer," Karen said, returning to her chair. "But we still have the evidence that he acquired Chinese computer chips."

"Well, that's good," Alicia said.

Fallon noted Karen's concerned look. "What else?"

"Massey claimed someone stole his supercomputer and when they did it triggered a countdown that will launch a drone attack on all the server farms running Archipelago."

"In all the states?" Alicia asked.

Karen nodded. "Chip said there could be hundreds of drones across the country armed with explosives."

Alicia shook her head. "That's not believable."

A memory from the cabin on Beaver Island emerged in Fallon's head.

> *Massey is seated across from him on the couch with a devious look on his face. "Well, I'm planning a little beta test down the road in case they need further convincing." He shifts in his chair and asks him, "What sort of beta test?" Massey gives him a wry smile. "Just a small demonstration of our ability to use force if necessary to get our way."*

"The attack on the *Emerald Isle* last summer was a demonstration of what he is capable of doing," Fallon said. "He told me that last summer in the cabin. I think he's serious."

The room went silent for a moment.

CHAPTER 50

"You remember that?" Karen asked.

Fallon nodded.

"Does Chip know where Massey staged those drones?" Alicia asked.

"He thinks they're housed in mini storage units near the server farms," Karen said. "He wants us to confirm that."

"How?"

Karen showed her phone screen to Alicia and Fallon. "There's one south of Lansing at the State Secondary Complex."

"Let's check it out," Alicia said.

"Shouldn't we get some backup?" Fallon asked.

Alicia gave Fallon a puzzled look. "Mr. Do-It-Myself wants backup?"

Fallon shrugged his shoulders, eyes locked on Alicia.

She took a deep breath.

"I'll have my security detail join us," Karen said as she made her way to the front door. "We need to verify those drones are there without creating a scene."

CHAPTER 51

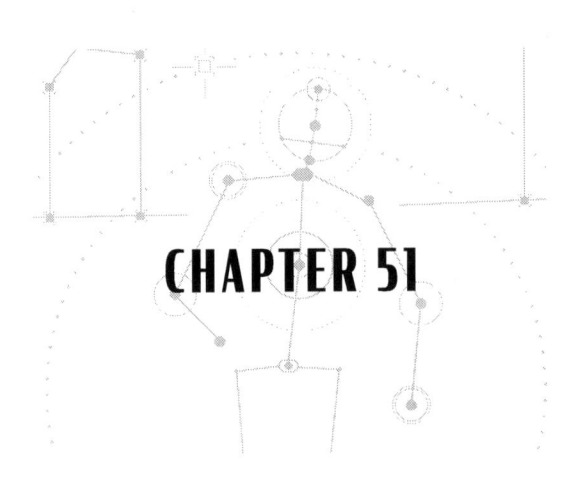

Sitting in the back seat of the SUV parked a short distance from the storage facility entrance, Fallon tried to avoid making eye contact with the member of the governor's security detail sitting next to him. It was obvious to him by the look on her face that she didn't think they should be here or that the governor should be driving, but she remained quiet. He glanced at Alicia on the passenger side in the front seat. Through the windshield and his side window, he studied two long, narrow buildings set inside a chain-link fence that circled the property. He counted twenty garage doors on each side of the buildings, marking the location of individual storage units.

"We're at the storage facility," Karen said to Chip over the phone connected to the SUV as she sat behind the wheel. "What are we looking for?"

"I need you to confirm the drones are inside those storage units," Chip said through the speakers.

"We're parked in the driveway near the front gate, and it's locked," she explained. "It has a keypad. Can you open it?"

"I can't help you, sorry."

"How much time do we have?"

CHAPTER 51

"We're down to thirty minutes."

"We'll figure something out. Thanks, Chip."

"We have to get in there," Alicia said from the front seat.

"I'm going to ram the gate," Karen said as she slipped the transmission into Drive. "We don't have time to waste."

"Hold it," Alicia said as she pointed toward the gate.

Suddenly, a car pulled up to the front gate. Someone opened the window, typed in a code, and the gate opened.

"Hurry, drive in after them, the gate's closing," Fallon said.

"No need to." Alicia held her phone for Karen to see. "I videotaped them punching in the code."

Karen drove up to the gate and typed in the code. The gate opened. She pulled the SUV inside the fenced-in area with two long rows of twenty identical, metal-sided storage units with locked garage doors. The car that pulled in before them was parked on the far end. The gate closed behind them.

"How do we know which units house the drones?" Alicia asked as they all climbed out of the SUV.

They all stood a moment scanning the storage units.

Fallon watched the car on the far end unload boxes into an open storage unit. "I think large, armed drones would have a difficult time flying out of a unit through a garage door. It would make more sense for them to have roof-mounted doors."

Karen tilted her head toward the roof. "How do we get up there?"

"Hoist me up." Alicia motioned to Fallon. "On the side over there where that guy putting stuff in his storage unit can't see us."

He rubbed his arm. "I don't think I should."

"I got you," Karen said as they went to the side of the building where she made a step with her hands.

Alicia put one foot on Karen's hands and stretched her hand toward the edge of the roof.

"Help me boost her up," Karen said as she motioned to her security person.

A moment later Alicia scrambled up the side of the building and disappeared on the roof for a moment.

"All the units on one side of the building have roof doors." Alicia said as she poked her head over the side of the roof. There must be twenty of them!"

Fallon put his hand over his eyes and squinted at her. "Can you confirm there are drones in those units?"

Alicia disappeared for several seconds. Creaking metal could be heard as she walked across the roof, followed by the thud of metal hitting metal. Suddenly, she reappeared, looking down on them from the edge of the roof. "I tried to open several of the roof doors. I need a little more muscle up here."

"Are they locked?" Fallon asked.

"They don't appear to be. I can pry the door up a few inches, but there's too much resistance. The doors must have a motorized opener holding them down."

"Apparently they didn't expect someone to try to access the drones from the roof," Karen said.

Fallon lifted his foot. "Hoist me up."

"No, Fallon. Your arm—"

"Give me a lift."

They stared at each other.

"The clock's ticking, Karen."

Karen cupped her hand as her security detail helped Fallon scramble up the side and onto the roof. He knelt on the roof for a second and rubbed his arm. Then he stood and limped to Alicia.

"Get down," Alicia snapped as she pointed toward the car parked by the neighboring building with storage units.

Fallon saw the man closing the garage door on his storage unit and start walking to his car. He dropped down and laid flat on the roof with Alicia and looked at his watch. "We must be down to twenty minutes before those drones launch."

They lay on the roof listening to the car leave the facility. Fallon thought about the buzzing sound of drones flying out of the storage facility. He could hear the entrance gate closing as he saw Alicia jump to her feet.

CHAPTER 51

"Help me pull this up," she said as she grabbed the edge of one of the roof doors.

Fallon groaned as he helped her tug on the door with his uninjured arm until it opened part way. Pain shot up his leg as he used it to brace himself.

"I'll hold it open," Alicia offered, her voice straining. "See if there's a drone in there."

Fallon bent down and peered inside. "There's a large drone on a rack with yellow, green, and red flashing lights."

"Call Chip and see what that means."

"Can you keep holding it open?"

She groaned. "Just hurry!"

He quickly pulled out his phone and called Chip. "I confirmed there's a drone inside one of the units with a roof door, and it has a yellow, green, and red flashing light."

"It's initializing," Chip said over the phone speaker.

"Wait, now only the yellow light is flashing."

"It's warming up," Chip said with a bit of panic in his voice.

Fallon sat up on the roof as Alicia let the roof door down. "How do we stop these drones?"

"If we don't get the password to stop them from here—" Chip began to say.

"I'll put a stop to this right now!" Alicia shouted. "I'm taking out the satellite antenna."

Fallon looked up at Alicia as she pulled out her gun and fired at a small satellite antenna mounted on the far end of the roof. He watched the antenna shatter to pieces and winced as the gun fired.

> *Echoes of a memory . . . the sound of an automatic rifle firing . . . images of Alicia standing in the back of the boat, rifle pointed skyward. More deep breaths.*

He couldn't return to the field, freezing like this every time he heard gunshots.

"Did Alicia just shoot out the satellite dish?" Chip asked with an alarmed tone in his voice.

"She did."

"Without that dish antenna, the drones won't receive the command to stop the attack. That's if we're able to get the code to stop it."

Fallon, with the phone in his hand, looked up at Alicia standing next to him. "How much longer before these drones attack the State of Michigan servers?"

"We're about to slip below fifteen minutes. You have to find a way to stop those drones at that mini storage facility."

"How?"

"I don't know."

"But you're the tech expert."

The phone was quiet for a few seconds.

"Are you there, Chip?"

"Yeah . . . Maybe there is a way . . . drones operate on electric power. If you can find a way to short out their motors, that might stop them."

Fallon looked at Alicia, her lips pressed tight together, eyes narrowed. "And how do you plan to stop the rest of the drones across the country?"

"It looks like our only option is to get the passcode from Massey."

CHAPTER 52

Chip took a deep breath and exhaled as he slipped his phone back in his shirt pocket. He sat in front of the computer screen and watched the timer in the corner slip below fifteen minutes as DEFCON 2 flashed. "There has to be a way to bypass his system."

"How?" Daniel asked.

They turned to see Evan drag Massey back into the room.

"I've agreed to give him immunity if he types in the passcode to stop the drone attack," Evan said as he uncuffed Massey.

Massey turned and glared at Daniel, then Chip.

"No, Evan!" Chip said.

Evan pointed to the timer. "We have no choice."

Chip felt anger surge inside of him as he looked at Massey's smug face. His phone rang and he looked at the screen with the notification "Potential Spam" and an unknown number. Curious, he stepped outside the room and answered the call.

"Have you seen the movie *War Games*?" someone asked.

"Who is this?"

"Have you seen the movie?"

"Yes."

"It's Henry's favorite movie. He likes to use one character's name in particular for passwords—the computer scientist from that movie."

"Who is this?"

The phone call ended.

"Who was that?" Daniel asked as Chip stepped back into the room.

"I'm not sure," Chip said, deep in thought.

"What did they want?" Evan said.

Chip walked to the other end of the room and looked at the walls and the computer screens on the other end. His mouth half open, he tried to recall the name of the character in the movie. The old cold war bunker where he stood and the DEFCON levels reminded him of the closing scenes in the movie when they were on the brink of nuclear war. He glanced at Daniel, Evan, and Massey staring at him from the other side of the room. He noted Massey's smug look and how much enjoyment he seemed to be getting out of the suspense.

"What are you doing?" Daniel asked as he walked over to Chip.

"How old is Massey?" Chip said in a hushed tone.

"What does that have to do with anything?"

"Just tell me."

"He's roughly Fallon's age."

"He was a teenager in the 1980s?"

"I guess so. What are you getting at?"

Chip turned to see Evan with his face in front of Massey.

"Unlock this computer!" Evan barked.

Massey sat down and placed his hand on the screen. A green outline of his hand appeared with the words "Accessed Granted."

"Now the code, Massey," Evan said.

"My immunity first."

"First the code," Evan fired back as he showed Massey the tablet in his hand with the immunity document. "We sign these after you stop the countdown."

"I got this," Chip whispered to Daniel. He walked back to the computer screens, stepped in front of Evan and looked at Massey seated in the chair. "That biometric software is quite impressive."

Massey smiled. "You like that?"

CHAPTER 52

"I'm impressed with the complexity you've built into this software—all the thought you put into calculating the different scenarios and the stopgaps you put in place."

Massey nodded. "You like computers?"

"I do." Out of the corner of his eye, he noticed a window appear on the computer screen requesting the system password. "People who aren't geeks like us don't appreciate complex yet elegant programming like you've done here."

Massey's eyes narrowed. "Where are you going with this?"

"This whole scenario you've set up with DEFCON levels reminds me of an old movie I saw years ago," Chip said.

"We don't have time for this," Evan said, panic in his voice.

Chip waved his hand at Evan.

Evan threw his hands up in a huff.

Massey's face brightened. "You know the movie?"

"I do."

"I can't believe someone as young as you knows about it."

"Only real geeks do."

Massey's head tilted with a nostalgic look. "I loved that movie. My brother and I watched it several times. It's what got me interested in computers."

"What *are* you two talking about?" Daniel asked with an annoyed tone.

"*War Games,*" Chip said.

"A great movie." Massey smiled.

That was all the confirmation Chip needed. He leaned over in front of Massey and tapped at the keyboard, watching dots appear in the box for the password. Nothing happened. He was panicked as he stared at the password box.

"It didn't work!" Evan said as he put the tablet in front of Massey.

Massey took the tablet and the stylus.

"Wait!" Chip said as he grabbed the tablet from Massey and tossed it on the desk.

"What are you doing?" Evan asked.

Chip began typing.

"You only have one more guess after this and the system will lock out," Massey said with a grin.

Suddenly the clock in the corner of the screen disappeared and the word DEFCON 5 appeared. The timer stopped at five minutes and a few seconds.

"How did you do that?" Massey asked, his face frozen in shock.

"The one character in the movie *War Games* that you would most want to be like would have been Dr. Stephen Falken," Chip said. "His name is your password." Chip cleared his throat. "With no spaces between the names and the word doctor abbreviated with a period. I didn't do that in my first try."

"Too bad this isn't a movie," Evan said as he pulled Massey out of the chair and cuffed his hands behind his back. "This drone plot alone is enough to send you away for a long time as a domestic terrorist."

Chip watched Evan drag Massey out of the room. He looked at the screen, then at Daniel.

"Who called you and tipped you off about the password?" Daniel asked as he leaned against a wall near Chip.

"I'm not sure."

"Check your recent calls list. We can trace the phone number."

Chip pulled out his phone and looked up the recent calls. "It's not there." Then he saw the call from Fallon on the list. "Oh no!"

"What's wrong?" Daniel asked.

"I just remembered. Alicia shot out the dish antennae on the mini storage facility in Lansing. The drones there won't get the message that we've stopped the attack."

CHAPTER 53

Fallon eased himself down the side of the storage building, fingers gripping the edge of the corrugated steel roof as his foot caught the toehold created by the governor's security detail directly below him. He rubbed his arm and throbbing leg as Alicia lowered herself down and stood next to him.

"What do you mean they will still attack?" Karen asked as she pressed her phone against her ear. "I thought you stopped it?"

Fallon noted the panic on Karen's face. "What's wrong?"

Karen lowered the phone from her ear. "The good news is that Chip was able to call off the attack from Massey's estate," Karen said. "The bad news is that because Alicia shot out the satellite antennae, the drones here didn't get the message and will still deploy."

Alicia threw up her hands. "Oh great! How much time before they launch?"

Karen put her phone on speaker and held it in front of her.

"The timer on the screen stopped here at five minutes, and that was a couple minutes ago," Chip replied. "You need to find a way to short them out."

A whirring sound from inside the storage units caught Fallon's attention. They all turned toward the building as it became louder. The sound of creaking metal could be heard above them from the roof of the building.

"That must be the roof doors opening," Alicia said.

"What if we cut the power source," Fallon said into the phone in Karen's hand.

"They're powered by batteries," Chip said. "That won't stop them."

Alicia held up her hand to her ear. "What's that buzzing sound?"

Fallon jerked his head skyward and expected to see a drone but instead spotted several high-voltage, electric transmission lines spanning the mini storage facility. "These buildings are all metal," Fallon said as he pointed to the power lines.

Alicia pulled out her gun. "If I shoot out that line, it'll drop on the metal building and send a high voltage surge through all those drones."

"That's a pretty small target."

Alicia took aim at the buzzing power lines. "I always beat you at skeet shooting."

"Your dad taught you well," Fallon said. "Have at it!"

"Wait!" Karen held up her hand. "We should be away from these buildings before you do that."

Gun still pointed skyward; Alicia turned to look at Fallon. "I need to stay here to get a better shot."

"But—" Fallon said, eyes locked on Alicia.

"Go!" she said.

Fallon joined Karen at the entry gate, away from the storage buildings. He turned and noticed the roof doors were fully open and the whirring sound from the drones was getting louder. Alicia fired several shots that echoed against the metal buildings, but the power lines remained intact. Fallon held his hands to his ears and cringed as Alicia took aim again. He turned away, trying to block the flashback triggered by the gunshots. His body tensed as a memory flashed in his mind of her standing in the boat with the automatic rifle, firing at the drone. Suddenly it faded as quickly as it had appeared. He opened his eyes as his body began to relax.

"Don't worry, I'll get it!" Alicia shouted as she fired more rounds. Suddenly one of the power lines snapped and curled as it fell onto the

CHAPTER 53

roof of the mini storage building. Sparks began to fly from the roof as the power line writhed off the top of the building and dangled on the side. A moment later, thick smoke began to rise out the open roof doors as the whirring sound slowly faded.

Fallon closed his eyes with relief, ignoring his aching body. He felt a pat on his shoulder and opened his eyes to see Karen struggling to hold back the tears welling up in her eyes.

"You did it!" Fallon said as Alicia ran to him.

They embraced, tightly holding on to each other for a moment. He was safe in her arms, reassured everything would be all right.

"I always was a better shot than you," Alicia laughed as she released Fallon and slipped her gun back into the holster under her jacket.

Suddenly, the sound of approaching sirens filled the air. Fallon turned to see three state police cars screech to a halt in front of the closed entrance gate to the storage facility. Uniformed officers jumped out of their cars with guns drawn.

"Hold it right there!" one officer said as he stepped to the chain-link fence between them. "Hands in the air!"

They quickly raised their hands.

"Officer—" Karen said as other troopers gathered along the fence.

"Keep your arms up!" the officer shouted. "We're responding to a call about gunshots in the area."

"Governor?" another officer uttered as he lowered his gun.

"Fallon?" another officer asked with a confused look on his face.

CHAPTER 54

"What happens to the supercomputer once it's in the train tunnel?" Ferguson asked as he sipped his champagne, eased back in his seat, and looked at Sophia. He noted the devious look on her face, not sure what to expect as she set her glass down and picked up her phone.

"I have a phone call to make." She set the phone on the small shelf next to her seat and put it on speaker. "I want you to hear this."

"Helen Massey—it's Sophia. You're on speaker. I have my special guest with me."

Not the person he expected to hear on the other end of the phone.

"So good to hear from you, Sophia," Helen said over the phone. "And hello to your special guest."

Ferguson nodded.

Sophia crossed her legs. "Where are you?"

"I'm in my office at our Colorado estate. The FBI is keeping me here while they tear apart our place."

"Where's Henry?"

"I asked an agent and all he would say is that he's being questioned

CHAPTER 54

first and then they'll get to me. They took my laptop a few minutes ago and left me here alone."

"Can you talk?"

"Yes. I hear you picked up the package."

"Thanks to your help. Within the hour, it should be at the location we agreed to."

"Very good. That will give my tech team time to run the AI software to remove any reference to me and Arpa. Only data pointing to Henry will be left on it."

Ferguson listened intently. Sophia had used him, but in the end they both got their revenge. This was certainly better than prison. He couldn't help having a big grin on his face, knowing justice would finally be served on Henry Massey.

"The FBI will be talking to me very soon. Of course, I'll act like the innocent wife who never knew anything about her husband's plans to seize data from all those states or all those drones he had staged across the country. Even if they suspect, they'll have no proof when we're done with the supercomputer."

"Things are unfolding just as we planned." Sophia leaned back in her seat. She appeared pleased with herself.

"We should be done scrubbing the data by tonight," Helen said. "Tomorrow an anonymous source will send the location of the supercomputer to the FBI. The shipping information will show that the supercomputer is going to China per Henry's instructions."

Sophia folded her hands in front of her. "Perfect."

"Henry is going away for a long time, so it looks like I'll be assuming control of Quick Connect with our majority shares in the company. His stock options revert to me if he is convicted of any criminal activity."

"You should've been CEO from day one, Helen. It was your vision, tenacity, and business sense that turned Henry's little software program into the world's largest social media platform."

"Thanks for all your support, Sophia," Helen said. "We'll have to get together for lunch when the dust settles from all of this. Oh, and there's one more thing. Tell your special guest it was so nice to meet him on the loading dock and thank him for delivering that special package."

Sophia ended the call and looked at him.

"Henry Massey's wife, Helen, was your inside operative?" Ferguson smiled. "So she's the one I met on the loading dock who disabled all the security around the supercomputer?"

"I'm surprised you didn't recognize her."

"You two were collaborating on this all along."

"Good things come to those who wait," Sophia said with a look of satisfaction on her face.

Ferguson extended his glass toward Sophia. "A toast to new things."

Sophia clanked her glass against Ferguson's. "May we forget the former things."

CHAPTER 55

Chip turned to Daniel as he ended the call. "That was the governor. They shorted out the drones and disabled them."

Daniel took a deep breath and gazed at the screen still flashing DEFCON 5. A wave of emotion washed over him as he suddenly realized his undercover assignment was complete. It had been so long since he could simply be himself that it now felt foreign to him. "I can't believe it's finally over."

"We still don't know where the supercomputer went."

"Does it matter if we locate it?" Daniel leaned against the wall. "All those state government server farms are still intact."

Chip looked at the computer screens on the metal desk and then at the empty bunker. "But that supercomputer holds the whole truth about Massey's plans."

"There's still enough to send Massey away for a while," Daniel said as he thought about Helen and what would happen to her. Was she in on Henry's plans? He wondered who would run their businesses. Would their girls pick up the pieces if Helen and Henry were sent to prison? Quick Connect's stock would likely tank after this with all the uncertainty.

"We need that supercomputer," Chip said. "Who knows what else Massey was thinking about doing."

"Any idea where it might be?"

Chip sat down in front of the computer screens. "There's no way to trace it if it was physically moved from here."

"It's up to Evan and his agents to locate it." Daniel patted Chip on the shoulder. "You did good work here today. Have you ever thought about being an analyst with the FBI?"

Chip lowered his gaze to the floor.

"What's wrong?"

"I don't think Fallon will return to his position as state police liaison for the governor. He hasn't been the same since his head injury. He's really struggled."

Daniel's heart sank. "I thought therapy would help him recover."

"It's been almost a year now. He's made a lot of progress, but he's still experiencing gaps in memory."

"If he's not working for the governor, what will he do?"

Chip shrugged. "I just don't know. He's been a detective all his life. It's what he loves to do. What's next for you?"

Daniel stood silent for a moment.

"You don't know?"

"I think I have just the ticket for Fallon," Daniel said as he left the room.

CHAPTER 56

Daniel stood on the bluff of the township campground on Beaver Island looking at Garden Island in the distance. To his left the deep orange sun slipped closer to the horizon. It was hard to believe that only a few weeks ago he was undercover. He took a deep breath, letting the fresh smell of Lake Michigan and the cedars refresh him. He was finally camping on Beaver Island. He heard someone call his name and turned to see Cally step next to him. He put his arm around his shoulder. "I told you I would make good on my promise to take you on a road trip."

"You made that promise to me when you got your license in high school," Cally said.

"Better late than never."

"I didn't think we'd see this day."

Daniel released Cally. Their eyes locked on each other. "I never gave up hope. It's what kept me going."

"I can't believe you were undercover with Massey all that time."

"Don't speak a word of it to anyone. That's just between you and me. The FBI doesn't want word to get out that they were infiltrating a political campaign."

"And me too," Fallon said as he stepped next to them.

"You too." Daniel lightly punched Fallon on the shoulder.

"I'm glad you joined us," Cally said.

"I didn't want to barge in on your family time," Fallon said.

"No, we wanted you to be part of this." Daniel turned back to the sunset. "You're like family to us."

"We're glad you're here," Robert said as he joined them by the bluff.

Daniel stared into his dad's gentle and caring eyes. His dad smiled at him.

"I hear you're not going back to work for the governor," Cally said.

"That's right." Fallon leaned against a tree and rubbed his leg. "I had to accept that I could never go back to who I was before the attack on the *Emerald Isle*."

"I don't think any of us can," Daniel said.

"So, what's next?" Robert asked.

Fallon shrugged. "I don't know."

"There's a scripture in the Bible—" Robert began.

"Not that religious stuff again, Dad," Daniel said.

Fallon waved his hand. "It's okay."

Daniel tried not to roll his eyes.

"There's a verse that talks about Jesus being the vine and we are the branches," Robert continued. "I think if you stay connected to God, it will become clear to you. He'll show you the way."

"I wish God would just send me a text. That would be a lot clearer."

"Be patient and prayerful. God will give you a sign."

"I'm tired of waiting around," Fallon sighed. "I want to know what's next."

"You can always call me to talk." Robert pulled out a flip phone and chuckled. "I don't text."

"You're missing the sunset," Daniel said as he pointed westward.

He glanced at all of them for a second, then at the sun as it slipped below the horizon. He took a deep breath and soaked up the peace and quiet, staring a long time at the golden glow reflecting off the glassy water of Lake Michigan. Above, the sky illuminated with hues of orange and yellow, slowly dimming as darkness settled in.

"I'm heading back to the campfire," Cally said.

CHAPTER 56

"Me too," Robert said.

"I'll be there in a minute," Daniel said as he watched them head back to the campsite.

Fallon stepped next to him. "It sure is peaceful."

"It is," Daniel said as he glanced at Fallon. "I'm surprised you're not going back to work for the governor."

"Chip is taking over my position. He's ready for it. It's perfect for him."

Daniel looked at the distant look on Fallon's face—light hues of the sunset orange tinting his face. He looked deep in thought. "Have you ever had a point in your life when you've been unsure of what's next?"

"Never. I've always had a plan. It reminds me of my dad when he was the Michigan Attorney General. His dream was to work in the White House. He tried several times to run for governor but never won. He finally resigned as attorney general so he could manage Bill Clinton's Michigan presidential campaign."

"Was that in 1992?"

Fallon nodded. "Clinton won, but my dad never got a spot in the Clinton White House. He never recovered from that and sunk into depression. He was aimless the rest of his life." Fallon shook his head. "I don't want to end up like my dad."

"You've never liked politics, Fallon. All those stakeouts we did together, you would talk about your frustration with politics. Maybe it's better you're no longer working for the governor."

"Sometimes I think my granddad had the right approach to life. He wasn't afraid to try new things."

"Ever think about having a place on Beaver Island like your granddad?"

"I don't know; it's pretty remote here."

"Give it time." Daniel smiled. "Come on, let's go back to the campfire and enjoy the evening."

"Thanks for bringing me along, Daniel," Fallon said as he followed him. "I needed this."

Daniel sat on a log near the glowing fire. He looked at his dad and Cally seated across from him in folding camp chairs as Fallon joined him on the log.

"I remember camping here when we were kids," Daniel said.

His dad smiled. "That was a long time ago."

"Who wants a beer?" Cally opened the cooler next to his camp chair.

"I have something better," Fallon replied. "I want to share a toast with all of you."

Daniel grinned. "To Massey's downfall?"

"Something much better," Fallon said as he went inside his tent and returned with a whiskey bottle and four metal camp cups. "I want to toast my granddad." Fallon set the cups on a small table near the campfire and poured some whiskey into each glass.

Daniel noted the content look on Fallon's face and the sparkle in his eye as he talked about his granddad.

"I never got to say a proper goodbye to my granddad's boat last summer. I kind of left here in a hurry," Fallon said as he handed a cup to Daniel and Cally, then offered a cup to Robert.

"No thanks," Robert said as he held up a cup in his hand. "I'll toast with my Vernor's Ginger Ale."

Fallon set the fourth cup back on the table. "That's just as good."

"To your granddad," Daniel offered as he raised his glass.

"To Granddad," Fallon said. "May his spirit remain alive on this island."

They clanked their cups together and took a sip.

"Wow! That's good stuff," Daniel said with a hoarse voice as the whiskey burned down his throat.

"It's an original from my granddad's whiskey operation," Fallon responded in a hoarse tone. "I saved a bottle to give him a proper tribute."

"Are you staying on the island for a while?" Cally asked.

"Alicia is coming here tomorrow," Fallon said. "I'm leaving camp in the morning to spend a few days with her."

"Are you two getting serious?" Daniel asked.

Fallon looked at the fire. "I honestly don't know."

"We're leaving in the morning, too, but we're just a phone call away if you need us." Daniel raised his cup toward Fallon. "To friends and family."

They clanked their cups together as he exchanged a reassuring nod with Fallon.

CHAPTER 57

The latch clunked open as the guard unlocked the thick, metal door to the prison meeting room. "In here," he said as he pointed to the open doorway.

Daniel stepped inside the stark room brightly illuminated with an overhead fixture. His eyes met those of Henry Massey seated at a metal table, hands cuffed and secured to a metal ring attached to the table.

"Nice jumpsuit," he said as he sat down across the table from Massey. "Orange looks good on you."

"How did you get in here?" Massey asked. "You're not on my visitor list."

"You're not calling the shots anymore, Henry," Daniel grinned. "I'm FBI, remember? I have access so I can interrogate you."

"Why are you here?" Massey sneered. "You betrayed me."

"I wanted to give you the news in person before it goes public."

"I don't care what you have to say. Go away!"

"You can't make me do anything." He leaned closer to Massey's face. "You can't even make a phone call without permission."

"Shut up, you traitor."

Daniel leaned back in his chair and locked eyes with Massey. He could feel the rage radiating from him. "It doesn't matter how many lawyers you have or how much you pay them, you will never beat the charges that are piling up against you. We had to create a database to track all the charges as we pull information about your plans to seize control of all that state data from the supercomputer. The armed drones you had staged across the country are grounds to prosecute you on domestic terrorism charges. I can't believe you sourced the bombs for those drones from Russia. Who's the traitor now?"

"I trusted you, Daniel," Massey said. "You were like a brother to me. How could you betray me?"

"When I enlisted in the air force, I took an oath to defend the US Constitution against all enemies, foreign and domestic. I took the same oath when I joined the FBI. My allegiance was to my country first—to do what I had to do to defend against enemies like you."

"You're as dirty as they come," Massey spewed. "You were part of Peninsular when I met you. They provided security for a lot of questionable, high-profile clients and you catered to them even if they posed a threat to your country."

Daniel laughed.

Massey frowned.

"Peninsular was created by the FBI as a way to infiltrate groups like yours." He relished the shocked look on Massey's face. "They recruited people like me right out of the military. You were played, Henry. I've always been an FBI agent."

"You were undercover all along?"

He nodded. "I had to put up with you hoping this day would come when I would see you in an orange jumpsuit."

"So why did the FBI have you leave Peninsular to become an agent?"

"They were concerned you and I were too close, that it might blow my cover. They wanted some separation, but when the crime ring came after my brother, Cally, we saw an opportunity to exploit our friendship."

Massey's face sank. "You were my most trusted advisor. How could you do this? You could've been my lieutenant governor when I won the election."

"Are you familiar with the oath of office when you become governor?"

CHAPTER 57

Massey shrugged his shoulders. "It's just a bunch of words."

"That's the problem, Henry Massey," Daniel said as he leaned in. "You put yourself first. If you had won the election, you would've taken an oath to defend the Constitution of the United States and of Michigan. It's a matter of honor. You planned to break that oath. I kept my oath."

Massey glared at Daniel, silent. The chains securing his handcuffs to the table rattled as he shifted in his seat.

"You can't win this one, Henry." Daniel stood and looked down at Massey. "Helen is going to make a great CEO of Quick Connect."

Massey growled as he tugged at the chain holding his cuffed hands to the table.

"Too bad it had to turn out this way. There's a part of me that thinks we could've been friends. After all, you did help me clear things up with my brother, Cally."

Massey's eyes narrowed. "I wanted to set things right for your family."

Daniel nodded. "Archipelago is an amazing tool for good, but in the wrong hands it became a means for nefarious purposes and selfish gain. I also wanted to set things right."

"Are they going to take down Archipelago?"

"That's the ironic thing about all of this. They're going to keep using Archipelago, only with better safeguards in place. You could've been the hero in all of this, but you let revenge consume you."

Massey sat silent as if in a trance. His face pale. His look somber.

"Goodbye," Daniel said as he knocked on the door to call the guard. "By the way, Governor Karen Bauer has asked me to run as her lieutenant governor for the fall election," Daniel said with a big grin as he stole a glance at Massey. "She should have an easy victory in the election this fall, so it looks like I'm going to be second-in-command after all."

A guard opened the door and Daniel exited the room. He was glad to hear the door close behind him, pleased he would no longer have to deal with Henry Massey.

CHAPTER 58

"Did you have a good week camping with Daniel and Cally?" Alicia asked Fallon as they sat on a double glider watching the sunset on Donegal Bay on Beaver Island.

He looked at her sitting next to him. "It was great." He put his arm around her and glanced at the large, orange sun sinking closer to the horizon. "The last time I went camping was with my granddad."

They sat a moment in silence as the glider swung back and forth, squeaking as it swayed. Alicia close to him and the sound of the waves sloshing against the shore soothed him.

"They offered me Trevor's job," Alicia said. "Turns out he was in on Massey's plot all along."

"I'm not surprised they offered you the regional director job." He looked at her. "I *am* surprised Trevor used the line about national security being threatened to coerce my therapist, Grace, to give him updates on what I recalled about the terror attack on the *Emerald Isle*."

"We're learning a lot more from the supercomputer about how Trevor was tied to Massey's plot. It's amazing the level of detail Massey had mapped out. His target was to eventually seize control of federal government data with his Archipelago software."

CHAPTER 58

"It's going to take a while to put all the pieces together," Fallon said. "It's a wonder none of it leaked out to the authorities."

"A few people did try to report it, but it sounded so outlandish that no one would believe them."

Fallon watched the sun sink toward High Island in the distance. "Did you hear Chip is now the official state police liaison to the governor?"

"How do you feel about that?"

"It's good. He's definitely ready. Besides, I was just his front man."

"Hardly," Alicia said as she glanced at him, then the sunset. "The governor should easily win reelection now that Massey is out."

Fallon looked at the orange tint on her face from the setting sun. Their eyes met. *Oh, those hazel eyes.*

"Why are you staring at me?"

"You could move here."

Alicia turned away toward the sunset.

Fallon watched the sun slip out of view behind High Island.

"If I take Trevor's job, I'd be the director for the Great Lakes Region. I would have to relocate to the Detroit area."

"You should take it."

"You just want me closer to you."

Fallon smiled and shifted his attention to the sunset.

"What's next for you?" Alicia asked.

"There's something I haven't told you," Fallon said. "I haven't told anyone about it."

Alicia frowned.

"When I was sorting out my mom's finances after she died, I discovered that my granddad formed a trust with the money he made when he sold his car company to the Dodge brothers back in the 1930s."

"Your parents never told you about it?"

"My dad told me there was nothing left after Granddad paid off his debts from the sale of his car company, but apparently there was a lot of money left. I inherited ownership of the trust."

"Why are you telling me this now?"

Fallon stood, looked at Alicia, and extended his hand.

"Stop playing games and tell me," Alicia said as she grabbed his hand.

"Come on, I'll show you," Fallon said as he took her hand and walked her to his car in the parking area on the other side of the gravel road by the beach.

As they approached his Dart, Alicia stopped to admire it. "I can't believe the people on Beaver Island got together and fixed your car. It looks like new."

Fallon looked at the polished fenders on his Dart reflecting the orange hues from the sky above. "The people on this island are the most generous and caring people I've ever met," he said as he climbed in behind the wheel.

"Where are you taking me?" Alicia said as she joined him on the passenger side.

"You'll see."

A few minutes later Fallon turned off King's Highway onto a driveway and stopped his car. The headlights illuminated a gate with a "For Sale" sign.

"Why are we stopping here?" Alicia asked.

Fallon climbed out of the car and waited for Alicia to join him at the gate.

"I was up here last week before the camping trip with the guys, and I saw this sign. I thought about how my granddad made a fresh start when his car company failed. I called the number, and the Realtor told me it's a vineyard for sale."

"And?"

"I made an offer on this place."

"You what!" Alicia exclaimed as her head whipped around.

"I put in a cash offer."

"From the trust?"

Fallon nodded. "Maybe I missed my calling all along. I should've followed in my grandad's footsteps instead of my dad's legacy of crime fighting."

"You know nothing about running a vineyard, let alone a winery."

"Todd and his son Gregg offered to help."

"Your friend who owns Blackbird Brewery in Charlevoix?"

"They'll also help me market the wine and recruit a staff to run it all."

CHAPTER 58

"Just how much is in this trust fund?"

"Enough."

"But Fallon . . ."

"I know it's not like me to be impulsive," Fallon said as he tapped his head and stepped next to Alicia. "Maybe the head injury was a good thing."

"I don't know," Alicia said.

"Maybe it's time we both settle down."

"But what about the regional director position?"

"Take it. You earned it."

They stood a moment staring at each other, then Fallon looked up at the stars emerging against the encroaching black velvet skies of evening. "The stars sure are amazing on Beaver Island. So clear. No light pollution—nothing to diminish the view." He looked at Alicia. "When I was at Cally's parents' house, his dad told me that sometimes God humbles us to help us see things about ourselves."

She returned his gaze with an empathetic face. "And what do you see now?"

"A future that includes you."

"I don't know . . . You've sprung a lot on me. I need time to think it all through."

"I understand. Give it some time."

They hugged, keeping their gaze skyward toward the stars.

"Let's get some dinner at the Shamrock," Fallon said as he pulled away from her a few minutes later.

Alicia smiled. "I could use a shot of whiskey."

"Me too," Fallon agreed as he climbed back in the car and started it. He looked at Alicia sitting in the passenger seat holding a book.

"I meant to ask you why you have a Bible in your car," she said as she picked it up. "Is there something you're not telling me?"

"Oh, Robert gave that to me when I visited their house."

Alicia opened the Bible. "There's a bookmark in here."

"He highlighted a verse for me."

"'For I know the plans that I have for you,' declares the Lord, 'plans for welfare and not for calamity to give you a future and a hope,' " she read.

"That's the verse."

"And what do you think those plans are for you?" She closed the Bible and set it on the bench seat between them.

"I'll tell you over dinner," Fallon said as he backed the car out of the driveway onto King's Highway and drove toward town. He reached his hand across the bench seat and took Alicia's hand, feeling very content for the first time in a long time.

EPILOGUE

"Congratulations to the new lieutenant governor," Fallon said to Daniel as he embraced him under the rotunda of the Michigan Capitol.

"Well deserved," Alicia said as she shook Daniel's hand. "That was such a nice inaugural."

"Thanks for being here," Daniel replied.

Fallon stepped back with Alicia as Daniel's family walked up and gathered around him. He watched as Robert, Liz, Sheila, and Cally took turns hugging him.

"Can you believe my brother is lieutenant governor now?" Cally said with a big grin on his face.

"Can you believe my little brother is now a computer expert?" Daniel asked as he hugged Cally, then pointed to Alicia. "I hear you're now the Director of the Great Lakes Region for Homeland Security and now living back in the state."

"It required a move to Detroit from Washington," Alicia said.

Daniel winked. "So you're closer to Fallon now."

"Hey Fallon—Alicia!" Chip waved as he emerged from the crowd of

EPILOGUE

people gathering under the rotunda. He stepped next to Fallon and looked at Daniel. "Is this your family?"

Fallon watched Daniel introduce his family to Chip. There was something comforting about seeing them all together.

"How does it feel to be the governor's state police liaison?" Daniel remarked as he looked at Chip.

"I have pretty big shoes to fill," Chip nodded.

"My shoes aren't that big," Fallon said.

"I need to get going, Fallon. I'm meeting Victoria," Chip said.

"The courier who delivered the documents proving Massey took delivery of the supercomputer." Fallon raised an eyebrow. "Is this serious?"

"I have to get going—"

"You're blushing."

"I need to go." Chip turned to exit the rotunda and called over his shoulder. "Let's do lunch next time you're in town."

"What's this I hear about you buying a vineyard?" Robert asked.

"Can you believe it?" the governor said as she approached with her security detail following behind her.

"I didn't expect to see you here, Karen," Fallon said.

"Congratulations on your second term, Governor," Alicia said.

"I saw all of you here and I had to stop by to personally thank all of you before I'm whisked off to all the festivities for the inaugural." Karen's voice trembled a bit. "I couldn't miss a chance to let you know how much I appreciate all of you. You'll be formally recognized in a few weeks for everything you did."

"Thanks, Governor," Daniel said as he glanced at his watch. "I'm sorry, but we have a celebratory luncheon we need to get to."

"Great to see your family here," Karen said to Daniel. "We'll talk tomorrow."

"Don't forget you promised to visit me sometime on Beaver Island," Fallon called after Daniel and his family as they turned to leave.

"We will," Robert responded as he left with Daniel and the rest of the family.

"I'll miss having you down the hall from me," Karen said. "I hope everything works out for you and your vineyard."

EPILOGUE

Fallon took a deep breath. He was getting choked up. "It will. I'm steadily improving. I was able to sit through the nineteen-gun salute they did after you took the oath of office, and it didn't trigger my PTSD."

"I'm glad you're making progress," the governor said.

"However, he did squeeze my hand through it," Alicia added.

Karen smiled at them. "I'm looking forward to visiting both of you on Beaver Island." She looked up at the stars on the dome of the Capitol, then returned her gaze to Fallon. "Thank you for everything, Fallon—for your friendship. And thank you, Alicia, for being there for him."

"We need to get to the next event," her husband, Jack, interrupted as he approached Karen with their daughters. He looked at Fallon and Alicia. "Thanks for being here."

"Wouldn't miss it."

"Keep in touch," Karen said as she turned to leave.

As Fallon watched her exit with Jack and her daughters, he fought back tears. For a brief second he saw the image of his father in the same spot, leaving the rotunda after he announced he wasn't running for reelection for attorney general.

"Are you okay, Fallon?" Alicia asked.

"Never better. Are you heading back to Detroit now?"

"I should get back to the office. Seems there's no end to the threats out there."

"Have time for lunch before you head back?"

Alicia paused a moment. "I think the country will be safe for an hour."

He took her hand, and they walked down the long corridor toward the large, ornate exit door, heels clicking on the black-and-white-checkerboard marble floor.

"We've known each other for a long time." She tilted her head slightly toward Fallon, the corner of her mouth raised. "What do you think about us as a couple?"

"I think our relationship is kind of like a bottle of fine wine," Fallon said as he squeezed her hand. "The longer you wait, the better it gets."

*It is better to be humble in spirit with the lowly
Than to divide the spoil with the proud.*

—Proverbs 16:19

ACKNOWLEDGMENTS

Writing and publishing a book is a marathon. I am blessed to have such a great team behind me.

A big thank-you to my wife, Joanne, for her continued support of my writing and publishing journey. As an avid reader and fan of crime thrillers, she has always been the first one to read drafts of my books. I appreciate the hours she spent offering insight and edits that enhanced this story. I am grateful for her love and support over all these years and for traveling with me on this road called life.

I also want to thank my daughters for the way they inspired me to tell stories when they were kids and for how they continue to encourage me to keep on writing. Thanks, too, to my granddaughter who keeps my creative skills sharp with her vivid imagination and artistic skills.

Thank you to all my editors who provided feedback and suggestions on how to revise this book. I am particularly grateful for those who agreed to be on my launch team. You provided valuable insight into the early draft and what might be next for the characters in the sequel. It all helped to make this book better. Also thanks to the team at Iron Stream and Brookstone who patiently worked with me through multiple revisions and changes to the schedule.

A special thanks to Brian Preuss for another amazing cover design. I

ACKNOWLEDGMENTS

am always impressed by his photography and design skills. His expertise adds the finishing touch that gives this book shelf appeal.

Also a shoutout to those who helped promote *Islands of Deception* on podcasts, with reviews, in articles, and on social media. I was overwhelmed by the support. And thank you to those who hosted book talks and signings. It was a privilege to meet so many of you and hear firsthand your thoughts and questions about the book. So many of you encouraged me to write this sequel.

Finally, I extend a heartfelt thanks to all you readers. I am truly blessed to have such a great team of people cheering me on.

Who can you trust when nothing is as it seems?

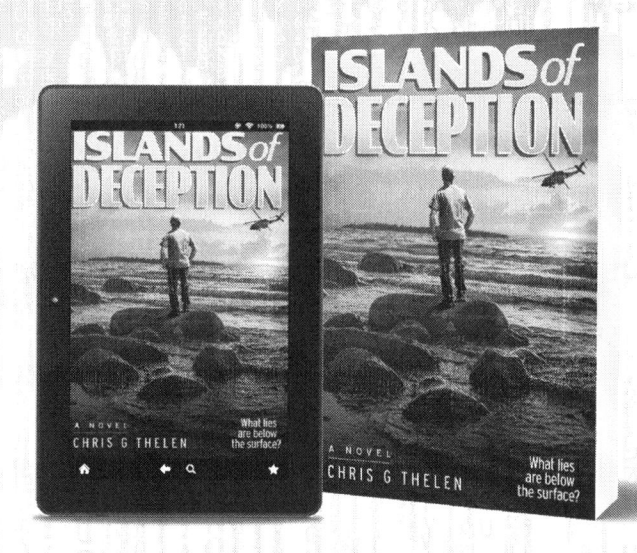

Political schemes, a billion-dollar tech empire, a wrongful conviction, and a detective's determination to get to the truth...

SCAN ME!

Book 1 in the Islands series.

Made in the USA
Middletown, DE
26 April 2025